PENGUIN BOOKS

THE SECOND WIFE

Denise Robertson, prolific writer of short stories, radio and television plays and radio documentaries, is at present the highly acclaimed and popular agony aunt of ITV's *This Morning* programme. She is also a panellist on Radio 4's *Any Questions*. Penguin have published *The Land of Lost Content*, a trilogy originally published separately in hardback as *The Land of Lost Content* (1985), winner of the Constable/Northern Arts trophy for fiction, *A Year of Winter* (1986) and *Blue Remembered Hills* (1987).

Denise Robertson lives near Sunderland with her husband, three of her five sons and an assortment of dogs.

DENISE ROBERTSON

The
Second Wife

PENGUIN BOOKS

PENGUIN BOOKS

Published by the Penguin Group
27 Wrights Lane, London w8 5TZ, England
Viking Penguin Inc., 40 West 23rd Street, New York, New York 10010, USA
Penguin Books Australia Ltd, Ringwood, Victoria, Australia
Penguin Books Canada Ltd, 2801 John Street, Markham, Ontario, Canada L3R 1B4
Penguin Books (NZ) Ltd, 182–190 Wairau Road, Auckland 10, New Zealand

Penguin Books Ltd, Registered Offices: Harmondsworth, Middlesex, England

First published by Constable and Company 1989
Published in Penguin Books 1989
1 3 5 7 9 10 8 6 4 2

The lines from 'Disobedience' in A. A. Milne's
When We Were Very Young quoted on p. 45 are
reproduced by permission of Methuen Children's Books,
London, and McClelland and Stewart, Toronto

Filmset in 10/12pt Linotron 202 Palatino
by Rowland Phototypesetting Ltd,
Bury St Edmunds, Suffolk

Made and printed in Great Britain by
Richard Clay Ltd, Bungay, Suffolk

[1]

On the surface it was like any other morning. Beside the window, Richard waited for the kettle to boil, feet bare, pyjama collar awry, running fingers through tousled hair. Ellie lay propped up on pillows in the wide bed with its aqua sheets. But it was not like any other morning. Richard was still angry, still unable or unwilling to understand her misery. He glanced occasionally at the hissing kettle but never at the bed.

If it had been an ordinary morning he would have smiled at her and shaken his head in mock reproof at her laziness. On special mornings he would have crossed to take her in his arms, recapturing the memory of the night before. But there had not been a morning like that for a long time.

The kettle boiled, the tea brewed, and he poured it carefully into Minton cups.

While Ellie drank her tea she looked around the bedroom. Pale aqua walls, deep aqua curtains, grey Wilton carpet splashed with cabbage roses, the mirror of the Georgian dressing-table reflecting the water-colour of the Jena bridge on the opposite wall. All beautiful, all carefully chosen so that no trace of Julia should remain. Replacing the cup in its delicate fluted saucer she remembered Adele's words: '*I do hope it's what you want, Ellie. We were afraid you might feel overwhelmed if we left it as it was. Julia had such style . . . this was very much her room.*' So Julia's possessions had been banished, her stamp removed from fixtures and fittings, but the spell of her remained. Thinking of her now, Ellie closed her eyes.

Last night she had begged again for reassurance and Richard had flinched at her words. 'What do you want from me, Ellie?' he had said at last, and she could have wept for the weariness in his tone. Afterwards she had put out a stealthy hand to feel him feign sleep, knowing he was awake like her and staring down the dark.

'More tea?'

She shook her head and Richard went into the bathroom. She heard the shower door open and close, and then the sound of water. In an hour he would be gone.

From the window she could see the horse-chestnut and beyond it the roof of Adele and Frank's house. Twin houses built by brothers for their brides: Frank for Adele, Richard for Julia. Julia! Inside her head the images arose. Richard and Julia together, newly wed and greedy. '*I love you, Julia. I love you, love you, love you.*'

The cup and saucer rattled in her hand and she put it down carefully on the bedside table. Julia was dead. That was fact. 'I am Richard's wife,' she said aloud, but the aqua walls were unconvinced. She closed her eyes, squeezing the lids together to shut out sight and sound of Julia, of Julia with Richard. But they were still there in her head, writhing, coupling, exulting in one another, always more savage in coition than she and Richard could ever be. She put a hand to her mouth and tried not to think about Julia.

Outside, November winds were struggling to strip the horse-chestnut. Individual leaves clung desperately for a moment and then were whirled away. One pressed against the windowpane and hung there, quivering, caught in a spider's web, reminding her of other autumns and a sycamore growing from the concrete of a northern yard. They had cut it down in the end because it shut out the light and its leaves blocked the drains. She hadn't thought of it for years.

It was good to stand in the shower's flow. Richard felt some of the tension drain out of him as he soaped and lathered, rinsed and soaped again. He pushed the pads of his fingers hard into the sockets of his tired eyes and winced as the soap penetrated and stung. How much more could he bear? And what could he do? Psychiatric mumbo-jumbo was getting them nowhere, as he had feared from the start. They said, 'Hold on,' but never for how long. And he had given up asking why – no one had an answer for that.

He leaned back, feeling the tiles strike cold against his shoulders. If he had known what would happen, that day in the park, would he have gone ahead? He raised his face and let water trickle between his parted lips as though to wash away the guilt he felt at having doubts.

In the beginning, the fact that he had been married before had not seemed to be a problem. Ellie had let him talk about Julia, even encouraged him. It had been a relief to let out the pain of his young wife's death and then to live again, as though departing grief had left space for new love to grow. 'Marry me, Ellie,' he had said at last, and had felt nothing but excitement when her answer was 'yes'. Perhaps second marriage was always a mistake. Love, yes, cohabit certainly, but make no commitment. Except that Ellie was not cut out to be a mistress.

He reached for the soap and began to lather his thighs. On their wedding night she had stood there, shyly, until he had taken her in his arms and carried her to bed. Perhaps he had been wrong to bring her here, to the house he had built for Julia. Perhaps he should have waited, given her more time. Perhaps, perhaps . . . the whole affair was a welter of maybes. If only someone would give him some facts, a prognosis, something to quantify and break into component parts until it could be dealt with and filed away. But all the psychiatrist said was, 'Patience.'

Adele had warned him: '*Julia will be a hard act to follow, Richard.*' But even she had been hopeful. '*We'll all help. It's time this house had a facelift. I'll do it, if you want me to . . . you know I love that sort of thing, and Frank holds an inquest if I even want to re-cover a chair. It's the accountant in him, I suppose. Let me do up the house for the bride. It'll be easier for Ellie if she feels she has a home of her own.*'

Except that Ellie, a year into marriage, still behaved like a visitor, like someone dwelling not in dreams but in nightmares.

He groped for the shower control and turned it to COLD – FULL FLOW. He must get through to the psychiatrist, make him understand the need for progress. And if a move would help they would go. He had never wanted to build a house in the first place; bricks should be mellowed by age. The new house had been Julia's idea. Perhaps that was all Ellie needed, a change of setting?

Across the gardens with their dividing walls and their dying roses, Adele Marriner was wide awake. She turned on her side and slid an arm round her husband. 'Wake up, you lazy sod. It's after eight.' Frank groaned and turned on his face, sliding his arms under the pillows. 'Up,' she said, and pulled away the duvet. His body was the body of an athlete and still pleased her, even after fifteen years of marriage and two daughters.

She had picked him out on the rugger field: 'Who's he?' Someone had said, 'Frank Marriner,' and she realized he was the second Marriner son. She had tried to flirt with Richard later on, in the clubhouse. And then Julia had put a proprietory hand on Richard's arm, and Adele had settled for what she could get.

Frank was out of bed now, padding towards the bathroom. 'Lay out my things, Adele, there's a good girl. I don't want to be late.' She rose obediently and began to sort through his drawers in search of socks and underpants. She had a lot to be thankful for. Complete security, a nice home. New bricks were common but the house was beautiful.

She closed the drawers, remembering her father's disapproval of the plan to build. But Julia had been adamant and Julia always got her way. *'I don't want a mouldering pile of brick, Del. I've lived in one all my life. I*

9

want something unique, something I created. And you must
live next door, so we can be like the Cosa Nostra and keep the
Marriner brothers in their proper place.'

So she had given in to Julia, like everyone else, and
she had been happy. Really quite happy. And if Frank
decided to go to Japan later this month and take her
with him, it would be heaven!

Ellie sipped a second cup of tea as Richard dressed. He
was not ashamed of his body, walking naked to select
shirt and socks. In the beginning she had found such
boldness surprising. In every other way he was a very
private person. She had been his wife for more than a
year and still felt as though she hardly knew him. But
she knew his body, reed-thin and brown, thighs and
forearms well muscled, skin smooth and almost hairless
except for dark lower belly and underarms which gave
the lie to his blond crown.

If she had been Julia she would have gone to him
now, pressing herself against him, kissing the flat belly,
the pelvic bone, nuzzling each vertebra until his spine
vanished between the firm buttocks. But she was not
Julia and there was more than an expanse of carpet
between them. She narrowed her eyes and tried to
concentrate on the horse-chestnut, weaving and bobbing to outwit the autumn winds.

Autumns in London had been fun, especially when
she had moved in with Terri. On Saturdays they had
shopped for groceries and afterwards walked in the
park, swinging their Safeway bags and trailing their
feet through the piled leaves when they thought no
one was looking. And then one day a handsome little

boy had moved into their path, holding out his camera. She had taken it from him and focused on father and sons, happy to be doing something to please. That was before she had known about Julia.

'I cannot stand this pain,' she whispered, but felt no answering sympathy from the room that would always belong to Richard's true wife, the mother of his children.

As he knotted his tie, Richard watched Ellie through the mirror. The first time he had seen her, that day in the park, he had been struck by her gravity, unusual in such a young woman. Dark hair springing from a wide forehead, straight brows above grey eyes. Not a beautiful face but a thoughtful one. When she had spoken to the boys her words had come out carefully, like small woodland creatures emerging into a world of danger. And then she had smiled and he had felt a sudden leap of spirits.

Now she seldom smiled. He thought of her last night, the words tumbling from her: '*But how did you love her, Richard? What did you say? . . . do? . . . I have to know!*' He realized he was standing motionless, fingers still holding the knotted tie, eyes closed against the memory. He opened his eyes and looked at his wife's reflection.

She appeared to be smiling and then her face clouded over suddenly and she seemed to shrink in the bed. What was she thinking? He contemplated crossing to her, taking her in his arms, kissing her firmly, savagely even, until he knocked the doubting out of her. But it was not in him to make extravagant gestures. He could not even say, 'I love you.' But he did love her, perhaps more than he had loved Julia.

Guilt came and went. Julia had been his friend and she had given him his sons; they had shared a deep happiness, and life without her had been a waste-land. But what he felt for Ellie was more. If only he could put it into words . . . but he had not been brought up to be demonstrative. He had come silently to Julia and she had not seemed to mind. She had enjoyed every moment of their marriage, and now he hardly ever thought of her, except when Ellie reminded him or when he saw the turn of her head or her wide-set eyes in his sons. They both had Julia's eyes. He recognized them in the boys and yet he could not remember Julia's eyes in her own face.

His fingers scooped change from the dressing-table and fed it into his trouser pockets while his mind scrabbled desperately to summon up his dead wife's features. If only Ellie knew how little he remembered of Julia. If only he could find words to tell her.

He crossed to the bed. 'I'm off, then.' He still felt remnants of last night's distress and it made him awkward. 'What do you plan to do with your day?' She murmured something about London and shopping, and he smiled. 'Good idea. It's not the weather to do anything else.' He bent to kiss her, gingerly holding her bare shoulders.

'I love you, Richard.' Her words and the vehemence behind them took him by surprise.

'I know,' he said, and then cursed his own inadequacy all the way downstairs.

*

Terri held the shirt to her face and felt dampness return as the warmth of the iron receded. Damn!

'Is it ready yet?' Mike yelled from the bathroom and she gave it one last despairing flourish before passing it through the door.

'It's still wet!' His protest was heartfelt and guilt consumed her.

'Do your own fucking shirts in future,' she yelled and went in search of coffee.

She was still at the kitchen table when he emerged, tucking in damp shirt-tails.

'Sorry!' They spoke simultaneously and laughed.

'I'll try to improve,' Terri said, holding up her face to be kissed.

His lips slid from her mouth to the gaping neck of her dressing-gown and then he reached for her hand and kissed her protesting palm. 'I'm a pig. You're wonderful. Besides, it hardly feels damp at all now.'

He was reaching for toast and cramming it into his mouth. Wild thoughts of balanced breakfasts rose up, and she quelled them: even if she had time to cook them, he would never have time to eat them. He lived on business lunches and it showed. 'I love you, love you, love you,' she said and kissed him again, but she could feel his yearning for the door and the tube and his overloaded desk.

When he had gone she looked at the clock. Eight-forty-five – she was already late so there was no point in busting a gut. She poured another coffee and glanced around the cluttered kitchen with its cheap, mass-produced units. Before Mike, she had shared a flat with Ellie and they had kept it neat as a new pin. Now there

13

was never enough time or money. Especially money. Diana's latest demand, a skiing holiday for herself and the children, had come this morning. 'Tell the bitch to go to hell,' she had said when he opened the letter. The row had lasted twenty minutes.

The phone rang and she looked once more at the clock. Too soon for Stephen to be ringing from the newspaper office to scold her for her absence. She lifted the receiver: 'Terri Benedict.'

The voice at the other end was a surprise and she shifted the receiver to her other hand.

'Ellie! I was just thinking about you . . . and the flat. I used to grumble about it but, God, I miss it. And I miss you. How are you?'

She listened to Ellie's reply but her mind was on the ticking clock, the whereabouts of unladdered tights, the chaos in the tube, the feature on showbiz marriages that was refusing to come together. And then the word 'doctor' intruded into her consciousness.

'What do you mean, doctor? Are you ill?'

The news that the doctor was a psychiatrist calmed her. Nowadays she only worried about cancer and Aids, and sometimes Hepatitis B. If one didn't get you, the other would. 'Well, take care,' she said at last, alarmed now at the lateness of the hour. 'And come up to town soon so we can talk and talk.'

In the bedroom Terri looked at herself in the mirror. She looked vile. It was weeks since her roots had been done, and her face was drawn. Perhaps she should revert to mouse, and age gracefully? Except that Diana had her hair done twice a week, reeked of Chanel, and sunbathed on the veranda in Twickenham when she

14

was not on the Costa Helluvalot at her, Terri's, expense!

She lowered herself to the dressing-stool. She didn't want to go to work, but that was only half of it. She wanted to be a full-time wife and mother. She wanted to breed, be fecund, bring forth and multiply. She wanted to be No. 1 wife, the mother of Mike's children. Except that she quite liked her job . . . well, most of the time. Would like it a lot better if she could get to grips with the Stallone break-up and move on to Alvin Stardust/Liza Goddard.

A cacophony of horns started up in the street below – London tempers fraying already, and the day hardly begun. She reached for skin tonic and began her make-up.

Driving the Jaguar with its REM 21 number-plate soothed Richard as it always did. Getting away from the house helped, too. He hoped the shopping expedition would do the same for Ellie. She was disturbed, perhaps seriously disturbed, but she was not ill.

A junction loomed and he took the Slough turn. After all, Ellie had taken on a lot . . . a husband with a first marriage behind him, two teenage sons – the worst age, so the pundits said, and yet she was never so happy as when she was with the boys. It was Julia she couldn't come to terms with . . . or rather, Julia's memory. They would be happy together, laughing even – and then something would trigger it off. He would feel her grow tense in his arms and then the questions would begin. Last night her face had been contorted with jealousy – or fear. He had given up trying to decide which particular devil was driving her.

He must stop thinking about last night. Whatever happened, he couldn't let his marriage affect the running of the firm. He must finalize plans for the western extension today, and talk Frank into the Japan trip. No time to agonize over Ellie . . .

A parking sign neared; he turned into the lay-by and reached for the car-phone. Ellie had a sheaf of credit cards and an allowance, but he couldn't imagine her on a shopping spree, not unless she had encouragement. Her northern thrift was too ingrained. When they had chosen an engagement ring together her mouth had formed a small O of disapproval at the cost. He was smiling as he dialled his sister-in-law's number.

'Adele? I wonder if you could do me a favour . . . ' If he was honest, he had never really cared much for Adele, but she was always good in a crisis.

Adele had been crossing the hall when the phone rang. 'I'll get it,' she called, hearing the au pair coming from the kitchen. She had put crop and gloves on the side-table and unstrapped her hard hat. Now she fingered it as she talked. 'Of course I will, Richard . . . I need to go up to town this week, anyway. I'll ring Ellie now.'

The thought of Snow, saddled and waiting, was frustrating but it was good that Richard still needed her. Through the hall window she could see the cotoneaster, vivid along the dividing wall. She must remember to tell Ellie that Julia had planted it.

She shouted instructions to Solange as she ran upstairs to change. No doubt they would trail from one dreary chain store to another, Ellie's instincts being definitely off-the-peg. Still, it meant Brownie points with Richard and would have to be endured. And Ellie would be grateful. Gratitude would positively ooze from her! Yuck!

When Richard had announced he was marrying again Adele had felt an almost physical shock. She had grown used to acting as his hostess after Julia's death, keeping an eye on his children and monitoring his house as well as her own. She had enjoyed it. And then Ellie had appeared, mousy little Ellie with the faintly northern accent and deeply northern principles. Batty little Ellie who already needed a psychiatrist and would probably end up in the nut-house.

She was not jealous, no matter what Frank might think; it was simply bad luck that he had been born after Richard. She hadn't minded when Julia was alive, had never begrudged Julia her place . . . well, hardly ever. But Ellie was different. Ellie was not her school-friend, as Julia had been. She was not jolly like Julia and, it had to be faced, she did not belong to their class. She was not equipped to be the chairman's wife, and never would be.

Adele took a tan wool dress from the wardrobe and threw it on the bed while she searched for matching shoes. She found a leather belt in her dressing-table drawer and paused to look at her reflection. Her figure was still good and she had never had a problem skin, not even in adolescence. She leaned closer and grimaced so as to inspect her teeth. They were her strong point, large and even and without flaw. She looked what she was, a well-bred, well-groomed English-woman of thirty-six. Young enough to have another

17

baby. Except that it might be a third girl, and that would never do.

She straightened up. She could get her hair and nails done while she was in town, and shop for a new Barbour. And she would need a whole new wardrobe for Japan. She was not going to ride shotgun on Ellie all day – why the hell should she?

Mrs Withers appeared with a breakfast tray before Ellie could go down. 'Now eat up. You don't take in enough to keep a bird alive.' The older woman was grey-haired and kind and Ellie felt tears prick her eyes. 'There now, I'll put it here and I want it cleared.' There was an egg under a cosy, a bowl of muesli, a rack of toast, and home-made jam.

'You're a dragon,' Ellie said, glad of the chance to joke and restore her composure. If she broke down or acted strangely Mrs Withers would ring Richard. She had done it before.

'I'll come up in half an hour.' The older woman's voice softened. 'Make an effort, that's all I ask. We can talk about dinner tonight when you come down. We haven't had pork for a while. Mr Richard likes a nice shoulder rolled with sausage-meat and kidney.' She looked at Ellie, hoping to see signs of salivation.

'That sounds lovely,' Ellie said, trying to look involved.

'Well, I'll leave you to get on with it. The dogs are waiting patiently at the stairs. They don't draw breath until they've seen you.'

When Mrs Withers had gone Ellie carried the tray to the window-seat and gazed down on the garden. There

was a brightly berried creeper along the dividing wall
and a magpie in the branches of the horse-chestnut.
Not all black and white, but iridescent green when it
turned its back, and somehow menacing. She looked
at the house opposite, mirror image of her own. They
had stood side by side for sixteen years, seen birth and
death, joy and sorrow. Once more a picture of Richard
and Julia flashed into her mind . . . walking hand-in-
hand up the grassy slope to inspect foundations. And
then the walls rising, handmade bricks in autumn
brown, sash windows under a dark red pantiled roof,
and French windows to all the reception rooms, so that
there could be parties on the terrace. That had been
Julia's idea.

Perhaps they had come at night to inspect progress
and made love in a welter of bricks and masonry. She
shook her head to rid herself of the image, only to have
it replaced by the sight of Julia, dressed for a ball as
she had been in so many photographs, descending the
curved stair with its wrought-iron balustrade while
Richard waited adoringly below. Violins started up in
her head and for the first time that day amusement
brought relief. She ought to be writing for Mills and
Boon! She selected a piece of toast from the rack and
took a dutiful bite.

She was still in the window-seat when the phone
rang, and it was obvious from the start that Adele
would not take no for an answer. 'I saw Richard as
he was leaving this morning and he mentioned you
were going up to town. I said "Good, so am I."'

Ellie had watched Richard drive away and there had
been no meeting, so he must have phoned Adele.

There was a vast conspiracy to keep her prisoner. She sat down on the window-seat again and covered her mouth with her fingertips while she marshalled her thoughts, then she crossed to the wardrobe. Her loose-fitting red wool dress with the cowled hood, low-profile tights and pumps, all topped by the blue fox coat. The huge gold ear-rings and her largest bag, the red leather pouch she had bought in Madeira and had then thought too ostentatious to use. She had hated the blue fox coat ever since Richard gave it to her – it was wrong to kill for vanity. Today, though, it would serve its purpose.

When she was ready she went out on to the landing. The boys would be home for a weekend soon, bursting into the house to tell their news. She pushed open the door of Gavin's room, a shrine to formula racing: stickers from Silverstone and Brands Hatch, a photograph of Nigel Mansell and enough motoring magazines to stock W. H. Smith. Then Jeremy's room. Studious Jeremy. Books piled everywhere, novels, biographies, some poetry . . . and a photo of Julia on the tallboy. There was a penholder on his desk, a funny blob of a creature on a spring which jumped about if you pressed it. She had put it in the toe of his stocking and he had spent Christmas Day making it perform. She pressed it and watched it squirm. For the first time that morning she felt a twinge of doubt. And then she noticed Julia, squinting into sunlight from her silver frame, smiling, always smiling.

Terri had to fight her way on to the tube at New Cross Gate and stand, arms at sides, hemmed in by other bodies. When the train stopped at Surrey Docks her holdall was almost wrenched from her grasp by the surge of alighting passengers, but a seat appeared and she beat all comers to reach it.

She still felt guilty about the shirt and angry with herself for feeling guilt at all. Prehistoric hang-ups about keeping the cave clean, that was all it was. She tried to think about work instead. The deadline for the marriage piece had already been extended; if she didn't complete it soon it would be dead meat, and she would earn a black look at morning conference.

What she should really be writing was a book on second marriage. Rule 1: Assassinate your predecessor. Rule 2: Drown her offspring. As the train rattled to a halt at Rotherhithe she relented. The girls were super, really. And they were Mike's kids, she must never forget that. Half of their genes were his. If she had a child they would be its half-sisters. Except that there could be no baby while Diana made so many demands. Life was fucking unfair!

She fished her memo pad from her bag and wrote 'Meat for tonight'. She would make a meal with real veg. Peeling things always made her feel virtuous – it was proper cooking. If she could get around to proper laundering, all would be well.

If she finished her piece and got a rise she might employ help? Ha! She realized she had snorted aloud and raised guilty eyes, but no one was looking at her. They were all too sunk in their own misery or lost in their Sony-Walkmans. The girl next to her was reading a dog-eared copy of *The Female Eunuch*. It must be out of the ark . . . All the same, Mike *could* do more to help. If he couldn't stand up to Diana, at least he could iron his own shirts – or buy drip-dry.

Lucky Ellie, marrying money. Except that money didn't matter. Richard and Ellie were made for one another, just as Mike was made for her. She was alighting at Wapping before she realized the significance of omitting to say she was made for Mike.

Adele brought the car to a halt on the drive and honked the horn. While she waited for Ellie to appear she admired the elegantly dressed windows. Working with a blank cheque had been joyous. Not that Frank was mean, but his training in accountancy meant he was aware of money. If he'd gone straight into the firm like Richard, instead of taking articles, he might have had more power now, but it had been Old Man Marriner's decision and his word had been law.

Ellie was coming out on to the steps with Mrs Withers, the dogs capering around her. Julia's labradors, old now but still perfect specimens. What on earth were they talking about? She could hardly honk the horn again but she looked pointedly at her watch and hoped they would notice.

She had always coveted Mrs Withers, had even tried to steal her when Julia died, but the old woman's loyalty had been to Richard and his orphaned children. Now she was besotted with Ellie. Northern working-class solidarity, probably. Withers came from some God-forsaken place near the Scottish border and Ellie from Durham, where everybody worked in the coalmines.

Ellie was bending to pat the dogs and Adele's eyes widened as she took in her sister-in-law's appearance.

Ellie was not usually guilty of bad taste, rather too restrained if anything. Today, though, she was dressed to kill. Fox coat, red dress, *Dallas* ear-rings. Could she possibly be meeting a man? Was Richard suspicious rather than anxious? The idea of being a detective titillated briefly, but she dismissed it. Ellie was too goody-goody for such carnal pursuits.

'We're only going to London, not Baluchistan,' she called to speed up the farewells, and switched on the ignition as a further hint.

'Have you noticed how magnificent the cotoneaster is this year?' she asked as Ellie climbed into the passenger seat and fastened her seatbelt. 'Julia planted it. She was so good with gardens.'

Trumper had broken away from Mrs Withers and was following them down the drive, leaves skittering around him in the wind. Ellie twisted anxiously in her seat, and Adele's eyes flitted to the mirror. 'It's all right, he won't come beyond the gates. He's a lovely beast, isn't he? Julia always meant to show him. Wonderful blood-line . . . that's everything, in dogs and in people.' She thought she might have gone too far but Ellie appeared not to have noticed and turned to settle in her seat.

Adele's conscience pricked. Julia had always brought out the best in her; was Ellie bringing out the worst? She didn't look like a usurper today, just a tired woman in a rather gaudy outfit. 'The children'll be home for a weekend soon . . . still, you like it when the house is full, don't you?' The M4 junction appeared and Adele slid into the flow, trying desperately to think of something absolutely unbitchy to say.

*

23

Terri brought up the Stallone details on her terminal and scanned them half-heartedly. No inspiration there, and not much to be borrowed from adjoining desks. Stephen was deep in a moody because his feature on office politics had been shelved. Meryl and Eddy were arguing over angles to take on the NHS piece, and Greta was weeping down the telephone because she wasn't pregnant. Earlier she had cried for a week, thinking that she was.

She cued in the Alvin Stardust/Liza Goddard details, hoping for a spark; but there was nothing. Star marriages on the rocks had seemed such a good idea when she had voiced it. Pictures had positively glowed at the prospect, and the Editor had overruled claims from showbiz that it was their province: 'It's not the stars we're interested in, it's marriage. That's Terri's forte.'

My God, if he only knew! She pushed her chair back and closed her eyes: if people saw you like that they assumed you were hatching a brilliant idea and left you alone. Not that there was anything wrong with her marriage – most of the time it was good. When they were allowed to get on with it, it was very good. Even brilliant. It was only the past that caused complications – Mike's past, blessed by Holy Mother Church and never quite off his lapsed Catholic conscience. She couldn't blame it all on guilt. He still had something going for Diana, as he had admitted once, in an unguarded moment. 'I did love her, Terri, but I never liked her.' And she had looked into his face and seen that the past tense was for her benefit.

She opened her eyes and hitched her chair desk-wards. No point in torturing herself. She punched in 'Collins/Holm' and waited for the saga to unfold.

Adele dropped Ellie at Harrods' entrance with a promise to meet in the Georgian restaurant at one-thirty. Ellie had been admiring Adele's skilful negotiation of the London traffic so the question about where she wanted to shop took her by surprise and Harrods had popped into her mind from nowhere.

She smiled at Adele when she got out of the car but refrained from touching her sister-in-law's arm in a gesture of farewell. 'See you later,' she said and stood to watch the car thread its way back into the flow.

The fur department was on the first floor and she made her way towards it. She heard music and saw there was a young girl on a dais, face rapt, fingers stroking a harp. 'Somewhere over the rainbow . . .' Judy Garland on a yellow brick road. Ellie stood to listen, wanting to enjoy it but disturbed, as she always was, by music. In the recesses of her mind another tune was playing; she felt the familiar choking sensation, and then the urge to get away.

The fur department was a forest of eyes, assistants guarding a king's ransom. Ellie turned towards the boutique and moved along the racks until she was unobserved. It took only a moment to slip out of the blue fox and place it over another coat on a hanger. The store was warm and the relief of shedding the coat enormous. She pulled the red cowl from her head, smoothed her hair and straightened her neckline. Stage One was complete.

An assistant saw a tall, bare-headed customer in an

expensive red dress, but the woman was not behaving suspiciously so she returned to reconciling her stock sheet.

A few moments later, in the privacy of the scented loo, Ellie struggled out of the red dress, revealing fine grey wool separates beneath. The dress was soft and rolled into a ball. When she emerged from the cubicle she checked her make-up until the attendant was looking the other way, and then dropped the ball into the waste container. She was trembling and in the mirror her eyes were bright. Too bright. She took her Reactolite sunspecs from her bag. The lenses were slightly tinted and gave her an owlish appearance. They would do very well.

Ellie couldn't believe she was doing this, behaving like a secret agent, she who had A levels in back-peddling. But she *was* doing it, even enjoying it. She felt better with each layer she shed, as though she were ridding herself of a burden.

The bespectacled woman in the grey two-piece attracted no attention when she left the powder room. Her outfit was unremarkable except for the large red bag and the attendant's thoughts were elsewhere. She did not notice the woman pluck out the huge ear-rings and drop them into her pocket.

In the luggage department Ellie bought a large navy holdall; in the cab that she took from the main entrance, she removed wrappings and price tags and put the red bag inside the holdall. When she left the taxi at Wimpole Street no trace of her former appearance remained except for navy stockings and shoes.

She walked into a branch of Lloyds Bank and cashed

a counter cheque for £100, then she walked down Orchard Street to the Oxford Street branch, where her cash card yielded a further hundred. Added to the £380 pounds already in her wallet, this gave Ellie £580. She would not be able to use cash card or cheque book again without betraying her whereabouts. At the first convenient drain, she bent as if to tie her shoe, and dropped cheque book and cards down the grid. It was eleven-thirty and her train left King's Cross at noon. It would have to be another cab. She stepped to the kerb and raised a hand.

The station was large and echoing and crowded. Pigeons sauntered between scurrying feet and flew about the rafters. Ellie checked the departures board and bought a single ticket, second class, and a daily paper before she took her place in the queue for Platform Three. There was little chance of encountering anyone she knew but she kept her eyes lowered and was relieved when they began to inch forward. How long before Richard discovered she was gone? Adele would wait for an hour and then press the panic button. By then she would be two hundred miles away.

Richard was clever, with money to buy detection, and the field of search would not be infinite. Paul Weidenek would know in which direction she would go. She had liked him so much and that had loosened her tongue. In the end, though, psychiatry had not been able to help her. He had probed and pried, and she had grown afraid of what he might discover. What was hidden in the recesses of her memory might be innocuous or it might be terrible. She must know which, before she could share it.

She found a seat in coach E, near to the buffet. She was longing for a cup of coffee but not until they were under way. She shook out the paper as the train began to move. Tomorrow she might merit a line on an inside page: *'Businessman's wife in shopping mystery. Sister-in-law sparks search.'* They would gather to compare notes . . . or else to wash their hands of her. Her ears popped as the train entered a tunnel. Her journey had begun.

[2]

As soon as they left York Ellie began to watch for the Cleveland Hills. It was eight years since she had seen them recede into the distance. Now she was going back.

A fallow field appeared and was gobbled up by the speed of the train, but not before she had seen the dog, ahead of its owner, looking back now and then for reassurance. Two hundred miles away Trumper would be watching the door for her return. She realized she was smiling foolishly and quickly turned back to the window, but the other passengers, reflected in the glass, were absorbed in their own concerns.

She loved both dogs but with Trumper there was a special affinity. He it was who had come to her in the black moments, pushing at her with his huge head until she ceased weeping and reached for him. She had never before known the comfort a dog could bring, had even avoided them if she could. There had been a cat at Grandma's and the Harpers had kept a budgie in a cage, but she had never had anything of her own until the day she had walked into Richard's home and Trumper had signified approval with a threshing tail.

He had been Julia's dog in the beginning, but she had come to terms with that.

The long line of hills gave way to the fringes of Darlington and she began to gather up her bags. Darlington passed and a sign came up: 'Durham 8 miles' . . . and after that the fairy-tale castle set on a hill, the cathedral behind, a collection of dolls' houses tumbling below.

It was a relief to Adele when Slough appeared. On the way out of London she had marshalled her case: *It's no use blaming me. I'm not her keeper.* There might have been new developments since she phoned. Perhaps Ellie had run off with some man . . . that would cause a stir, and no one could blame her then. Except that it wasn't going to be that simple. Ellie had probably thrown herself under a bus somewhere and Richard would go berserk. Worse still, Frank would despise her. She had caught him looking at her oddly once or twice when she had been beastly to Ellie.

As the needle of the BMW flicked to eighty she acknowledged her real fear. If Ellie died she would live on, a constant reminder to everyone that she, Adele, was an eighteen-carat bitch! Oh God, let her be all right, OK, sitting at home when they got back, brows raised at all the fuss, that stupid little-girl-in-a-day-dream look on her face.

She had phoned Richard at two-thirty: 'I am sorry, Richard, I hardly took my eyes off her . . .' If it all came out he would know she had lied. She had in fact never given Ellie a second thought once she dropped her off. Emil had given her the latest bulletin on the Sangsters while he did her hair, she had had a manicure and a back rub, and had arrived at the restaurant ten minutes late.

She had been affronted that Ellie was not there, waiting. And then she had blamed crossed wires. The idiot would be somewhere else, checking her watch and feeling abandoned. She watched the doorway for Ellie to appear, flustered and apologetic. But she had not come, and eventually the call to Richard could be delayed no longer. Richard had ordered . . . there was no kinder word . . . ordered her to the plant and then put the phone down on her so he could ring the psychiatrist. No doubt *he* would blame her too. And Frank would be livid.

The 'Marriner Engineering' sign appeared, and Adele slowed the car for the barrier to be lifted.

Paul Weidenek eased the Volvo into the kerb and switched off the engine. The Norton Commando was parked at the kerb. Gary had come back! There were patient files and two tapes on the passenger seat beside him but he made no move to collect them. Once he got out of the car and entered the house, it would begin again. What would it be? Love or hate, feast or famine, a deluge of good spirits or a cold front to end all cold fronts?

The Nursing Officer had walked with him to the door of the hospital when he left, bemoaning her own domestic entanglements and envying him his bachelor state. 'You're lucky,' she'd said as he went down the steps. 'You have no complications in your life.' Which showed how much anyone knew about anyone else's affairs.

He could hear the phone ringing as he fumbled for his key, and then the ringing ceased. Gary was standing in the hall when the door opened, the receiver to his ear. Their eyes met and then the boy said, 'He's not in,' and put down the phone.

'Who was it?' Paul said, trying to speak equably.

'How should I know? Some man. If it's important he'll ring back.' The words were defiant but there was an uncertain note in the voice. It was that hint of vulnerability behind the bravado which defeated Paul every time he meant to make a stand.

He moved forward to place the files on the marble-topped table. It was time for an olive branch. 'We could eat out tonight, if you'd like? Chinese, Indian . . .?'

The thin shoulders under the black leather rose and fell to demonstrate lack of interest. 'We might. I don't know my plans yet.' The boy turned and began to mount the stairs.

'Gary . . .'

There was a moment's hesitation and then the ascent continued. The memory of their row over money hung between them, a barrier neither of them was ready to dismantle. *I ought to handle it better*, Paul thought as he moved towards the kitchen. But the old saw of the cobbler's wife being the worst shod was true. A training in psychiatry was no guarantee of a quiet mind.

He made instant coffee in a mug and added saccharine from the container in his pocket. There was mail on the kitchen table, mostly circulars, and a letter from his parents in Stoke. They were so proud of him and so blind. He carried letter and coffee through to his study and sat down at his desk.

Up above music blared out, discordant and aggressive. If he asked for the volume to be turned down, there would be another battle, and he wasn't up to it. He sagged in the chair, watching steam rise from the coffee. On the cabinet the wildlife miniatures beckoned. He reached for the first silver frame and set it on his desk for inspection.

The harvest mouse was round and brown, bright-eyed and full of life so that it seemed to quiver on its cornstalk. He looked at it and tried not to think of the beautiful, mutinous face in the bedroom above. After a while he reached for a vole emerging from its hideaway. The boy's capacity to hurt was infinite; the wildlife miniatures were balm.

He had replaced the vole and was engrossed in a winter hare when the music ceased. He moved into the hall as steps crashed on the stairs.

'Going out?' Paul said, and was rewarded with a scowl. He put out a placatory hand but it was pushed aside. 'Shall we eat out tonight?' The front door was already thundering shut as he spoke. He heard the Norton Commando start up in the street and roar into the distance. It would be hours before Gary came back – perhaps days. And he couldn't live without him.

The Lalique glass clock on the mantel chimed a quarter to three. He had a long list this afternoon – time to go. If Gary . . . when Gary came back they could mend fences, and at the weekend they would get out of London. Gary always enjoyed an uninterrupted weekend. Or pretended to enjoy. That was the hardest part of all, not knowing how much was make-believe.

*

As the details of failed, star-studded marriages flashed up on her terminal, Terri tried hard to feel interest. It was death to a piece if the writer felt uninvolved. But these marriages were celluloid and remote. What a piece she could write about the real thing, except that the Editor would say it was boring. 'Find me something juicy,' was his constant cry. Perhaps she should murder Diana! That would be worth a few lines.

She pushed back her chair and went in search of coffee. 'Heard the latest one about Maggie Thatcher?' Trevor's jokes were even weaker than the coffee but she tried to look expectant. He had an invalid wife and his contract was up for renewal. 'She's not recommend ing anyone for a knighthood because she doesn't understand the meaning of "Arise". Get it? A rise. See?'

Her hearty laughter was over and she was back in her seat before the penny dropped. What would everyone do for jokes when Maggie went?

On an impulse she dialled Mike's number. 'Hallo, you.' He sounded harassed and she began to regret making the call. She never felt she had the right to ring him. But she was his wife, God damn it!

'I'm cooking tonight . . . proper cooking. No micro.' She was on to the veg when he interrupted.

'I'll be late, Terri. Diana's just rung to remind me about the school concert.'

Terri moved the cup on her desk a fraction to the right, trying to keep her feelings under control. 'What concert?' She had picked up a pen and was writing *Bitch*, *Bitch*, *Bitch* on a letterhead.

'Some charity thing. She did tell me about it ages ago

34

and I forgot. I need to pick up Diana and the girls straight from the office.'

'Why can't she go in her own fucking car? We bloody well pay for it.' Work had ceased around her as ears were cocked and she bent her head closer to the phone. 'It isn't fair, Mike. She behaves as though you were still together: "Come here, do this, go there."'

The injured note she had been expecting moved into his voice. 'You know I can't let the girls down, Terri. We agreed that at the beginning. It's not Diana, you know I don't give a damn for her . . . but I can't let down the girls.'

There was no counter-argument and she hated him for that. 'Sod off, Mike,' she said and slammed down the phone.

On either side her colleagues started working like crazy. God bless eavesdropping, nothing like it for getting noses back to grindstones. She hitched up her chair and tapped in 'Geldof/Yates'. Work, for all its demands, kept you sane.

The shrill of the phone took her breath away. He was ringing back and she would grovel, grovel, grovel. Disappointment dulled her wits when the voice was not Mike's. 'Richard? Richard who? Oh, Richard . . .'

The woman started to cry and Paul Weidenek passed her a tissue. 'I'm sorry.'

He smiled at her. 'No need.' It was growing dark outside but switching on a light would spoil the mood. He had been waiting three weeks for her to give way like this.

The light on his handset glared. Someone was calling

him. If he didn't pick up the receiver the operator would tell the caller to ring back. His patient was sobbing with relief now and it would be a pity to break the spell. He leaned back in his chair and the light went out.

Paul enjoyed his work. That was the one saving grace, getting it right sometimes. Opening the attic that was the mind, letting in light and air, throwing out the debris of years . . .

'I'm ever so sorry, doctor.'

He passed another tissue. 'I'm not. You needed that. Now, I suggest you go and freshen up. Put on some lipstick.' That always brought a smile and the woman's chin came up a little. 'Then we'll talk. If you want to, that is.'

While she was gone he pressed the intercom switch. 'Who was that? Mr Marriner? OK . . . Yes, get him for me as soon as Mrs Sullivan leaves.'

Ellie Marriner's folder was already on his desk. He looked at it, thinking of the bombshell it contained. Ethically, he should break the news to Ellie before he revealed it to her husband, but he was not sure she could cope with it. And time was ticking away. In the beginning Ellie Marriner's malady had seemed like simple anxiety over a dead and charming predecessor. But it was much, much more.

There was a timid knock on the door and he put thoughts of Ellie aside. One patient at a time was a good rule.

The hotel room had apricot curtains. Ellie's room in the Home, the room to which she had graduated on her

36

fifteenth birthday, had boasted apricot curtains but they had been cotton rep. These were velvet with watered silk pelmets to match the bedcover.

Her bag stood on a luggage rack at the foot of the bed, but she couldn't be bothered to unpack. Tomorrow she would have to buy a nightdress and a change of clothes. The red bag had had room only for bare essentials. No use worrying too much about money, but she couldn't afford to stay here, that was sure. Besides, it was the sort of place Richard would look for her, a former mansion converted to an hotel, recommended by the taxi driver who had brought her from Durham station. She must move on.

The excitement of escape was ebbing. She wanted a pill, but they must be saved. There was a well-stocked bar in the room but it would show up on her bill tomorrow and could not be afforded. Tomorrow! She took refuge from an unknown future by conjuring up the past.

Gatcombe Street: creaking stairs covered by a paper-thin carpet strip and always a smell of cat food. Pussy's pieces fetched from the fishmonger wrapped in news-print, boiled in a scabby pan while the cat kneaded the clippy mat in an orgy of anticipation. Clippy mats, that was something she had forgotten until now . . . wondrous concoctions of old rags, warm to the feet and full of dust. All your old clothes there, cut into strips and threaded through hard.

The cat had come to them as a stray and never had a name except Kitsa. When Gran had died they promised her it would go to a good home, but she

37

had seen the lie for what it was, a sop to a grieving eight-year-old.

She crossed to the drinks cabinet and turned the key. Remembering was painful and she needed a drink. Gin and tonic, just one to oil the wheels of memory. She poured, and let herself remember the Home. *'You're a clever girl, Elldis. Put your background behind you and make something of yourself.'* They had given her Life Preparation classes and taught her to boil eggs and mend nylons – but not how to cope with love or pain, or discover hope where hope did not exist.

She must find hope. Or at least facts. She had spent years trying to forget her northern heritage, but now she must remember. And if the truth, when she found it, was very terrible she must never see Richard or the boys again.

On impulse she crossed to the rack and unzipped the holdall. Jeremy's penholder looked out of place on the ornate dressing-table until she set it away to jiggle about and make the place its own. He wouldn't mind her taking it. He had always seen the need in her, just as she had sensed the need in him that day in the park. Perhaps she could phone the boys – but she must think it through first. She had already made one grave error in allowing Dr Weidenek to tape their conversations. There was something safe about the spoken word; even if it lived in memory it lost its sting. But words captured on tape took on a greater, a growing, menace. 'He knows me,' she said aloud, and then sucked in her cheeks in dismay. If she started talking to herself, who knew where it would end?

She took the flowered cosmetic bag from her case

and shook one pill into her palm. She had emptied all the bottles with their neat labels before she left the Garth. The pill was round and blue and potent. Just one. Just tonight. Just to begin.

Terri tried to relax in the car, taking in the deep leather seats, the leather-clad doors and chrome fittings in the bulkhead separating passengers from chauffeur. She had offered to get a train but Richard had been adamant: 'It'll be an enormous help to me if you're here, Terri, so we can all pool what we know. The least I can do is send a car.'

She had known Richard was a wealthy man but the car was something else. And a driver in a peaked cap! Any other time she'd have enjoyed the ride, but not today.

If only she hadn't been so screwed up over that damned shirt this morning she'd've realized something was up. She and Ellie had lived and worked together for four years, and Ellie knew the morning score. She would never have rung at nine o'clock on a working morning unless she'd been in trouble. She'd never indulged in casual calls, anyway. When they had lived together it was Terri who had hogged the phone; Ellie had hardly touched it. 'No one to phone,' she'd said once, when Terri had joked about it.

This morning she had put Ellie's call down to boredom. Any woman who didn't work must surely be subject to that! And any woman who did work was harassed to death. Still, a situation like this put everything into perspective. She tried to remember what Ellie had actually talked about. Richard seemed to think it was terribly important: 'You're her greatest friend,' he had said. But in reality this morning had amounted to nothing much more than an exchange of greetings and promises to meet at some unspecified future date. Except that Ellie had been vague about when . . . as though she might not be around in the future.

No, that was silly. She hadn't given Ellie her full attention this morning and now she was reading all sorts of nuances into a perfectly normal conversation. But Ellie had not mentioned that she was coming to London today, and that was strange. Perhaps she had wanted to avoid a lunch invitation? But they were old friends, and had no need of such evasion.

The car was leaving the M25 now and Slough was appearing on the signboards. She had never seen the Marriner plant although Richard had once issued an invitation. It was like so many things, there had never been the time. They drove between twin gate-houses and drew up at a glass reception area. Flags fluttered, a Queen's Award for Industry, a Union Jack and others Terri couldn't identify.

The chauffeur helped her out of the car and she walked up the steps.

'Mrs Benedict? Mr Richard is expecting you.' And then she was in a walnut-panelled lift and ascending to the floor marked Chairman.

Richard came forward as the lift doors opened. 'This is kind of you, Terri. I appreciate it. You know my sister-in-law, Adele?'

Terri remembered Adele from the wedding, handsome and as sweet as an armoured car. Her husband was a younger edition of Richard, except for the moustache, rising from his perch on the corner of a huge desk to greet her. The grey-haired home help, whom Ellie had grown so fond of even before her wedding, was sitting, knees together, on an upright chair, looking worried to death. This was beginning to look like a wake.

She took a swift glance round the office. By day there would be breath-taking views from the huge windows – Slough in the distance, with Windsor Castle behind it, perhaps even the Chilterns. Now, there was a fairy-land of lights strung out as far as the eye could see.

'And this is Paul Weidenek, the doctor who has been helping Ellie.' She put out her hand and felt a firm pressure. The psychiatrist's eyes were warm and shrewd. Bearded men always looked like Augustus John and frequently turned out to be Tiny Tim. This one was different, for reasons she couldn't yet define.

She accepted a cup of coffee from a secretary and took a chair.

Richard was moving to the seat behind his desk, a tall man in a well-cut suit, a powerful man who could summon aid at the press of a button. So why did she sense fear in him, as though he was a man being sucked into a vortex?

Richard had known something was dreadfully wrong as soon as he heard Adele's voice on the other end of the line: *'Richard? Look, Richard, it's probably nothing and I'm making a fuss far too soon, but I seem to have lost Ellie.'* Now they were all here, in his office, waiting for him to take charge and make it all come right. Adele, Frank,

41

Mrs Withers, Paul Weidenek, and Terri with her eyes fixed on his face.

He cleared his throat. 'Everyone got tea or coffee? Good. Just leave it there, Janet, we can help ourselves if we want more.' His secretary was gliding from the room. No further chance to procrastinate.

He laid his hands palm downwards on the desk. 'I propose we all describe what happened today. What we saw or said or did in relation to Ellie. And if anyone has ideas on where she might be, this is the time to trot them out.' He looked around but there was no dissent and the psychiatrist's eyes were reassuring. Richard tried not to let his own hostility show but it was difficult. If it hadn't been for Dr Weidenek urging caution, this might never have happened.

'Very well, I'll begin. Today was much like any other morning. I made tea and gave Ellie a cup . . . two cups. We didn't talk much . . .' He wanted to gloss over the previous evening's row but it was too important. 'I was still upset about an argument we'd had the night before . . . the usual thing. Ellie was seeking reassurance, and I made the devil's own job of giving it.'

No one was smiling reassuringly at him now, but perhaps he didn't deserve it. 'I asked Ellie what she'd be doing today and she said "shopping". I came downstairs to breakfast . . . I said goodbye to Ellie in the bedroom, quite amicably . . . we kissed goodbye . . . and then I left for the plant. On the way I started thinking about Ellie on her own in London so I spoke to Adele on the car-phone and she agreed to keep Ellie company.' He clasped his hands on the blotter. 'And that was that until Adele rang me at two-thirty.' Frank was looking at him sympathetically and he signalled his gratitude with an upturn of the mouth. 'That's about it. Except that there was nothing this morning, between Ellie and me, that would make her run away.'

Terri shifted in her chair. 'Are we sure she *has* run away? I've gone missing before. Bumped into friends or decided to see a film . . . I mean, she's not sitting at home now wondering where everyone else is, is she?'

Heads were swivelling, eyes locking with other eyes, seeking a get-out. Time to bring them to order. 'I'm afraid not, Terri. One, Ellie failed to meet Adele for lunch as planned. Two, she's not at the house. Mr Withers is there, standing by the phone. If Ellie had come home or been in touch, we'd know by now. Three, she has not been well lately, as Dr Weidenek knows. And four . . . and perhaps most important . . . Mrs Withers has checked her room. Her toothbrush is gone and her pills – the empty bottles are there but no contents – some photographs and one or two pieces of jewellery. I think we can take it that she meant to go.'

'And there's her outfit.' Adele was leaning forward, the light of superior knowledge in her eyes. 'As soon as she came on to the steps I knew it was bizarre. She hated fur . . . I'm sorry, Richard, but if you'd asked me about buying her fur I'd've told you. And she never dressed for effect, but this morning she looked stunning. Tarty, but stunning.'

Paul Weidenek was smiling. 'Tarty?'

Adele shrugged. 'Well, gaudy. Red dress, huge red hood, even bigger red handbag and the fox on top. It simply wasn't her.'

Richard was watching the doctor's face. 'Do you think it means something?'

Paul was nodding. 'Yes, I think it's interesting. That, and the fact she took her toothbrush. If you're intending suicide you don't take your toothbrush. I think she means to get up tomorrow morning – but where is another matter.'

Ellie had unpacked her toothbrush and placed the photographs on the dressing-table. The boys and Richard on the steps of the *Sacré Coeur*. She and Richard in profile, her favourite photograph of them together. Richard with Trumper, holding a tit-bit so that the dog stood erect, nearly as tall as its master.

And Julia. Julia in virginal white on her wedding-day, discovered between layers in one of Richard's drawers. Beautiful Julia, who drew her as the candle draws the moth. Damn Julia, she was going to cry, and if she cried she would look a mess and someone would put two and two together and give her away. She swung her legs off the bed and returned to the drinks cabinet. One more small gin with lots of tonic. A bracer, that was all. And then she would make plans, a neat list of things that must be done.

She carried her drink to the writing table and pulled a letterhead from the rack. On an impulse she reached for the cord and pulled back the curtains. There was Durham, cathedral and castle floodlit against the night sky, looking like a fairy kingdom waiting for a once and future king. She had been born here, in this kingdom by the sea. And yet she felt nothing, no sense of belonging, no singing in the blood. Nothing. And she had felt no kinship with the south. Perhaps she was condemned to live in limbo like the Flying Dutchman.

She uncapped her pen and held it above the page. If she didn't make concrete plans, time would run out. Or money. If she was careful she could make the money last, but eluding Richard would be more difficult. She put the end of the pen to her mouth and touched it with her tongue. Perhaps at this very moment he was setting the wheels in motion. 'Lost – one wife.' Correction: 'One second wife.' *'Last seen wandering vaguely, quite of her own accord . . . she tried to get down to the end of the town. Forty shillings reward.'*

That was a poem by A. A. Milne. And if she could remember reciting that in a childhood schoolroom, why couldn't she remember the rest of her past? She reached for her glass. Why did she feel she had always known Julia, when the idea was patently absurd? She glanced at the dressing-table. Julia in white, lifting the veil from her face, blowing out the birthday candles. *'Blow Ellie, blow. Blow the candles out for Julia. That's a good little girl.'*

Ellie sat up sharply, so sharply that gin slopped from the glass and stickied her fingers. Perhaps she was going mad. There had never been a birthday cake for Julia, not within the ambit of her memory. She must be going mad. She crossed to the dressing-table, seeking reassurance, but the woman who looked back from the mirror was a wild-eyed stranger. Tomorrow they might print her picture in the papers: *'Mrs Richard Marriner, whereabouts unknown.'* And they were sure to mention Julia . . . the first, the proper, Mrs Richard Marriner, whose father had been a knight of the shires. How could she hope to compete, she who could remember no father at all?

They had all been talking for an hour now and still facts came tumbling out. 'She said I should put the winter-weight duvets on the boys' beds. I wondered at the time, with them not coming back for a fortnight. Now I can see why she said it.'

Mrs Withers' eyes were suspiciously bright, but Paul Weidenek was thinking of Gary, pulling himself up on the pillows, hugging the duvet: *'I'm gasping for tea. Ta.'* He was always like a child in the morning, shorn of leather and denim, the lines of discontent sponged from his face by sleep. He was twenty-one years old and a hundred and nineteen. Paul shifted in his seat and tried to concentrate on the conversation. Time enough for Gary when he got home. Please God let him be there.

'She's so naïve . . . amazingly naïve, really, considering she worked on a paper.' Adele managed to make Ellie sound educationally subnormal and rolled her eyes to deplore the fact. Irritation flared at the back of Paul's mind. There had been too much of Adele on the tapes, too much altogether.

'I wouldn't call her naïve, Mrs Marriner. She has a certain innocence . . . but there is also intellect there. That has been one cause of her trouble, I think – too great a degree of awareness, of sensitivity, leading to depression. There is no need for antidepressants on a ward for the mentally subnormal, you know. It's the intelligent among us who suffer.'

There was no mistaking the reproof and Paul saw

Adele's eyes flicker towards her husband Frank, who was looking directly at him.

'You're right, of course, Dr Weidenek. If Ellie had been less sensitive she'd have had an easier time. We all underestimated what it must be like, coming into a ready-made family. I know I did. So if there's anything I can usefully do . . .' He was looking towards his brother now but Richard's eyes were fixed on Paul, as though in challenge. Weidenek stood up and moved to the desk.

'If I may sum up . . . we know Ellie meant to go. She made arrangements for the running of her home to cover the next few weeks, so she means to stay away for a while. She must know we are all worried and she cares about that. The phone call to Mrs Benedict this morning was meant to reassure – she couldn't say what she intended to do, but she wanted to imply that all would be well. I think she'll ring again soon but I don't think she'll return. Not yet. I think she's gone in search of her past. We've talked a lot about that over the last few weeks. Ostensibly she knows who and what she is, but there's something else, something shelled over like grit in an oyster. I would have got to it in time . . . Perhaps that's why she chose to go now – because I was coming close.'

'Does she know what it is, this secret?' Adele was leaning forward as she spoke.

'Not with the conscious part of her mind,' Paul said. 'But it's there. I think she's almost certainly travelled north, to Durham, the place where she was brought up, hoping that old scenes may bring it back or that she may find actual evidence.'

There was silence in the room except for a faint sibilance from the strip lighting. Paul looked at the faces. Adele Marriner agog, excited by what was happening; Terri Benedict genuinely concerned; the old woman from the house confused and distressed. The two brothers were the least affected, on the face of it, but that was the English public school and its infinite capacity for turning out poker players.

There was a knock on the door and the spell broke. Richard's secretary looked in.

'I'm off, Mr Marriner, if there's nothing else? Masters is waiting downstairs to take Mrs Benedict back to London.'

Paul looked around. They were all moving in their chairs, glad of the break in tension. If only Ellie had let him use sodium pentothal, but she had been afraid to let him probe too deeply. He thought of other patients, voices guileless under the influence of the drug, telling him the most intimate details without shame. If only Ellie had trusted him. If only . . . that was half his work – and half his life.

The door closed and five faces turned expectantly towards him. 'I don't know exactly what she'll do because I don't completely know her. I have tapes of our conversations and I hope to do some work on them. I think we must register her as missing, but I'm fairly sure she won't do anything foolish . . . not before her curiosity is satisfied.'

'And then?' Richard Marriner's voice was even, only his eyes betrayed fear.

Paul searched for words. Monstrous to cause greater fear, equally wrong to give false reassurance. 'I don't know. I would like to find out how many pills she has with her – I'll give her GP a ring and check her prescriptions. In the mean time we must assume she has . . . enough.'

'She'd never do herself harm.' Mrs Withers had come to life, hands clasped on her handbag, mouth resolute. 'She's not that selfish. Not after what Mr Richard and the boys has been through. I know she's poorly and not herself, but she'll never hurt anyone and that's a fact.'

Richard was nodding. 'I'm sure Mrs Withers is right. Ellie adores the boys, and I think she'll come back for their weekend at home. In the mean time we need to organize. The phone must be manned round the clock. I'll inform the police . . .'

He was all right now he had something to manage. Paul sat back as they all volunteered and shared out burdens. In a moment, with any luck, the others would go and he could break the news to Richard. After that he must persuade him not to do anything precipitate. And that would not be easy.

Adele felt a terrible excitement as she drove home. At first Frank was behind her but she lost him at a roundabout and he didn't overtake. The needle flicked beyond eighty and settled at ninety but her thoughts were breaking limits. Pregnant! Trust that little bitch to play the trump card. And Richard had lain down and rolled over at the news! It was sickening.

She had taken Mrs Withers to the loo and then gone back to Richard's office. Frank was taking Terri down to the car and Richard was alone with the psychiatrist.

She had put out a hand to the door and heard her brother-in-law's voice, slurring with shock. 'Pregnant? But she can't be, she wanted to wait . . .'

And then Dr Weidenek: 'I'm afraid she is. Probably five or six weeks. That's why I'm worried about the pills. She's on Dervinox and Imprival, harmless in ordinary circumstances but not advisable in pregnancy. And there's another thing: I can't be sure of her reaction. She didn't want a child, so what will she do when she finds out? I want her to be back here, under my care, before that happens. That's why I didn't mention it in front of the others. But time is running out, we can't keep it quiet for ever.'

There had been movement then and Adele had stepped back from the door and walked unsteadily back to the cloakroom. When Mrs Withers emerged from the loo she was powdering her nose at the vanity unit as though she had been there, preening, all the time.

Now she pressed the accelerator to vent her fury. It wasn't fair, that was what stung. It simply wasn't fair that Ellie should walk in from nowhere, from somewhere dubious if Dr Weidenek was to be believed, and take everything! She would now be the centre of attention. However it worked out, they would all fuss over her, even Frank. When she'd arrived at Richard's office this afternoon he'd looked at her with positive dislike. His own wife! 'I thought you were looking after her,' he'd said, as though she had deliberately got rid of Ellie.

They wouldn't let her go to Japan, not now. She would have to stay tied to the phone like a hen on eggs, waiting for a silly, neurotic bitch to ring and say she was coming home. Back to Julia's house. To have babies.

It had been so good when Julia was alive. Friends since childhood, eager to live cheek-by-jowl and share everything, the way they had always shared things. They had come back to school that first summer and compared notes about their lost virginity. *'I'm going to marry Richard and you and Frank will live next door and we'll both have a baby every year for ever and ever.'* Julia had sat on the edge of her bed, hugging her knees, and devised the plan for the two houses. *'Simply super places with French windows everywhere and great sweeping staircases. And near enough for us to shout to one another whenever we choose.'* As usual, Julia had got her way, and then she had died.

'I won't let Ellie spoil it all,' Adele said aloud and changed into overdrive.

Ellie had tried the television, operating it from the remote control in the bedhead, but there was nothing to interest her. War, war and rumours of war. Ships in the gulf and freedom fighters in Afghanistan. Guerrillas in El Salvador and pompous politicians trading insults and calling one another by their Christian names as though they meant no harm. It was funny really. Hilarious.

She lay back on the pillows and contemplated the ceiling until the light blurred and swelled, beating on her closed lids. Open your eyes, Ellie, mustn't settle to sleep. That was when thoughts came about Richard with Julia – locked together, a beast with two backs, endlessly making babies. The ultimate sin. There had been retribution, even for Julia. She had died, which was funny really. Absolutely comical.

Tomorrow she must buy a nightdress. For tonight she had pulled her waist-slip up over her breasts but it felt wrong, even in the closed, air-conditioned bedroom. Too much expanse of thigh, too much skin. Wickedness – that was what it all stemmed from, really. She started to cry and tried to work out why. Perhaps she was crying because she was not dead like Julia? She had to live and feel this pain. She had already had two pills but another drink would do no harm. If she had another drink she might forget about Julia, block out the sight of her in Richard's arms, drown the sound of his panting breath, the way he called out 'Julia' at the last exquisite thrust.

Suddenly she was filled with self-disgust. Where did these thoughts come from? And what was she doing here in this strange hotel room? She had thought of her journey as an odyssey but it was no such thing. She was not being clever or brave; she was a stupid, cowardly, dirty-minded, probably crazy woman who had not been able to go forward. Now it was too late to go back.

On the dressing-table Julia stared back at her but Ellie could not meet those serene eyes. She had never locked gaze with anyone in her whole life. She thought of the face then, the unyielding face that was Richard's and not Richard's, and still the face of every man she had ever met. Thought of it, and drained her glass.

When she tried to stand up the room tilted alarmingly but she couldn't waste the tonic left in the bottle. She could never quite manage to finish the tonic, so there had to be more gin. But then there was not enough tonic so she had to open another, and the whole tarra diddle began again. She slid down the side of the bed and sat on the floor to laugh. It was good this thing, drink and pills. It didn't stop you thinking but no thoughts stayed for long enough to hurt. Unless they were funny, in which case they stayed and stayed.

Her nose was running and she reached for the apricot coverlet. No, the mucus would make a mark on the watered silk and revolt the next guest. *'Be a lady, Ellie'*: Mrs Harper had been keen on people being ladies. People! Pee-pul. The word was explosively funny. *'Pee-pul, pee-pul who need pee-pul.'* She managed to turn on to her hands and knees and began to crawl, pains-takingly, in search of a tissue.

'Where the hell have you been?' Mike was standing in the kitchen doorway, a tea-towel in his hand. Behind him the microwave whined and gave its final ping. 'I didn't expect you'd be back,' she said, closing the door behind her.

'Obviously. I came back early because you behaved like a shrew on the phone. So I dumped Diana and the kids at the school and gave them cab fare home. I felt ashamed, Terri, but I did it. I got back here at seven. No Terri. I've waited and waited for this miraculous meal you thought more important than my kids, and when I got too bloody ravenous to care I shoved some chemical muck into the microwave. So much for wed-ded bliss!'

Terri put down her bag and started to shrug out of

her coat. 'I thought you were out with Diana and the kids. Richard phoned to say Ellie had gone missing. He needed to talk so I went over – he sent a car. If I'd known you were here, waiting, I'd . . .' But she would still have gone! Ellie was a friend and she was in trouble.

Mike had shovelled the plastic bags of rice and curry on to a plate and was trying to snip the tops. 'Let me.' Not for the first time she wondered why they didn't invent an easier way. The kitchen scissors baulked at the plastic and when she tore it open with the tip of the bread-knife half the contents remained in the bags and defied squeezing.

'Has Ellie turned up?' There was no quarter in Mike's voice and Terri felt her own resolve harden.

'No. She's missing and the police have been called in. I'm sorry if that minor occurrence interfered with your fucking supper but she happens to be a friend of mine.'

He had taken a few mouthfuls of food. Now he pushed the plate away. 'And Gemma and Alison happen to be my kids. Flesh and blood which, I might remind you, is supposed to be thicker than water. It's always the same – you react every time I try to do something for them. Not content with breaking up their home, you seem to want to deprive them of any contact with their father.'

He was taking out his guilt on her and they both knew it but that wouldn't stop them.

'Your marriage was a bloody waste-land long before I came on the scene. Put the blame where it belongs, lover: on your bitch of an ex-wife, whom you could not handle, cannot handle and will not be able to handle in the future. And why? Because you're a wimp. A grade A, first-class wimp.'

He was through the doorway when he turned. 'I'm going to bed, Terri. To sleep. Don't get in beside me and touch and snuggle and make up because it'll be a waste of time. I couldn't make it tonight if you were Selina Scott . . . which, needless to say, you aren't. And if you're going to repeat one of the more insane of your accusations, that I've been bonking Diana tonight and am therefore shagged out, forget it. The truth is that I don't fancy you, that's all!'

The courgettes and veal she had bought in her lunch hour were still in her bag. She took them out and placed them carefully in the fridge. There was a small bowl on the bottom shelf with a healthy growth of fur on the rim. Pork drippings. She scraped it into the waste-bin and put the bowl to steep.

The bedroom light went out as she crossed the living-room. He was going to make her get undressed in the dark and creep into bed like a thief. 'I love you,' she whispered as she flicked the switch but she was careful to say it too quietly for him to hear.

[3]

Ellie woke in the early morning. No light filtered through the thick curtains and when she pulled them back she looked out on a still-darkened world. Trees were garlanded with mist and loomed ghostly in the light of old-fashioned street lamps dotting the hotel grounds. She closed the curtains and turned away.

Her tongue felt huge in an arid mouth and waves of nausea were sweeping over her. On the dressing-table glasses and bottles gave mute evidence of last night's drinking. She must never do that again. She felt a sudden wave of sickness and made for the bathroom, but nothing would come. Sweat had broken out on her brow and she gripped the sink's porcelain sides. Oh God, she felt awful. Tears squeezed between closed lids and trickled down her face.

In spite of her woes she smiled. If she went on like this, her voyage of discovery would turn into a lost weekend! She switched on the kettle and as she scalded tea the papers she had ordered the night before slithered under the door.

In the bathroom she stepped under the shower and turned it to cold. The icy water hit her, cutting off breath and making her move smartly out of range. She adjusted the temperature and let the water take her, washing away the imagined grime of the previous night's excess. A sachet of shampoo was thoughtfully provided by the management, and she lathered her hair. Ten minutes later she was back in bed, turbanned and cosy inside a huge bath towel, ready to drink her tea.

None of the papers carried a word of her departure, much less a photograph. A crazy thought struck her: perhaps they would simply let her go? Carry on as though nothing had happened, as though she had never existed? Perhaps, at this moment, Richard was whistling as he shaved, Mrs Withers was humming as she grilled bacon, and no one had noticed she was gone? There would be no mark, no sign that she had ever been there. The house would sigh with relief and settle to being Julia's house once more. It could happen. She had never been more than a ripple, a gnat skimming the calm pond of their existence.

She turned to television for relief but it was useless. One side had a woman bobbing about in a mad set of physical jerks and the other side had not even begun to transmit. As soon as light broke she would walk in the misty gardens, gingerly in her high-heeled pumps, but as far as she could go. And after she had settled her bill and vacated the room she would go into Durham city and buy some sensible shoes.

When she went back to the window the sky to the east, where it showed above still-dark tree tops, was pale pink. To the south she could see the outline of the cathedral tower, four-square and black against a grey sky. She still felt slightly sick and pain hammered at her temples but it was impossible to watch dawn break without an uplift of spirits. She moved at last to the chair which held her clothes and began to get dressed.

Richard made tea at four a.m. and climbed back into bed to drink it. At five he abandoned any pretence at sleep and began to prepare for the day. He had listened to the World Service through the night and it was a relief when he could switch to the familiarity of Radio 4. As dawn broke he was standing by the window looking out on the deserted garden and his brother's house opposite, its windows still dark. 'She'll come back,' Frank had said last night but there had been more sympathy than conviction in his voice.

Richard thought of his visit to the police station. The inspector had been bland and almost uninterested. 'The most likely outcome, sir, is that your wife will ring you . . . from a friend's or some family member's home. If she'd been visibly disturbed, acting strangely, anything like that, we'd've heard by now. Someone always rings in. We'll put out feelers – the dress and coat sound quite distinctive. We're contacting the Met about Harrods. Perhaps you could give the WPC all the details you know . . . but my guess is you'll soon be ringing us to say "Panic over".'

So he had repeated Ellie's description to a WPC hardly old enough to be out of school, let alone in uniform. And all the while it had seemed like a scene in a bad television play that would be interrupted any moment by an advertisement for coffee. He'd asked about press involvement. 'I think tomorrow's soon enough, sir. We don't want to stir up a mare's nest. We'll contact you tomorrow morning and if there's been no word from Mrs Marriner we'll take it from there.' Not that he had much faith in press coverage. Ellie's face, though beautiful, was not distinctive. She looked like any other intelligent, well-behaved twenty-eight-year-old woman, until you looked into her eyes or heard her speak, softly, as though in awe of her own voice.

Oh God, if she came back, if she only came back, he would be different. He would explain, explore. He would *communicate*. He had never really told Julia he loved her, not even at the end. He had always expected her to take it for granted. She had behaved as though she did, but perhaps he had been wrong about that too; perhaps Julia, like Ellie, had wanted more? They had never really talked about life, about anything other than the humdrum details of everyday existence and how jolly it all was – not even when they had looked at the children they had made together. Privately he had felt each child to be a miracle but he had kept it to himself.

And then Ellie had come into his life and he had had a second chance. But if anything he had been less forthcoming, less free with his feelings. Something had held him back: guilt, perhaps. A feeling that to be more open with Ellie would be a betrayal of Julia. The fact that Ellie had no family had been easy to accept, convenient even. He winced, remembering how uninterested he had been in his second wife's background.

Across the garden a light sprang up in an upstairs room. Frank must be awake too. They had always

59

shared things, the good and the bad. On the night of Julia's death Frank had tramped beside him for mile after mile, not speaking or comforting, just being there. A bird was being impossibly cheerful in the horse-chestnut and behind him on the radio the *Today* programme was under way. Tuesday was beginning, an ordinary day for the rest of the world and with luck a day of relief for him.

Paul poached eggs and drained them carefully before putting them on an empty plate. Gary hated soggy toast, preferring it cut into crisp fingers on a side plate. Orange juice, coffee, the hideous tabloid Gary swore by, and a solitary letter. When they were all on the tray he carried it up to the bedroom and set it down on the bedside table.

The boy was curled in sleep, knees almost up to chin, mouth slack, one slender brown arm behind his head, the other flung into the space Paul had vacated.

'Wake up, lazybones. Some of us have to work!'

As the words left his lips he regretted them. Yesterday morning they had rowed about money: '*Your* house, *your* car, *your* furniture; oh God, the very food I eat is *your* food. I've got nothing, I do nothing, I am nothing. Go on, say it.'

But today there were to be no recriminations. Gary smiled and stretched, without opening his eyes. 'Jealousy gets you nowhere.'

Paul tried not to show relief. 'Come on, sit up. Eggs and coffee. I wouldn't do this for everyone.'

That was also the wrong thing to say, but again the good mood endured. Last night they had been close, vowing, showing one another tenderness, and even in the cold light of day some of it remained.

'Anything special today?' The juice stayed on the upper lip, a faint orange moustache, and the blue eyes were full of anticipation. He shivered a little and Paul crossed to the ottoman to fetch a sweater.

'Put this on. The year's changing.'

The boy pushed head and arms into place and pulled the jersey down under the duvet. 'You do fuss, I'm tougher than I look. Good toast though. And you haven't answered my question.'

If Paul sat on the bed any longer he would reach out, pull the blond head to him and make a fool of himself. Gary would despise him for showing weakness, nothing more. Instead he crossed to the window and looked out on the almost empty street. 'Much the same as usual. I've one patient who's gone AWOL, though. A woman. I think she'll be OK but I'll be glad when she's safely home.'

Gary was grinning. 'Nutters! I can't get over you being a shrink. Everyone thinks it's a gas.' *Everyone* being the slightly sinister crowd he knocked around with, Paul thought, and turned back to the window.

'It's a living. Anyway, I'll be back early tonight and we can eat out. Anywhere you like.'

'No, it's my treat.' Gary was speaking with his mouth full. 'I'll bring something in and we'll eat in style.' Last night Paul had given him ten ten-pound notes so he was feeling generous. 'I'll even clear up afterwards if you behave yourself.'

*

Terri knew Mike was gone as soon as she woke, before she reached out and touched the empty space. It was probably just as well. If they had come face to face, both feeling rough in the early morning, there might have been another ding-dong. All the same, he was a swine to leave her sleeping when it might have made her late for work.

Her anger evaporated when she saw the note on the kettle. 'Sorry! Hope Ellie turns up well. Ring me before lunch, I might make a pint and pie. I love you. Mike.' Euphoria carried her through to the bathroom and back to the bedroom to choose something nice to wear. They would sit in the pub, knees touching under the table, eyes locked, mouthing platitudes across the noise. It would be bliss!

Suddenly and remorsefully she thought of Ellie, out there somewhere, on her own, while she, Terri, was meeting the man she loved at lunchtime. She was mad to be jealous, mad and double mad. Mike had walked away from Diana, in spite of the kids. And he had married her when she had been quite ready to accept a looser arrangement.

She sat at the dressing-table to do her make-up and then, in an orgy of wifeliness, swept make-up and assorted debris from the top of the dressing-table into a drawer to be tidied later. Mike was quite right about her being disorganized. Not that she wanted to turn into a *hausfrau* but there was a happy medium. Last night had not been her fault, but there'd been other times. Once Ellie was safely home she'd get down to some real planning. She looked round the bedroom. There had not been time to decorate, and it showed. It needed vinyl silk emulsion on the walls and some decent curtains. The home Mike shared with Diana had been decidedly *Homes and Gardens*, if she was to believe all she had heard. How he must hate all this tat!

Suddenly, Terri felt depressed. Even if lunch went well and tonight was a veritable love-in, it would only be a matter of time before they were again at one another's throats. She must do a feature on second marriage. Everyone was at it nowadays, or would be if the statistics were correct. Though you could never be really truthful if you were relating your own experience. As she wriggled into her good navy suit she thought about Ellie. Marriage to a widower ought to be a breeze: no alimony, no demands, no comparisons. Except that the dead had a habit of achieving sainthood, whether or not they deserved it. Perhaps a live rival complete with warts was better than a sanitized predecessor. And if Terri's instincts were right, Adele would make sure Ellie didn't have too easy a ride.

She juggled priorities for a moment, weighing the need to placate her husband against her friend's need for help. She decided to postpone decisions. Ten to one Ellie would turn up during the day, and Richard and the nice psychiatrist with the gimlet eyes could sort it all out. If not . . . well, a mate was a mate.

She twisted her Liberty scarf round so that the scorch mark was hidden and squirted herself liberally with Ysatis. God help anybody who got in her way today: they'd be felled at the first sniff.

Adele walked with Frank to the car, both of them trying to pretend there was not an atmosphere between them.

'See you tonight,' he said, brushing her cheek with his moustache.

It was not enough and she clutched his jacket. 'Hold on. Kiss me properly.'

Frank smiled, but the second kiss was as perfunctory as the first.

Last night he had sat on the edge of the bed with his back to her, making a big thing of taking off his slippers. 'Have you any idea why she went, Adele? Did anything happen . . . between you, I mean?'

She had been about to swear innocence when she changed tack. 'I must say that's cool, Frank. I've run myself ragged trying to help her settle in, and now you're suggesting I've driven her away.'

He had twisted around to face her. 'I'm not suggesting anything. Merely asking for facts.'

She had bounced from the bed and paced the floor to defend herself but his expression had said it all: 'You're my wife, Adele, but I don't always like you.'

For a moment she'd been tempted to blame everything on Ellie's pregnancy: 'Women often do strange things when they're preggers. You can't blame me.' But some instinct told her to keep the secret. The information might be useful at some stage . . . and anyway, she was not supposed to know. If he found out she'd listened in to a confidence he would despise her even more. So she had argued her case as best she could, pleading her own innocence and Ellie's complete unsuitability to be Richard's wife. In the end Frank had called a halt. 'This is crazy. Richard's going to need us tomorrow. We'd better get some sleep.'

At seven a.m. he had phoned Richard in the hope

of news, but there was nothing. Now, as they stood at the car, he looked across at the other house. 'Do your best for him today, Del.'

Her conscience smote her at the sound of the pet name. 'I will, you know I will. I'll chain myself to the phone and the minute she calls I'll ring you.'

He smiled and nodded. 'Good.' He had to fold himself into the car, the long legs coiling under the dashboard. 'See you tonight, then.'

She watched as the car churned gravel and then sped towards the gates. She would do her best today – she didn't wish any harm to come to Ellie, she just wanted her to disappear. Especially if there was going to be a baby. Julia's sons taking precedence over her daughters was a pain; a Richard/Ellie baby would be the absolute end.

Ellie packed her few possessions and checked that nothing had been left behind before she went down to breakfast. She was never really at ease in hotels, she had come to them too late for that. But it was not insecurity that made her look under the bed and push her hand down the sides of the armchair. You never knew what would give you away. She had tried to leave at home anything bearing her name, even jettisoning the pill bottles, but you could never be too careful.

The dining-room was almost deserted. She still felt vaguely nauseous but some breakfast might help. '*Put a lining on your stomach*,' – that had been Grandma's injunction on autumn and winter mornings. And spring and summer mornings, come to that. She took orange juice from the side-table and carried it to a corner.

'Coffee or tea, madam? And could I have your room number?' She ordered a Continental breakfast and opened *The Times*. At the next table a man was shuffling through morning papers, stopping occasionally to read beyond a headline and then carrying on. He looked up and caught her watching him.

'Nothing in 'em. Still, it pays to check.' He finished the *Sun* and added it to the pile. 'All tits and tittle-tattle.'

Ellie didn't like him but he was only trying to be friendly. Besides, if she shied away he might get suspicious. She smiled. 'Have you got *The Times*?'

'Yes, ta, I get 'em all. Tax deductible in my business.' She had marked him down as a rep, but a compulsory study of current affairs was hardly *de rigueur* for a commercial traveller.

'Look, we might as well share.' He was moving himself and his cup to her table and taking the opposite seat. 'Dave Smith.' He held out his hand and Ellie licked her lips. Must, must, must get the name right.

'Caroline Shaw.' Was that the name she had given when she registered? She was suddenly aware of the name she had wanted to use: *'Julia. I am Julia.'* That was what she had wanted to say but instead she had written 'Caroline Shaw' in a firm hand. At least, she thought that was what she had done.

Confusion made her hand shake and tea slopped from her cup, but he seemed not to notice. He was looking around the high-ceilinged room with its William Morris wallpaper and huge, antique sideboards. 'Nice place. Stay here often?'

Ellie shook her head, but the piggy eyes were fixed on her face. She would have to give him something. Fear sharpened her wits and she gave up worrying about the recesses of her mind. There was only here and now, the pink-clad breakfast table with its single carnation, the chrome teapot and water jug, the curious face opposite and her own desperate need to survive.

'Actually, I'm here to work.' She gave what she hoped was a simper. 'I'm starting a new book and I find it pays to get right away for a few days, just to get under way.' His eyes had flicked to her wedding finger. 'My husband is taking care of the children. He's very good.'

The man was visibly impressed. 'Shaw you said, didn't you? Catherine Shaw? I've heard the name.'

She nodded. 'Actually, it's Caroline . . . I write romantic fiction. You've probably seen it about.' Now to carry the battle into the enemy camp. 'What do you do?'

He had taken a cigar case from an inside pocket and was preparing to cut the end. The satisfied set of his mouth told her he was proud of his profession but he didn't answer immediately. 'Do you mind?' He held up the cigar until she shook her head, then he snipped and lit up with a slim lighter. 'Ah.' He blew out smoke and smiled. 'I have to confess, I'm a politician.' He grinned in mock embarrassment. 'Couldn't you guess from the way I was scanning the filthy capitalist press? We're always hungry for a mention.'

For a moment Ellie considered that this might be some strange surrealistic game they were playing, and his story no more authentic than her own, but there

67

was the sleek, well-satisfied air of the bureaucrat about him.

'Tell me more,' she said archly and began to top up her cup.

The boy had ceased to fidget and was staring impassively at the floor. In the adjoining chair his mother pursed her lips and looked at Paul. 'See?' her eyes said, 'This is what I have to put up with.'

He gave her a half-smile, hoping she would not see it as confirmation of her view. Too early to come out and say what he thought, that she was more than half to blame for her son's withdrawal. He turned to his patient. 'Last week you said you liked Weather Report, David.' The boy's eyes lifted for a second, then dropped again. 'I have two of their albums . . . *Night Passage* and *Domino Theory*. We might play them on your next visit. There's someone else I think you might enjoy: Pat Metheny. Have you heard of him?'

There was a tiny shake of the head.

'Well, I'll bring him along and you can tell me what you think.' He pushed back his chair to show the consultation was over but the mother was not satisfied.

'You go on, David. I want to talk to the doctor.'

The boy's gait was uneven, his progress to the door painfully slow.

'Well . . .' the mother said, turning back to face Paul when the door closed behind her son, 'we don't seem to be making much progress, doctor, do we?'

He forced a smile to his face and leaned forward to speak.

When she had gone, resigned to the fact that he must

see the boy alone next time, he pressed his intercom switch. 'You can get me that number now, Susan; the Sunningdale one.' He flipped open Ellie's folder and checked her GP's name. The pregnancy test was uppermost, its verdict ringed and ornamented with an exclamation mark. It was routine for the lab to do a pregnancy test when they were making other checks. Modern drugs were a powerful weapon but had to be used with care, and the patient's entire condition was a vital part of any equation. So the urine sample had been tested for a wide range of possibilities. Only the pregnancy test had been positive, and Paul had been amazed. Husband and wife had both stressed at interview their joint desire to prevent conception, Ellie for reasons of her own, about which she had been vague, Richard because it had been his wife's wish in the beginning and now he was too concerned about her mental state to want any complications. The responsibility for contraception had been his.

Paul closed the folder and then opened it again as the ringing tone commenced on the line. 'Dr Mortimer? Paul Weidenek here. You may remember you referred a patient to me, Elldis Marriner . . . ?'

Mike was waiting at the bar, Terri's half of Carlsberg ready. 'Hallo, darling. Can you squeeze in?'

All around them people were laughing, talking, jostling about, ample excuse to move close until they touched.

'Sorry about last night.'

'Me too.'

'Forgiven?'

'It was my fault.'

'No, it wasn't, it was mine.'

'All right, it was yours.'

'Oh, God, you're a cunning swine.'

'Drink up and shut up, woman.'

They carried their drinks to the first vacated table and strained to see the blackboard with the day's menu. 'Chilli, I think.'

'Me too.'

Mike came back with slopping plates of chilli and rice. 'It's watery,' he said in disgust and stirred the rice with his spoon.

'Never mind, I'll cook *cordon bleu* for supper, or as bleury as I can manage.'

'I love you, Terri Benedict.'

'Yes, I rather love myself.'

'Touché! Now, tell me about Ellie.'

She had rung Richard at nine a.m. and got Mrs Withers: 'There's been nothing, Mrs Benedict, not a word. But Mr Richard says no news is good news.' Her tone had asked for confirmation and Terri gave it.

'I'm sure he's right. She'll probably just walk back in some time today, you'll see.'

Now she chewed on lukewarm rice and lumpy mince with one or two kidney beans struggling through an onslaught of chilli powder and contemplated the riddle of Ellie's departure.

'Do you think they'd had a row?' Mike said.

She shook her head. 'I don't think so. For one thing, I don't think either of them knows how to fight.'

He grinned. 'Unlike another couple I could mention. Still, they're not going to do it again.'

She rolled her eyes. 'Sure?'

He grinned and licked the corner of his mouth where sauce had lingered. 'Fairly sure.'

Around them the pub heaved and erupted with noise. 'I love you, Mike – that's why I'm such a bitch about Diana. I know you loved her once and I can't really believe that it's me you love now.'

He wanted to come to meet her but his eyes were wary. They had tried to reason things out before, usually with disastrous results.

'I still care for her in a way, Terri; I have to be honest about that. We shared a lot and there were some good times at the beginning. But I don't like her any more. Perhaps I never did. She's a scheming, manipulative bitch. I never had with her what I have with you. We're mates. Partners. You take the bad times . . . I haven't been able to offer any good times so far, but I will, if only you'll believe me.'

She wanted to, oh how much she wanted to, believe. 'Finish your drink and I'll get you another,' she said and began to fumble in her bag.

The hotel bill came to £63, £8 of it for drink. The hotel receptionist's manner was cool and efficient, her long red fingernails flicking over the computer until it clattered out the total. There was no smile, no wish for a pleasant journey, and Ellie felt irrationally put down.

What did it matter? Why the agonizing as though the girl's coldness had been her fault? Why did she mind so much what people thought of her, even people she was unlikely ever to see again? Why, when she closed her eyes, did the face appear, a male face closed as the Bastille?

She picked up her bags and moved to the door. It was chilly outside and she realized she would need to buy a coat. Leaves stirred at her feet, pale brown from the trees, blood-red from the creeper-clad walls.

'Taxi, madam?' The hall porter had followed her on to the steps. She would have preferred to take a bus into Durham and save some money, but a guest who walked down the drive lugging her cases might stick in his memory.

'Yes, please,' she said.

While she waited for the cab to arrive she kept an eye out for Dave Smith, the MP. He too was leaving this morning, travelling into Newcastle to make some TV appearances. 'I never stay on top of the job,' he'd confided when she'd asked why he didn't stay in Newcastle itself. 'Doesn't do for the rank and file to see you enjoying the fleshpots. No use telling them the telly pays for it . . . they think you should pig it with the rest of them. Always offer to put you up. I tried that in the beginning, when I was green – bunking in with the lodger in someone's back bedroom. Mug's game! You have to conserve yourself in this job. I believe in equality but . . .' and he had tapped his nose . . . 'some of us are more equal than others.'

She saw him suddenly, walking towards the doors, but to her relief he stopped and went back to Reception. He was asking a question and the receptionist was turning away to check something for him. While Ellie watched he reached for the file of guests' registrations and rifled through them. Why was he doing that?

What was he looking for? It could only be her card: no one else would have lied about their name. She was the only one with something to hide. She had given a false name and address. Caroline. Caroline Shaw. She had written that . . . or had it been Julia? In her mind's eye her hand executed the name, finishing with a flourish.

In spite of the cold wind, sweat trickled down her back and her face tingled. She was going to be exposed.

A hand descended on her arm and she turned. 'Your taxi, miss.' She was safe in the womb of the cab, her bags beside her on the seat, the MP a bad dream retreating behind her. He would never be able to find her now.

On the way down the drive she calmed herself by thinking about Richard. It was almost eleven o'clock. He would be drinking coffee now, poring over figures or consulting schedules. The thought that he might be disturbed by her flight, might well be sitting at home wringing his hands, occurred briefly and was dismissed until she recognized the dichotomy of her own attitude. With one half of her mind she believed he would not even miss her, with the other half she feared his pursuit.

The river gleamed suddenly at the corner of her eye and she saw they were crossing the bridge. She had asked to be put down in the city centre and the taxi drew up in a market square with a statue of horse and rider. 'Thank you,' she said, 'this is fine.'

She walked into the main shopping street and looked for a chain store. A temporary charity shop loomed up and she went inside. It was dark and foisty and piled high with second-hand clothes. Two women chatted beside a till and pictures of woebegone animals plastered the walls.

She rifled through a rack of coats but there was nothing to fit. A table piled with handbags caught her eye, most of them plastic and tired. She glanced towards the till. No one was looking.

It only took a second to open her holdall and slip out the empty red shoulder bag, another second to slip it into the pile and close the case. It was a relief to be rid of the last tangible fragment of her old identity and she took her time choosing a navy handbag before she carried it to the counter to pay.

Richard had decided to go in to the plant. There were loose ends to be tied up if he wanted free time over the next few days, and if he stayed at home, waiting for the phone to ring, he would go mad. Frank had advised work: 'At the moment there's nothing you can do, old chap. Adele will be glued to the phone, I've made sure of that. If she takes time off to breathe, one or other of the Withers will be there. And besides, isn't it possible that Ellie will ring your office when she decides to make contact? That's where she'd expect you to be – during the day, anyway.'

So he had come to his office and covered his desk with plans of the new extension, but he couldn't concentrate. The picture that forced itself upon him at five-second intervals was of Ellie, alone, taking pills that might harm her and the child within her.

At eleven Paul Weidenek phoned, and Richard offered to give the psychiatrist dinner. 'At home – or I could come up to London if it makes it easier for you? I can get someone to cover the phone.' He didn't really like the idea of psychiatry, but he mustn't ignore any avenue.

But his invitation had come too late. 'I'm afraid I'm tied up, something I can't put off,' Paul said, thinking of Gary's offer. 'But we do need to talk. Perhaps tomorrow. I'll keep in touch.'

When he put down the phone Richard walked to the window and looked out over the yard below. Men were coming and going, joking with one another, their breath steaming in the crisp air. They looked happy and he envied them. Inside him, a knot of despair had formed: talking to Dr Weidenek might have helped. He needed advice, my God, how he needed it. Ellie's case was unique but there were always patterns, projections, educated guesses.

It had shocked him to realize, that morning, how little he really knew about his wife. They had known one another for only four months when he proposed, seven when they married. Ellie had sketched in a bleak childhood: grandmother, foster-parents, children's homes. But there had been no hint of real trouble nor any suggestion that she felt especially deprived – and he had never pressed her. If only he had demanded detail! But Ellie had shied away from in-depth discussion, preferring to talk about her time with Terri and the life they had shared together in London.

Richard went back to his desk and pressed his intercom. 'I want Mrs Benedict. You'll find her at the number where you reached her yesterday. Keep ringing until you get her.'

His door buzzed twice: Frank's code. He touched the

button that freed the door catch and crossed to the cabinet. 'Just in time. I've got to have a drink. I know it's a crazy hour but I need it. Join me?'

Frank did his John Cleese funny walk to the window and peered out. 'The sun is definitely over the yardarm. Make mine a Scotch.'

They sat either side of the desk, both outwardly calm, both inwardly concerned. 'Where is she, Frank?' Richard said at last.

'I wish I knew.' Frank leaned towards him. 'But I don't have bad vibes, if that's any consolation.'

They drank in silence for a moment and then Frank spoke again. 'Adele is arranging dinner at your place. We assumed you'd like company and wouldn't want to leave the phone.'

Richard nodded. 'Thanks. I asked Paul Weidenek to join me but he was tied up. Now Janet's chasing Terri Benedict to see if she's free. Otherwise, I'll be glad to have you and Adele there.' He tilted back his chair. 'I want to use every minute, talk to everyone, amass every single scrap of information. When I know more, I'm going after her.'

Frank's voice was reassuring. 'Good thinking. But with luck Ellie will come back of her own accord before you need to go looking. Which brings me to another matter . . . when do we start the extension?'

They were discussing possible dates when the phone rang. Richard had hoped Ellie would ring, had ordered that she be put straight through, but the sound of her voice was still a physical shock. He felt a fierce agitation in his chest, as though someone had let free a flock of birds, and turned his back on his brother.

'Ellie! . . . In God's name where *are* you? How could you *do* this . . .' Frank was moving round the desk, shaking his head and lifting an admonitory hand. 'Ellie . . . !' He wanted to go to her, to take her in his arms, but the first fragile contact must be made with words. And the right words would not come.

There was a sigh from the other end of the line, and then the dialling tone.

The atmosphere in the kitchen was cool, not to say frosty. Adele had stated at the outset that she didn't mean to interfere but Mrs Withers had signified her disapproval with a tightening of the lips. Failing to poach the old bat had probably been a blessing in disguise. 'I just want to help,' she said but the older woman refused to meet her eyes and went on clattering pans.

Adele meant to serve Richard a tempting meal; it was the least she could do, and it would please Frank. She separated eggs for a lemon mousse and began to beat in the sugar. It was bound to bring them closer, the three of them. They would talk about Ellie, certainly, but they would grow closer all the time, and that must be an advantage. Mrs Withers was sweeping eggshells off the table. 'I can finish on my own, Mrs Frank, if you've got other things to do.'

She was sick of the mousse but if Withers took over dessert as well, she could hardly claim any credit for the meal. 'I'm fine, thank you. Almost done! I'll finish this and then I'll go home to change. You will stay by the phone, won't you?'

The implication that she was capable of deserting her

post annoyed the housekeeper as Adele had meant it should. Served her right for the 'Mrs Frank' bit. After Julia died Mrs Withers had promoted her, the only surviving 'Mrs Marriner'. But at Ellie's advent Adele had been relegated to junior status once more, and it rankled.

At half-past five she went home to change. Trumper sat disconsolate in the hall but when she invited him to accompany her he buried his nose between his front paws and stayed put.

'All right, stupid dog. But I'm all you've got now. You'll have to come round in the end.'

As she walked across the gardens guilt smote her. She was talking – no, thinking – as though Ellie had gone for good. Wishful thinking probably . . . except that pregnant women popping antidepressants would not figure high in an actuary's table. She didn't want Ellie back, but her disappearance must be painless. Nothing tragic, or they would all be sunk in gloom again and that was not to be contemplated.

She decided on her green wool challis suit, which was quite restrained, and stuck to pearls. Mustn't look like a Christmas tree in the middle of a family crisis. As she stroked Patou's Joy behind her ears she wondered if Richard would tell them about the pregnancy test. She must be amazed if he did, too wide-eyed for words.

She laid out a clean shirt for Frank and made her way back to the house as Richard's car came through the gates.

'Gin and French all right?' She had the glass ready as he came through the door, and held out her other

78

hand for his briefcase. 'Come and sit down. Is Frank behind you?'

Richard was explaining Frank's absence when the phone rang.

'Oh, Weidenek. You *can*? Good. Yes, seven-thirty will be fine. And you're sure you don't want me to come to you?'

Adele could have borne his turning her out for the psychiatrist if it had not been for the satisfaction on Mrs Withers' face as Richard explained to her. 'Just the two of us. We have a lot to talk about. Mr and Mrs Frank will be dining at home, so if you dish up I can see to the rest myself. I expect you'd like to get away.'

Terri was home by six and attacking the vegetables by two minutes past. When Richard had phoned and invited her out for a meal there had been a momentary temptation to say yes, or at least to invite him to supper, but she had resisted it. She couldn't leave Mike unfed two nights running, and she wasn't up to cooking for a tycoon.

She had compromised by agreeing to meet Richard for lunch tomorrow and in the mean time to rack her brains for anything useful that Ellie had ever said to her. As she peeled and chopped odd phrases popped into her mind, but it was a rag-bag. Ellie had been . . . was . . . her best and truest friend and yet she knew almost nothing about her. What had they talked about for four years? Men mostly. Well, she had talked and Ellie had listened. There had been the odd double date, but no real man in Ellie's life until Richard. She herself had already been head over heels for Mike by then.

The newspaper had been changing over to computers, and Mike was the software consultant brought in from outside . . . Terri realized she had ceased to chop and was staring into space. They had been so happy then. Still, enough day-dreaming! He was going to have a balanced meal tonight if she died in the attempt.

She was skinning onions when he came in, advancing on her with a paper cone of unopened carnations. 'Best I could do,' he said, apologetically. 'It should have been roses.' He put his arms around her and kissed her forehead. They both knew what would happen, both wanted it.

As they moved, still locked together, towards the bedroom, she cried halt. The frying-pan was already smoking; if she had forgotten it they could have been burned to a crisp. 'At least I'd have died happy,' she murmured as he began to unbutton her shirt.

'What are you talking about?' he said fondly as they crept hastily between the sheets in the unheated room. But when she tried to explain he covered her open mouth with his, and thoughts of burning pans faded from her mind.

Afterwards they lay curled together, closer than new banknotes.

'Penny for them?' he said, his mouth against her ear.

'You expect me to say that was wonderful, don't you?' she answered.

His hand came round to clutch her belly, fingers tensed. 'Be careful what you say, woman. You're vulnerable.'

She turned in his arms, loving the feeling of moist flesh on flesh. 'I was thinking that was wonderful,' she said obediently '. . . and a bit about Ellie. It seems heartless to be so happy when we don't even know if . . .' She couldn't bring herself to finish the sentence but he understood.

'She's alive, all right, my love. Other than that, I admit I'm not sanguine. You have to be pretty far gone to just take off. I mean, if you'd gone you'd've left a note, wouldn't you, or at least phoned?'

She wriggled against him. 'I might, I might not. It'd depend how you'd treated me.'

His hand fingered her scapula then moved to the nape of her neck. 'You'll have a hump when you're an old woman. A dowager's hump. I can see you . . . like a little camel.'

'That's it, chum. You've asked for it.' She was up and astride him, tickling as and where she could.

He caught hold of her hands and then, fetching one to his nose, let out a roar. 'Onions! My God, you stink of onions. Other men get Opium or at least L'Air du Temps. I get Eau de Cabbage Patch.'

She was laughing so much she could hardly bear it. She was still laughing when he drew her down beneath the sheet and began to love her again.

It had been five o'clock when Ellie got off the Durham bus in Sunderland. Too late to look for lodgings, burdened as she was with her purchases. She walked to what she remembered as the town's only hotel and took a single room. Tomorrow she would find somewhere cheap and cheerful, and there would be no extras on the bill tonight. She would make sure of that. Except that she needed a drink. Or a pill. Or both. Anything to blot out the sound of Richard's angry voice. He was right; she had caused chaos, and the boys would feel confused and rejected.

There was a pay phone in the lobby. Could she ring them and put their minds at rest? She wanted to, but she was not sure of her ability to handle it just yet. Perhaps tomorrow, with a carefully thought-out script so that she would give nothing away. But she would never again ring Richard to hear the contempt and fury in his voice.

She thought of the boys as she brewed tea and ate two digestive biscuits from the tray in her room. If she could not go back, Adele would care for them. She was fond of them and they were used to her. 'She's OK,' Jeremy had said once when she had asked about his relationship with his aunt. 'She goes on a bit, about the family and that sort of thing. But she's OK.' And Gavin had chipped in. 'Better than Sara and Emma. They're gruesome.' He had rolled his eyes in horror at mention of his cousins, and Ellie had tut-tutted in mock reproof.

She drank her tea at the window, looking out on a lake set within a park and lit by street lamps. There had been swans there once, she could remember them. And tiddlers. A hand had clutched the back of her coat for fear of her falling in, and she had watched the small creatures wriggling beneath the surface. That must have been before Grandma, and the hand at her back thus her mother's. Or her father's. If only she could remember!

Panic gripped her. Where was she going to begin? She had been gone for twenty-four hours and had achieved nothing. It had seemed so simple – go in search of the truth. But what was the truth, and where would she find it? Apart from the birth certificate in her holdall she had nothing, and the certificate told no more than her parents' names and the address in Liverpool where she had been born and lived for the first four weeks of her life. *'And then you came north,'* Grandma had said when she queried it. *'Now let it go, it's water under the bridge.'*

She switched on the TV and began to unpack her new clothes. Lace-up shoes with cuban heels, a cheap camel coat with a tie belt, a nylon nightdress and two pairs of cotton briefs. She had not been able to afford a new bra or waist-slip; she would have to wash the ones she was wearing each night and go without if they weren't dry by morning. She had bought an acetate head-square, too, and some thermal gloves and two hand-towels. The kind of accommodation she was seeking would not run to towels. She had saved the sachets of shampoo and soap from the Durham hotel and would clear out the bathroom here before she left. After that she would have to buy toiletries, and that sort of thing ate up money.

A familiar voice from the television stopped her in her tracks. Dave Smith, the MP who had shared her breakfast, was being interviewed on the evening news magazine. He was, he said, glad to come up and share the privations of a north-east starved of funds by a government that cared only for the rich. He was a man of the people and understood their needs.

She heard the words, but fear had returned to hammer at her ribs. His eyes were on her. He could see her, here in this room, and he knew her for what she was, a liar and a cheat.

Paul Weidenek and Richard carried brandy to the fire and sat down either side, dogs at their feet. 'They miss her,' Richard said, 'especially Trumper.'

There was silence for a while as each man contemplated his own misery. Paul had arrived home early, a tissue-wrapped bottle in his hand. He had come into the hall and known, even as he was calling Gary's name, that there would be no answer. He was telling himself the boy had gone in search of supper ingredients when he saw the note: 'Chance to go to Brighton, too good to miss. Back tomorrow. PS Sorry about the supper.' Now he made a conscious effort to overcome his own pain and help the man opposite. For Richard at least, there was hope.

He was about to open the conversation when Richard spoke. 'Did you get hold of Mortimer?'

Paul nodded ruefully. 'I did. As I feared, there was a fairly sloppy procedure – if you handed the receptionist an empty container you got a scrip for another. According to them, Ellie has had two repeat prescriptions of each drug. Hopefully, she used them as she went along. If not . . .'

'If not,' Richard said slowly, 'if not, she's wandering around with a few hundred tablets.'

Paul put down his glass. 'Don't get it out of proportion. Two hundred are no more lethal than six.'

'What about the baby?' Richard asked, and the psychiatrist sat forward.

'I'd avoid thinking of it as a baby, Marriner. For the

time being, at least. At the moment it's a microscopic group of cells, no more. My guess is she's missed only one period – so it's early days. But pregnancy will be an extra burden on Ellie's already fragile mental state. When we find her we may have to consider a termination.' He saw the other man wince and hurried on.

'If we get to Ellie, help her to sort herself out, she may be able to come to terms with the pregnancy. I don't know. I'm not sure of anything except that none of us really knows your wife. She doesn't know herself. Sooner or later she's going to find out who she is.'

'Perhaps she knows she's pregnant,' Richard said suddenly. 'Perhaps that's why she went?'

Paul shook his head. 'I think not. The manner of her going, everything about it, says no. If she had discovered she was pregnant, she'd have behaved differently.' His tone was sombre as he considered the possibilities.

Richard was offering the decanter and had obviously missed the implication – that was good. He should have been more careful. He held out his glass. Important to be fit to drive, but he needed something to ease the pain of thinking of Gary in Brighton, turning on the charm for someone else.

'What are you going to do about your boys?' Paul had seen Richard's sons as part of his casework. They had sat side by side on the sofa, giving polite answers to his questions, volunteering nothing, and he had recognized in them a sense of loss. They had seemed genuinely fond of Ellie; now it was possible they were going to lose again.

Richard was murmuring something about Adele

stepping into the breach but Paul knew he was thinking of something else, and at last it surfaced.

'If . . . when she comes back, this new version of herself . . . what will she be like?'

Paul shrugged. 'I don't know.' His teeth glistened in his beard as he smiled. 'You're wondering if she will still want you?'

Richard's face betrayed nothing but he did not deny the allegation and Paul continued. 'The answer is that I don't know. But I can tell you one thing. If she does come back she will no longer see you as a father figure.'

The other man's eyes widened as he took in the meaning of the words but he didn't speak. They sat on silently as the coal burned down in the grate and the dogs inched stealthily towards the fender, and then Richard spoke.

'I must be honest and say I have doubts about your advice that we should wait. It seems to me that we've lost valuable ground over the last few weeks, and now Ellie is gone. I made such a hash of her phone call to me, I can't just sit and do nothing. She's my wife!'

[4]

Ellie carried her bags into the park when she had checked out next morning, and sat down by the lake. Around her feet pigeons pecked for crumbs, behind her Sunderland throbbed, but her eyes were fixed on the lake with its islands and resident ducks.

She could remember being there, actually remember walking along the cobbled edge – and then someone had swung her on to the stone lions that guarded the wall. It had been a summer's day, the stone flanks warm against her thighs, and then she had been lifted down and hurried to a waiting bus.

She closed her eyes and tried to summon up a face, but there was nothing. It must've been her mother. A sudden grief seized her, so that she almost cried out aloud. *'You are the wages of sin, Ellie.'*

A voice sounded over to her right. 'Come away, Andrea. Don't disturb the lady.' The voice was sharp with anxiety, and Ellie opened her eyes to see a child, its eyes fixed on her face. The little girl was four or five, clutching a doll and curious at the spectacle of an adult apparently sleeping in a public park.

'I'm sorry. She's so nosy.' The mother had advanced

and was grasping her daughter's hand. In spite of Ellie's smile of reassurance she hauled the child away.

Bile rose suddenly in Ellie's throat and she grimaced. She must start eating properly. Her digestion was usually excellent but in the last two days she had barely eaten at all. She got to her feet and looked around. There was a bus station in the town centre, presumably with buses that ran to the seaside: she seemed to remember living beside the sea. She began to walk, the half-empty holdall banging against her leg. She would have to leave it somewhere.

There was a nip of autumn in the air; shop windows were dressed in browns and greens with piles of artificial leaves and stark trees for background. Last year at this time she had been preparing for her wedding-day. Now she was running away.

She wanted to ring someone. 'I'm all right,' she would say, 'please don't worry about me,' and then she would put down the phone. They were clever with telephones nowadays. She might stammer out her speech and turn to see a policeman leaping from a Panda car.

She checked the holdall into a locker at the railway station and tucked the key in the inside pocket of her handbag: there were fragments of tobacco there so the previous owner had been a smoker. She turned into W. H. Smith and bought a packet of peppermints. She still felt sickly and it was not a pleasant feeling.

There was a news-stand by the till, every newspaper under the sun, all of them boasting front-page pictures – but none of them were of her. It was going to be as she feared; they were not going to miss her at all.

Slinking around in a chain-store coat and sun specs was a totally unnecessary precaution. She could leap on to the roof of the nearest parked car and yell, 'I am Ellie Marriner,' and no one would care. And if some passing policeman put her under restraint and notified her next of kin, no one would journey up the M1 to claim her.

But even as Ellie formulated the thought she knew it was nonsense. Richard took his responsibilities seriously; she was his wife and he would come in search of her, for that reason if no other. It was up to her to make sure he did not find her.

A few moments later she was sitting in the upstairs front seat of a bus, glancing out at shops on either side. They gave way to the bridge across the Wear and then the town centre was behind her. Lamps were strung along the roadside and a sign welcomed people to the illuminations. At night those bulbs would sparkle red and green and blue; now they waved alarmingly in the wind that had sprung up, a wind that was blowing litter along the pavements and causing passers-by to clutch at caps or tug at wayward skirts.

The bus bore right after the bridge. She saw a library and then an ancient church above the river – St Peter's, Monkwearmouth, where the Venerable Bede had penned his manuscripts. She was remembering half-forgotten lessons in history and northern pride when tall cranes came into view and she knew they were nearing the sea.

Richard had made a list of urgent tasks and was working through them one by one. The police had been slightly less offhand this time, as though they were beginning to scent more than a domestic tiff. 'We've got it out to other forces, sir. A picture would help. Head and shoulders, without a hat if possible, black and white for preference. I'll send a car to pick it up, and if I could have the name of Mrs Marriner's medical adviser . . . ?'

Richard had wanted to protest that Ellie was more than a crazy woman, that there was purpose in her flight, but he had a feeling that that would draw another bland assurance that it was 'all in hand'.

'You do have somebody by the phone, sir?'

He gave details of the arrangements for manning the phone, and replaced the receiver. Now for the boys' school, Avebury.

The Head was courteous and genuinely concerned. Richard was an old boy and a governor, and generous into the bargain.

'I'm driving up tomorrow. I want to tell Gavin and Jeremy what's happening before they see it in the press. There may be something in the papers tomorrow morning . . . can you vet them? And if there's any question of the boys being harassed by newsmen . . . I hardly think it likely, but you never know . . . could you contact me? I don't want to bring them home before their weekend if I can help it but we'll have to play it by ear.'

While the Head sympathized, Richard thought of Ellie's first visit to Avebury. Round-eyed at the Victorian splendour of the school, standing beside him in Chapel when Jeremy was confirmed, sitting forward with parted lips when Gavin said his five lines in the

Christmas play. She had loved to go and collect them for home weekends and holidays and write the letters he had always been so remiss about. She had been good to them, and he had never thanked her.

He put his elbows on the desk and rested his head in his hands. Tomorrow he would have to face his sons and explain. Last night he had asked Weidenek about possible effects and the answer had not been reassuring. 'Children can take one loss, however close, even a mother. The second is harder. I think your mother's death was their second loss. If there should be a third they will begin to see a pattern of loss, to make their relationships on the basis of impermanence. And that does not augur well.'

Richard was glad when Frank's buzz came at the door and he was wrenched back to business. 'We can't put it off any longer, old son. Do I go to Japan or do we let the deal go?'

Richard wanted to have Frank beside him, but a foothold for their vehicles in Asia was too lucrative a prospect to dismiss. He reached for his diary. 'Could you go? If you fly out on Monday . . . that's the 30th . . . you could be back in this country by Sunday the 6th. Or you could go on the 3rd . . .'

Terri sat back and laced her fingers behind her head. The marriage piece was *fini*, *kaput*, gone down to Subs and out of her hands. She had done her best, but it had come out a dog's breakfast. Right up to the last minute she had hoped for something else to break, a great big news story that would have them all running round like mad and fill two pages. Anything to give her more time! Another week and she might have made something of it. There was too much to say about marriage . . . any marriage . . . to confine it within a single page. Throw in Hollywood and alimony, not to mention toy boys and drugs, and the whole thing was hopelessly out of control. If it hadn't been for Ellie going missing . . . no, that was unfair. She had been floundering long before that. And now she'd have to think up something fresh for morning conference.

She picked up a pencil and twiddled it hopefully over her notebook, hoping for inspiration. Around her the office buzzed: arguments from two corners, raucous laughter from a third. Carole was holding up prints, looking for a pic for tomorrow's piece on pigs. She wrote 'Factory Farming?' on her pad and then crossed it out. 'Child Abuse?' Done to death. 'Missing persons?' She had thought of little else for two days, but she could hardly do it while Ellie was missing. Afterwards, perhaps.

How did you set about finding someone? To turn it on its head, where would you go to hide if you wanted to get away? A big city – country people were notoriously quick to notice strangers. Perhaps Ellie was here in London, in one of the million small hotels that lined every street.

'London hotels – the big rip-off?' That was a possibility! She put thoughts of Ellie to one side until she met Richard at lunchtime, and got down to work.

The beach was golden yellow, the sea a long way out. Ellie walked on the lower promenade, shivering inside her camel coat, taking great lungfuls of sea air. In the distance she could see a big ship emerging from the Tyne, going who knew where. A gust of wind caught her hair, whipping it cruelly into eyes and mouth. It was nearly noon. In a few hours darkness would come, bringing with it that terrible sinking of the spirits. Before then she must be safe inside a room of her own, door locked against the world.

She left the promenade at the next opening and began to make her way back to where accommodation might be found. Above her, strings of lights jiggled and creaked with each gust. Set pieces swayed alarmingly as the wind took them briefly, shook them and passed on. There was no one about, except an old man walking his dog and a woman alighting from a bus.

Winter seasides were sad places, and a feeling of futility overcame her. What was she doing here? If she had hoped for a revelation, an open sesame to the closed recesses of her mind, it had not come. It was all too vast, hundreds of streets, thousands of houses. A needle in a haystack. She saw a coffee shop and scuttled gratefully into the warm.

The coffee was hot and frothy and delicious. She sipped it slowly, both hands round the cup, feeling warmth flood back into her limbs. There were two attendants behind the counter and a boy and girl, clad in identical jeans and bomber jackets, holding hands across a corner table. As Ellie watched, the boy detached himself and moved to the juke-box. A moment later the *EastEnders'* theme tune flooded over them. 'Anyone can fall in love' – the boy was making mock gestures of distaste but the girl was loving it, humming along with the music while he put fingers in ears and gazed dotingly at her.

'No one has ever looked at me like that,' Ellie thought. 'I have never been doted on in my life.' A voice in her head urged fairness: she had been loved, but never totally. Never with abandon. There had always been someone else taking precedence.

Recklessly she crossed to the counter and ordered another coffee. She had pocketed her change and was about to turn away when a thought struck her. 'I don't suppose you know of anyone round here who takes paying guests?'

The woman behind the counter was small and plump, her face washed clean but her long nails, of which she was inordinately proud, painted shocking pink. She touched her cheek with one index finger and pondered.

'Lodgings? Well, there's plenty takes people in the summer but I don't know about now. Elsie!'

The other woman came from cleaning tables and her colleague outlined the problem.

'You want to be at the Roker end. The terraced houses. Or you could try the Civic Centre, they've got a list there.'

The grey mantle of late afternoon would soon descend, so an assault on the Civic Centre back in the town was out of the question. Ellie thanked them and made her way to her table.

Stevie Wonder started up on the juke-box now: 'I just called to say I love you.' A sharp picture of Richard flashed into her mind: Richard waiting by the telephone, his face care-worn as she had seen it so many times lately.

He had been sharp with her yesterday but she had deserved it. Oh God, why was she doing this to him?

Outside in the street a child started to cry. And then, like something splitting open in her mind she heard another tune, insistent above the sound of the crying child. The same musical phrase repeated again and again. Her heart was hammering. She must get out. Now, before it was too late! She could hear the child, above the music, crying in her head – and then the face, the man's face, implacable and hostile. She stood up suddenly, so that the spoon caught in her belt and clattered out of the saucer. She had to get out, get away. Faces were turning to her, startled, but she was too frightened to care. Nothing mattered but to get to the street, and she let the door bang behind her.

In spite of the cold, she felt over-heated, her skin tingling with panic. She put up a hand to her mouth to stifle a sob and at the same moment saw the policeman on the other side of the road. The sight of him was enough to restore her senses. She took her gloves from her pocket and pulled them on, put up her collar and turned away, no other thought in her mind than to escape his curious eyes.

Gary was there in the driving seat of the car when Paul came down the steps. 'Hi! Long time no see.'

Paul settled into the passenger seat and reached for the seatbelt. He had learned the foolishness of reacting too quickly. 'Hi yourself,' he said. 'Where are we going?'

The boy put the car into reverse and edged out of the consultant's parking bay. 'Anywhere you like.

Lunch is on me . . . seeing as I let you down last night. Sorry about that. Grovel, grovel and abasement plus, plus. It won't happen again.'

A heaviness had settled on Paul's chest. 'I've heard that before. Where did you get the car key?'

That went home! For a second the triumphal smirk slipped. 'I found it lying around . . . on the hall table . . . somewhere . . . how the hell do I know?' There was an ugly note in his voice now, and Paul felt a shiver of apprehension. And then the thrill that always followed.

Gary had got a spare car key. Some time when he had borrowed the Volvo for a 'spin round the block', he had taken it to a garage and had a spare key cut. Paul glanced out of the window. 'There's a pub down here. We can get a sandwich.'

The boy frowned. 'I can afford more than that. I told you I was buying.'

Careful, careful. Mustn't spurn his peace-offering. 'I only have half an hour and I'd hate to rush a good meal. Can we leave it until tonight, when we can both relax? I want to hear about Brighton.'

For a moment it hung on a knife-edge and then Gary smiled. 'OK. Point out your grotty pub. God, you're a pleb.' As usual when he could feel equal he became expansive. 'You don't take care of yourself, I keep on telling you! We'll eat well tonight, God's honour.' The pub came into view and he drew the car into the kerb.

At least he had come back. That was something. Paul unfastened his belt and tried to summon up an appetite, but a gnawing feeling that he couldn't take much more was already filling his gut. He both loved and feared the boy but escape would not be easy. Gary, when crossed, could be dangerous. Perhaps that was what made him exciting.

Terri knew the restaurant Richard had chosen. It was small and crowded, a rabbit warren where a drink of water would call for a mortgage.

He rose at the sight of her and smiled the rather grim smile that made him look like a young Charlton Heston. Wolfish . . . except that the eyes were kind.

Terri knew he wanted to talk about Ellie, and sensed that he would find it difficult. She decided to put him at ease. 'I've never taken you up on your offer of a visit to your works. Is that the right word? It's too big for a factory, isn't it?'

He nodded. 'Works . . . or plant. It started as a factory, in 1922. My grandfather made motor parts – one-off jobs, some of them. He was very proud of keeping beautiful motors on the road. The big leap came in my father's day. The war changed a lot of things. Now we're mostly into construction vehicles . . . the Marriner Two-Way is quite revolutionary.' He smiled suddenly at Terri's bemused expression. 'I mustn't get too technical. Suffice to say it's big. We're hoping to get it into Japan.'

A waiter was filling a glass for Richard to taste but he waved his hand and the man filled both their glasses as spinach terrine was placed in front of Terri.

'You wanted to compare notes,' she said, when the waiter had moved away. 'Well, I'll rabbit on and you stop me if anything interests you.'

Relief showed in his face. 'That's fine . . . but enjoy

your food.' He was looking at his own plate of *crudités* with less than relish, but Terri picked up her fork and began.

'I didn't know anything about her going away, Richard. Please believe that. She never ever mentioned it to me. I didn't even know she was seeing a psychiatrist until she rang me on Monday, which is pretty amazing when you think how close we are.'

There was pain in his face and an awful care-worn look. No man should look like that, and a lot of them did. On Monday night, when Richard had given his halting account of Ellie's demands for reassurance, she had wondered if that was what she did to Mike.

'Now that I've had time to think about it, Richard, Ellie never talked about the past. She was an orphan: that was it, basically. You sensed it was a bit painful, so you let it go. And, if I'm honest, I didn't much care. We were two young, provincial girls loose in the big city. There was so much happening day to day we didn't have time for post mortems.'

She bit her lip. 'And if I'm really honest, I was too taken up with my own affairs. I should have shown more interest in her background. But Ellie was a home-bird. I'd come in late at night and we'd have a nightcap . . . hot chocolate mostly; it was all we could afford. I'd tell her where I'd been and who with, and we'd turn in. Weekends we shopped and cleaned and washed smalls. Sometimes I went home for the weekend. She never did, but that was because she had no home. Once or twice she came up to Lincoln with me. I could ask my mother if she ever said anything to her?'

He nodded. 'Please. Anything that might help. And

if you'd talk to Dr Weidenek when you have time . . . I gave him your number.'

They talked of other things then, but Ellie was in both their minds, and it made for stilted conversation. Terri was tackling a raspberry *vacherin*, exulting in the taste of cream and ice, when she looked at her watch. It was two o'clock. Ellie must have eaten by now, somewhere, wherever she was. She put out a hand and touched Richard's wrist. 'She'll be all right, Richard, you'll see. I know she's mixed up at the moment, but there's a lot of sense there too. And she loves you. I don't think I've ever seen anyone so much in love.'

Richard was trying not to betray a response. Thank God Mike could emote when the occasion demanded!

Terri took her napkin to her lips and dabbed. 'Richard, I have to go but I'll keep in touch. Thank you so much for lunch.'

When he stood he towered above her, but on impulse she stretched to kiss his cheek and saw he was touched by the gesture. Poor Richard, she would have to find a way to help him.

Ellie was almost at the end of her tether when she saw a corner shop and the row of cards in its window. 'Mothercare pram. Brand new. £15.' 'Kittens free to good homes.' 'Clean lodgings with board if preferred. No DHSS.' She felt a surge of fellow-feeling for the disadvantaged, and glad of the wad of notes in her bag. There was still no room at the inn if you were short of money and without a job.

The address on the card was two streets away, a narrow terraced house painted mauve and white, neat privet hedge round a microscopic front garden, every window shrouded in net. She rang the 'Avon-calling' bell and waited. A curtain twitched in the downstairs bay and a moment later the door opened to reveal a tiny, elderly woman with a teenage hairstyle.

'I'm sorry to bother you but I saw your card in the shop-window. I wonder, have you a room available?'

The hall was narrow and dark and smelled of polish. An oak carver chair stood by an oak hallstand, its mirror flanked by two handsome copper-backed brushes that had never suffered the indignity of use. There was just room to manoeuvre past the furniture and up the creaking stairs.

'It's a back room, I'm afraid. Still, there's a sea view. I like a reference . . . you can't just let anyone into your home, can you? It's £18 a week or £35 with breakfast and evening meal. No meter for gas and electricity, everything provided, but I need a signature on the inventory before you move in.'

The sea view turned out to be a vest-pocket triangle between adjoining roofs, but the sight cheered Ellie.

'It'll take me a while to get a reference, I'm afraid, but I could pay four weeks in advance.' She tried to look as little like a psychopath as possible but it was the sight of her bulging wallet that tipped the scales, together with a heart-rending tale of a quick trip north to the bedside of a dying aunt.

Ellie had already decided that the best cover story was a detailed one leaving no space for conjecture, but she was amazed at her own ability to produce detailed lies out of thin air. She talked of her family back home in Luton, her part-time job in a wool shop that she hoped would be held open for her return, and family feuding that had forced her to seek accommodation other than in her aunt's home.

'People can be wicked,' the landlady said. 'Especially where money and wills are concerned.'

Ellie nodded gravely. 'That's the trouble here.'

The woman's eyes shone. A tenant with a loaded wallet was good. If she was also an heiress it was Brownie points. 'I'm Irene McReady,' she said, extending a veined hand heavy with rings. 'And I'm sure we're going to get on.'

Ellie elected to cater for herself – 'I'll be out a lot, so it's best if I don't impose' – and explained her baggage left behind at the station.

'There's a phone for emergencies,' Mrs McReady said, 'and if you want to ring your hubby I'm sure we can work something out.'

Downstairs Ellie parted with £72 and received a front-door key and a key to her own room. 'There are two other guests at the moment,' Mrs McReady said, scribbling a receipt. 'I'll have a rent book for you tomorrow . . . and that's the phone number if you want to leave it at the hospital.'

Her yellow hair had the unhealthy glow of a cheap tint, her greying brows had been darkened with pencil, and although her figure was trim the legs above the three-inch heels were spindles.

'There's no Mr McReady,' she said as she let Ellie out of the front door. 'But we live in hopes.'

Ellie gave what she trusted was an all-girls-together laugh, and left. If any of the lodgers were men they would have to keep their wits about them.

She was almost back to the corner shop when she realized her gait had changed. Even the way she held her handbag was different. She had taken on the guise of a harassed housewife who worked in a wool shop and was up from Luton – just as she had enjoyed being the romantic novelist in the Durham hotel! Did she relish these other personalities because she had none of her own? Or was she sliding into unreality and from there to madness? The shop loomed up, its sign proclaiming that it was an off-licence. The prospect of a drink carried Ellie over the threshold and up to the counter.

Adele carried coffee through to the breakfast-room at the Garth and curled up in the window-seat. She was bored, bored, bored but there was no escape. If Ellie had intended to ring she'd have done it by now, but until Richard gave her leave she would have to stick it out, hour after boring hour.

She looked at the clock. Twenty minutes to five: an hour, at least, before the men came back. She looked across at the sideboard. There was a bottle of Courvoisier in there and at six p.m. precisely she was going to have a generous sample of it.

She had found it this morning. Looking in the Garth's cupboards and drawers had been the only light relief in an otherwise bloody day, and no sympathy at all from Withers. The old woman was tight-lipped and silent except when she was poking her nose in. She had appeared in the door of Ellie's bedroom looking like the wrath of God and not even made an excuse for pushing home the bedside drawer. Adele had considered making some excuse about looking for clues, and then thought better of it. Once you started explaining yourself to the hired help, you had trouble.

She couldn't even ring people in case it blocked the line. Frank had been quite specific: 'I know what you're like, Adele. You look on a receiver as an extension of your middle ear. No calls, except in an emergency.'

She looked at the clock again. No harm in a quick call. If Ellie decided to ring she'd keep trying till she got through, and if Frank tried to ring and got an engaged signal she'd simply say it had been someone ringing to ask for news.

She dialled her mother's number and waited for the familiar voice at the other end. 'Mummy, you're not going to believe what's happened here . . .' Half an hour later she replaced the receiver and picked up her empty cup. She was half-way through the doorway when the phone rang, and she carried on to pick up the hall extension.

'Adele Marriner.'

There was a pause and then Ellie's voice, indistinct as though on the other side of the world. 'Adele? Is everything all right?'

Adele jabbered out an answer and demanded Ellie's whereabouts, but all she got was, 'I'll ring you again.' The phone clicked and there was the burr of a dead line.

Adele stood there for a moment, devoid of power, and then she jabbed at the rest and began to dial the works' number. She had almost reached the last digit when she changed her mind and replaced the receiver.

*

Paul closed the hall door behind him and pocketed his key. The kitchen was blitzed but the smell from the cooker was good. The relief of knowing Gary was there was overwhelming, and he felt a foolish grin creep over his face.

'Don't say anything. I'll clear it all up when I've finished,' Gary said, waving a tea-towel.

Paul advanced on the cooker. 'What are we having?'

The frying-pan heaved and sizzled. 'Pork curry, pilau rice. Melon for starters and pitta bread. Don't touch anything. I'm in a hurry.'

Paul grasped the significance of the final sentence and disappointment rose in his throat. 'Are you going out?'

Gary kept his eye on the pan, stirring vigorously. 'Yeah. A gig. It was all last-minute but I can't turn it down. Sorry and all that, but you know the score.' He lifted a grain of rice from the lidded pan and bit it tentatively. 'Just right. *Al dente* . . . or is that pasta? Anyway, clear the table . . . and don't droop. I'll be back before twelve, if the thought of your face doesn't turn me into a pumpkin.'

They ate in a welter of debris, but the food was good and Paul was coming to terms with the change of plan. Gary was twenty-one years old, a musician: he had to take work when he found it, and he was always in a good mood after a gig. 'Leave the washing up,' he said. 'I've got some work to do but I'll have time for this lot. I'll still be up when you come back, and we can have a nightcap.'

He helped Gary to lug his drums into the lobby, and a roadie in a sleeveless T-shirt hefted them down the steps as though they were feathers.

'Have a good night,' Paul said, 'and thanks for the meal. You're improving.' He wanted to reach out, but it wouldn't do. Instead he stood on the steps and watched the banged-up van swerve down the street.

In his study the animals waited patiently: small woodland creatures, eyes bright, captured for ever in idyllic backgrounds. In nature they were all too often left, dead and bloodied, on the ground. He put a Steve Hackett tape into the stereo and turned the volume down. There were other sounds to compete for his attention – Ellie Marriner, talking haltingly about her problems.

The first tape was a jumble of feeling. '. . . *and she was beautiful. Always smiling. Adele told me she was a very happy person.*'

And then his own voice. '*Do you resent Julia?*'

The reply was too quick. '*No. Oh, no. It's just that . . .*' The voice was more childish now. Paul reached for his pad and made a note.

'*It's just . . . there doesn't seem to be a place for me. It's no one's fault . . . everyone tries. Adele gave me all her photograph albums so I could know about Julia . . . about Richard's life . . . not feel out of it. Everyone's kind . . . I'm sorry. I'm sorry, this is silly. Yes please. Thank you.*'

He had handed her a tissue then and she had blown her nose, precisely, like a little girl. There was a definite regression towards childhood.

Paul stopped the tape and began to write. In time she would have come to trust him but time had run out. He reached forward and started the tape again.

*

Terri set up the ironing board at the back of the living-room and watched television as she worked. Everything in the ironing basket had been there for too long and seemed impervious to heat. Bloody creases. If you wanted them down the front of trousers they wouldn't come, and if they were in and you wanted them out they wouldn't budge.

In the end she rejected half of the clothes and put them back into the washing basket. Next time round, she would catch them damp and it would all be easy. The thought that some of them had been recycled in this way more than once intruded, and was firmly put down. They were having a *nice* night. Nothing must be allowed to spoil it.

The Channel 4 news came to an end, and Mike used the remote control to change channels and lower the volume. 'Right,' he said, wriggling into a more comfortable position on the sofa, 'tell me about your day.'

Terri grinned. He was enjoying being the master of the house, watching the little woman do chores. She selected a tea-towel from the pile and flicked him with it. 'Lazy sod! If you're really interested, my day was fraught! I finished the break-up piece. Then I saw the first run-off before I left, and it was dire . . . cut to ribbons. I don't blame them, most of it was padding. But they'd cut the bit about in-built failure which I thought was quite inspired. *C'est la* bloody *vie*, I suppose, but it still rankles.

'Then I met Richard. Oh, Mike, I feel so sorry for him. Here's this great big guy, power at his fingertips, and he's completely out of his depth. God, I wish I could do something for him. I should have known Ellie better, then I could be more help.'

She finished a collar and turned the garment over.

'Where do you think she is?' Mike asked.

Terri shrugged. 'I haven't the foggiest. If I had even a glimmer I'd be on a train to bring her back. I rang Mum today to see if she knew anything.'

'Did she?'

Terri put the newly ironed shirt over the back of a chair. 'Not off the top of her head. She said she'd think. She did talk to Ellie when we were up there once, but it's a slim chance that Ellie said anything significant.'

She was disconnecting the iron and setting it to cool. 'Anyway, when I got back Stephen had come up with this bright idea about a Who's Who of who's in and who's out. You know, "Barry Humphries is in. Bruce Forsyth is out." It's all part of this "let's-go-for-the-upwardly-mobile" thing. I don't fancy it, but he's keen.'

'By the time you've done it, it'll be out of date,' Mike said gloomily and then, hoisting himself on the cushions, 'I had a drink with Sam at lunchtime. He's looking for an investment. Around the £30,000 mark. He fancies property, but he'd get nothing in London for 30 thou. So he suggested we went in with him.'

Her hoot of laughter was genuine. 'I've heard of optimism but this is something else.'

He was sitting up now, warming to his theme. 'No, wait. He puts up the deposit, we get a mortgage. We live in the house and pay the mortgage.'

She knew there must be a catch somewhere. 'What's in it for him?'

'Profit! Say the house costs 90 thou. He owns a third of it. In ten years we sell it for 150. He makes an extra 20 thou.'

Terri struggled to sift the figures but it was useless. She needed to see things in black and white. 'Could we afford a £60,000 mortgage?'

'We could if we both earn.'

That was it then, the sting. Stay in a poky flat with no room for a child, or move to a house with space for a child but stay barren. And all the while Diana was bringing up Mike's children in green and pleasant Twickenham.

'Where are you going?'

She was already half-through the bathroom door. 'I need a pee. Back in a sec.'

She was bathing her eyes with her cupped hands when the doubt about her pills crept in. She always took them first thing – every day! But the action was so automatic, what if she forgot, like you could get used to traffic lights on a familiar road and never know whether or not you had driven through them? It wasn't until she had retrieved them from her bedside cabinet and checked the days that she could draw a comfortable breath.

It was eight o'clock when Ellie got back to her room, struggling with holdall and handbag and plastic carrier of provisions. She let herself in as quietly as she could but not quietly enough. The door of a downstairs room opened and light streamed into the passage. 'Oh, it's you, Mrs Cheshire. Did you manage?'

The landlady was weighing up the bags. Behind her

in the room a comedian was eliciting roars of laughter from a studio audience.

'You're welcome to come and watch a spot of telly, seeing as it's your first night. I know what hospital visiting's like, I've done some in my time. I could tell you tales . . .' *And probably will*, Ellie thought resignedly.

'Thank you very much, Mrs McReady. Actually, I'm hoping to get an early night. But I'd like to ring my husband if I may? Just a quick call and I'll pay, of course.'

Mrs McReady waved a generous hand. 'We don't need to worry about that tonight. He's bound to be anxious . . . and I've got all the charges down somewhere. We can work something out.'

The evening paper with the required number was safe in Ellie's bag. She smiled her thanks to the landlady and carried on upstairs.

The room was small with T-fall ceilings either side of the dormer window. Cheap floral paper covered the walls but the white paintwork was clean and the gold cord carpet looked almost new. The double bed with its floral counterpane took up a third of the space. The remainder contained an easy chair, a gate-leg table bearing a vase of plastic flowers, two upright bentwood chairs, a single wardrobe and a kitchen corner with a table-top grill and electric kettle.

Ellie put down her bags and took the half-bottle of gin from the carrier. She poured a small measure and topped it up with tonic, then she sank into the easy chair and contemplated the glass. It must be the only drink of the night. She couldn't afford it and there was an even better reason. On his very first consultation Dr

Weidenek had asked about her drinking habits. 'Do you drink alone? In the house?' He had warned her solemnly of the dangers of drinking by herself, his only stricture of the session. If she drank, it would addle her wits and she must keep her wits about her if she was to uncover anything useful.

She tried to think about her cover story. She was all right when she was doing something – plotting, planning, carrying out a scheme. It was when her mind was idle that trouble began. That was when the snake crept into Eden.

She knew then that she was going to think about Richard with Julia. The two of them together. The snake, the writhing snake, the evil, evil thing that ended in ultimate sin.

She put down the glass and covered her ears but the voices were in her head. 'Wicked, wicked, wicked.' She was wicked, the very evocation of sin. In the corner shop she had wanted to steal, to take without paying – it was her turn to have something for nothing. She was tired of paying. She picked up the glass and drank, but the taste of gin did not come through and she reached for the bottle.

In supermarkets some people walked around, munching. Trying anything they fancied. She had read that somewhere. They were called 'grazers' and they cost the economy a zillion pounds a year. She was laughing heartily now, thinking of supermarket aisles filled with Friesians and Ayrshires, all of them chomping fit to bust. But still Julia was there . . . Richard had enjoyed sex with Julia; Adele had told her that. 'You're lucky to have such a good lover. Julia was a virgin and he taught her everything. He's quite something, I believe. Insatiable. Well, according to Julia . . .' And then, seeing Ellie's face . . . 'We were very close, you know. You can't grow up together and not share things.' But Ellie's look of shock had had little to do with Julia's indiscretions. She had been trying to equate the insatiable Richard of Julia's story with the gentle man who shared her bed. No wonder he had preferred to sleep with Julia!

She was reaching for the bottle again when reason overcame her and she picked up the newspaper instead. 'Sweet Talk. Are you lonely? Need to hear some loving words? Call Love Line.'

She scribbled the number on the back of her wrist and made for the stairs. A thin sliver of light showed under the door of the back parlour and she made her way towards it.

'Come in, dear. I'm sure your hubby's dying to hear from you.' The phone was on the sideboard, covered by the skirts of a crinoline lady. Mrs McReady removed herself to a discreet distance and huddled over the telly. 'Take as long as you like, dear. Hubbies get anxious. There's a second hand on the clock so we can't go wrong.'

Ellie smiled and dialled. A moment later, as a voice dripping with syrup billed and cooed in her ear, she told her Luton husband all the doings of the day, gave him Mrs McReady's number for use in emergencies and instructed him not to ring her as ten to one she would be at the hospital and it would only disturb her hostess. She would ring him whenever she got the chance.

Across the room the other woman was totting up minutes with one half of her mind and waiting for something juicy with the other. You could see it in her eyes. Ellie decided to give full measure. 'I'll miss you tonight, darling.' She paused for effect and gave Mrs McReady an arch twinkle. 'Me too. No, I'll be a good girl. Just till I get back!'

Mrs McReady was glowing visibly. This was better than Barbara Cartland. At the other end of the line the sugared tones were drooling on.

'Bye, bye, darling. Take care – and be good!'

When Richard had switched off the lights he drew back the curtains on a moonlit garden. The branches of the horse-chestnut were bare now, except for odd leaves clinging stubbornly, looking like roosting birds in the darkness. In the distance, lights gleamed. In homes up and down Britain weary husbands were setting alarms, rueing the day gone by or worrying about the day ahead, climbing into bed to move close to the yielding bodies of their wives. That was the best thing about the marriage bed, the closeness. Not sex, important though that was, but closeness.

He glanced towards the bed, gleaming ghostly in the moonlight. Big enough to swallow one diminished man. Somewhere Ellie was climbing into another such bed. He felt a tiny lift of spirits. She had always enjoyed being with him: that could not have been pretence. She must miss him as he missed her. And when she came back . . . oh God, how he would love her then. He found he had clasped his arms, hugging himself in an ecstasy of longing.

Why hadn't she rung again? Down below the grand-mother clock chimed the hour. It was one in the morning. He closed the curtains and felt his way towards the bed, but not before he had checked the card in his wallet: 'Jackson and Hawkes. Private Inquiries. Discreet and Confidential'. If there had been no call from Ellie by noon tomorrow he meant to summon help.

[5]

Light filtering through the thin curtains struck Ellie's
opening eyes and she shut them again. She must stop
the night-time drinking. She felt awful – sick, cold, and
when she tried to sit up the room swirled alarmingly.
A tear of self-pity formed in the corner of her closed
eye and ran down into the folds of her neck, adding to
her misery. She must *do* something, but where was she
to begin?

She had been three when she left Sunderland, and
gone to Belgate with Grandma. The age of that child in
the park yesterday, thumb in mouth – seeing, certainly,
but not comprehending. Forgetting instantly. You
couldn't recapture your childhood unless there was
someone to tell you how it had been. And she had
no one. She closed her eyes again, squeezing them
together as though by concentrating she could summon
up someone, anyone, who would offer to be her guide.
But there was only the man's face, unmoved and eye-
less.

She pulled herself up on the pillows, brushing her
eyes. This was foolish and counter-productive. She
would have to take a pill, just one pill to dull the pain

of living. Suddenly she acknowledged what she had tried to ignore, that the day might come when she would take the pills, all of them, one by one until the end.

She realized then that she was going to vomit and hurtled out of bed, but the vomiting was nothing more than water, scalding throat and mouth and disappearing without trace into the swirling plughole. Waterbrash! The word popped into her mind and with it her grandmother's face. A hand on her brow when she had suffered the sickness of childhood: *'It's only waterbrash, pet. A nice drink of tea'll settle your stomach.'*

She made tea and carried it back to bed. Now that she had made the effort to get up she felt better. Today she would go back to the Home that had taken her when Grandma died. No one there knew her as Marriner and they would not connect her with the missing wife of a millionaire tycoon, not in her grey two-piece and camel coat. There would be a file on her somewhere, and she meant to see it.

The tights she had washed the night before were still damp but they were all she had so she wriggled into them, feeling them cling to crotch and toes. At the Garth she had had a stocking drawer filled with tights in every colour. If only she had slipped a few pairs into her bag. She would have to buy some today, along with a face cloth and some tampons. She couldn't remember the date of her last period but another one must be due any day.

She was suddenly struck by an awesome thought. If she couldn't go back she would have to begin again, accumulate once more the thousand tiny necessities of life. How would she pay for them? How would she get a job without a P45 and a reference, without a name that would stand up to scrutiny? When her money ran out she would be reduced to living like a bag-woman, shuffling from town to town on feet bound up with rags. Once she had seen such a figure, tousled grey hair under a stained felt hat, shapeless figure inside an assortment of dirty clothes. She had fished in her purse for money and the face had come up for a moment, revealing eyes, youthful and blue in a discoloured face.

Ellie put up a hand to her mouth, nauseous once more and terrified into the bargain. It was not lack of money she feared; she had always been poor, until Richard. As she chewed on a slice of wholemeal bread she thought about childhood clothes. Always bought for serviceability, never to compliment a thin little girl with unfashionably brown hair and an anxious expression. Once she had shown Terri a school snapshot and Terri had dubbed her Little Orphan Annie and hugged her by way of compensation.

Memory was stirring. Once or twice a year Grandma had taken out a 'club' and they had gone shopping. To big stores and to Sillett's warehouse, a dark cavern full of terror and delight where shoes in boxes were fetched from darkness at the top of a swaying ladder. But pleasure at new finery had always been short-lived. The 'club' had to be paid for, week after painful week. When there were bad weeks, when gas and electric bills came together and the 'club' money was hard to find, there had been hostility in Grandma's eyes. Once she had spoken of 'bearing other folks' burdens' and Ellie had known beyond doubt that she was the burden.

She finished buttoning her blouse and reached for her coat. It was coming back, piece by piece, swimming up to the surface as Dr Weidenek had promised it would. If she went on searching the truth would emerge, the creature from the deep that had always haunted her. She picked up her handbag and made for the door.

The police were already in Richard's office when Paul arrived but the black plastic evidence bags were still untied. 'Dr Weidenek – thank you for coming. This is Inspector Corkhill.' Richard was indicating chairs and the Inspector was taking out a tagged exhibit, the blue fox coat.

'We believe this belongs to Mrs Marriner, but we'd like confirmation. Harrods were able to identify it as having been one of theirs. You bought it there, I believe?'

Richard nodded. 'Yes, earlier this year.'

'It was found on a rail in their fur department. They have expensive merchandise there and their stock checks are rigorous . . . and frequent. It surfaced yesterday. They knew it wasn't new stock because there was a handkerchief in one pocket. Fortunately the buyer notified management, and they knew of our inquiries.'

He put the coat aside. 'Now we have something else, also found in Harrods.' The red dress was limp and grubby. 'Can you identify it as your wife's property, sir?'

Richard shook his head. 'I'm afraid not.' He grimaced. 'I'm not terribly observant. It could be hers. My sister-in-law would know, or our housekeeper.'

The Inspector laid the dress down. 'If you would get it formally identified, sir . . . but I think we can be fairly sure it belonged to your wife. It matches your sister-in-law's description, and it was found in the waste-bin in the powder room at Harrods.'

Paul saw Richard's shoulders sag slightly. He had been expecting worse news and was relieved. 'You mean it had been discarded?'

The Inspector nodded. 'It looks like it. When it came to light at closing time on Monday the attendant thought it was probably stolen – people often take things and then lose their nerve. She notified the fashion buyer who recognized it as French and not one of hers. Someone put two and two together when the coat turned up, and notified the Met.'

Richard was shaking his head from side to side. 'I don't understand it. She went into Harrods and started to take off her clothes . . . it doesn't make sense.'

Paul spoke. 'I think it does, Marriner. In fact, I've been expecting it ever since I heard about the flamboyant way she left the house. I'm sure your wife thinks she had good, practical reasons for shedding these things but in fact she was obeying an inner compulsion to strip away the top layer of her identity, her persona as your wife. So she sheds the expensive clothes and she does it in a public place. She is removing the mask in order to see the face.'

The Inspector cleared his throat. 'Does this mean Mrs Marriner can be classed as . . .' he was seeking a word Richard would find acceptable . . . 'as mentally disturbed?'

'In the sense you mean, Inspector, no. She is not

mad. She is simply curious. She is no danger to anyone else . . .'

The Inspector jumped in. 'And to herself?'

Paul raised his hands, palm upwards. 'I can't say. I think not. In my own mind I'm almost certain. But we are dealing with imponderables here. It's impossible to be definite.'

Richard's tone was impatient as he interrupted. 'Forgive me if I'm less concerned with my wife's mental state at the moment than with her physical safety. It seems to me that the nuances of her behaviour can be left until she is back in her own home. I think I should tell you that I intend to employ a private detective.'

Paul saw the Inspector's eyes narrow but he stayed silent as Richard continued. 'I know Dr Weidenek is less than enthusiastic about this but I'm afraid I must use my own judgement. He's a good man, recommended by my solicitor. His name is Jackson of Jackson and Hawkes . . . do you know of him?'

The Inspector nodded. 'Yes. He's a reputable operator but I have to say that I think his intervention would be premature. Your wife has been missing for a very short time . . .' His eyes had travelled to the crumpled red dress and he fell silent.

When the Inspector had left, the two men faced one another across the desk. 'It doesn't look good, does it,' Richard said. It was not a question but a statement.

Paul sought for the right words. 'She's out there, doing her best to find a way back to you. But it has to be a way she can accept.'

Richard stood up and turned to the window. 'I feel as though she's in another country,' he said. He had loosened his jacket; now he put his hands into his trouser pockets. The defiance of a few moments ago had left him. 'It's my own fault. I married a girl and I didn't make allowances for that fact. If it had been a business move I'd've commissioned surveys, done costings, held briefings. But when it came to the most important move of my life I simply assumed we'd live happily ever after.'

Paul felt pity for Richard: he was as ill-prepared as anyone else to deal with the pain and difficulty of loving, and ill-preparedness was not something he relished. When Paul had interviewed Richard alone, early in his casework, he had formed certain conclusions. A man of deep, even passionate feelings, totally incapable of expressing them, even to those he most cared for. A man of little sexual experience and with no great thirst for more knowledge. He had not come to his first wife a virgin but Paul was prepared to bet Richard Marriner had sown few wild oats, none at all where it mattered. He had probably had a few minor flirtations, mostly with girls whose families were friends of his own, visited a prostitute once or twice in his late teens and then settled down with a jolly girl who was possessed of great sexual energy but little emotional depth. If Julia had lived they would have grown old together in great contentment, seen their sons reach manhood, enjoyed their grandchildren and been brave and upright in old age. Certainly, Richard would never have been unfaithful. There would have been passion towards his wife, but men of his type did not see other women in a sexual light. And then Julia had died, and the neat edifice of Richard Marriner's private life had tumbled. Now he was in torment and unless he could be restrained he might do something that would send Ellie over the edge.

Mrs McReady was hovering as Ellie came downstairs. 'Just off? She must be bad if they're letting you in in the mornings.' Today her accent was broader and yesterday's gentility was slipping a little. 'I'm beginning to be one of the family,' Ellie thought wryly.

Mrs McReady advanced and dropped her voice. 'Have you met them yet?' She nodded towards the stairs.

Ellie shook her head. 'Not yet. I haven't heard a sound from either of them.'

Mrs McReady came closer. 'He . . . the big front . . . is very nice.' She sniffed. 'As for her in the off-shot, she's a born stirrer. I could tell you tales . . . I've asked her to look elsewhere but she knows when she's on to a good thing. Thinks she's a proper lady but it's all fur coats and nee knickers if you ask me. Pardon the expression.'

Ellie was edging towards the door but Mrs McReady stuck with her. 'I hope you get better news when you get there. You look really peaky.' Her tone implied that Ellie would be lucky not to land in a hospital bed herself.

'I'm all right. I never have a lot of colour.'

On Mrs McReady's cheeks rouge stood out in two triangular patches. 'Well,' she said, looking Ellie up and down, 'you ought to take care. Still, I mustn't keep you.' She glanced again at the stairs. 'Mr Corkhill'll be down any minute. I must catch him.' She adjusted her ruffled blouse and perked up her yellow hair. 'I'll tell you what, you pop in when you come back and we'll have a nice chat.'

It was a relief to be out in the street. Ellie made for the newsagent and bought an *Express*, a *Mail* and a copy of *Today*. The sea was blue, with few whitecaps, stretching to a deeper blue horizon where ships came and went, grey dots fading to infinity. She had forgotten how exhilarating it was to live within sight of the sea. She breathed deeply, inflating her lungs, then she sat down on a seat and opened the first paper.

There was nothing in the *Mail*, but she merited four lines on an inside page of the *Express* and six lines in *Today*: 'Fears are mounting over the whereabouts of Mrs Elldis Marriner, wife of industrialist Richard Marriner. Mrs Marriner left the couple's £500,000 home on Monday and has not been heard of since. The police have been informed but a spokesman for Mr Marriner said they were anticipating Mrs Marriner's early return.'

The piece in the *Express* was much the same. Not a word about Julia, not a single, solitary word. For once she had held the stage alone. The thought was comforting, and then frightening. Ellie folded the papers and got to her feet. Behind her the sea, ahead of her a maze of houses where once she and her parents might have lived.

Street gave way to avenue, opened into shopping thoroughfare and closed again into narrow terraces, but there was nothing to strike a chord. Most of the houses had been renovated. They had modern windows and imposing doors in teak. If the doors were painted they had been wash-leathered until they gleamed and bore shiny brass knockers and keyholes. Windows had frilly nets behind brightly patterned geometric prints, with here and there a Venetian blind or a pot plant. All were eminently respectable but not in the least familiar.

Ellie retreated to the park, a ravine that led to the sea, and sat down on a wooden seat. The sun had come out and with it the pushchair brigade. The children, released from their prams, laughed and clattered along the wooden seats, chased each other on unsteady legs and had to be retrieved from the flowerbeds. She liked to watch children but the thought of holding a baby in her arms filled her with distaste. There was something terrible about babies. She realized she was tense and tried to relax. Silly to worry about things like that.

One child, bolder than the rest, had advanced and was regarding her sympathetically. Children often did that . . . looked at her as though she were in need of comfort. The child in the town-centre park, a child on the train, Jeremy, sometimes even Gavin . . . she frowned at the thought of the boys. Perhaps she could ring them? A quick call . . . but to say what? No reassurance to offer, not yet.

A child was crying in the distance, a mother leaning to kiss better a damaged knee. In her head the music started . . . the same phrase repeated. She held her breath, willing further recollection to come, but there was nothing.

Getting to her feet, Ellie began to walk home. She felt queasy again, the taste of her morning toast rising buttery in her throat. When she got back she would make tea and drink it with her feet up. That had been her treat in London, at first alone and then with Terri. They had sat on rainy Sundays, toasting bare feet at the gas fire, talking about work and Terri's latest love-affair, putting the world to rights and drooling over the fashion pictures in the supplements. Once they had made a list of all the clothes Terri wanted that season and added it up to twelve hundred pounds' worth. The resultant laughter had carried them through to Monday.

'Do sit down.' Richard moved round the desk and sat in his own chair as the private detective settled opposite him. The man was not what he had expected. He was young; no shabby raincoat, no air of sleaziness. He was snapping open a framed briefcase and taking out pen and notebook.

'I've got the general picture from your solicitor but you'll appreciate I need background detail; the more I get the more quickly we can get things moving.'

Richard nodded, moving objects on his desk in an effort to put off his answer. How did you tell a fresh-faced boy that you could live with a woman, sleep with her, and make no effort to explore her past? For a moment he tinkered with the thought of a smoke-screen, blowing up what little fact he had to create an illusion of depth. But lies would not bring Ellie back and that was what he wanted.

'I'm afraid what I can give you is pitifully little . . .' He cleared his throat. 'My wife and I married a year ago. I was a widower. I have two children, boys. My wife had not been married before.'

The detective's eyes were on him and they seemed

to hold a doubt. But Ellie had been a virgin. There had been no previous marriage. Richard raised his voice slightly and continued. 'She had not had a happy childhood – she was orphaned as an infant. That period is all rather vague, I'm afraid. Her grandmother took her, and she too died. Ellie then wound up in care and stayed there until she was old enough to be self-sufficient. She was reticent about these circumstances, and I respected that reticence . . .'

The man's eyes were on him again, doubting. Or was the doubt in him?

'The fact is I never took the trouble to understand my wife's background. I bitterly regret it now, but I'm afraid it's fact.'

The detective was nodding, as though ignorance were the easiest thing in the world to understand. 'What about friends? And what papers have you? There must be birth certificates, documentation?'

Richard grasped at the proffered straw. 'There's a birth certificate, but it won't tell you much, I'm afraid. Still, I can arrange for you to have a copy.'

Terri made lists of names and worked out a structure. Perhaps it might gel after all. She ran her eye down the 'In' list. Barry Humphries, Bruce Oldfield, Phil Collins, Michael Crawford, Anouska Hempel . . . but it couldn't be a simple list of 'Ins' and 'Outs'. She had to have an angle. If you were 'Up' there was always 'Down' yawning below, which must be a pretty daunting prospect. If you were 'Down' you had everything to hope for and nothing to fear, except being down for ever. She doodled a face and then turned it into Pamela

Stephenson. She was an 'In' who behaved as though she wanted someone to put her 'Out'.

Terri drew a squiggle through the face and tried to concentrate. Royal 'Ins' and 'Outs'? Possible, but done to death. 'Ins' who had fallen from grace through an act of folly? No, that could be tacky, and not her mark. 'Ins' and 'Outs' in tandem? Married couples who were both powerful? The Kinnocks, the Owens, Pinter and Fraser, Holroyd and Drabble . . . a moment later she was scribbling away.

At noon she put her work aside and went to the washroom. She was meeting Mike in the pub and wanted to look her best.

'Going somewhere?' Greta said as they stood at adjoining handbasins.

'Mmm . . .' Terri finished outlining her mouth and clamped lips together to spread the colour. 'I am meeting my better ten-per-cent in the pub.'

Greta had recovered from her abortive pregnancy but was still feeling low. 'It must be nice to be hitched. Absolutely safe in a good marriage.'

Terri rapped an imaginary breastplate. 'Like having the strength of the insurance companies around you.'

As she walked to the pub she marvelled at the deception implicit in her reply. She did not feel safe inside her marriage; in some ways, she had felt safer before they married. Then, Mike's very presence had been proof that he wanted to be with her. Now she could never be sure whether he was with her from choice or because he could not again face the trauma of divorce.

He was waiting at the bar and he smiled at the sight

of her. His raincoat was grubby and the cuff of his suit jacket ready to fray. She wanted to reach out and smother him with kisses and then drag him off to the nearest bespoke tailor and spend and spend and spend. Instead she hoisted herself on a stool and accepted a half of lager.

'Any news?' he said.

She knew he meant about Ellie. 'No. We ran five lines on page seventeen. I asked News to tell me if anything breaks – I don't like to bother Richard all the time.'

Mike was nodding. 'Every time the phone rings he must feel sick to his stomach. I know what I'd feel if it was you . . .'

She smiled, feeling happiness well up inside her. He loved her, he really did!

Adele sighed and changed the position of her legs. If she had to stay here much longer, trapped between Mrs Withers' jaundiced expression and the four walls, she would go mad and join Ellie on the psychiatrist's couch. Opposite her, the telephone sat like an obscene Buddha, dominating the room, tying her to the chair. There was no possibility of Ellie's ringing the Garth – when the call came it would come to Adele, in her own home. But she couldn't tell that to Richard, so the dreary business of manning the phone had to continue. The temerity of what she had done threatened to overwhelm Adele. If Frank found out she was in touch with Ellie . . . her mouth went dry and she made an effort to switch her thoughts.

She might have been out on Snow now, reining him

in until roads and traffic were behind them, then giving him his head. She loved the gallop, the sensation of flying, the thunder of hoofs on baked earth, the rush of wind that would threaten to pluck her off his back so that she had to lean low on his neck and hang on for dear life.

And afterwards, when they had both exorcized their demons, the quiet canter through fields striped by the plough, white birds on black furrows. Fields of burned stubble, or green with winter wheat. She felt a stir of pleasure at the thought of the English countryside and then it was spoiled by the thought of her old home, a conference centre now with neat direction signs on the walls where water-colours had once hung. On her wedding day she had left that house proudly on her father's arm: now her father was dead and her mother lived in a ghastly red-brick villa. How perfectly bloody life could be.

Adele rose from the chair and moved to the window. For two pins she would walk out now, tell Withers to take over the phone and to hell with the consequences. But it wouldn't do for Richard to ring and discover her desertion. There was still a minute chance she might get to Japan if she behaved herself. She wanted that trip. She deserved it. She looked back at the room, filled with Anstruther furniture. Lucky Julia, to be left the lot. She herself would get a few good pieces when Mummy died, if they had not already been sold off, but that was all.

Julia had always been lucky . . . except that Julia was dead, which showed the bloody impermanence of happiness. She *must* get to Japan! You had to take happiness, it didn't fall into your lap. So she must use her contact with Ellie to advantage. Please God, let the silly little bitch ring her this afternoon, as she had promised.

There was a rattle of cups from the hall and then Withers with a tray. About time, too! Adele sat down with her tea and pondered how best to bring Ellie back . . . or drive her away for ever.

Richard waited for the boys in the Head's study. It looked much the same as it had looked twenty-five years ago, on his last day at Avebury. There was shelving now where the huge bureau-bookcase had been, and the wallpaper had grown more florid with each succeeding headmaster's wife, but the same photographs adorned the walls and the scuffed leather chairs still flanked the fireplace.

He looked at the sagging seats. When he had come there at eleven his feet had barely touched the ground. Now he was forty-two years old and he was tired. He wanted to stretch out in the old chair, put back his head and sleep. Instead he looked out on the walled garden and wondered what to say to his sons.

When they came in there was apprehension in their faces and he hastened to reassure them. 'We've got a bit of a problem at home, I'm afraid, but it isn't bad trouble.' The Head was making a discreet withdrawal and Richard was starting to explain when Gavin interrupted.

'It isn't Trumper, is it?'

In spite of himself, Richard smiled. 'No, old chap.

Both dogs are fine.' He hurried on. 'Ellie hasn't been well lately, I think you know that. She's all right . . . not at death's door . . .' He was making the most awful mess of it and the strain was showing in their faces. 'She's gone off somewhere to think things out and we don't know where. She'll come back eventually but in the mean time there's bound to be some talk. I wanted you both to know the truth in case you hear wild rumours.'

The relief of having it out in the open caused him to overdo things. He reached out and ruffled Gavin's hair. 'Come on, don't look tragic. This is just a temporary thing.'

But their faces had adopted the world-weary expressions of those who have been reassured too often and are not prepared to believe again. He felt a sudden anger. How could Ellie do this to them? They had been through more than enough already.

He took them down to the Crowborough Arms and ordered cream teas in the beamed dining-room, but there was none of the usual thrill of eating out while comrades were left behind. They ate dutifully, cleaning knife-blades of jam and cream, wiping their mouths of crumbs, answering his questions but asking none of their own.

At length he ran out of topics and took the plunge. 'You must want to ask more about Ellie.'

Jeremy tried to oblige. 'Did she leave you a letter?'

Richard shook his head. 'No, but she telephoned. She sent you her love and said no one was to worry.' Jeremy nodded and sat back.

Gavin was folding his napkin into smaller and smaller

triangles. 'If she doesn't come back does that mean we can't talk about her any more?'

Richard looked at him in amazement. 'Of course not. She *will* come back, but what made you say that?'

The boy took refuge in a shrug and it was left to Jeremy to supply an answer. 'Aunt Adele said we mustn't mention Mummy any more. Ever . . . for fear of upsetting Ellie.'

It was his son's flat tone that angered Richard, more than the words themselves. 'I must say I think that was a profoundly silly thing for your aunt to say. I'm sure she meant well but it was utter rubbish.'

He should have said more, but he couldn't bring himself to be too critical of Adele – she was family, after all. And what could he say about Ellie? Instead he pressed them to more cake, more cream, and when they refused substituted a ten-pound note apiece, before driving them back to school and making the usual embarrassed goodbyes.

'Shit!' Terri said when she saw the message scrawled in Stephen's hand: 'Ellie phoned. May ring again.' She crossed to his desk and waved the early edition of the *Standard* under his nose. 'You only had a missing person on the line and you let her go with a one-line message.'

He took the paper and followed her pointing finger. 'Oh,' he said, 'sorry. If it's any consolation, she sounded perfectly normal. I thought it was just one of your *many* girl-friends.'

Terri retrieved the paper and went back to her desk. Who did she tell, Richard or the police? She swung round and called to Stephen: 'Did she say where she was ringing from?' But she knew the answer would be 'No' before he spoke.

She called Richard's office and found he was not there. Instead she left a message giving him news that was really no news at all. 'She may ring me at home tonight,' she told his secretary. 'I'm not going out, so if she does call I'll be there.' They had intended to go for a drink at the Duke but it would have to wait.

Waiting for the tube Terri checked her bag to make sure the chops were there, and tried to plan ahead. Making a decent evening meal was a doddle if you planned ahead. The trouble was she always had to compromise. If the recipe called for barley she would find peas and lentils and three types of rice but no barley. If she wanted nutmeg she had every spice but. Her store cupboard had galloping alopecia and the bald patches moved around so that they were always in the wrong place at the right time. Still, it was chops and healthy baked potatoes tonight and they were safe in her bag. Nothing could go wrong.

Mike was working from home today, so the flat would be warm and welcoming, a bottle of plonk nicely chilled and the immersion heater on for a bath. It was ages since they had bathed together, not since they were married, in fact. She tried to think randy thoughts but they wouldn't come. Somewhere Ellie was sitting alone: however much you tried not to think about it, you couldn't escape it.

She turned out of the tube, hoisting her bag on to her shoulder so that she could run the quarter of a mile to home. If Ellie rang early and all was well, they could have an early night. But she must resist peeling onions – the second time round would be a turn-off.

She called Mike's name and looked into the living-room before she saw the note. 'Diana rang. They have a day-time prowler. Girls upset. Will be back as soon as I can. Am leaving lights on just in case.'

Terri put one chop into the pan and the other in the freezer, peeled a potato and chipped it into a bowl of water, thinking all the while of the magnificent damage the chip-pan would do to his veins. When the chop had ceased to run blood she turned out the hotplate and locked herself in the bathroom. She was down to bra and pants when she decided to have a large gin and tonic. She carried it back to the bathroom and balanced it on the soap dish while she stepped into the suds. It was a very large G and T. If it went to her head and she slipped under the water it would serve him right.

She felt the hair at the nape of her neck grow wet and start to straggle. She sank lower until the thought of Diana moving back in before she was decently interred brought her bolt upright and reaching for the loofah.

The lights gave everything a dream-like quality: brilliant patterns at a distance, close up a criss-cross of steel and wire, the bulbs set like jewels in the frame. Ellie had followed them for miles, enjoying the feeling of people all around her. There were only two nights of the illuminations left and it seemed the world had come to view before it was too late. At first the strollers were families – children in fathers' arms, mothers with push-chairs – but the children were gone by nine-thirty and

133

the teenagers came into their own. The cruising cars vanished, too, and traffic flowed normally along the coast road.

At ten o'clock Ellie bought chips from a van, showering them with salt and vinegar, eating them with relish from a cone of newspaper. She had needed to get out of the house so she had invented a supper invitation after the hospital. 'The family are coming round, then?' Mrs McReady said, nodding satisfaction. 'I should think so, as well. Still, you can't expect much from families. God chooses your friends and the Devil sends your relations, as my old mam used to say.'

Ellie had felt the usual elation at another fairy-tale well told. She was becoming an accomplished liar, so that increasingly it was hard to distinguish lies from truth. And she would have to be careful. Mrs McReady was nobody's fool in spite of always wanting to know the ins and outs.

'Ins and outs': a Belgate phrase she'd forgotten. 'The ins and outs of a cow's behind' – that had been the full quote. '*Well, she'll get nothing from me.*' Her grandmother's voice had been sharp. '*She wants to know the ins and outs of a cow's behind, but she'll get nothing from me.*' No one had ever visited them. They had had no friends and that was unnatural, but Ellie had never thought of it till now.

The chips had grown cold and grease stood on her lips. She grimaced with distaste and scrubbed her mouth with her hand. There was a waste-bin nearby and she threw the chips away.

Pieces of the past were floating into her mind all the time now, but they were only fragments, too insubstantial to be of use. It wasn't fair. If life had been fair Grandma would have lived, and she would have grown up in Belgate and married a miner, sitting by the fire to knit chunky cardigans for chunky children, the only agony in her life the saccharine agony of *Dallas* or *Dynasty*.

Except that staying in Belgate would have solved nothing: the damage had been done before she went there. In the distance the fairground music rose and fell and she tried to shut her ears against her own music, the tune that came constantly and stayed until it was banished, as always, by the child's crying. And then the drain, the black mouth of the drain with rain trickling towards it along the gutter.

Ellie turned and began to hurry back along the seafront. It was cold suddenly and the air was sharp with the coming of winter. Around her couples walked, starry-eyed in an illuminated fairyland. Only she, Ellie Rowe, had no one. She could never go back to Richard. She started to run, dodging couples, sometimes jarred by a passing shoulder or kicked by a stray heel. Once someone turned. 'What's up with her? Seen a fire?' And then laughter.

Laughter! *'Elldis is a stupid name.'*

'But who am I? What am I?'

'Little girls with long noses get them cut off, Ellie Rowe. You'll know what you're told and no more.'

'But what about Julia?' A giant Humpty-Dumpty looked up, outlined in glitter. *'That's enough about Julia. Mention her again and I'll tan your backside.'* But Julia *had* been there. She had, she had!

The lights came to an end and she turned up a

135

dark back street. Quietly now, Ellie, mustn't attract attention. *'Keep quiet, Ellie. You're not supposed to be here.'* She must walk calmly into the house, close the door gently, mount the stairs. And then a pill. A pill to put out the lights, stop the music and kill the pain of it all.

Richard looked at the plate and then at Mrs Withers' anxious face. 'I've kept it small, sir, so as not to put you off.' The steak was medium rare garnished with onion rings, mangetouts and small potatoes. Richard didn't feel like eating but he would have to try. When he had told Mrs Withers of Ellie's attempted call to Terri her face had glowed. 'There you are, sir. I told you she'd ring someone.'

'I'm not frightfully hungry but it does look good. Will you sit down with me? I want to talk to you, if you're not in a hurry.' Mrs Withers was already sinking into a chair and he crossed to the sideboard for a second glass. 'Try this . . . it's one of the better reds.'

She sipped at the glass and nodded. 'Very nice. Now you eat up.'

It was easier to eat with the incentive of her pleased expression. He ate a third of the steak before he began. 'I know you've talked to the police and to Dr Weidenek, but I wondered if there was anything . . . any little thing, however unimportant it might be . . . that might help? We have to find her soon.' He wanted to tell her about the baby but Weidenek had said no for the moment.

She was shaking her head. 'I've racked my brains. I mean, there's things I could tell you, things that upset her . . . but they're not much help now.'

He topped up her glass against faint-hearted protests. 'What things?'

Her lips pursed. 'Well, I think there was too much harking back. She was shown too much of . . .' she hesitated and then went on . . . 'of the first Mrs Marriner, before she had time to find her feet.'

'But who by?' He saw her eyes flicker. Adele! It must have been Adele. 'Still, we won't go into that now. Just tell me what happened.'

She was leaning forward. 'There was one time, we were up in the box room. You know what it's like, all clutter. She picked up a box. "What's this, Mrs Withers?" she says and opens it.'

He couldn't wait. 'What was it?'

'It was the first Mrs Marriner's wedding veil, Mr Richard. It should never have been in the box room and someone had left it beside a radiator, I don't know who. The colour had gone, so all the mother of pearl was grey and the veil had gone brittle. Mrs Marriner lifted it out of the box and it fell to bits. Just shredded. "Give that to me," I said but the damage was done, you could see that.'

He pushed aside his plate. 'I've done my best. It was very good, but I'm not in the mood.' If only he had cleared the house; better still, razed it to the ground. If only he had thought twice about Adele. God, on Monday he had set her on to Ellie himself!

The housekeeper was waiting, her eyes on his face.

'Well,' he said, trying to reassure, 'we're making some progress. There was the call today: it's unfortunate that Mrs Benedict was out, but Ellie did leave a message. It's not much, but it's something. Then there's the newspaper publicity – that might produce results. And I've hired an excellent private investigator. He'll probably want to talk to you soon. If we only knew where Ellie came from. The psychiatrist is certain she's gone back to her roots. You come from her part of the world, don't you? Did you ever compare notes?'

'I come from Northumberland, sir. Mrs Marriner came from Durham. That was all she ever said, just Durham. I never asked where in Durham because it wouldn't have meant much if she'd told me.' She smiled. 'We don't all live on top of one another up there, you know.'

So Mrs Withers had never asked and Ellie had never volunteered. Ellie had been his wife for a year and he had never been interested enough to demand details: he could hardly expect more from an employee.

'Well, if you can stay by the phone as much as possible. I'm going to tell my sister-in-law she can ease up a bit. She's done very well over the last few days. I think we'll give her some time off.'

The tightening of the old woman's lips denoted satisfaction and confirmed his suspicions. 'Just as you say, sir. You can trust me. I'll never be out of earshot, not for a minute.'

Paul could hear it emerging quite clearly now on the tapes – a distinct aversion to discussing sex.

'Do you think sex is important, Ellie?'
'Quite important, but it's not everything.'
'Would you say you were sexually experienced?'
'I'm not sure what you mean by that.'
'Have you had lovers?'

'No.'

'But Richard is your lover, surely?'

'It's not the same thing. I'm his wife.' And then a clatter of tea-cups.

He stopped the tape, remembering. They had been sitting in the garden at the Garth, which was her favourite, windows wide open on to a terrace. The housekeeper had brought tea on a tray and Ellie had made a great fuss with the tea-things whenever she wanted to divert him.

He leaned forward and restarted the tape. *'Julia was his wife, too.'*

'Yes.'

'Are you jealous of Julia?'

'No. Of course not.'

'Do you fear her?'

'No. It's not like that . . . it's just . . .' There had been a long pause but he had waited, determined not to let her off the hook. '. . . *it's just that there's a lot of her here, in the house. Even though they try. I keep wondering if . . . wondering what . . .'*

There was another long pause and then she started again, as though talking to herself. '. . . *we went into the box room. Gavin wanted his skates that weekend. It was a nice day and the sun was coming in through the fanlight. There was a box there. It was Julia's veil. I shouldn't have touched it. It was so beautiful, a crown of orange blossom. She looked perfect in the photographs.*

'*It was my fault. I picked it up . . . just to look at it . . . and it disintegrated. Tiny little pieces of it were spinning in the sunlight, on and on, swimming there as if they were never going to stop, as if they were going to hang there for ever.*

*The flowers . . . I could feel them coming apart in my fingers
and I couldn't stop it. I didn't want to spoil things. I just
want to please everyone but I don't know how.'* Her voice
was rising and breaking, and then came the sound of
his own voice, soothing.

Paul rewound the tape, pressed the replay button
and listened once more. It must have been disturbing
to find the veil, the trapping of a former ceremony
more elaborate than your own. He did not know details
of Richard's marriage to Julia but he could imagine:
garlanded pews, penguin ushers and bridesmaids ga-
lore. Yes, the finding of the veil must have been traumatic but he could sense something more there. Ellie
had not been apologizing for the accidental destruction
of Julia's veil. She had been apologizing for her own
existence.

On an impulse he crossed to the bookcase and looked
along the shelves until he found what he wanted.
Matthew Arnold – *Collected Poems*. It took only a moment to find the line. 'Resolve to know thyself and
know that he who finds himself loses his misery.' Ellie
must find herself and he must make sure she is left
free to do so. All the same, it would not be easy with
Richard building up a head of steam that could fuel a
locomotive.

He was still reading the poem when he heard the
door and Gary came into the room. 'You look tired.'

Paul smiled. 'I am. It hasn't been the best of days.'

Gary moved to take the book from his hand. 'Come
on, I'm in charge. I have had a good day, in fact a
bloody good day. I want some food . . . we'll eat in the
kitchen and you can moan as much as you like.'

Paul felt the tension ebb from him. It was going to be all right. He could forget his fears for Ellie, forget the terrors that nibbled at the corners of his own mind – for tonight, at least, there was peace.

He followed the boy to the kitchen, marvelling at the difference one human being could make to the happiness of another. 'I love you,' he said as he sat down at the kitchen table.

'I know. Silly old sod.' The words were harsh but the tone was devoid of menace.

Paul sat on, luxuriating, as the smell of food began to fill the kitchen and the worries of the day took flight.

Frank and Adele went up early, turning off the lights together and mounting the stairs side by side. It was a ritual and one Adele enjoyed. Frank had not mentioned Japan at the dinner-table and neither had she. Softly softly catchee monkee.

'Richard's light is still on,' Frank said, the curtain cord in his hand.

Adele was stepping out of her dress. 'I don't expect he sleeps much. Ellie is creating havoc for everyone. It's totally inconsiderate. Not even to ring and let us know . . . it's too bad.' She kept her eyes down in case he saw she was lying. For a moment panic fluttered in her. If he knew about the phone call this afternoon . . . !

Frank pulled off his tie and threw it on to the Wellington chest. 'She's not to blame for her behaviour at the moment, that's patently obvious.'

'And neither am I,' Adele wanted to say but bit it back.

141

'It's strange, really,' Frank said, moving back and forth between wardrobe and dressing-table. She loved his precise morning and evening rituals; her father had had them too, and they made her feel safe.

'What's strange?'

He had dropped his shirt on the floor and was following it with pants and socks. 'The way life goes on. Something pretty cataclysmic happens: a very much loved wife vanishes. And yet the petty little things go on. The milkman calls, the window cleaner. You get out the car, go to the office. Clean your teeth. Change your shirt. It's bizarre.'

'I know what you mean. It's different this time, though. In one way, nothing has happened. I mean, if someone dies you have a funeral; it's like punctuation. It's sad, but it's over. But this time nothing's really changed. Ellie exists, she isn't dead. She's just gallivanting around on a wild-goose chase, wrecking Richard's nerves in the process and doing God knows what damage to the boys.'

He was padding towards the bathroom and Adele knew she had gone too far. But it irked her to pretend she was sorry for Ellie – if the little fool had any sense she'd have a good dose of ECT and get on with life. She sped across the room and caught him before he had stepped into the shower.

'I'm sorry,' she said, winding her arms around him. 'I'm sorry. I'm a hard bitch and you don't love me.'

There was no response. Nothing. He stood there, unmoved.

'Darling,' she tried to sound seductive, 'I can't remember when we last made love. It's yonks.'

He was reaching for her hands and removing them from his belly. 'Sorry, Adele. I was wrong just now when I said life went on as though nothing had happened. As far as I'm concerned, Richard is in a hell of a mess and Ellie, whom I rather like, is probably in a worse one. Even if I could make love I couldn't give it my full attention, which rather negates the process, don't you agree?'

He moved to the shower and Adele turned away, humiliated. God, she was sick of this business. When Ellie rang again she would tell her she was pregnant and make her come home, double quick! Before things got even worse than they were.

[6]

Ellie had woken from a nightmare at six a.m., sitting bolt upright in the bed until cold prickled her bare arms. It was a dream, she told herself, only a dream. Predictable stuff about hiding from nameless, faceless soldiers in some strange terrain. But the terror persisted, defying attempts to sleep, so that she finally climbed out of bed in darkness and put on her coat. She would have to buy a cardigan. She was always cold now . . . and sickly. She made for the sink, retching and retching, producing nothing except acid that burned her throat.

She climbed back into bed to drink tea, wishing she could afford a radio. She had always liked radio, preferring it to television. Now there were no news broadcasts to punctuate her day, no familiar landmarks like *Any Questions* on Fridays or *Gardeners' Question Time* on Sundays. Outside this house the world would be ticking. Hospitals, news rooms, police stations . . . Richard must have been to a police station to report her missing. Or perhaps he had done it by phone, impersonally, like someone reporting a missing umbrella. She drained her cup and set about getting ready as dawn began to break.

'Going out, dear?' The blue eyes were tired this morning; the face sagging slightly, powder and rouge lying on the skin as though they would blow away at the first breath.

Ellie continued down the stairs, tying the belt of her coat. 'Yes. I've some shopping to do.'

'There's a nice cup of tea in the pot. Come in for a minute. I won't keep you long.' The puffed-up hair had divided to show pink scalp beneath, and the hairs around the pencilled-in browline were white. 'She is pathetic,' Ellie thought and followed her into the sitting-room.

There were plants everywhere, vivid cyclamen in even more vivid pots; wandering sailors roaming over sideboard and china cabinet; a spider plant dripping obscenely on the television. 'Now sit yourself down and I'll top the pot up. I miss a woman's conversation.'

Mrs McReady patted a frilled cushion behind Ellie's back. 'There's some you can't talk to . . . her in the off-shot for one . . . still, we won't discuss unpleasant subjects this early. You haven't rung your nice husband lately.' She smiled. 'Mustn't neglect him, must we? Give him a ring tonight in the cheap time.'

She poured tea into flowered cups and handed one to Ellie. 'I knew we'd get on as soon as I saw you. I go by faces. That and a nice background. I won't take DHSS. The welfare state has a lot to answer for. Not that I'm not sorry for them but I've always paid my way. I've run my feet off, some of the jobs I've had. I wound up doing check trading . . .'

She realized Ellie was bemused. 'Of course, you

don't come from up here, do you. Not that you sound Cockney but still . . . Well, we used to call them "clubs" in the old days – now it's shopping checks. You take out a "club" so you can buy on tick, and then you pay it back – with a little bit extra for the agent's trouble. I did quite nicely out of that, enough to fit this place up.'

The blue eyes filled. 'Then Ernie went. The best-laid plans . . . still.' She blew her nose on a lace edged handkerchief and tucked it back up the sleeve of her turquoise cardigan. 'Yes, I've done all right. Well, I have got a nice place, haven't I? Nice things.'

On the mantelpiece china ornaments jostled for place. 'I'm a devil for bric-à-brac. Junk, Ernie used to call it but he liked nice things as much as I did.' She sighed. 'You're lucky to have your hubby. Ernie was only sixty-four. It was a strangulated colon. Still, mustn't depress you when you're off to the hospital.'

She jumped to her feet. 'Take your aunt this pepper plant. I always think they look cheerful.' The white seed pods were turning orange and red.

'Yes, it does,' Ellie agreed, wondering how and where she would dispose of it. 'Are you sure you can spare it, though?'

Mrs McReady's nod was emphatic. 'I'm sure. Cast your bread on the waters; you'll get it back tenfold.' From the look of the room she had cast quite a few pot plants, and Ellie felt her lip twitch.

'It's a pleasure to have you here, pet,' the landlady said as she set Ellie to the door. 'I have to be careful . . . I mean, this is my home. But I go by the face. That's how I took Mr Corkhill, on a hunch. Of course,

I fell down on her upstairs but you can't be right every time. She says she's a civil servant but I have my doubts. I shall get to the bottom of it, though, sooner or later.'

Her hand was on the door catch. 'She called me a glorified doss-house keeper!' Her face defied Ellie to believe the calumny. 'She did! Me, that's got slides in my back room of near enough every holiday resort in Europe.'

There was a plop as the morning paper came through the letter-box and fell to the floor. She picked it up and turned to a middle page. 'Ooh. "You are coming to the end of a testing time and will overcome all opponents." That's nice. What are you, dear?'

'Gemïni,' Ellie said, immediately regretting that she had not transposed her sign. It was by such tiny truths you were betrayed.

"An encumbrance will be lifted today."

I'm sure it will, Ellie thought, shifting the pepper plant to her other arm.

She was still feeling wryly amused as Mrs McReady read out the rest of her fate in the stars – and then she saw the photograph. Blurred and unflattering, but unmistakably her. She was panicking until she remembered the sun specs. She had grown so used to wearing them that she had almost forgotten they were there.

Mrs McReady was closing the paper. 'I mustn't keep you but I've loved the chat. I get lonely sometimes. Look in on your way back.'

Ellie was opening the gate when the bombshell came. 'Ask for Sister Bollon at the hospital – her mother's a

147

good friend of mine. She'll see you all right. She's a good girl to her mother. Just mention my name.'

'Terri!' It started as a howl of rage and degenerated into a wail. She came to the bathroom door, mouth foaming with mild mint, toothbrush in hand.

'You've done it again!' Mike was looking down at his half-buttoned shirt.

'What?'

He gestured, holding the edges away from his chest towards her. 'You haven't ironed the edges. They're all curled up.'

Inwardly she cursed her own forgetfulness: he was a fanatic about pressing buttonholes. Aloud, she said, 'Tough,' and went back to the bathroom.

He was waiting in the kitchen when she emerged. 'Sorry,' he said and then, 'That's all I seem to say. I should be shot!' Normally, such contrition would have carried her straight into his arms but not today. She was angry with herself for neglecting something he had complained of before, with him for being so hard to please, most of all with life for putting them under so much strain that little things could cause a furore.

'Forget it,' she said, feeding bread into the toaster. He had come up behind her and was nuzzling the back of her neck. 'Give up, Mike, we're late already. You can be sure of lunch; I can't. This toast may be all I get.' He moved away and clattered tea-cups.

Watching for the bread to jump from the toaster, she groaned inwardly. Damn Diana. She had phoned at eleven last night to remind him that fees for Alison's ballet classes were overdue. He had tossed and turned all night, and now she was being mean to him. She wanted to turn and make up, but she couldn't. She just couldn't. Why should she? Why must she always be the one to compromise? Diana never gave an inch.

'Where's the sugar? This bowl's empty.'

His tone was curt and she made her own even sharper. 'In the usual place. Use your eyes.'

'I've looked in the usual place. There's none there.'

She stalked across to the unit to collect sugar and brandish it in his face. There was none. She thought for a moment: own up, or defend by attacking? 'We're out of it. I can't remember everything.' His answering snort was a masterpiece, and it maddened her. 'You do the stocking-up, if you're so worried about it. Any-way . . .' she looked at his midriff . . . 'doing without sugar won't do you any harm.' That stung!

'God, you're so childish, Terri. You can't just say, "Sorry I forgot", like any other woman. Oh no, that's not enough for Terri. She has to make it one more episode in the battle of Man v. Woman.'

The toast leaped and she began to butter it with short savage strokes. 'Any other woman? I like that. By any other woman I suppose you mean your lady wife? Or perhaps your mother, that retired gentlewoman who is not averse to the odd gin or two or seven? Of course she ironed your frigging shirts . . . when she could see straight.'

He was looking at her with loathing. 'You have a vicious streak, Terri. I've often suspected it, now I know.'

She sat down at the table and began to pour tea. 'OK, so now you know. I'm vicious. Worse than that,

I'm undomesticated. What a disappointment for you. Well, I'm sorry. I can't do everything. And remember this, lover . . . I may not be Superwoman but I have my advantages. I work, which is more than your Number One Wife ever did. I work and I earn. I make the difference between living in a Grade C dump or a Grade A dump, and don't you forget it.' Why was she doing this when she loved him so much? But she still couldn't stop. 'So I don't iron your buttonholes. The cardinal sin! I'm not around long enough to do anything properly. I work on the hoof, I iron on the hoof, I do the week's shopping in three minutes flat before they close the supermarket. And why?'

She had pushed back her chair and risen to face him. 'Because I have to earn money to keep your frigging wife and kids in the manner to which you've let them be accustomed. Because I'll never get the chance to be a full-time wife . . . not to mention mother . . . while your past life is round my neck like a bloody millstone!'

She threw the last words down the stairs after his departing figure, and then she returned to the table to weep as she chewed on her granary toast.

The chrysanthemums were still abundant but up close they were brown and dying. Adele searched the garden for something else she could pillage. Alpines were useless in flower arrangements, and there was nothing else. It was crazy to have a flower festival in November. If they wanted a patronal festival they should've called their damned church after a sensible saint who had his feast day in high summer. When Julia died the vicar of St Andrew's had suggested Adele take Julia's place on the PCC. She had jumped at the chance, seeing it as one more token that she was *the* Mrs Marriner. It was the one office she had subsequently pressed on Ellie when she became Richard's wife, but even Ellie had had too much sense to say yes and Adele was stuck with it.

The trug was full of greenery and she rested it on the stone balustrade. It was going to be a boring day, cooped up in the church with moronic villagers wearing holy expressions on their normally mean little faces.

This morning Frank had told her the weekend with the Chestertons would have to be put off. 'We can't leave Richard at the moment, Del. Besides, I've too much on, with Japan looming up.' She had rung Flicky Chesterton and given a guarded version of events but there had been no probing questions in return so obviously Flicky was *au fait* with the facts.

Mrs Withers was toiling up from the lower terraces, her arms full of branches of fir that reeked of funerals. Still, it would have to do.

'Julia made a good job of it, didn't she?' They were gazing over the garden Julia had planned and Adele felt a painful tugging at her throat.

Beside her, the older woman was wiping secateurs on a corner of her apron. 'Yes, she loved her garden.'

For a moment Adele was tempted to explain, perhaps even gain an ally. '*She loved it all*,' she could say, '*she created it, garden, house, everything. So you see why we mustn't let Ellie . . . let anyone . . . spoil it.*' But you couldn't talk like that to staff. It always had repercussions. She picked up the trug and led the way round to the yard where Mr Withers was waiting with her car, its boot full of expensive hothouse blooms that had cost her the earth.

She had been in the church for only ten minutes before her fingers became cold and sore from bending stems and twigs. Next year she would find an excuse.

'Oh my, that's splendid, Mrs Marriner.' The vicar's wife was tall and stooped with a hairy chin and an Honours Degree in Oriental Art. It had done nothing for her arrangement of chrysanthemums and Adele took the bowl from her.

'Better let me finish these for you. You can clear up.'

Released from the need to be creative, the vicar's wife bundled wet paper and stripped leaves into a waste-bin. 'I know it looks lovely when we've done, but it's such a task, isn't it? And all to be dismantled after Sunday. Still, dear St Andrew is worth it.' She came closer and dropped her voice. 'I do hope you've had word of your sister-in-law. No? Oh dear. The vicar was hoping . . . she's being prayed for, I can assure you.'

And a lot of good that would do, Adele thought, giving a frozen smile to indicate the subject was closed.

The chrysanthemums looked as though they had been shot from a gun. She sighed and began to put them right, plucking a bloom here, reinserting one there. She was good at it, so it wasn't surprising they kept on asking her. Up and down the church women worked, intent on putting into practice what they had learned at the Flower Club. Adele despised them. You didn't go to classes for flower arranging; it was some-thing you did, taking over from your mother after years of watching. Mummy had done the flowers every single morning. People made such a fuss about things now.

She pushed the last bloom home and carried the bowl towards the font. Beyond, the altar was piled with flowers spreading jewel-like, everywhere. It was beautiful.

Adele put a hand to her chest, suddenly stirred. Perhaps life *was* miraculous and commandments there to be obeyed. Except that they didn't make sense. Turning the other cheek was for ninnies! She put a five-pound note in the offertory box and made her goodbyes, feeling the cosy glow of duty well and truly done.

Ellie found a place for the pepper plant in a garden ruled by a stout gnome in a red hat, fishing-rod poised vainly over a gravel sea. His rosy cheeks and blue eyes reminded her of Mrs McReady so it seemed appropriate, and she went on her way relieved. She had felt sickly all morning and she paused outside the Home gates to unwrap a peppermint and slip her wedding ring into the inside pocket of her handbag.

The place had changed. The gates were no longer closed and there was a gaggle of motor cars in front of the main door. A tennis racket lay abandoned on the lawn and she could see a red enamelled climbing frame. It looked at once seedier and more alive than it had when she had left it nearly twelve years ago, but the smell of polish and pine disinfectant was the same and the front door on the right was still marked 'Inquiries'. She knocked and waited obediently for permission to enter, just as she had done in the old days.

The secretary showed her into Miss Davison's office but the woman on the other side of the desk was young, not more than thirty-five, smartly dressed in a Gatsby-style cardigan and ethnic beads. 'Liz Southern . . . and you're Elldis Rowe. We spoke on the phone, didn't we? Do take a seat. Could we have coffee, Sally? White for you, Miss Rowe?'

Ellie had given her maiden name when she made the appointment. She would have preferred an alias but if she wanted answers to questions she had to start from a position of truth.

'Now, what can I do for you?' The smile was expansive, the voice positively warm but the eyes were twin computers, totting away the minutes. She smiled again. 'Take your time.' And then, before Ellie could speak, 'Perhaps I can help you? You said you were here in the seventies. You'd find it very different now. We've learned an awful lot, I think. Modern social work practice is very different.'

Ellie resisted the impulse to scamper for the door and opened her mouth. 'I came here in 1967 and I was here on and off until 1975. I was wondering if it would be possible to check my records.'

The eyes across the desk had narrowed. 'I'd have to know why. It's not usual – not after such a lapse of time.'

Ellie hastened to appease her. 'I don't want to cause any trouble; that's the last thing I want. It's just that I want . . . I need to know more about my background.'

'Ah, of course. There's always a need to know, isn't there? Were you the subject of an order? I mean, did we take you into care, or were you placed with us voluntarily?'

Coffee came in china mugs but they went on talking.

'My grandma died. She brought me up after my parents' death. There was no one else.'

The chest under the Gatsby cardigan heaved slightly. 'Poor thing, no wonder you feel a bit lost. We have a counselling service . . .' She was fishing in a desk drawer. 'You can contact the Duty Social Worker on that number.'

Ellie took the card but stayed seated. 'I've had counselling . . . in Scotland. They thought I ought to find out the facts about myself. I wondered if I could see my admission notes?'

Miss Southern's voice had hardened. 'But surely you'd get all that sort of information when you left? We're meticulous about giving family detail. It's crucial.'

Ellie shook her head. 'No one told me anything. I knew my name, my gran's name, where we lived, that sort of thing. There was a little money from the sale of my grandmother's things, my birth certificate and a few personal possessions they'd kept for me – but that's all.'

Miss Southern looked at her watch. 'Well, I don't really see what I can do. I'd like to help.'

Ellie tried not to sound desperate. 'Anything really. That's all I want . . . anything about my parents.'

Miss Southern had risen and was coming round the desk. 'Look, love, I know how you must feel, but I do really think you need some trained counselling. Even if I had the records . . . and they'll be back at County

Hall by now . . . even if I had them, I doubt it would be wise to drag up the past without some preliminary work.'

Her hand was on Ellie's shoulder and the expression on her face was benevolent. Ellie wanted to say, 'You smug bitch,' but the intensity of her anger frightened her. Instead she said, 'There was a Miss Davison here in my day. Is she still around?'

Miss Southern's laugh was as patronizing as her gestures. 'I'm afraid not. She went long ago.'

'Is she dead?' Ellie asked flatly.

Miss Southern's eyes were on the clock. 'Oh no, I shouldn't think so. I don't want to rush you but I'm due at a case conference . . .'

Ellie stood her ground. 'Do you know where she lives now?'

Miss Southern was gathering up files and shovelling them into a tapestry holdall. 'I don't know. She left here in '79 or '80 and went to an Assessment Centre for a while. I think she lives in the city, in a flat somewhere. And it wouldn't be ethical for me to tell you if I did know. If you'd do as I suggest and contact the Duty Social Worker, she might help.'

Terri finished the 'famous partners' piece and sent it to Subs, knowing it was competent but uninspired. The morning after next it would be propped against tea-cups and skimmed by eyes feverish for famous names, but it would not move the world, which was what she had always wanted to do. She looked at the clock. She had fifteen minutes to spare before meeting the psychiatrist. She could tidy her muck-heap of a desk or she could think up some brilliant ideas for morning conference.

She began to tidy her drawer. What would happen when she got home tonight? They had parted on the worst possible terms. Mike had been unreasonable about the shirt, but she *had* been vicious. She had known about his commitments when they married, and throwing them in his face now was a putrid thing to do. The trouble was, she and Mike were always on edge. *We have never had a chance to be happy*, she thought and then, remembering Ellie, felt suddenly ashamed. Over the last few days she had thought a lot about Ellie.

She pushed back her chair and marched purposefully towards the Features Editor's door. 'Stephen . . . I've been thinking.'

He swept some files off a chair. 'Sit down . . . you shouldn't take unaccustomed mental exercise. It's bad for you.'

She was not in the mood for badinage. 'Shut up, Stephen, I'm serious. You know that friend of mine, the one who's gone missing?'

He nodded. 'Elldis Marriner, wife of Richard of Marriner Engineering, as profiled in the FT. Squeaky clean in and out of business, and boring. I've thought of you doing a piece but there doesn't seem to be much there . . . unless . . .' His eyes lit up. 'Unless you're in possession of a guilty secret or two?'

Terri shook her head. 'No, there's nothing steamy. They're pillars of the community . . . but she feels she has to go. Why? And more important, where? If we did a piece now, I could guarantee the inside story once she was back.' Even as she spoke, her heart was sinking. She was used to selling ideas to editors, but this was a friend she was haggling over.

Stephen was still looking dubious. 'Is there likely to be anything juicy? You know the old man . . . he's only interested in two kinds of stories: high achievers and perverts. If I go to him with something about a respectable woman gone missing for a day or two, no real press speculation, low profile, little or no police interest, he'll ask where the beef is. Tell you what, start on it in your spare time and we'll see how it goes.'

She knew he was fobbing her off but at least she had tried. And there was one more thing she could do. She sat at her desk and reached for her list of stringers. Contacting the northern stringer, a freelance employed to round up news stories not important enough to be covered by a staff reporter, was a long-shot – but anything was worth trying. Stringers had their ears to the ground in their own patch. Perhaps this one could help.

'Sorry,' the stringer said when she explained her reasons for ringing him. 'I've heard about it, of course, but there's not been a monkey's up here. What makes you think she came in this direction?'

Terri gave him a potted version of Ellie's life-history and explained her own interest. 'So, you see, she's a mate as well as a former colleague. I want to help.'

At the other end of the line he was whistling through his teeth. 'There's someone who might know,' he said at last. 'If she's come up here to uncover something, there's one man who might have an idea what she's after. If it made news at the time, that is . . .'

When Terri rang off she had his predecessor's name and number on her pad. 'He was here for thirty years,' the stringer had said. 'Mind like a steel trap. Give him what you've got, and if there was anything he'll have it.' She was so excited she tapped out the number incorrectly and had to try again.

'Mr Prentice?' She tried to sound calm and confident and as though she had all the time in the world. 'I'm Terri Benedict, I'm with the *Record*. I've just been talking to Ted Lavery in Newcastle. He gave me your name.'

The voice at the other end was a bark. 'Well, he had no bloody right to. For your information, young woman, I was retired. Forcibly retired. Scrapped like a surplus Olivetti. So if you've any intention of picking my brains you can think again. I'm not here to be made use of by people too lazy to do their own research.'

'Please, I'm not ringing you about work. It's a personal matter.'

At the other end of the line there was silence and Terri's mouth opened in apprehension. 'Well, trot it out, then,' came the bark. 'You're not ringing at the cheap time, you know.'

Even as she began to speak she realized the hopelessness of what she was asking. 'I'm looking for something that happened about twenty-five years ago. Something you might have heard of, concerning a child of two or three . . . because Ted Lavery says nothing happened on your patch without your knowing.'

There was a snort from the other end of the line that might have been pleasure or contempt. 'There's no need to slaver, young woman. I'd help if I could but think of this . . . I could give you a hundred incidents involving toddlers, right now, off the top of my head. But twenty-five years ago! You're not asking much.'

She acknowledged the vagueness of her own request and they parted amicably enough. 'Come back when you know what you're looking for. And now can I get back to my garden? The morning's gone, thanks to you.'

She put the phone down as Stephen loomed over her.

'If I hear one more word about stock market crises I'll go berserk,' he said, perching on her desk. 'He wants money on every page – yuppies – puppies – vanished lifestyles. He's using Debbie's piece on that friend of hers . . . the one who got the push from his broking firm . . . very suicidal, as you'd expect, but he thinks it's great. He wants you to ring round and get prognoses. Celebs: are they worried about their money? Will they invest in future or keep it under the bed? You know what he likes.'

The world's stock markets were teetering on the verge of collapse and still they were looking for a show-biz angle! Terri raised her eyebrows at Stephen and then went through her contacts book, ringing familiar numbers for predictable answers. Celebs never refused an opinion, unless they became super-celebs and too lofty for words.

At noon she knocked off and went to get ready for her lunch date. Debbie was already in the cloakroom, looking smug at the thought of tomorrow's half-page spread.

'What's happening about your house?' she asked, trying to demonstrate her lack of egocentricity.

'We're meeting soon,' Terri said. 'But it's all up in the air. I'm hopeful, though.'

In the pizza joint she looked at Paul Weidenek across the table. He was attractive, dark hair greying at the temples, neat beard, good hands. All very fanciable, but the eyes were the real turn-on. While he ordered wine by the glass for her and lager for himself she sought an adjective. 'Liquid' was a yuck word when applied to eyes. 'Soulful' suggested a spaniel, and there was nothing of the household pet about Dr Weidenek. 'Piercing' wouldn't do, the eyes were too kind. She settled for 'compelling', but even that was off the mark.

'It's good of you to meet me at such short notice,' he said. She had chosen the pizza parlour because it was near to the office, and they both ordered Hawaiian Regulars, deep pan. 'Not at all. I'm glad to do anything I can to help find Ellie. It's very frustrating, wanting to get to her and not knowing how. I feel sorry for Richard. The strain must be tremendous.'

She was going to suggest that Richard and his stiff upper lip might be half the trouble, but something in his face told her it would be a waste of time. He would parry any attempt to discuss personalities. If her guess was correct he wanted information about Ellie, nothing more. This would not be a cosy lunch to exchange opinions. *You mean to suck me dry, Dr Weidenek*, she thought and gave herself up to the draining.

They talked about how she met Ellie while they ate. 'We weren't particularly friendly – just two girls working on the same paper. She was on the picture desk, I was already doing features, so we'd work together occasionally. I'd got a flat, just a small place but I thought it was Buck House. I couldn't really afford it so I was looking for someone to share. And then someone said, "Ellie Rowe's in digs; she wants a place," and I thought, "Ellie's a nice quiet girl. She won't give me hassle," so I asked her.'

They had grown closer once they moved in together. 'She never blew her top. Not once. Now that I think about it, it was unnatural. I'm a volatile type – show me a row and I'll have it. But Ellie was too much the other way.'

He was nodding, as though he already knew. 'How much did she tell you about her life?'

Terri chewed for a moment. 'Well, not a lot . . . but I don't think she was being secretive. She just didn't have a lot to tell. She'd lived with her grandmother when she was a kid. The grandmother died when Ellie was eight or nine and they put her into a Home. She wasn't unhappy there: in a funny way I think she liked the security. She talked about foster-parents . . . I don't think that worked out. She used to laugh about them sometimes, about customers in their corner shop and the budgie they kept called "Captain", but it had a hollow ring. Anyway, she wound up back in the Home and when she was sixteen they put her through a typing and commerce course and sent her out into the world.'

Paul put knife and fork together, part of his pizza still in the pan. 'So from the time she went to her grandmother until she started work, her life was a relatively open book?'

Terri nodded. 'I think so. No big traumas, anyway. And she talked quite a lot about the jobs she'd had after that. Newcastle, on a local paper. Then London. The usual ups and downs, but nothing out of the ordinary.'

'That only leaves us with her early years, doesn't it?' He was leaning back, one arm over the back of the chair and she thought once more that if she were a free woman he'd have to run for his life. How old was he? Thirty-eight to forty probably, but with beards it wasn't easy to tell.

'She wouldn't be aware of much before she was three, would she? I suppose if she was beaten or abused it would leave scars but . . .' She cogitated. 'I can't remember a thing before about five. Vague bits . . . sun always shining, that sort of thing. Nothing more.'

'But it's there.' Paul's voice was suddenly eager. 'All neatly documented and filed. If you underwent narco-analysis it would come out.' She raised quizzical eyebrows at the medical term. 'It's interrogation under the influence of drugs,' he explained. 'Sodium pento-thal for choice.'

'The truth drug?'

He was smiling. 'As beloved of Hollywood and the CIA? Yes. It simply removes inhibition. You tell things as you saw them, without tailoring your answer to fit.'

Terri was intrigued but not by the truth drug, which was fairly old-hat. 'You mean we remember everything and retain it in memory, even if we don't realize it?'

He nodded. 'Have you ever been on a train journey and wondered why sitting still for a few hours had made you so tired? It's because you've captured every-thing you've seen, as though your eyes were a camera lens snapping and recording every house, every curtained window, every field . . . almost every blade of grass.'

She opened her bag and jotted 'Memory' in her diary. 'There's the makings of a marvellous feature in that,' she said, 'when all this is over and I have time to get around to it.'

He had two more questions for the coffee. What did she know about Ellie's drinking habits, and could she tell him anything at all about the timing of Ellie's menstrual period? 'It's the hormonal balance, you see. I'd like to know what her monthly cycle is, where she is in that cycle now. It could give a clue as to her moods.' He didn't meet her eye, being busy with cream and sugar, but Terri had a feeling he wasn't being totally honest.

'She doesn't drink. Well, not what you'd call drinking. She used to have a draught sherry sometimes in a pub, but just one and never a schooner. As for the curse, I wouldn't know about lately. When we were together she was always the week before me. That would mean she was due . . . the week after next. Yes, that's right. But that could be well adrift now. It's over a year since she moved out.'

They came out into the crowded street and turned towards her building. 'I've enjoyed that,' she said and smiled her thanks.

'Not at all. It was my pleasure.'

It was time for them to part. 'Was it any use?'

She sounded doubtful and his teeth gleamed in his beard. 'Of course. This is a composite we're building, a jigsaw. Everything is useful. Besides . . .' he held out his hand . . . 'I enjoyed your company.'

As she went up in the lift Terri indulged in a nice little day-dream of being the psychiatrist's wife but it was easy enough to put it aside when the lift doors opened. There was only one man for her, worse luck.

Ellie took a bus into Durham city and made for the nearest phone booth. There was a tattered directory there and she thumbed through it to Davison. Davison A. Davison A. L. There were hundreds of Davisons! What had Miss Davison's Christian name been? Dirty Flo, the boys had called her. She ran down B, C, D and E and found four F. Davisons. One was a men's outfitter so three remained.

The first two numbers proved useless. The third one failed to answer. She looked at her watch. One o'clock: if Miss Davison were out she would probably come back during the afternoon. Ahead was Silver Street, narrow and winding, leading to the cathedral. She waited until the traffic lights halted the flow of cars and crossed the road.

It was years since she had toiled up the bank to the Palace Green and she had forgotten the glory of the cathedral. Leaves blew here and there on the Green, some of them plucked from Virginia creepers. A pyracantha flamed by a doorway, and a uniformed attendant stood out of the wind directing cars to parking places. Ellie walked around the square of grass and between ancient gravestones to the cathedral door. Gran had brought her here once, in springtime, when bright daffodils had bobbed everywhere and the church had been dressed for Easter.

Inside it was smaller than she had remembered, but

still mysterious. The organ was playing Bach and she slipped into a pew and bowed her head. 'Please God, let it be all right. Help me to know it all, and let it be all right. Find me a place.' She was gnawing on the fingers clenched beneath her down-bent head. Mustn't make a scene in church. Mustn't ever make a scene.

And then that other tune began, in counterpoint to the organ. Oh God, don't let me be frightened . . . But the impulse to run, to get outside into the open air was overwhelming. She rose to her feet, clattering against the row of seats in front as she stumbled towards the aisle to tug at the huge door.

The man beside her wore the white mac and mandatory camera of the tourist. He opened the door with ease and she sped past him without a word of thanks, not drawing breath until she was safe in the recesses of a coffee shop.

She did not like churches! Grandma had cried in church, holding her hand and the light coming through the window red and blue, making patterns on the polished wood. She closed her eyes, trying to bring the memory into focus, widen its parameters. They had been in church, and there had been sobbing. A funeral then . . . but that was not what terrified her. There was that other crying, a child crying out in terror and the music playing on and on inside her head. She pushed aside the coffee and rose to her feet.

Safe in a telephone box she looked up Miss Davison's number once more. The voice was huskier than Ellie remembered but still firm. 'Elldis Rowe? Yes, I remember you, Elldis. You left in '75 or '6. Come round now, but I can't give you long, I'm afraid. I have a committee meeting tonight and there's an agenda to prepare.'

Still organizing, Ellie thought, and smiled. Miss Davison might have been dead or moribund or gaga; instead she was alive and well and remembering dates.

She bought a box of shortbread with a pensive Victorian urchin on the lid, and a bunch of spray chrysanthemums, and made for Miss Davison's address.

It was a neat terrace built on a slope above the river. The house fronts were narrow and clad with clematis and red-leaved creepers. Miss Davison had a buddleia springing from a tub and a brass door knocker shaped like a fiery dragon's mouth.

Ellie was taken aback when the door opened. The lean and athletic Miss Davison who had marched off many a six-foot malcontent in her time had shrunk to a tiny grey-haired doll. But the eyes in the doll's face were still shrewd and . . . more than that . . . welcoming.

'Come in, Elldis.' Odd to hear her name correctly pronounced. She had been Ellie for so long.

She followed Miss Davison through to the tiny sitting-room. A water-colour of the cathedral on the wall, an overstuffed three-piece suite, faded velvet glimpsed beneath frilled chintz covers, pot plants everywhere, like Mrs McReady. Is this what childless women came to in the end, nurturing green shoots in brass cauldrons and flowered chamber-pots?

They sat in the chintz armchairs to drink tea from china cups with finger-trapping handles. 'Now, tell me all your doings,' Miss Davison said, helping herself to a piece of the gift shortbread.

Ellie's wedding ring was safe in her bag. She could invent what she chose, but with this listener she would have to be careful. 'I'm a secretary. In a big engineering works.' The words came out neatly and she sensed a certain secretarial primness overcoming her as she spoke. 'This is my annual holiday. I had to take it late this year because of staff shortages. And I thought this was the time to look back a little. I really don't know much about my background.'

The faded eyes were on her face and she thought she detected scepticism in them. 'What is it you want to know, Elldis?'

'Just details . . . anything really. I went to the Home but they said my records would be at County Hall. They couldn't help.'

Miss Davison sniffed. 'Your records are probably lost! Once things get into the hands of the administrators that's the end of it. Not that the records would tell you much.'

She was pondering and Ellie held her breath. 'I'll tell you what I know,' she said eventually. 'I was always fond of you, Elldis. You were a strange child but I had a soft spot for you, and it can't do harm to tell you now.

'We first got wind of you when your grandmother had her stroke. You were with the next-door neighbour who handed you over to a welfare official. And then we found that there was no official record of you. There was a birth certificate, but your parents had gone from that place years before leaving no forwarding address. Your grandmother was not in receipt of any benefit for you. At your school they'd been told your parents were dead and your grandmother was your guardian. You weren't registered with a doctor. In other words, you'd

168

slipped through the net. As far as the state was concerned, you didn't exist.'

The room had gone quiet except for the hissing of the gas fire. The air above the mantelshelf seemed to shimmer and Ellie felt her senses slipping away. 'Drink your tea, dear, and don't look so tragic. You've done very well, in spite of it all.

'Anyway, you came to us clutching your satchel and your mackintosh. No doll, no teddy. You were a little old woman cut-down, we used to say. You knew your birthday was in June; you knew you were eight years old; you knew your parents were dead, and there was no one else. "Only Grandma", you said. "Only Grandma".

'I went to see her, you know. She was a tragic figure, lying in the bed, mouth all twisted. "Take care of Ellie," she said but not a word about the circumstances. I had several goes at her and the Chief Welfare Officer went along, but we couldn't budge her. She died a week later and you were made a ward of the county. I went through your grandmother's possessions . . . with the solicitor's clerk, I might add . . . but there was nothing to tell us any more. Only that brief birth certificate, which didn't help.'

'What about the neighbours?' Ellie said. She had regained her composure but despair had settled on her like a dead weight.

'They were no use. Nice enough people, typically colliery women, good-hearted. But your grandmother had kept herself to herself. "Toffee nosed," they thought, and gave her a wide berth. She was a northerner . . . no doubt about that. But she appeared in

Belgate out of nowhere, bought the house and installed herself and you in it. And that was that, until she was struck down and it all came out.'

But it hadn't come out. The secret, the dreadful, terrible secret, was still just that. Except that it must have been something unspeakable. 'So my parents could still be alive?' Ellie said.

Miss Davison's smile was kindly but the shake of her head was emphatic. 'No, my dear, disabuse yourself of that idea. If ever I saw an orphaned child – and I saw a few – you were it. Desperate for love. Desperate for a father figure. That was what put the Harpers off in the end. Well, put her off – Mrs Harper was not a nice human being! You were always hanging around Mr Harper, and it got too much for her.'

So that was why her foster-parents had sent her back! Ellie had often wondered what particular wickedness had been to blame. She reached for her cup, trying to disguise the trembling of her fingers, and began to drink the lukewarm tea.

Paul Weidenek's home was in a rambling Victorian terrace in North London. Richard had been reluctant to accept the invitation but the psychiatrist had been quietly insistent.

They settled in the study, in deep leather chairs, and in spite of himself Richard felt a sense of comfort. It was a man's room, a place where someone lived and worked but not in the least functional or bare. There was a fern on a stand in one corner, a clutter of miniature water-colours on a cabinet and books everywhere.

'I'm glad we could get together,' Paul said, opening

the folder on his knee. 'I'll make tea in a little while but there are one or two things I'd like to get out of the way first, if I may?'

Richard nodded. 'I thought we'd talked ourselves out but if you think it will help . . .' He had not meant to sound hostile but it was there in his voice. He looked at Paul for signs of umbrage but the calm eyes were patient, the lips unmoved. He tried to make amends.

'When all this started . . . at the beginning . . . well, almost until now, if I'm truthful . . . I've seen this as an illness. Ellie's illness. Nothing to do with me, in a way, except in so far as I was affected by it.'

Paul was smiling. 'You mean you felt no responsibility for what had occurred?'

'Not exactly. I thought it was just a terrible misfortune . . . like Julia's cancer.'

He was searching for words and Paul took pity on him. 'And now you're not sure. You wonder if you were partly to blame? Could you have done more? Have others contributed to the present débâcle?'

So he knew about Adele. Richard felt a surge of relief. If Weidenek already knew he need not feel disloyal about criticizing his brother's wife. 'I have wondered about Adele. She and Julia were so close, almost like sisters . . . perhaps I expected too much of her when I brought Ellie home. And on Monday, when I knew Ellie was at breaking point, I deliberately threw them together.'

Paul closed the folder and put down his pen. 'If you think you precipitated Ellie's flight, you're wrong. Your sister-in-law has played a part; her name crops up frequently in the tapes of my discussions with your wife. Perhaps deliberately, perhaps thoughtlessly, she has emphasized your first marriage. But Ellie's leaving was not Adele's fault. You might almost say it was inevitable. We can be influenced in our actions, but ultimately we do what we want to do, what we feel we must do.

'Second marriage is not easy: secondary status seldom is. If it is to be successful, husband and wife must build something new and quite unique. I'm not talking about bricks and mortar, although that can help, I'm talking about something entirely intangible. They must be able to say, "This feeling I have now belongs to you and to no one else. We created it together."'

Richard tried to think. Was that what he had given Ellie, that all-important feeling? Paul was smiling. 'Cheer up. As we talk, I think you'll see that you bear very little responsibility in all this. That's one reason why I asked you to come today. Of course you could have said more, done more, shown more concern. Is there a human situation where any one of us could say less than that? But you didn't drive Ellie away. And now I'm going to make some tea. You look as though you could do with it.'

It seemed an age before Paul came back with a brass-railed tray. 'There. Help yourself.' The tea was curiously scented when Richard lifted the cup to his mouth but it was refreshing and he drank gratefully.

'So you're saying all this was somehow pre-ordained?'

'Yes, I think Ellie has an area of pain inside her – well covered over the years, even forgotten. Marrying you brought her great joy but it also stirred her

172

emotions. She became, in an instant, wife and mother, mistress of a gracious home, wife of an influential man. The layers, that careful cocoon of protection, were shaken.'

'Then I *am* to blame?'

Paul shook his head. 'If not you, it would have been someone else. The only alternative was that she should live a life devoid of emotion, and I think you'll agree that would have been a waste.'

Paul was opening the folder again and Richard hurried to get in another question. 'What is it then, this time-bomb? Until we married she seemed perfectly all right.'

'Did you sleep together before you married?'

Richard felt his colour heighten but this was too important to duck. 'No. Not because of reluctance on my part. Nor did Ellie ask me not to. It just didn't happen.'

'And afterwards?'

Richard looked away, trying to find the words. 'There was no reticence. Now that I think about it, though . . . the passion was mine. She co-operated. And it seemed to make her happy.'

'I'm sure it did. I think she wanted, above all else, to make you happy, so that you would love her. And when she began to make you unhappy by her constant demands for reassurance, she went away. Before you came to hate her.'

'What does it all mean? If she saw . . . our lovemaking . . . as simply a means of pleasuring me, does that tell us anything about what is upsetting her?'

'I told you I was going over the tapes. At the time

you're watching, assessing, making notes. Afterwards you simply listen and you see landmarks. One is a certain reluctance about sex, particularly sex when a child is the end-product. Ellie loves children, but I think she detests the mechanism of their production.'

'Are you suggesting she was sexually abused as a child?' It seemed to be what everyone talked about nowadays but he had never thought it would impinge on his life.

Paul was shaking his head. 'No. There are certain connotations to child abuse, and those are not present in Ellie's case.'

'This baby – I've wondered how she became pregnant. I was always careful.'

'I'm sure you were. But no form of contraception is a hundred per cent certain.'

And I'm no expert, Richard thought wryly but did not voice his thoughts. He put fingertips together, raising them to his lips. 'If she finds out about the baby, it could bring her back?'

'No.' Paul's tone was sharp. 'I think it might well tip the scales, but in which direction? She is not ready to be a mother; she is too busy seeking a father. I sense that in everything she says. I think she married you because she loved you, which is not the same thing as being *in* love. And when she found herself falling in love with you, the situation got out of hand.'

It was too much for Richard. He could not understand the tangled skein of emotions Weidenek was describing. Loving, in love . . . surely it was all the same?

'I need some answers. Can you remember the date

of Ellie's last menstrual period?' Seeing his embarrassment, the psychiatrist continued. 'She must have missed one period already and it's gone unnoticed in all the confusion. I think the second missed period will alert her. I'm going to talk to the obstetricians tomorrow, and if they have anything to offer I'll come back to you. We're running out of time, I'm afraid. If Ellie has other symptoms – nausea, breast changes – she will know.'

He was looking at Richard, demanding answers, but Richard had no help to give. He had never entered into his wife's affairs, not in either marriage. Sometimes, if he had reached for them and they had gently turned away, he had put it down to the time of the month and been content. But he had never known or wished to know about such private things. And yet Weidenek expected him to know. Perhaps other husbands did know. Perhaps this was one more area in which he had failed.

'I'm sorry, I'm afraid I can't help. I wish I could.'

Paul inclined his head. 'Never mind. There's one more thing I have to ask you. Will you call off the investigator? Please? I'm very afraid of what might happen if Ellie is subjected to pressure!'

'Chicken curry or chilli?'

Mike wrinkled his nose. 'Tinned?'

'Yes,' Terri said. 'Of course you could bring in a chicken from the backyard and I'll wring its neck, pluck it and joint it. Failing that, it's tinned. And before you ask, the rice is tinned as well. Give me any more argument and it'll be pudding rice, not Patna.'

He held up his hands. '*Kamerad!* It's a good job I get meals out from time to time. The standard of cuisine in this establishment is less than *haute*.' He leaned towards her. 'I love you, though.'

She accepted his kiss. 'You still haven't said which.'

He pondered. 'Chilli. Tinned chilli is marginally less horrid than tinned curry.'

Terri relented. 'There's some gammon in the fridge. You could have gammon and pineapple and green beans.'

'Done,' he said. 'You do the gammon, I'll slice the pineapple. Where is it?'

She looked at him in amazement. 'In the tin cupboard. You didn't think I meant fresh, did you?' Tomorrow she would stock up with fresh food, get a book on *nouvelle cuisine*, count his calories and monitor his cholesterol. For tonight she held the pineapple slices under the tap to rid them of syrup and trimmed the fat from the gammon.

'I made a good deal this lunchtime, in spite of diversions. Rog was pleased. Wouldn't be surprised if he signalled his approval in some tangible way.'

Terri emptied her mouth. 'What diversions?'

He was smiling. 'Talk about Britain being a fiddlers' paradise. There were these two couples at the next table: polytechnic lecturers, at a guess. Anyway, teachers. The female in one couple had just been ripped off by an ex-boy-friend. He'd broken in to the flat and cleared the place of everything he could lift.'

Terri took a sip of wine. 'Filthy greed or vengeance?'

'Bit of both probably. He claimed it was all his. Anyway, the guy – the one at the table – who was now shacked up with her had told her to say it was a burglary. The police asked if they had any idea of who'd done it, and they'd both looked the fuzz straight in the eye and said "No".'

Terri was looking puzzled. 'Why did they do that? Because she still had a soft spot for the first guy?'

'No, idiot. So they could claim on insurance. She had a new-for-old policy, so they'd be quids in.'

Terri was trying to work out the ethics of the story but it wasn't easy. 'Do you think that's wrong?'

Mike chortled. 'It's wrong, all right. On several counts. Withholding information, wasting police time, making false claims . . . and I bet there are half a dozen further misdemeanours in there somewhere.'

She was still unconvinced. 'But would you have done it?'

He frowned. 'I don't know. I'd like to think I wouldn't, but I don't honestly know. We all bend the rules nowadays. I mean, everyone. One of the chaps at work found he could use his credit card in the all-day car-park machine near his tube station. It's the magnetic strip or something. Does it all the time now and saves a fortune. Well, that's theft. What's more, he stands on the platform telling everyone else to do it. He's proud of it. Years ago, if you'd done it, you'd've kept it quiet.'

They were both suddenly glum. 'It's all the fault of plastic,' Terri said. 'It's not like stealing real loot, it's like playing Post Offices with Monopoly money.'

'What did you do for lunch?' Mike asked, refilling her glass.

'Ate out with a *very* attractive man,' she said. 'You'll

have to look to your laurels, lover, or you'll be replaced.'
And then she thought about Ellie, and the impulse to
tease Mike into the bedroom suddenly left her.

Paul had found it in a side street, in a window crammed
with silver-backed brushes and papier-mâché trays. It
was a long-tailed wren on an almond twig, and he
knew it was a Kathleen Nelson before he saw the tiny,
almost invisible, signature and the date, 1986. What a
prize! He had entered the shop and parted with the
£80 asking price without a quibble.

Now he took it from his briefcase and unwrapped it,
feeling the familiar joy of owning such perfection. He
had twenty-six of the miniatures now; this made
twenty-seven. And three of them Nelsons. He wiped
the frame with his handkerchief, breathing on the glass
to polish it. The bird looked back at him, eye gleaming,
plumage lit by a sunlight that would never fade. He
sighed with satisfaction and settled to work.

'Julia loved the boys. I know she did.' Ellie's voice on the
tape was fragile. 'But she wanted a girl, so there'd have
been other children. Adele told me Julia wanted a daughter
who would go to her old school, the school she and Adele went
to together. They were all very close. Julia met Richard when
they were very young. It was love at first sight, Adele said.
And then Julia introduced Adele to Frank.'

Paul had started to doodle, and he pulled off the top
page and aimed it at the waste-basket. Adele, Adele
. . . it always came back to Adele. But no one person
could break down another's defences. There had to be
a crack, an enemy within.

It was his own voice now. 'Do you love Richard's

children?' And then the reply, confident but tinged with resignation. *'Yes, I do love them but they are not mine.'*

'Is this your home, Ellie?'

He sat forward now as the voice on the tape rang out, childish and troubled. *'It's Julia's house. I don't like touching Julia's things.'* He had noted it at the time, that strange inflection as though she were talking about her childhood, not about the possession of another woman's home but about the possession of her toys, the trappings of childhood.

'I picked it up and it was so beautiful, velvet and the little flowers were raised up in some sort of silver wire. I'd seen it in photographs. They'd had a holiday in India once so she must have bought it there. I knew I shouldn't touch it, just put it away somewhere; but I wanted to try it on. I had to try it on. I walked to the mirror and I fastened it round my waist and I looked in the mirror . . . and it was as if it was Julia there! As if they were all saying, "Don't touch Julia's things. Naughty Ellie! Don't touch Julia's things." And I could never please him.'

His own voice then, gently insisting, *'Who said "don't touch", Ellie?'*

'Everyone.'

'But you are the mistress of the house. No one could tell you what to do.'

Now the regression into childhood, the voice an octave higher. *'No, it's not my house. Julia built it. It belongs to her.'*

'You said you could never please him, Ellie. Who did you mean when you said "him"?'

Ellie had cried then and become confused, and the session had ended inconclusively.

Paul switched off and leaned back, rubbing the bridge of his nose. It was as though there were two pictures, two exposures, one superimposed on the other. As though she had known Julia since childhood, deferred to her for a lifetime.

He pressed 'Play' again. They were in safe areas now – routine questions about the children which she answered readily enough. No difficulties there. Most women had at least some difficulty in accepting another woman's offspring, but Ellie, it seemed, had none. And then Adele cropped up again. He grimaced, seeing the petty tricks for what they were. But Adele was not a real villain, she was too afraid for that. Real villains were confident. Adele had been Julia's acolyte and she had liked the position, it made her secure. Now, with Ellie, she had to jostle for place again and it was making her nasty.

He stopped the tape and sat back once more, reviewing the facts. They were a strange family, all of them with hang-ups except perhaps the husky, rugger-playing brother. What sort of relationship had existed between Richard and Ellie if there was no discussion, no sharing even of simple facts like menstruation? And how was he, Paul Weidenek, expected to predict the actions of a woman he had met for five hours over a period of two weeks if her own husband didn't know her? She had Dervinox and Imprival enough to kill a street, more than enough to warp a foetus. If she was taking them, even in the stated dosage, she could be in trouble.

Paul's eye caught the envelope on the mantel. He must write to his father, keep up the fiction that all was well. His father had escaped from Poland in 1939 without shoes on his feet; now his son was a doctor, a professional man. That was all his father had, the vision of his son's perfect life. Paul couldn't destroy that vision, so he kept up a charade. Just as Ellie had done.

There could be only one end to his relationship with Gary: disaster. One way or another it would end in pain. Even death. The boy's lifestyle was hazardous beyond belief, and he was sharing the danger, knowing all the implications but powerless to desist. Even roused by the squalor of it all. He closed the folder and put it on one side, then he moved to his miniatures: water vole, shrew, harvest mouse among meadow-sweet and ragged robin. What was it in the boy that turned him on? Was it fear? Up close the harvest mouse had jewelled eyes. If he put out a finger he would find them moist.

He was still rapt when the boy clattered through the hall and into the room. 'Hallo there. Have you had a good, nice, peaceful evening? Mine has been a gas. Mega-good. I am playing like an angel.' His speech was slurred but his eyes were shining. Speed, probably, or perhaps just joy of living.

'Do you want some food?'

'No, ta, we had kebabs on the way home. But I'll make coffee. You look whacked. Poor old Paul – working hard to keep the wolf from the door? You wait till I make it. I might have this chance of a gig at Dingwall's . . . no money but good music-wise. Come on, let's go into the kitchen and I'll tell you what I'll do for you if the ship comes in.'

His hand on Paul's shoulder was light, the touch of a child. 'You'll soon be tucked up in bed, all your worries behind you. And we'll do something together this weekend – get right away. So you can start cheering up. That's an order.'

If something upset him, Gary would become a devil incarnate, but for now all was sweetness and light. Better make the best of it.

Adele had changed into a yellow silk shirt and trousers after her shower and taken extra care with hair and make-up, but it did not have the desired effect.

'It's a business trip, Adele. It won't be all *sayonara* and cherry blossom, it'll be hard slog, talks in offices suspiciously like the one I inhabit usually, trips round industrial complexes suspiciously like my own, signing – God willing – on dotted lines, and catching the plane home. I'm only going for a week. No sightseeing, no carousing and definitely no shopping! So I can't see you being madly interested.'

She ignored the implied insult and tried a different tack. 'We haven't had a holiday this year . . . not a decent one. I just like the idea of jetting away together, even for a few days. I am so sick of that house and the wretched phone and Withers going round like the Avenging Angel. It's all very well for you – you get away from it. I'm the one who's left to hold the fort. I know you have Richard to cope with, I appreciate all that . . . but I still think the onus is on me, and I need a break.'

He was struggling into a clean shirt now. 'Well, it can't be Japan, Del. Apart from anything else we couldn't both go off and leave Richard, with things as they are. He looks wretched. When this is over I'll take time off . . . you have my word. We could take the girls to Davos, we've always intended to do that. And we could take your mother along. She told me last time we were over that she misses Switzerland.'

Adele was less than enchanted with the idea of a family holiday, but at least he was trying to meet her half-way. 'Well, we won't talk about it now. Richard will be waiting. What worries me, though, is that this could go on indefinitely.'

He nodded. 'I can't understand how a person can simply walk into oblivion like that. Someone must have seen her.'

Adele wrinkled her nose. 'She's awfully ordinary. Take away good clothes and she's positively non-descript.' Her mind was working furiously. She had said Ellie's disappearing act might go on indefinitely, but Ellie was pregnant and that would impose a time limit of sorts. She would have to come out of the woodwork once she knew she was preggers. And any time now she would spill her actual address. Perhaps even during the next phone call.

'When did you say you go to Japan?' she said, trying to sound like a dutiful wife resigned to staying at home.

Mrs Withers withdrew once they were served. Richard offered the gravy boat. 'No thank you, not for me.' Adele would have liked gravy but if she was firm with herself she could lose five pounds before Japan. 'No word from Ellie, Frank tells me?'

Richard shook his head. 'No, nothing since the call

to Terri Benedict. But I'm sure she'll be worried about us . . . She must know the boys' weekend is coming up.'

Adele put down knife and fork. 'If she's so concerned, why doesn't she come home?' She could feel Frank's eyes on her but she refused to meet his gaze. Someone had to say it! 'Don't think I'm unsympathetic, Richard. I'm *dripping* with sympathy, positively dripping. But there are limits. I can't bear to see what this is doing to you. You look awful, you're simply moving your food from one side of your plate to the other . . . where's it going to end? I can see Frank disapproves of my speaking out, but I can't help that. Someone should tell Ellie . . . to pull herself together.' She had almost used the forbidden word 'pregnancy' and bitten it back just in time.

'You'll have to forgive Adele, Rich.' Frank's voice was icy. 'She has a dreadful capacity for over-simplification. Now, unless you want to discuss it, I suggest we change the subject.'

A flush had broken out on Adele's neck and chest at the thought of what she might have revealed. She would have to be more careful. They must never know about the phone calls: that would ruin everything.

They carried their coffee to the fire, the dogs were petted and encouraged to settle away from the flames, and all the while she saw Richard gearing himself up for an ordeal. When it came it was not what she expected and her look of surprise was genuine.

'Adele, I'm sorry to turn to somewhat . . . personal matters but Dr Weidenek tells me I must. It's the date of Ellie's last period. Her menstrual period.' She could see he was using terminology supplied by the psychiatrist. What a hoot! 'It's a question of hormonal imbalance – that's why he needs to know.' So she was not to be trusted with the truth and told that batty Ellie was preggers and would throw a fit at the next missed period. 'I've asked Mrs Withers but she can't help. You're the last hope.'

She pretended to be thinking hard while she considered the possibilities. If she was sympathetic now she might coax the truth out of him; it wouldn't take much doing. He must be dying to share it with someone. Perhaps he *had* shared it with someone, perhaps he had told Frank, who was keeping it from her? It wouldn't surprise her. They were thicker than thieves.

Still, she was better off seeming not to know, then no one could blame her if Ellie found out the truth. She shook her head and met Richard's hopeful eyes. 'Sorry. I can't remember it ever being mentioned.'

Ellie had managed to stay out all day and most of the evening, wandering around and repairing frequently to the coffee bar.

Now she was safely back in her room, out of the distinctly crumpled grey suit, and eating cheese on toast. Best of all, she had not had a drink. She was finished with waking in the morning feeling like death. She had tired herself out quite deliberately today, and would get into bed and drop off, without drink or pills or counting sheep, or any outside aid.

She was feeling drowsy when the knock came at the door. Mrs McReady! She put the camel coat over her nylon nightdress and opened the door a crack.

The man on the landing was small and bald. A finger was to his lips in a plea for silence, and above the plump cheeks his eyes were imploring. 'Sh . . . keep your voice down. She's got ears like a bat.' In his other hand he held a small glass jug, still creamy where it had held milk. 'Can I come in a minute, pet? I'm sorry to disturb you but I daresn't for the life of me ask anyone else.'

There was nothing for it but to open the door.

Inside with the door shut, he relaxed. 'I've come for a drop of milk, pet, if you can spare it.' He was looking round. 'How much is she stinging you for this lot? I've got the big front cheap – that's because she's after my body. Not that it's much of a catch, mind . . .'

He was chuckling and she felt a smile creep over her face. If she asked him to stay he would talk and talk – she knew the type. The night lay ahead, the dark night of terror and sleeplessness. If he stayed, even for a little while, he would push back the border of that dark country.

'There's some tea in the pot,' she said. 'Would you like a cup?'

He took a bentwood chair and drew it up to the table. 'I won't say no.'

She proffered the last bit of cheese on toast and he took it. 'Ta. I've seen you tiptoeing in and out, trying to give her the slip. We all do it.' He rolled his eyes. 'I've met a few over-sexed women in my time but she takes the biscuit.'

Inside Ellie a chuckle was growing. *'Middle-aged tenant preyed on by nymphomaniac landlady!'* – what Terri would have made of that!

'You don't fancy her then?'

His teeth had slipped down, stuck to the gooey cheese, and he tongued them back into place. 'Oh, she's a little cracker all right. Keeps herself nipping clean, neat little backside. I took her to the club once and she did me proud. But I'm a bit too fly to get caught again, I had enough trouble with the last one. No, I'm off to Australia soon. I've got a daughter settled out there . . . the papers'll be through before long and I'll be off.'

He moved closer and dropped his voice. 'If I was some men, I'd take what I could get while the going was good. It's there for the asking. No, I'm misjudging her – I wouldn't need to ask. But that's not my way. She'd be hard to shake off and I'm all for a peaceful life. Pint at the club, game of dominoes . . . fly off to the sunshine, see the grandbairns.'

His teeth dropped again and he gummed them into place. 'You only love once . . . well, that's my contention. I had a good wife. A tartar, mind, when it came to the house, but a good wife. They say you marry for companionship second time around, but that's not what her downstairs has in mind. I'm lucky to get up these stairs intact. It's scandalous.'

The chuckle inside her had died and left a whimper. *'You only love once in this life'*: no room for Ellie, no right to be there at all. But if she could get him out of the room she could pour a drink, put out the light and take refuge in the creaking bed.

Instead she sat on in the chair when he had gone, drinking her way steadily down the bottle until once more she could see the funny side of it all. She was laughing so much she could hardly bear it and she couldn't remember why. Her glass was empty and she got to her feet. Whoops! The room swirled and steadied and she sat down again. Mustn't have another drink. Last night she had got into bed to escape dizziness but the room had continued to spin around her closed eyes, and when she was slipping into sleep the spinning got worse so that she had to force herself awake. She couldn't face that again tonight. She clambered to her feet, using the arms of the chair, and made her way unsteadily to the window.

Below, the yard gleamed in the light from Mrs McReady's living-room. A cat walked along the wall, tail erect and yowling for a mate. Beyond the dark roofs, lit here and there by moonlight, were the lights of the sea-front and lovers in dark corners.

She started to cry for the sadness of it all and then she saw the star, the all-seeing Eye of Heaven. It made her laugh, thinking of God up there with his eye to the keyhole. It was bloody funny! She put down her glass and lunged at the right-hand curtain to close it. The exquisite fun of missing it again and again took her into the centre of the room. She began to gyrate, as though to music. But the music clicked and clicked.

She felt a choking sensation in her chest and clawed at her collar. Must get out, get out, get out! Must get out before the music, the clicking, clicking music stopped.

But her legs would not carry her and all she could do was crawl into the bed, burrowing into the blankets and pulling them over her face.

*

Richard turned on the step for a last look at the stars – programmed by computer, winking away, and one brighter than the rest. The Eye of Heaven: Ellie had told him that. 'The Eye of Heaven' she had called it, and there had been fear in her voice, as though Heaven's Eye was not a partial one.

'Come on, boys. Baskets!' When the dogs were settled he locked up and switched the telephone back from the Witherses' extension. The clock showed midnight. Please God he would sleep tonight. He twiddled the knobs of the radio, hoping for a voice and finding instead a cascade of violins. He recognized the tune – 'These Foolish Things'. It came to an end, the disc jockey enthused about the 'golden oldie' and put on another record, but the words of the previous song continued to flood Richard's mind. It was the foolish things that reminded you, that had the power to cause you pain.

The phone sat, ivory and round, on a side-table. At the beginning he had watched it all the time, expecting it suddenly to leap and jingle as phones did in Tom and Jerry cartoons. Now he knew it would not. He knew a lot of things. He knew it was not sex you agonized over when you lost it, or the need for sex that kept you awake. He had discovered that when Julia was ill and it was equally true with Ellie. It was love you needed.

But Julia's death had taught him about survival. However much you might want an ending, life went on. It had to be lived, each painful day with its share of problems and decisions to be made. Tonight, as Mrs Withers bustled to welcome him home, he had taken the bull by the horns. 'I think we must plan for the boys' coming home, Mrs Withers.'

She had shaken her head. 'You don't think Mrs Marriner will be back by then?'

He had moved to the sideboard where the decanter and glasses stood. 'I still hope she'll be back – I hope that every day. But we have to be sensible. We have only the sketchiest idea of her whereabouts. The press have lost interest . . .' he didn't add 'until they find a body', but the suggestion was in both their minds . . . 'and the police are on the look-out but not actively pursuing her. Hopefully the private detective will come up with something, but we can't be sure.'

'She will come back though, Mr Richard. I won't pretend I know what's going on in her mind but I know she'll come back. She loves those boys.'

He wanted to cry out his anger, to shout aloud, *Why in God's name doesn't she come back then, if she loves us all so much?* But it wouldn't do.

'You cut along now. It's late. And don't worry about me in the morning, have a lie-in. I'm up early at the moment, and making breakfast gives me something to do.' They had both known she would be in the kitchen at eight on the dot, but it made a nice fiction.

Now he paused on the landing, before he switched off the lights. This was still Julia's house, her creation. She might easily come through the archway into the hall and look up at him, smiling. Always smiling! As he put out a hand to the switch he realized that it was as though Ellie had never lived here. She had gone and the waters had closed over her. Perhaps she had never existed at all, except in his hungry mind.

Her négligé, discarded on the morning of her leaving, was draped over a chair in the bedroom. He held it to his face, breathing in, trying to catch some trace of her presence. But the silken folds betrayed nothing. If he got her back he would love her as no woman had been loved before. He would change. He had already changed: he had been frank with Weidenek, and it had not been easy to question Adele tonight. He had meant to do it through Frank and then had decided that that would be shirking. In the end it had not been so difficult. If he got another chance he would never shirk again.

Lying in darkness he thought about Weidenek's plea: *'Call him off, Marriner, before it's too late.'* He had said no, partly because the detective was his only hope, partly because he still resented Weidenek's part in the whole affair. Were they good enough reasons to ignore advice?

[7]

The bedside phone brought Terri back from sleep and a delightful dream of new furniture. 'Terri – get in here *now*! We've had a buzz about Sting: they say he's tying the knot today. In Newcastle. He has family there. I want you, Terri – now. We're sending a car.' The line went dead.

'What's up?' Mike said from the depths of the duvet, but Terri was already in the bathroom sluicing her face and running through what she knew about Sting. *Real name Gordon Sumner. Born Newcastle. Lead singer with The Police, turned actor . . . well, there were two opinions about that . . . film star, certainly. Married charismatic Shakespearean actress, Frances Tomelty, by whom he had two children. Now with Trudi Styler . . . Styler? . . . yes, that was the name. Two children . . . or one?* She stepped under the shower still adjusting her cap.

'I love you . . . see you,' she said to the bed five minutes later and sped down to the half-dark street in time to see the paper's limousine nose round the corner.

'Who else has it?' she asked as she hit the office.

'No one.' The Editor was unshaven and shrouded in

a huge mohair sweater. For once he looked human as he grinned his triumph. 'The northern stringer got the first sniff. He phoned it in last night. We can't find where the happy couple are right now, and that's significant. I've got showbiz doing the facts and the razzmatazz; I want you for the human interest. Go for "why" – why now? Why there? Who's there; his family, her family? Their children, his children by Tomelty. God, fancy leaving a woman like that – she's magic. Anyway, you know what I want. There's a train out of King's Cross at seven or thereabouts, Transport have the details. The ceremony's at the Civic Centre in Newcastle at eleven. If it's a gen. buzz, that is.'

'You want me to go up there?' Terri said. She was less than enthusiastic, it being Thursday and there being no food in the house. She had intended to slope off at lunchtime and shop and shop.

'Yes, I want you up there, Terri. It's the first bit of light relief we've had in an otherwise turgid week – I should bloody well think I want you up there. Unless you can find something equally exciting in WC1. Now get your butt out of here, it's turned half-past already. Clive is at the station now, getting your ticket. He'll see you off and give you anything that's come in meantime.'

As they threaded their way to King's Cross she prayed for a miracle. Clive was in the radio car: by the time she got there it might all be over. Exclusives like this had a nasty habit of fizzling out.

But Clive's face was lit up like a 150-watt bulb. 'Return ticket, cash float, dossier. The northern man'll meet you at Newcastle. You're in coach G – first class. Meals on the house. Indulge yourself.'

She climbed aboard and he slammed the door. 'Just don't come back empty-handed, darling. Toss yourself out on the return journey if you can't get the goods. It'll be less painful that way.'

Behind the chimney pots the sky was beginning to glow and Ellie felt the familiar lightening of spirit that came with dawn. She washed from head to toe in the tiny bathroom, using water that had just begun to heat. There were traces of Mr Corkhill everywhere, disposable razors in a tooth-glass, denture-fixative on the windowsill and a set of cellular underwear on the drying rack above the bath. Of the off-shot tenant there was no sign. She obviously disdained the communal bathroom or, if she used it, preferred to leave no trace of herself behind.

Ellie was ready by eight-fifteen, fretting behind the closed door of her room. This was when she missed a radio, but she had counted her money last night and once she had bought essentials like a cardigan there would be nothing over for luxuries. She heard the elusive Miss Summers emerge from her room and go downstairs, and then let herself out on to the landing.

Behind Mr Corkhill's door a radio was playing martial music. No danger there. She was half-way down the bottom flight when she heard the voice, faint and petulant but not to be disobeyed. 'Is that you, dear?'

Mrs McReady's door gave to Ellie's touch but the living-room was empty.

'In here!'

Ellie moved forward and pushed back the door to the bedroom. Mrs McReady lay back on frilled pillows, her face, devoid now of make-up, oddly drawn and topped by a coronet of brush rollers. 'Come in, dear. I've been watching out for you. I didn't want that one in, nor Mr Corkhill, not when I'm in this state. I've had such a night with my liver. I've rung the doctor. In the mean time there's one or two little jobs . . .'

The 'one or two little jobs' took an hour, and while Ellie did them Mrs McReady lay back on her frilled pillows and conducted an interrogation. 'Thank you so much, pet. No, I'll take the tray here, on my knee. That's right. Now, if I could just have my toilet water, it's there on the dressing-table. There . . . inside the black poodle.'

Everything on Mrs McReady's dressing-table was disguised as something else. Her ring tray sported a Japanese sunshade, a crinoline lady spread her skirts over the telephone, a Dutch girl did the same for the hand-cream and the black poodle, subjected to Caesarean section, revealed a bottle of Joie de Nuit.

'I saw my friend, Mrs Bollon, yesterday – you know, the one with the daughter at the hospital. She was asking all about you. "Well, I can't tell you much," I said. "She's a proper little clam."' She reached out and patted Ellie's arm. 'Just my little joke, don't go all huffy. Anyway, I said I'll find out all about her and you can tell your Edie to do what she can for her auntie. She's well up, Edie Bollon, you know. Next to the matron or something like that. What is your auntie's name, pet? I said I'd ask.'

Thinking of it as the bus left the town centre, Ellie

went cold. 'Carter,' she had said desperately. 'It's Carter, but I wouldn't want to make a fuss.' She had felt threatened and quite unable to argue when Mrs McReady had asked for another two weeks' rent. 'It's not that I don't trust you, pet, but my overheads are crippling – the lights and the phone and the hot water, not to mention wear and tear. I'm not one to boast, but I've never put in meters like some people. Make you pay for breath, some people would, but that's not my way. So if we could just keep a little bit ahead . . .'

The houses were slipping away now and there were fields on either side. The year was dying: as they travelled between hedgerows Ellie saw the touch of winter everywhere. She leafed through the paper she had bought, but there was no mention of the search and she put it aside.

Penshaw Monument came into view, modelled on a Greek temple, dominating the landscape in memory of some long dead Lambton, Earl of Durham. In the distance the Pennines ran south to north, low and mysterious, the sky striped turquoise behind. On either side, fields were black with new-turned earth, Durham earth. In spite of herself she was stirred, but it was the spare beauty of nature that moved her, not any sense of belonging. She had no affinity with this place.

The sea, blue-grey and calm, appeared and re-appeared as the road wound through colliery villages and on to Belgate, whose main street was at once familiar and yet strange. 'Can't you remember?' Miss Davison had asked yesterday, and Ellie had shaken her head ve-hemently. Too vehemently, perhaps, as though the person she wanted to convince were herself.

She walked away from the bus stop and looked around. There was the familiar gaggle on the street corner, a whippet-cross lifting its leg in a shop doorway, a torn poster flapping on the Welfare wall. All these had been there on the day she left. But the fish-and-chip shop was now the Hong-Kong Gardens and had crossed fans in the window instead of sauce and vinegar. The Golden Hind was closed, its windows boarded up and sprayed with graffiti, and the Methodist Church was a carpet warehouse. There were fewer people on the streets, more cars in the road. Ahead, round the pet-shop corner, lay Gatcombe Street.

'Come in, Mr Marriner. Do take a seat.'

At close quarters the Superintendent was huge and handsome in his bemedalled uniform. 'I've sent for coffee.' Behind him, the walls were covered in team photos and sports awards, and the calendar on his desk was silver with handles to adjust the date.

He put well-manicured fingers together on the immaculate blotter. 'Now, sir . . . what can I do for you?'

'I don't know if you're familiar with . . .' Before Richard could complete his sentence the Superintendent sat up and opened the folder that lay on his blotter.

'I certainly am, Mr Marriner. I've been very concerned about it, and I can assure you I've been kept informed. The trouble is . . .'

There was a knock on the door and a WPC entered, bearing a tray. Bone-china cups, crystals of sugar, petit-beurre biscuits, all on a stainless steel tray. They did themselves well!

'The trouble is', the Superintendent continued as the door closed, 'that your wife went of her own accord, has been in touch and is not, as far as we can ascertain, in any danger. That means that we are in no position to intervene.'

'You mean you won't help,' Richard said flatly, shaking his head to the petit-beurres. From the window he could see a crowded car-park, black and white cars, their blue lights unlit.

'We want to help,' the Superintendent said. 'Believe me, I'd like nothing better than to restore Mrs Marriner to her own home, safe and sound. But we're in a delicate area here. If she chooses not to let her family know her whereabouts, it's not up to us to overrule her.'

Richard bit down to control his rising anger. 'My wife is not well, Superintendent. She needs protection.'

The Superintendent's mouth was smiling but his eyes were bleak. 'I can understand your anxiety and you may well be right. But the facts . . . and that's all we can go by . . . the facts are that Mrs Marriner is not in any sense certifiably insane. Her psychiatrist does not think she is at risk; and there is no underlying medical condition that could cause concern. If we were to hunt her down we could, with some justification, be accused of harassment. Besides, I understand you've seen fit to employ civilian investigators.'

For a moment Richard considered telling him about Ellie's pregnancy, but Weidenek had been specific: '*No one, no one must know.*' He put his cup back on the tray. 'It appears I'm wasting your time,' he said and got to his feet.

Outside in the corridor someone was whistling Beethoven's *Ode to Joy*. 'I'm sorry, sir. If there's any change at all in the circumstances . . . any change . . .' A car started up in the courtyard and sped, blue light spinning, towards the gates.

Adele was sure Richard had cut her out of his calculations. It was quite obvious. 'Oh, by the way, Adele,' he had said, 'there's no need for you to be tied to the phone any more. Ellie is not going to keep in touch as I hoped she might at the beginning, so Mrs Withers can cope.'

Adele had blustered a little, and begged to be allowed to do her bit, but they all knew it was a *fait accompli*. And how Withers would love it, the old cow! But the laugh was on them: unknown to them she was the one that Ellie was in touch with. She had the power.

The visit to her mother must be kept short, so she could get back in plenty of time for Ellie's afternoon call, but she needed this little break. She left instructions for the evening meal, rang butcher and baker with the week's order, and went out to her car. There was a good stretch of road between here and Windsor. She would put her foot down and let the car show its paces, perhaps that would cheer her up. She got behind a transporter as she joined the M25 and spent the rest of the journey changing up and down and nipping in and out of jams.

Her mother straightened up from a flowerbed at the sound of the car. 'Hallo darling. Do go in. I'm afraid we've had the best of the chrysanthemums.'

Adele went through to the tiny kitchen with its

painted cupboards and plugged in the kettle. In the old house they had had a pantry bigger than this.

She looked in the fridge. Chocolate pudding, just as she'd hoped! Just as she'd found it every time she came home from school.

'Oh Mummy, you are a darling, you never forget.'

Her mother put down the trug and pulled off her gloves. 'We'll take everything through to the morning-room. I'll whizz these into jars and then we'll chat and chat. I'm longing to hear your news.'

Her mother's hairstyle had not changed in forty years, but the neat waves and curls of the mid-'40s still looked good on her, faded now to a distinguished white-gold. She hitched up her tweed skirt before she sat down to serve salad and fat pilchards.

'Tinned, I'm afraid, as the cupboard is bare, but the *Telegraph* is constantly telling me eating fish prolongs life, so I suppose poverty has its uses. No news of the Scarlet Pimpernel?'

Adele shook her head. 'Not a peep since that phone call.' The salad was crisp and delicious and tasted of lemon and thyme. Mummy's food was always scrumptious. A little knot of pleasure formed inside her at the thought of seconds and chocolate pudding to follow. And a chance for a lovely, long talk. 'The trouble is . . .' Must go carefully here: she couldn't bear it if her mother thought badly of Frank. 'The trouble is, it's casting the most awful blight over everyone.'

Her mother's eyes were shrewd. 'Well, you could hardly expect anything else, dear. Someone can't just vanish without it causing waves.'

'Yes, but . . . well . . . I did try with Ellie. I didn't

like her, I'm not going to pretend I did. But I did try. Even that last day I was running after her, following her round the shops when I'd far rather have been off on my own. And then she just walks off! Does this incredibly theatrical thing with the fur coat and dress, and literally disappears into the undergrowth. And everyone looks at me as though I'd engineered the whole thing.'

'You didn't, did you? So that's the end of it. Do your best for Richard and the boys, and for the silly girl, if she ever turns up. Richard will expect that. But don't moan, Adele. You're a loved wife, you have the dearest children, no money worries and an excellent constitution. But you're never happy!'

Inside Adele the glow of chocolate pudding faded and flickered out. She had been foolish to think she could confide in her mother. She would have to brace up and count her blessings. She speared an unfortunate radish and ground it to pulp with her excellent teeth.

Frank and Richard walked to the assembly shop together, pausing to admire the Marriner Two-Way parked outside. It was their latest product, a revolutionary excavator capable of shifting 1,000 tons a day and with a power-to-weight ratio far in excess of anything else on the market in its price-range of £250,000.

'She's a nice machine,' Frank said.

Richard patted the hub of one huge wheel. 'Get this into Japan and we're sitting pretty.'

Inside the assembly shop work was at a standstill. It was the three-monthly meeting, an opportunity for Richard to address the work-force, for them to bring grievances or suggestions to him. As usual Frank did the warm-up, laying facts and figures before them, painting a rosy picture of their joint future, producing a joke unexpectedly to relax the solemn faces. 'He's good at this,' Richard thought. 'Better at communicating with the men than I'll ever be.' His own skill was in prediction, seeing the future of their industry and anticipating demand. But he couldn't reach out to people.

He looked at the sea of faces. What was he doing here when his wife was missing, might well be dead somewhere, and never come back to him again? He had a sudden impulse to get to his feet, leap down from his place on the loading bay and walk past the astonished men to the nearest north-bound train.

But the upturned faces were expectant. They depended on him not only for themselves but for wives and children, dogs, cars, mortgages, their Christmas bonus. He was tied, had always been tied, since the moment of birth. No one had ever asked if he wanted to go into the firm; he had never been tested for aptitudes or encouraged to develop talents. He had been groomed from childhood to take over from his father. Even at school they had talked of his future with Marriner's, and by the time he got to Oxford he had had no desire to spread his wings.

Now he would be nothing without the firm. If it ever went down he was done for. He had never attended a job interview or prepared a CV, unlike every other senior member of management except Frank. If he had to begin again he wouldn't know how. He had succeeded at nothing except making use of inherited privilege. Last night, when his children had phoned, he had felt at a loss. 'No news is good news,' was a fatuous statement at the best of times – to a perplexed fourteen-year-old it was useless.

Frank was winding down now, and in a moment he must get to his feet and assume his responsibilities. He had no choice about today but he could change some things. He would talk to the boys when they came home, make it abundantly clear that they had a future with Marriner's only if they chose.

All eyes were on him as he moved to centre stage. 'We had a good first half-year,' he began, and felt an easing of his misery as he got on with his job.

When the meeting was over he went back to his desk for a ploughman's lunch. Half-way through he took a call from a components supplier in Cleveland, and then Paul Weidenek came on the line. 'I think we need to talk again. Are you free this evening?'

Richard felt an uplift at the prospect of seeing the psychiatrist, and it surprised him. 'I'd like that. The problem is the phone. My housekeeper mans it all day, and I take over at six. I could ask my brother but that would mean . . .' His words trailed away as he shirked maligning Adele.

'Of course.' As usual the other man grasped his meaning. 'I'll come to you. Shall we say seven-fifteen?'

The back lane of Gatcombe Street came first, cobbled and grey, doors in pairs painted brown or green. Ellie had played there as a child: *One potato, two potato, three potato, four.* She found she had clenched her fists and was stamping them together in the old childhood way.

And then the skipping game came into her mind: *Raspberry, strawberry, marmalade and jam, tell me the name of my young man.* Running into the rope, skipping through the alphabet – *A – B – C – D – E – F – G* . . . your life's partner chosen at the moment your foot tripped the rope.

On the corner the old red phone box was gone, replaced by a smoked glass cabinet. She could go in there and dial Richard's number, hear his voice: *Stay where you are, Ellie. I'm coming to get you.* But there was no point. She couldn't face that voice again, cold instead of welcoming, and the face implacable. There was no room for her anywhere because Julia had taken all the love available and there was none left over.

She turned and retraced her steps to the back lane. She would look at the house from behind and seek out her bedroom window. There had been a sycamore growing in the yard, a sapling when she came there, shooting up each year until it dominated the narrow concrete, threatened the brick walls and shut out light from the kitchen. Autumn had come one year, and with it two men who cut off the branches, and then sawed the trunk into pieces and took it away. She had shut herself in Grandma's front bedroom, hands over ears to shut out the screams of the dying tree. And then Grandma had slapped the tops of her legs 'for daftness' and sent her out into the street to play. 'Raspberry, strawberry, marmalade and jam . . .'

The sash window of her bedroom was gone, replaced by modern double glazing. She had to put up a hand and finger the numbers 1 and 3 on the door before she could accept it was the same house. There were double gates beside the yard door and the top of a carport above the wall. Inside a radio was playing . . . or a stereo . . . Elaine Page, the song from *Chess*: 'Isn't it tragic he can't be mine.'

She moved away and walked round to the front street.

How far back could she remember? Playing in the street, Grandma watchful at the gate. That must have been aged five or six. Before that . . . climbing the gate in a new coat. *'Clothes cost money, Ellie.'* And coming home from school to ask about her name: *Elldis isn't a proper name, Grandma. No one says it's a proper name.* A knife slicing through bread. *'Another of your mother's daft ideas. The wages of sin, I told her. But she would never listen.'* And the voices in the street, *'Elldis, Elldis, stupid name!'* And her own voice, indignant: *'My name is Julia'.* Julia! Photographs everywhere, photographs of Julia. The tune was starting up again, the record clicking. Ellie felt her senses slipping away and leaned against a wall.

'Are you all right, pet?' The man was keeping his distance but the eyes were concerned.

'I'm sorry. I felt dizzy suddenly.'

He was holding a boisterous puppy on a leash. 'Haway, pet, I'll get the missus. Y're as white as a sheet.'

They moved away from No. 13 to a house three doors down. 'Babs, get yersel' out here. There's a woman took bad.'

Babs was small and stout and took it all in with one glance. 'Give me that dog, Wilf. Get her arm. Fetch her in along of me. I'll put the kettle on.' And then to Ellie,

'You'll be all right in here, pet. I'll just put this dog out bye and we'll soon sort you.'

The dog was banished to the kitchen, the man to make tea. Babs took one of Ellie's hands between her own rough ones and rubbed. 'You're frozen. And you look peaky. You don't belong round here, do you?'

Ellie shook her head. She was beginning to regain her composure, here in the tiny sitting-room, a roaring fire in the grate and a budgie twittering its concern by the window. 'I used to live here once. Years ago. I came back, just to see the old place.' She loosened the neck of her coat. 'I thought I might see a few old friends.'

Wilf was coming from the kitchen bearing tea, a frenzied puppy, deprived of its outing, leaping at his heels. 'Will you get that dog out of here, Wilf! By, if you want something done in this house, do it yourself. Give me that tea and get that animal down the school.' She was pouring tea. 'He takes it down to see the bairns in the schoolyard when he's on tub-loading – he's daft about them. Now get that down you. Mind, I can see your colour coming back.'

She talked determinedly and asked no questions until she saw Ellie relax, then she leaned forward. 'Now, you said you lived here once. What number?'

'Thirteen,' Ellie said. 'But it was a long time ago.' There was a wooden clock on the wall, its pendulum a girl on a swing. Up and down she went, up and down.

'McKennas live there now,' the woman was musing. 'Temples were here then, and old Mrs Connor on the corner. But the rest of the street's newcomers. They're always up for sale, these houses – first-time buyers, on account of only two bedrooms. They come, but they don't stop long. The Wimpey estate, that's where you'll find most of them now. When did you say you lived here?'

'I left in 1967. I was only a child.'

Babs was holding the teapot to her chest. Now she let out a burp. 'Ooh, that's better. Whenever I have cucumber I suffer. I doubt you'll find anyone who's been here that long. Still, you drink your tea, and I'll pop and ask.' She brushed aside Ellie's protestations and left the room, causing the budgie to leap energetically about its cage and shout out, 'Givvus a kiss, Babs. Givvus a kiss.'

Ellie sat quietly, drinking her tea, in a room that was full of evidence of family life. Children's clothes on a dryer, a half-completed model on a side-table, a daily paper opened to the TV page, and knitting on a chair, its needles progged into a ball of wool. Progged! She hadn't used that word for ages. Proggy mats. Her grandma had made proggy mats, which were slightly superior to the clippy variety. She had lived in this street, in a house like this one. She *had* existed. *I am Elldis Rowe,* said the voice in her head but it was more of a question than a statement.

It was twenty minutes before the woman came back, rubbing her hands together to warm them. Her arms were rounded and firm with bracelets of fat around her wrists. 'By, it's nippy out there! There's no one remembers you.'

Relief flooded over Ellie and that surprised her. She had come to find out, so why had she been afraid?

Babs was brewing fresh tea. 'There now. Help yourself to sugar and that's my own stottie. Get a bit down you. You look all eyes. Anyroad, they've all moved in in the last ten years. There's only Miss Porter and she's in the Geriatric. But I've spoken to No. 13 – she says you can go across there later on and have a good look round.'

The bread was doughy and full of flavour, and Ellie ate it gratefully. This morning she had retched and retched at the sink but nothing had come, only the waves of nausea rolling in like the sea.

They went to No. 13 when the tea was drunk. 'I won't come in,' Babs said. 'She'll only think I'm after an eyeful. But I'll introduce you. She's all right. A bit full of herself, but that's nothing nowadays. Just don't let her get on about Tenerife or you'll never get out. They went last year when her man got his redundancy and she's never shut up since. My man calls it the Tenerife Embassy, she clocks on that much.'

The tenant of No. 13 was pink with exertion and still holding a duster. 'Been redding up, Mary?' Babs inquired sweetly. 'She's come for a trip down memory lane, you know, not a dust inspection.'

'Pay no attention to her,' the woman said as Babs retreated to her own door. 'I always take a duster over the furniture in a morning. You've got to in a colliery district, haven't you? It gets in everywhere.'

But Ellie was lost in contemplation of her old home, tiny and unrecognizable, striking not a single chord. They moved from room to room and she tried to look suitably impressed at the alterations.

'That would be a cupboard in your day. Phil knocked that out before we moved in. And the dividing wall was here. Well, I've always preferred through-rooms.

Now I'll just lead the way upstairs. You'll see some changes there, I expect.'

There was nothing to remind her, nothing at all to stir until they went into the yard for a rear view and she saw the stump. 'It was a sycamore,' she said. 'I remember when they cut it down. You could hear the branches creaking and groaning . . .'

The woman put out a toe and prodded it. 'It'll have to come out sooner or later. We're going to put a patio in once Phil's finished the kitchen extension.'

Around them the house was spreading, acquiring bits and pieces till it looked like a cottage from 'Hansel and Gretel'. 'You've got a handy husband,' Ellie said, and saw the other woman's lips tighten with pride.

'Had your holidays?' she asked as they went back inside. 'We went to Tenerife . . .'

'What was it like?' Babs asked when she got back. She was trying to sound nonchalant but her eyes were keen.

'Very nice,' Ellie said, looking round, 'but not a patch on yours.'

Babs offered to make her some dinner. 'The bairns stop at school, and he's on tub-loading so he'll be abed as soon as he gets back, but I can soon knock something up.'

The stottie was lying awkwardly on Ellie's stomach and she shook her head. 'It's very kind of you but I'm a bit off my food at the moment.'

Babs shifted in her chair. 'Pardon my asking, but you're not pregnant, are you? You're all eyes. And then, wanting to come back to your old house . . . a baby can take you like that. All I wanted, with my first, was to go down the school playground and hold the railings. He thought I'd gone light.'

Ellie smiled and shook her head. 'No, it's nothing like that. I just had some time to spare and I was up here on holiday so I thought I'd look round. You never know, nowadays; it might have been pulled down. I'm glad it wasn't.'

'Oh, they'll never pull Gatcombe Street down. Colliery houses are built to last, I'll say that for them.'

In the grate the huge, over-stoked collier's fire glowed and twinkled. Ellie could have sat on there comfortably, lulled by the other woman's serenity. But there was work to be done. 'You said there was an old woman?'

When they parted she had the number of Miss Porter's ward in the old cottage hospital that now housed geriatrics. 'I'll drop her a card,' Ellie said, 'just for old times' sake.' She left two pound coins for the children and promised to keep in touch. 'You've been very kind.' She bent to kiss the rosy, unpowdered cheek that smelled deliciously of Knight's Castile. For a moment she was tempted to come clean in the hope that the fat young arms would close around her and make everything all right, but in the end she went off down the street.

Miss Porter's house was on the corner, paint dull and peeling, one downstairs window boarded up. The old woman had left it on a stretcher three years ago and no one had heard of her since. 'She's still alive though. The vicar keeps in touch and he says she's thriving.'

Ellie pulled shut the gate and turned towards the bus stop.

Tears had coursed down the woman's face until her eyes were washed clean of mascara that now streaked cheeks and chin. Paul passed her another tissue, noting the tremor of her fingers.

'None of it was your fault, Anne.' This time there was no vigorous shake of the head. Perhaps she was ready to accept absolution. 'If you'd had counselling beforehand . . . if they'd let your husband be there with you . . . but you had to bear it on your own.'

A year ago, with an unemployed husband and six children, she had had a seventh pregnancy terminated. And still she could not come to terms with it. Now the marriage was in shreds and he was fighting to keep her out of a psychiatric ward.

'If I could just have a rest, doctor. I just want a rest. I just want to get away.' He had heard this before, from so many patients. The desire to enter the closed world of hospital, slip between crisp white sheets, never have to face up to anything or anyone again. But that was not the answer.

He came round the desk and perched there. 'I'm going to arrange for you to get away for a day every week. It's not a hospital, it's a day centre. You'll like it there . . .'

She was the last of his patients. Now he must catch up on paperwork. His secretary came in with a sheaf of folders. 'The file on the Johnson boy has arrived, at last. The District General want you to look in on someone in their Dialysis Unit . . . a possible schizoid. And there's a negative HIV here I can't reconcile. We don't have a folder.'

He kept his voice level. 'Who is it?'

She held out the Path form. 'A William Mole. It rings a bell.'

He had used that name before – next time it would have to be something different. 'Oh yes, it's a private patient. I'll take it with me.'

HIV negative! So he was safe once more and, more important, possibly Gary was safe too. He had tried to persuade the boy to have the test but it was impossible to get him to understand the gravity of it all. *'You do it if you want to, mate. I know I'm OK. Trust me. What do you think I am, some kind of idiot?'*

When the woman quit the room he folded the Path form and put it in his wallet. Relief was making him light-headed and he must concentrate. He picked up the phone. 'Can you get me Mr Wheeler . . . yes, the obstetrician.' And then, when the call came through: 'Chris, how are you? Yes . . . ages. I'd like that. Give Muriel my love . . . and the children. Now, look, I want to pick your brains. What would be the effect on a primigravida of twenty-eight of taking Dervinox and Imprival? The foetus is six to twelve weeks . . . No, I can't be more specific, Chris. The patient is missing . . .'

The obstetrician was vague. 'It all depends, Paul – you know the score. Potentially it's disastrous, but we see the foetus survive disaster every day. If you get more information come back to me.'

Paul thought about Ellie all the way home and was

212

relieved to find the house empty, the tape-machine waiting.

'Did you enjoy your wedding-day, Ellie?' The reply on the tape was a long time coming. *'Yes. Yes, it was a lovely day. I just felt . . . well, it was afterwards . . . I wondered . . .'*

An agonizing pause. Listening now, knowing words would come, Paul still felt tension until the halting voice continued.

'I didn't think enough. I wanted to make them all happy. I thought it would be easy this time because they needed me but there were other things . . . more important things.'

What things, Ellie? Paul thought. *What things?*

On the cabinet some of the wildlife miniatures caught the light from the window so that they appeared to stand in a dappled glade. In a little while he would rearrange them and feel the familiar easing of his spirits. For now, though, he must concentrate on his patient. Not for the first time he reflected that many of the people he treated were like woodland creatures, timid and afraid to emerge into the light of day.

'I dream sometimes. And then, when I wake up, it hangs over me. I can't cast it off.'

'What do you dream, Ellie?'

'Sometimes I'm trying to get through something. A space, a very narrow space. And it closes in on me so I'm caught there. I can't go forward or back.'

'Do you dream about Richard, Ellie?' The pause went on and on. *'Ellie?'*

'I think so. I know it's Richard . . . but he has no face.'

Paul's pencil was flying now. At last there was straw

with which to make bricks. *'And he won't listen to me. He won't answer me. I can't make him hear.'*

'What do you want to tell him, Ellie?'

A pause and then a little anger in the voice. *'I don't know. No one will tell me and when I wake up I don't remember.*

'Once I dreamed I was on the stairs, the top of the stairs. It was dark and I wanted to go to bed. And then Richard was coming up the stairs with Julia. Because it was her house. He had his arm around her shoulder and they came up towards me to go into the bedroom. I said, "Where will I go?" and Richard said, "The box room. Julia is back with me now. Your place is in the box room."'

And then his own voice: *'Did you go there, Ellie?'*

'No! I ran away but I couldn't get out of the house!'

The tape had come to a stop then and clicked, and Paul remembered how he had watched her fingers curl into claws at the sound of it.

Terri almost missed the sight of Durham cathedral, noble against a blue sky, and had to crane her neck to see it. She concentrated after that and saw a medieval castle set among trees, a town with a market place, and a monument like a Greek temple set high on a hill, dominating the landscape. And then the train was crossing the Tyne and disgorging into the huge Gothic station.

'Terri Benedict? Recognized you from your piccy. We've spoken on the phone before. Ted Lavery. I've got the car outside. We'll have to get a move on or the bastards'll make me pay 65p. You're only allowed twenty minutes, and the train was seven minutes behind.'

On the way to the Civic Centre Ted gave Terri the bad news. 'I've been sniffing around there since they opened and there's not a whisper of Sting's wedding. I mean, they went all round-eyed and weak-kneed at the mention of his name, but that's all. I know he has family here, so you can see why he might come back, but *I* think it's a dead duck.' And then, as he man-oeuvred into a parking space: 'Did you find that friend of yours? I heard you rang Charlie and got the bum's rush. He's an old bastard. Good at his job though.'

They were running up the steps of the Civic Centre and she saw he was not really interested in an answer about Ellie. He was after bigger game.

There was still nothing to discover. Disbelieving faces and shaking heads. 'Wish it was true,' one girl clerk said. 'We never have any excitement in here.'

They came out on to the steps again. 'Either they're better actors than the RSC or we're flogging a dead horse,' Ted said gloomily.

Terri looked at her watch. 'Well, we'll give it another half-hour, then I'll ring in.'

They walked around the Civic Centre, an odd but rather charming edifice. There was water spraying and a statue of the Great God Tyne on a wall, crouched in what seemed to be despair, his uplifted hand trickling water on to his downcast head.

'Seems like a nice city,' Terri said. 'Wish I had time to look around.'

Ted's face brightened. 'It's a good city. Plenty going on and some riveting architecture. John Dobson: good as Bath, any day, though you won't hear anyone say so. Travel five miles out and you're in the best landscape in

215

Britain, but no one mentions that either. According to them, it's all back streets and mean cobbles. I've given up, in a way. I take the bread and let it roll over me.'

In the distance a limousine glided to a halt and they both came alert. But it was only a couple of civic dignitaries. 'I think I'll ring in,' Terri said, and went in search of a phone.

Back in the office, voices were gloomy. 'Sting's supposed to be in Cannes. We're checking. Stay put in the mean time.'

Terri shrugged as she rejoined Ted. 'Zilch. Stay put, they say.' On the grass two winos were sharing a bottle of British sherry and railing at passers-by who dared to look in their direction.

'Oh God,' Ted said, shrinking into his anorak, 'there must be easier ways to earn a living.'

Next Terri tried to ring Mike, but he was out of his office. 'Tell him I'm in Newcastle,' she said. 'I'll see him tonight.' She rejoined Ted, who was looking wistfully towards a nearby pub, and they stood, stamping their feet against the cold.

'That old stringer, Charlie Wotsisname, does he live far out?'

Ted shook his head. 'Gosforth. Half a mile up the road.'

She considered for a minute. 'Lend me your car for five minutes?'

He handed over the keys reluctantly. 'What if something breaks here?'

Terri was still scribbling down the directions he had given her. 'It won't – I can feel it in my water, Ted. Anyway, you can cope, and I'll only be five minutes.'

She found the house without difficulty, a pleasant detached villa with weeping ash either side of the short drive. In London it would have cost £300,000 at least. Perhaps she and Mike were working in the wrong place. The woman who answered the door was wiping her hands on a tea-towel and pastry showed around her fingernails. 'He's in the garden, dear. Just go round the side.'

Terri passed through gloomy laurel and hawthorn and came out in a paradise of shrubs and lawns with alpine-covered rocks to mark one plot from another. At the bottom of the garden a bonfire was sending a trail of smoke into the sky.

The man tending it scowled at her appearance, and doubts about coming threatened to engulf her. 'I'm sorry to bother you but I couldn't miss this chance . . .'

Charlie heard her out and shook his head. 'It's like I said on the phone: twenty-five years! You're not asking much, are you? Anything fresh to go on?'

Terri winced. 'Nothing, I'm afraid. All I know is that she was two or three, and a grandmother whisked her away from whatever it was, so it was probably something fairly hairy.'

The garden obviously had a calming effect on retired newspapermen. 'I can think of a few cases . . . there was a vicar ran off with the cub mistress, wife topped herself. There was a two-year-old there, but it was a boy. And the name wasn't Rowe. There was a jeweller shot himself rather than go bust. Two little girls there, but I think that was late fifties. Couple of domestic murders: we have our fair share of violence up here. But unless you can narrow it down . . . And even if I could pinpoint the case, where would it get you? You're talking about a quarter of a century. Life moves on . . .'

Terri was regretting her excursion as she drove back to the Civic Centre. If something had broken while she was away she would be in shtuck and no mistake. And all for nothing! Except that Charlie had raised the issue of the birth certificate. She must speak to Richard about that.

Ted was still in place, hands in pockets, shoulders hunched, and the Great God Tyne was still sluicing his head. She didn't blame him: it'd been a hell of a morning.

'I've rung in,' Ted said. 'Half an hour after you went off for five minutes! They said to hang on, but I daresay we could ring again now. I've got a mouth like a birdcage.'

Terri dialled the paper's freephone line.

'Panic over: he's in Cannes,' Stephen said. 'Get yourself back. No hurry, but call in here when you arrive . . . just in case.'

Terri protested that it would be seven o'clock at night but he was adamant. 'Balls to you, Stephen,' she said, and put down the phone.

She caught the next train, and bought a brandy and dry ginger before she settled in her seat. She was going to get stoned on the way home to make up for an utterly, bloodily useless day.

Richard had poured himself a drink and was looking out of his office window at a darkening sky when the call came through.

'Mr Marriner?' The detective's voice was business-like and unexcited but he still sounded like a boy and Richard found this faintly embarrassing. What would the boy uncover; what question would he ask next? Would the time come when he would look at the boy and see contempt, or worse still, pity in his eyes?

'I thought I'd fill you in on what we've accomplished so far. The birth certificate was a dead end: no one of that name there in the last twenty years, certainly. No other known addresses for the mother. If I have no success up here I'll try the Central Register, see what turns up there. However, I've struck lucky here at County Hall. There were a limited number of children's homes your wife might have been in, and I found a record of her at the second I tried. I'm going there now.'

Richard's heart was hammering against his ribs as he heard Frank's signal at the door. He pressed the button and when Frank came in, motioned him to a chair. 'That's marvellous,' he said into the telephone. 'I didn't expect such progress.'

The detective's voice was smug. 'There's more. I rang the Home to make an appointment and it sounds as though your wife has already been there. Yesterday.'

Richard tried to keep his voice steady. 'So she's definitely up there, and she's all right?'

'As far as I can tell. The woman I spoke to says she seemed perfectly normal . . . a little agitated perhaps. And of course she used the name Rowe. I have the address of her grandmother's home in Belgate and I'm going there now. I'll ring in if I find anything significant. Your wife is obviously searching for something, and I'm not far behind her.'

Richard felt almost euphoric about the news but Weidenek's warning was still to be taken into account. He kept his tone even. 'I don't want you to do anything if you find her. Simply report back to me. My children are coming home this weekend but as soon as they go back to school I'll come up to you. Keep in touch. I'm very pleased with your efforts so far.'

When he had put down the phone he felt his eyes prick and a lump fill his throat.

'It's OK, old man, I understand.' Frank's eyes were full of sympathy, but it wouldn't do to give way.

Richard put a fist to his mouth and pretended to burp. 'It's nothing . . . just a touch of indigestion. That was the detective. Ellie's there all right . . . in Durham . . . but he hasn't located her exact whereabouts yet.'

Frank's smile was almost rueful. 'Good. That's a step forward.'

As Frank moved towards the drinks cabinet, Richard wondered why he had felt the need to cover his emotion. Frank was closer to him than any other human being, even Ellie; closer even than Julia had been. And he still felt the need to dissemble.

Adele gave Solange last-minute instructions about dinner and went upstairs. She must stop thinking about Ellie's call; the phone never rang if you watched it. Instead she would think about Japan. She was going there with Frank, by hook or by crook; she was going to walk the exotic streets of Tokyo and be jostled by its twelve million inhabitants; she was going to shop in the Ginza, drink sake and buy an embroidered kimono with a dragon on the back. On reflection, she decided dragons were Chinese and substituted cherry blossom, but the principle was the same. She was owed Japan and she was having it! Except that Frank was still being obdurate.

She decided to do her Fagin bit. Her mother had christened it that, finding her gloating over her treasures one day: *'Darling, you look like that dreadful Jew in Oliver.'*

Defiantly she took her tiered jewel-box from the dressing-table and carried it to the bed. The top tray was mostly costume jewellery; the goodies were lower down. She fingered the large gold-rimmed cameo her mother had given her, and the matching ear-rings that had been a gift from Julia. Frank had given her the pearls when Sara was born, and the opal ring and brooch as a thank-you for Emma's birth. She had wanted matching ear-rings too, but in the end she had had to buy them for herself. The aquamarines in the grey shagreen case had belonged to Frank's mother. Julia had got the sapphires while she herself had been fobbed off with aquamarines.

She had hoped to find the sapphires in Ellie's jewel-case when she looked around the bedroom. Or perhaps feared would be a better word. She couldn't have borne it if Ellie had got the sapphires – brooch, ear-rings and ring in exquisite settings. Perhaps she could ask about them when Ellie phoned? Ellie's conversation was so disjointed now, you could slip in anything. And it would be nice to know about the jewellery . . . Adele snapped shut the case on aquamarines suddenly grown pale by comparison, and bounced from bed to wardrobe.

Japan, Japan, that was the important thing. She had checked with a travel agent and Japan was pleasantly warm at this time of year, with cooler evenings. She would take silk and wool, thin layers, nothing heavy. That would cut down luggage. Frank was foul if he had to tote too many bags. She threw garments on the bed, dividing them into two piles, possible and definite, and was standing at the mirror, holding a hanger under her chin and squinting at her reflection, when the phone rang.

She picked up the bedroom extension.

'Adele?' It was Ellie.

Adele threw the hanger towards the bed and watched the yellow silk dress it held slither to the floor. 'Ellie . . . I was waiting for you to ring.' She pulled out the dressing-stool and subsided on to it. 'Where *are* you?' There was no reply and she tried again: 'I wish you'd tell me. I'm not going to tell anyone . . . you can trust me.' She must make progress. If she could find out Ellie's whereabouts, they could get her back. She herself would be free to go to Japan once Ellie was safely home or consigned to some neighbourhood asylum. And if she could produce an address, they would never check on how many calls from Ellie she had actually received. She tried to find the right words. 'Tell me where you are, Ellie. I won't tell anyone, not even Frank.' She pictured herself walking into Richard's hall supporting a drooping Ellie. 'I found her for you, Richard,' she'd say and everyone would be *pleased*.

She crossed her legs and took hold of her foot with her free hand. 'Ellie, let me talk for a while. I know what you're going through but I can help. I'm on your side . . .'

But when Ellie spoke, she also wanted answers. 'Are the boys all right? Is this their home weekend? How is Richard?'

The bitch deserved a little punishment, Adele thought – she was selfish; selfish and above herself. 'Richard's fine. He was worried about you at first, but you know men . . . business comes first. I'm sure he does think about you. Well, he must do, mustn't he? But it doesn't show. He looks . . . well, almost relieved . . . so don't worry about him. He's fine.'

Paul and Richard carried coffee and brandy to the living-room and the dogs rose to greet them, tails flailing. 'I take them out after dinner,' Richard explained. 'Since Ellie went I've usually waited until later . . . in case she should ring . . . but they don't understand the delay.'

'We could walk in the grounds,' Paul suggested. 'I could do with some fresh air, and we could stay within earshot.'

Richard moved to the door. 'Mrs Withers takes calls on her extension while I walk the dogs. I don't like to ask in her off-duty time, but the dogs have to get out.'

When he came back he was wearing a padded jacket and was carrying another. 'You'll need this. It's cold outside but it's a beautiful night.'

They left by the French windows, the dogs gone mad in an ecstasy of freedom. Underfoot the grass was crisping with the first suspicion of frost, and the trees were stark against a sky misted and

223

sprinkled with stars. 'You can smell winter now,' Richard said, bending for a twig. He sent it in an arc far out into space and the dogs tore into the abyss to catch it.

Paul let out his breath. 'It's a long time since I did this,' he said. 'It feels good.'

They walked down the slope in companionable silence, each busy with his own thoughts. Paul was thinking of the empty house he had left behind: if Gary went . . . when Gary went . . . there would be a void. He would fill it with work, with music, with his books and miniatures, good cinema and an orgy of redecoration. But the void would remain. Only his patients would assuage his pain.

Over dinner, they had talked of the stock market, its fluctuations and their effect on Marriner Engineering. 'I worry', Richard had said, 'because of the men. They depend on me, their wives and families. It's a terrible responsibility but in a way it's also a sheet anchor. I have to go on, for their sake.' Paul had nodded, knowing exactly what he meant. Now he broached that subject that was on both their minds.

'I've talked to an obstetrician and I'm beginning to form a more definite picture. You know I'm going over all Ellie's tapes? So much is becoming clear.'

As Paul had hoped, Richard found it easier to talk under cover of darkness. It was an English trait. 'I wish it was clear to me. I'm becoming more muddled by the minute.'

'Anything I can clarify?' Paul kept his tone deliberately light.

'I don't know,' Richard said. 'It's all so desperately

224

vague that it's difficult to pose questions. I mean, if she has this thing about sex . . .' In the darkness Paul smiled. The fatal word had been brought out, like a ferret from a bag. '. . . if she has a distaste for love-making, why did she choose to do it? I didn't force her.'

'You sound angry. No, don't feel guilty – you're entitled to feel anger and bafflement. They are very normal emotions in a situation like this.'

A dog emerged from the darkness, eyes like green glass, breath rising from its lolling mouth. 'There you are, boy.' A stick sped skyward once more and the dog disappeared.

'I do feel anger sometimes, even rage. And then I feel such utter, bloody remorse. It isn't Ellie's fault, any more than it's mine.'

'Hang on to that. The seeds of this thing were sown when she was a baby; perhaps before that, for all I know. And you were then a callow youth in short pants.'

'But if she has no knowledge of it, why does it have the power to hurt her?'

'She does have knowledge of it, but not with the conscious part of her psyche. The mind can only cope with a certain amount of emotion. Too much, and something blows. So there are cut-out points – in some people breakdown, in others a healthy anger at their situation. In others, a curtain is drawn over the cause of the pain: that's what's happened to Ellie. But it's all there, like cyanide in a capsule, ready to destroy. Ellie knows of its existence, but she doesn't know what "it" is. So she imagines the worst.'

Richard's voice was somehow forlorn. 'Imagines what?'

'I don't know . . . something desperate. I think she fears that she is illegitimate, but that is the lesser part. She fears that her mother was in some way tainted – mad, or criminal, or both. She sees herself as the illegal fruit of a tainted tree. And there's this other thing, this exaggerated sense of your first wife's presence. I suppose it's impossible that their paths could ever have crossed?'

'Completely impossible. Ellie's past is a closed book, more or less, and I can't tell you how bitterly I regret that I didn't find out more. But I have known Julia since I was thirteen. She was never in the north, and Ellie, as far as we know, never left it until after Julia and I were married and were with one another every day.'

They had reached a wooded copse and were walking, single file, between trees. 'Surely she'll realize she's pregnant before much longer?' Richard said.

'She may not let herself realize it,' Paul replied. 'The human mind has an infinite capacity for excluding the unacceptable. She may see and not see, and go on not seeing. Women have gone full term without acknowledging pregnancy, and as yet Ellie's pregnancy is hardly established.'

'What about the pills? I worry about them night and day.' In the darkness a small creature scuttled across their path.

'We'd have heard by now if she'd intended to use them. And the obstetrician is cautiously optimistic . . . as long as we find her soon.'

'What will the end be, Paul?' Between them in the

darkness, a bond had been forged and the Christian name was its token.

'Hopefully she will come back,' Paul said, 'if she's successful in her quest. There's a line from Matthew Arnold that sums it up: "He who finds himself, loses his misery." Ellie is trying to find herself.'

As they emerged into a clearing, the moon broke through, showing the dogs on the other side, dashing in and out, snuffling at roots and scrub. Richard was silent now, but Paul knew he had eased the other man's mind. That was good.

It was quarter to ten when Terri got home and all she could think of was getting into bed. She would put her head on the pillow, face unwashed, give one luxurious stretch and fall asleep. She nodded off in the taxi and came awake with a start at her door.

One look at Mike's face told her there was a problem. 'We've got guests,' he said, trying to sound cheerful and gesturing towards the sofa where his daughters were watching TV. 'Hi,' they said dutifully and in unison, before turning back to the box.

'What are *they* doing here?' Terri said when the kitchen door was safely closed behind them. Jesus, she sounded as though she hated them!

'I had to bring them. Diana had the chance of a weekend away, so it was bring them here or stay there with them, and you know what you'd've made of that.'

She sat down at the table. 'Where are they sleeping?'

He turned to fill the kettle, keeping his back to her. 'I've had to put them in our room . . . I can't ask them to sleep on the floor the one time I bring them here.

You can have the sofa, and I'll bunk somewhere . . . just let's have a peaceful weekend. Please!'

Terri had slept on the sofa before, during several of their many rows. It was too short to stretch out on, and the arm was too steep so that you woke with a crick in your neck.

'I'm tired,' she said. 'I'm fucking tired and worn out, and I need my bed. And your fucking ex has managed to screw up my life one more time.'

There was no sympathy in his voice, no trace of compromise. 'I hope you'll watch your language in front of the girls. I'll say this for Diana, she doesn't have a mouth like an Aussie stockman.'

He managed to duck as the stainless steel butter-dish flew past his head, coming apart as it struck the wall, disgorging its contents to smear obscenely down the patterned wallpaper.

The garden was silver in the moonlight. Adele tightened the belt of her dressing-gown and sat down on the sill. Across the way, the horse-chestnut was outlined in the light from Richard's window. So he was awake, too. Behind her, in the bed, Frank slept.

They had lain back to back until she heard his breathing slow and deepen and knew there was no possibility of his turning to her. She had not wanted sex, but she had wanted to possess him, to shut out the rest of the world for a moment and be in control.

Down below on the silvered lawn something was moving. Not a dog, too purposeful. Too big for a cat. A fox! The fox stopped suddenly and sniffed the air. Adele felt a dart of satisfaction. What did it all matter, as long as a fox could still go about its business? But winter was coming, a hard time for foxes, for everyone. She was thirty-six years old, more than half-way through her life and it had still not really begun. She had everything and nothing. Frank despised her, the girls would have lives of their own soon, and she was still waiting for her own life to begin.

Perhaps there was nothing. Nothing between over-ture, the moment when you became grown-up, and curtain-fall. *I'm frightened*, Adele thought. *Please, I'm frightened*. Today she had looked at her mother and thought that life was a treadmill. Cradle to grave. In-exorable. Her mother's face was blanching with time, losing colour like a leaf. She put up a hand to her own face, testing to see if the flesh was still firm. There had to be something. Something more.

Across the way the light went out. If Julia had still been there she could have confessed her fears and Julia would have laughed them away. But Julia was gone. She looked instead for the fox, searching the edges of the lawn in vain for signs of movement. But she was alone in a silent world, and morning a lifetime away.

If only she didn't feel so guilty. Keeping quiet about the first call had been almost inadvertent, but the sub-sequent secret calls had given her a thrill. Terror at the enormity of what she was doing, but still a thrill. Today, though, when she had rubbed Ellie's nose in it, the exultation she had expected had failed to materialize. 'He's relieved to get rid of you,' she had said, or words to that effect, and there had been no surprise in Ellie's voice, no anger, just a terrible acceptance.

Adele shivered a little but the warm bed did not

tempt her. Strange to think of all the little subterfuges she had once got up to in order to land a Marriner. The bills for clothes they couldn't quite afford, subscriptions to clubs, and sports equipment that was never used – all to make sure Frank swallowed the bait. All that effort for this: a seat in a cold window with only a midnight fox for companion.

Her mother had been behind her every inch of the way in those days. Daddy's money had been running out even then, but Adele had only had to ask and Mummy had found a way. They had been conspirators, and it had been such fun. And then had followed the building of the houses. Mummy had been scandalized at that. *'So many lovely houses going to seed, and Julia wants a vulgar red-brick mansion. And with her background, too!'* As the plans had escalated, the very size of the houses had impressed everyone. But it was Julia who had decided who should live where, Julia who had chosen the western aspect for herself. The stables had been Julia's and the Witherses had moved into the lodge to care for Julia's home and Julia's garden.

A cloud covered the moon, throwing the garden into darkness. Adele stood up and felt her way towards the bed, slipping between the sheets quietly like someone who had no right to be there.

'Try and get home early, Frank,' Adele said. 'The girls should be here around three.' They paused on the steps to look around a frost-spangled garden. The lawn was silver, with fallen leaves crouched here and there like small brown animals. 'You need a coat,' she chided him, and plucked an imaginary speck from his sleeve.

Frank ignored the remark and the gesture and went down the steps. 'I'll get back as soon as I can. They're coming with the Tryons, aren't they?'

'Yes, in the Roller. They'll love that, vulgar little beasts that they are! I remember Daddy telling me once that nice people never bought Rollers in the old days . . . between the wars. Something to do with them being the preferred motor of the profiteers. He would never touch one – Bentleys every time.'

Frank was smiling. 'Your father was the most awful snob, wasn't he? I liked him enormously, but he was a hoot. Anyway, love to the girls. I must go.'

She watched the car till it turned into the road and was lost to view. Eight-forty-five. In five and a quarter hours, if Ellie kept her promise, the phone would ring again. As she walked back into the house she wondered how long it could go on. For a while it would be OK: Ellie was so confused that no one would believe her if she claimed to have made the calls. But if it went on for too long it could be dangerous. Ellie must be made to reveal her whereabouts as quickly as possible. The only problem was how to make her crack. And when to play the trump card!

Paul had started on the tapes again at six o'clock, carrying the coffee-maker into his study and switching on the gas fire. Now, three hours later, he stretched and put down his pen to flex cold fingers. In the background Ellie's hesitant voice continued. *'I feel despair sometimes. I know I shouldn't. I'm a very lucky woman. I'm sorry for all this upset. I'm sorry for everything.'* There it was again, the apology for being alive.

'Christ! I knew I'd find you in here.' Gary was standing in the doorway. 'God, it gives me the creeps the way you sit there, lapping it all up. "I'm unhappy. I'm sad. I'm a silly, rich bitch with too much time on my hands. Lick my arse. Make me better." It's sick, Paul. You kid yourself it's all in the cause of medical science, but it's just another way of getting kicks. Face it!' Gary was still in pyjama trousers, bare-chested under the open dressing-gown, perfect feet slipperless and arched against the cold. He had picked up the harvest mouse and was squeezing the frame between his fingers as though he wanted it to break.

Paul reached to stop the machine. 'OK, don't go overboard. I'll stop now and see about breakfast.'

It was not enough. The head, hair tight-curled as always in the mornings, was turned in disdain. 'Don't stop on my account, please. I'm used to playing second fiddle.' There was menace in the voice and in the lip, stretched tight across the teeth.

Paul stood up carefully. Things were at flashpoint and he felt the familiar *frisson* of fear. 'What about scrambled eggs and smoky bacon? You like that.'

'I'll do my own; you stay and eavesdrop. She must be thrilling, the way she obsesses you. But I'm used to it. I'm wallpaper in this house, that's all. Background! Oh God, I'm sick. Help *me*, if you're so all-bloody-merciful. Do something about my hang-ups! I've got good reason to break down – I've got talent, but where will that get me in a bloody philistine country?'

The tide of his own misery was engulfing him, which was good – better than anger. It meant he would allow himself to be consoled. 'Come into the kitchen and we'll talk. You said the gig went well. And you're going into the studio soon . . . I told you I'd pay. A decent demo tape could make a difference, you'll see. I'm sorry about neglecting you. We'll do something special this weekend . . . anything you choose.'

For a moment it hung on a knife-edge. 'Oh, all right, don't grovel. I can't stand abasement. For Christ's sake get on with it, if you're going to cook something.'

They moved to the kitchen, peace restored except within Paul's mind. It was dangerous to be committed to this extent. It would end in darkness. And yet, seeing the danger, he could no more avoid it than take wing and fly.

There was a smell of urine everywhere, accentuated by a dreadful cleanliness that made it somehow more obscene. 'Miss Porter? Oh, you mean Sally! She's along the end. The chairs round the telly.'

Ellie moved along a corridor from which bays opened, each holding light hospital beds with a bedside trolley and chair beside them. Most of the beds were unoccupied in the early afternoon, sheets folded back neatly on counterpanes in a way that suggested a shoe horn would be necessary at bed-time. Here and there a bed held an occupant, but these were pathetic remnants, sunk into sleep, eye sockets blind, faces devoid of colour so that they looked like statues chiselled out by some demented sculptor. Where a limb showed above the bedclothes it was emaciated, the joint huge beyond a shank of bone, the skin dry and scaly like a fish.

The end bay held a colour telly but the volume had been turned down. Instead of Henry Kelly the floor was held by a vicar, tall and muscular in his cassock, an open hymn book in one hand, the other clenched behind his back. He was conducting a service but only a handful of the semicircle around him were joining in. One or two slept, one, bolder than the rest, craned to see the silent television whenever the vicar ceased to block her view. 'And now', he said, 'we'll have "The King of Love my Shepherd is". I know that's one of your favourites. Take your time from me. One, two . . .'

As the vicar broke into song a junior nurse behind him turned away, unable to hide her mirth. 'I nothing lack if I am His, and He is mine for ever.' He would never attempt another verse, Ellie thought, and was immediately proved wrong. 'Where streams of living waters flow . . .'

An old woman began to cry, unreasoned tears that did not dry up in spite of the nurse's blandishments. The vicar rattled to the end of the verse and called it a day, and Ellie moved forward, praying Miss Porter would be one of the hymn-singers and therefore more *compos mentis* than the rest.

'Can I help you?' The junior nurse had pulled herself together and was moving wheelchairs.

'I'm looking for Miss Porter. Sally Porter.'

The nurse nodded. 'That's her, behind you. I hope you've brought her some liquorice allsorts. She's been on all day about her gob.'

Miss Porter clutched Ellie's arm. 'What've you brought?' she said, disdaining the niceties of introduction. 'They keep you short in here. Prison grub'd be better.'

The junior nurse pushing her wheelchair was stung to response. 'You're on a diet, Sally. That's why we watch your food.'

The old woman cackled. 'Watch it? You'd need a bloody microscope to find it, some days. And you watch your own waistline, miss – never mind mine. It's done me for ninety years. I daresay it'll see me out.'

Behind her the nurse raised eyes to heaven. 'Eleven stone,' she mouthed. 'Try hitching her up in the bed and you'll soon know. And she's not ninety, she's eighty-eight.' She parked the chair by Miss Porter's bed and went on her way, puzzled by the beaming smile on the face of Miss Porter's visitor.

Ellie *was* pleased! Miss Porter seemed very much all there. 'I'm Ellie Rowe,' she said, putting down bag and gloves. 'I used to be a neighbour of yours. I've brought you some biscuits and a bottle of orange.' Before she could produce them the old woman gave a fierce shake of her head.

'Not now, not now. The snatch squad'll have them if you wave them round. Sly them under the pillow when they're not looking. You can put the orange juice on the top, they don't mind that. Now, who are you? I don't remember you round Gatcombe Street.'

Ellie sat down, trying to compose her thoughts. She was not really prepared for Miss Porter. She had expected a frail old lady in a high white bed, not a harridan in blue Crimplene. 'I used to live in Gatcombe Street, years ago. I left when I was eight in 1967, and I've never been back until today. I came up here on holiday and went to have a look, but everyone's gone. Except you. They told me about you.' She tried to sound rosy about this fact but she was wasting her time.

'They did, did they? Didn't say they've never been near hand, I bet. Not a bloody water biscuit in three years.' She leaned forward in the chair. 'Did you see my house?' Now, suddenly, she was vulnerable. 'They want to sell my house, you know. Over my bloody head. They're at me day and night.'

'Who?' Ellie asked, swept along by Miss Porter's passion.

'The government! Who else takes your property off you? The DH bloody S. But I'll beat them. As long as I'm here, in Geriatrics, they can't touch it. If I go to a council home they can sell it to defray costs. I'll defray their bloody costs for them. Here I am and here I stay!'

Ellie smiled. 'I saw your house,' she said. 'It looked

fine.' And then, taking her courage in both hands . . . 'I lived in No. 13.'

Miss Porter considered. 'Thirteen. When did you say? Nineteen-sixties. You're not a McArthur?' Ellie shook her head. 'Then you're a Botcherby?' Again Ellie demurred. Miss Porter pursed her mouth. 'Lived with your gran, did you?'

This time Ellie nodded. 'That's right. They called my gran Baxter.'

Miss Porter was nodding. 'Very stuck up. Kept herself to herself. I remember you now. By, you were a pasty bairn. Frightened of your own shadow. I told your gran, but she wasn't one to listen.'

'Do you remember when she came to Gatcombe Street?'

Miss Porter was nodding vigorously. 'Oh yes, it was '62. I mind that because my mam died along of Harry Jessop. They were both in the Sunderland Royal and they died in the May. His sister had his house on the market before he was cold. No. 13. Twelve hundred pounds she wanted. It was scandalous for a house that'd never seen a lick of paint.' Her face clouded over. 'What about my paintwork?'

Ellie thought briefly of the blistered door and windows of Miss Porter's house. 'It's fine,' she said, 'not a mark on it.' And then . . . 'So you saw my gran move in?'

'Oh yes. A proper van, it was. Piano, the lot. The bairns was hanging round the way they do, hoping for coppers for jobs. But she chased them. She stood there counting her bits and pieces and then she checked the van.'

Ellie could contain herself no longer. 'Where had she come from?'

Miss Porter looked vague. 'I don't know. She never let on and it was one of them big vans – Pickfords, mebbe. It wasn't local. She had the Durham twang, so she must've come from roundabout. Some folks asked her but she was a cheeky madam. "Ask no questions you'll get no lies," she told one wife. And she had no callers. Not a foot across her doorstep except the clubwoman, not in all the years. She kept herself to herself and she only let you out in the front street where she could watch you. It wasn't natural, the way she coddled you. It's a wonder to me you grew up straight.'

When Ellie had made her goodbyes she walked from the foetid atmosphere of the ward into a cold autumn day. There were rose-hips in the hedges as she walked down the drive and leaves turning to jewels with autumn, but all she could think of was Miss Porter's parting remark: '*A wonder to me you grew up straight*'. She had not grown straight and she had brought down misery on those she loved, first Grandma and now Richard, so that he was relieved to see the back of her. Adele had said it, but Ellie had already known it. Foolish tears were running down her cheeks and she brushed them away. Mustn't attract attention.

At the end of the drive a young man was paying off a taxi. The collar of his raincoat was upturned and he carried a framed briefcase. Perhaps he was a visiting consultant, or a lawyer come to execute a will. Whoever he was, she mustn't pass him with tears on her cheeks.

People remembered details like that. A gravel path wound off to the right, and she turned into it.

'Everybody is promoting something nowadays,' Terri said bitterly, to no one in particular. 'Breast reduction, step-parenting . . . this is a plug for lubricating jelly. Jesus, nothing's sacred any more.' She threw the rest of the junk mail into the waste-basket.

Greta was gathering up her notebooks. 'It's Thatcherism. Everyone wants to make a living without actually getting their hands dirty, so they service someone or take commission for providing something. It's all a terrible vicious circle, like pyramid selling. There'll be one hell of a crash before long.'

Terri tried to equate pyramids and circles and then gave up. 'Any ideas for conference?'

Greta's eyes rolled. 'You've got to be joking. If the Lord High Executioner expects fizz from me this morning he'll be lucky. Bloody lucky!'

Terri ripped open a stray envelope, '"Sexual Problems. The curse of the Modern Woman. You are invited to a seminar . . ."' As the invitation hit the basket she reflected that modern woman's only problem with sex was finding enough energy to stay awake for it. And her own bed to do it in.

Still, no point in dwelling on that now. It was resolved. She had screamed out all her fury and frustration, and for once Mike had not retaliated. Instead, he had moved to take her in his arms. 'Hush. Stop it. What are you scared of? We're a whole, you and I. A united front. No one outside can harm us if we stick together, not even Diana.'

Later he had tucked her in on the sofa and then huddled into his sleeping bag on the rug beside her. She had lain and listened to his sleeping breath, thinking of the girls, his children, sleeping in the next room. She would have been perfectly happy if the image of Ellie had not appeared, ghost-like, like Banquo at the feast.

The office had gone quiet. Everyone had gone into morning conference, which was where she should be. But all she could think of was Ellie. Ellie walking somewhere, hiding somewhere, shopping somewhere in a corner shop: *A small cut-white and some oranges, please.* Ellie waiting, Ellie weeping. Christ, there must be something they could do!

The Editor gave a jaundiced smile as she sidled in and sat down next to Greta. 'We can all stop worrying now, people – Terri has arrived. Come on then, Terri, let's have your usual flood of dingbat ideas. We don't mind you rolling in at your own time as long as you come up with a cracker.'

Terri smiled in what she hoped was an ingratiating way and waited for him to find a fresh target.

'Right, let's cut the crap and get down to it. Tomorrow's issue is so bland it looks like it's written in invisible ink. I'm going round this table and I want ideas, ideas, ideas. If you've got nothing to contribute, get out of the fucking way and make room for someone who has.'

No one moved but no one looked inspirational either. The Editor gazed round the table. 'Come on then. Where's the beef, Stephen?'

The Features Editor shifted uneasily. 'There's this new G-Plan diet . . . we could do a series, bring in a few celebs: "How the stars keep their shape".' His voice died away as the Editorial brow darkened.

'Is that the best you can come up with . . . a tired idea that's got brewer's droop, like our circulation? Who'll write it? You'll want to use freelances, no doubt. What you are paid for, cobbers . . . correction, grossly overpaid for . . . is to write. Get out and frigging well do what you're paid for.'

No one moved. There would be hell to pay if they did and they all knew it. He would go on like this, working himself into a state, until he could announce that he, unlike the rest of them, did have an idea worth printing. Terri shifted her weight and tried to avoid his eyes while still looking as though she hung on his every word.

When at last it was over and she made her escape, she looked at her watch. She was meeting Mike and Sam at twelve-thirty but she mustn't let her hopes rise. It was sure to come to nothing. And she had to remember to get something for the girls' supper.

She had emerged from the conference with no particular assignment: 'Come up with something about the beautiful people – about achievers – whizz-kids – entrepreneurs – from your angle. Give it some glamour. Take your time, make it good.' Around her the others were beavering away at something definite. Lucky sods. She tried to switch her brain to inventive lines, but without success.

She collected a cup of coffee, and then rang a former colleague who was sometimes willing to swop ideas. 'Sorry love, I'm scraping the barrel myself. I hear you went after that Sting story? There was never anything in it . . . I'm surprised it took off at all.'

'Thanks a bunch,' Terri thought, as she put down the phone. She was brooding too much about the house, that was the trouble. The house, and Ellie. If only she could do something constructive about her friend she wouldn't feel so guilty. In desperation she pulled out the piece she'd started on Ellie. Ellie was young and beautiful, in a classy kind of way . . . and Richard was certainly an achiever. But getting an angle without being totally insensitive to the central figures was far from easy. Thinking of Richard reminded her about Ellie's birth certificate. She reached for her phone and dialled the Marriner number.

'Richard? Terri Benedict here. How are you?' There was no further news of Ellie and she could tell from the sound of his voice that he was despairing. 'Look, I do want to help, Richard. The thing is that if I succeed in doing something in the paper . . . and that in itself is outside my control . . . if I do get something into print, it could come out in a different way to the way I intended it to.' God, she was making a verbal dog's breakfast of this. 'What I'm trying to say, Richard, is that I'm scared I might do more harm than good.'

There was silence at the other end and she knew he understood and was considering. 'Terri, I don't think things could be much worse. Time is running out . . .'

She eased herself in her chair. What did he mean? Running out for what? Surely Ellie didn't have some dread disease, or need insulin, or something?

'You feel there's a definite time-factor, then?'

That was a mistake. Even along the line she could

sense his withdrawal. 'No, I only meant to say that I think all publicity is good publicity in this situation. If you get a chance to widen the coverage, take it.'

'There's one more point, Richard. It's probably nothing but I was wondering about Ellie's birth certificate. It must have some details . . .'

'We've looked at that. It's the short version and it gives the place of registration as Liverpool, but Ellie left there just after she was born. The private investigator checked, just to be sure, but she wasn't known there.'

'If you could send me a copy, I could pop into St Catherines House and see the original. You never know what a fresh eye might pick up.'

Tonight she would go through her snaps for a pic of Ellie, and tomorrow she would go to St Catherines House in Kingsway and check.

Richard tried to concentrate on the rows of performance figures in front of him, but his mind kept slipping out of gear, so that he had to go back and begin again. It was eleven-thirty and he wanted to leave at noon to pick up the boys.

His intercom buzzed and he flicked a switch. 'I have someone on the line from the *Daily Mail*, Mr Marriner. Do you want to speak to them? It's about Mrs Marriner.'

His heart lurched and then steadied. Bad news would come via the police, not Fleet Street. 'Put them through.'

The voice on the other end was nonchalant. 'Just checking, sir . . . is there any change in the situation?'

Richard gave the facts, aware as he did so that there was nothing really to engage interest. Ellie was gone:

that was all. At the beginning there had been a little *frisson* over the manner of her going. Now the few news items that appeared were brief regurgitations of known facts. But the phone call finally convinced him of his inability to settle to work.

He replaced the receiver and closed the Marriner Two-Way folder. He pressed the key to his brother's room. 'Frank? Can you come up for a moment . . . when you're ready. Yes . . . I'm hoping to get away at twelve, so there's no panic.'

Frank would be with him as soon as he got rid of the works convenor. As he waited Richard walked to the window and looked out over the shed roofs, the town of Slough beyond, the fading countryside in the distance. December! Christmas without Ellie. Last year, their first Christmas together, she had filled him a stocking and sat, hugging her knees like a child, to watch him open it. Now he was standing, jingling the change in his pockets, doing nothing at all to bring her home.

She had been a virgin when she came to him on their wedding night, standing by the bed, her hair falling forward on either cheek until he lifted her down-bent head. 'It's all right, Ellie. I love you so much. I'll take care of you.' But he had not bargained for her lack of expertise. She was twenty-seven years old, a career woman who still waited for him to make all the moves. Not like Julia, who had been eager to explore and experiment. But he had loved Ellie's reticence . . . and now he did not even know where she was.

It was useless to say there was nothing he could do. He could beg, go on his knees to police, press, passers-by: 'Find her. Find my wife. I need her, I can't live without her.' Somebody would do something, then, if he bared his soul. That was how things happened. But he couldn't do it.

The phone rang again and he turned back to the desk. Please God let it be some perfectly ordinary business problem. Something he could fix. That was all he had at the moment, the balm of small achievements.

'Have you got any spare cash?' Mike's whisper was anguished and Terri's heart sank. So they were paying. Ahead of them Sam was threading his way towards a corner table, two waiters in tow. That was always a bad sign. It was going to be a mortgage job! As they seated themselves she struggled to extricate her last two tenners and pass them, under cover of the starched cloth, to Mike's waiting fingers.

'This is nice,' she said when it was done and Mike had ceased to look apprehensive. Menus were produced and flourished, and Sam became knowledgeable about the wine list. She looked down the menu and cheered up. Several items at three or four pounds. Except that the bill always came to some astronomical sum, and if you queried it they would take it to pieces and you would find they were right all along and you had egg on your face. If she and Mike got a decent house, though, it would be worth the price of a meal. She gave her order and looked expectantly at Sam.

'About this house,' he said and began to make lines on the white cloth with the points of his fork. Within minutes they were throwing figures around like confetti. Terri tried to take an intelligent interest but she had never been able to understand percentages. Around them Londoners wined and dined, waving expansive arms in the air and wiping dribbling chins between courses. It seemed remote from real life. Who were these people to whom money seemed no object?

'Terri?' They were both looking at her, expecting an answer.

'Sorry,' she said. 'Say that again.'

Mike put down his knife and fork. 'Sam is saying he could probably stretch to 40 thou, which means we could go for something better. What do you think?'

Suddenly she felt flat. They would never escape from the flat, not while the girls were dependent on them. Not while Diana was determined to bleed them dry. 'I think it's up to you,' she said weakly and saw surprise flare up in Mike's eyes. Guilt made her feel defiant. 'There's no point in my going on about what I want. It's a case of what we can get, isn't it? I'm grateful, Sam, for your offer and I hope we can make a deal that's satisfactory all round. But I'm not going to get excited, Mike. Not till I know there's something to get excited about.'

Sam looked suddenly chastened and Mike's jaw was jutting. He would be mad at her for showing him up in front of a friend. But all she had done was tell the truth.

'I'm sorry,' she said again. 'It's not that I'm not excited about the idea, it's just that I daren't let myself get carried away in case it doesn't come off.'

Sam patted her arm. 'It will come off, you'll see. Anyway, eat up and we'll change the subject. It's up to Mike and me to find suitable properties to view.

246

Now, tell me about this friend of yours. Mike says she's done a runner?'

Adele was expecting the girls at three. She had told Ellie to ring at two but at two-thirty she was still pacing the floor, half hoping the phone would ring, half wishful to tidy away thoughts of Ellie and get ready to welcome her daughters. She had made a chocolate gateau and finger sandwiches of smoked salmon, their 'most favourite' food. If only Ellie would ring and get it over, they could all settle down to tea by the fire.

The phone rang and she leaped to answer.

'Adele?'

She lowered herself to a chair, gripping the receiver with both hands. 'Ellie, I'd almost given you up. I'm so glad you've rung. The children are all coming home this weekend so it won't be easy. Let me have your number and I'll ring you back. I want to help you, Ellie. You can trust me!'

At the other end of the line Ellie was demurring. Adele raised eyes to heaven. 'No, I won't tell Richard. I'd have told him already if I'd been going to tell him, wouldn't I? I won't mention it, I promise you. And I don't think you should ring him yourself. Even if the phone is clear, we don't want to confuse the boys, do we? I wish you would give me a number where I could reach you. Let's work everything out together, you and I, and then we can make it turn out right. For everyone. It's not going to be simple. I'm afraid everyone is rather fed-up . . .'

Even to her own ears, her words sounded synthetic,

but she was unused to cajolery. 'Listen, stupid bitch, I am tired of you being the centre of attention,' was what she really wanted to say, but being the one who got Ellie back was the name of the game and there was no other way to do it than plead.

Adele did not succeed in getting an address or a phone number, but she did find out that Ellie had lodgings in Sunderland. The feeling of power as she put down the phone was heady. She was in the driving seat. Before long she would know Ellie's whereabouts and drag her home to all-round applause. *'I did it for the family, Richard.'*

She was still in her day-dream when the Tryons' Rolls crackled over the gravel to the front door.

'Bye! Ta-ta! *Ciao!*' While the girls said their farewells as though they were parting for a decade at least, Adele made small talk with Ben Tryon.

'Awfully good of you, Ben. I could've come myself, but things are a trifle fraught at the moment, so your offer was bliss.'

He inquired discreetly about Ellie and hoped Richard was bearing up.

'He's doing his best,' Adele said. 'We all are . . . but, as you can imagine, it's far from easy.' She sounded brave and sincere and, above all, loyal, and Ben Tryon's smile of admiration was all she could have hoped for.

The boys were waiting by the locker-room door, both dressed in aggressively casual leisure clothes. Richard smiled, remembering how good it had been to cast off the grey suit and regulation shirt when it was time to go home.

'OK, pile everything in. One in the front today, the other on the way back.'

There was the usual small argument and then Gavin slid into the front passenger seat and Jeremy into the back. The first manufacturer to design a family car with two front passenger seats would make a fortune, Richard thought – except that families with more than two children would still have problems.

'Is Ellie back?' They were circling the building, dodging homing boys and seeking parents.

'No, not yet. She's been in touch, though.' But not for days! It was days since Ellie had phoned anyone and that had been the unsuccessful call to Terri.

'Why don't you go and find her, Dad?' Gavin's tone was matter-of-fact.

'It isn't quite that simple, Gavin. I don't know where to begin.' Through the rear-view mirror he saw Jeremy shift slightly, a small frown between his brows.

'You could look for clues,' Gavin said cheerfully. 'Or advertise. Go on TV! I bet *Crimewatch* could get her back.'

'Don't be wet,' Jeremy said, and was rewarded with a lunge from the front seat.

'No fighting,' Richard said automatically as he slowed for the gates. Why had Jeremy scowled like that? Embarrassment over Ellie's departure? It must have been talked about at school. Or displeasure at his father's lack of effort? Richard might be excused for failing to find his wife, but not, perhaps, for failing to look.

As they drove along winding country roads, his hands tensed on the wheel and he forced himself to relax. Mustn't get uptight in front of the boys. 'What are you going to do with yourselves?' he said. 'I'm hoping to make time for an expedition or two. Any ideas?'

Paul carried the pile of folders from the consulting room to the Medical Records office. There were letters to dictate tomorrow, appointments to make, tests to arrange. Miss Frey had been in Medical Records for years and was one step ahead of him most of the time. 'Right, doctor, you can leave all this with me. I do have one message for you. It's about Jenny Dean; you remember her?'

He nodded. 'She hasn't done it again, has she?'

Miss Frey knocked the folders on the desk to bring them into line. ''Fraid so. Wrists again. Superficial. They've got her in 21, mild sedation only. I think they're hoping you'll go up.'

He had wanted to get away early but the one time you walked away was the one time you shouldn't have done. He took the stairs to 21 two at a time and pushed open the swing doors. 'Oh, Dr Weidenek, I was just going to ring for you again. You've heard about Jenny . . . she's creating. Says you won't forgive her this time.'

Patients were lurking everywhere, ears cocked for tit-bits, faces expectant of his time, his attention, his love. *I am being eaten alive*, he thought but he still smiled and put out a reassuring hand as he walked towards the sideward.

Jenny lay still in the high bed with its dolly-mixture-patterned counterpane which matched curtains and wallpaper. There was a small, tight smile of triumph on her lips but the hands below the bandaged wrists were clenched.

'Hallo, Jenny.'

She kept her eyes on the ceiling. 'Hallo yourself.'

He sat down by the bed. 'Why, Jenny?'

Still she did not look at him. 'Felt like it.'

'Why? I thought we agreed this wasn't the way? If you want my attention you only have to ask. I listen, don't I?'

One hand untensed, the fingers flexed and then curled again. 'I was fed-up, wasn't I?'

He stayed silent. Her council flat with its meagre furnishings was enough to sicken anyone, and she had no one. No one who cared, anyway.

'You signed me off,' she said suddenly.

He looked up. 'I haven't! You're due for review in something like a month.' Her hair was a greenish yellow except at the roots, where it was a rusty black. He felt a terrible pity for the raddled face beneath, the mouth down-turned in misery, attenuated cheeks the colour of putty. 'I hadn't signed you off, had I?' he pressed.

She shook her head and blinked furiously. 'No.' A tear formed and began to run towards her mouth. That was good.

'I won't get rid of you, Jenny. Not till you're ready to be rid of me.'

She was half smiling, licking the tear into her mouth. 'Fat chance.'

He reached for her arm and patted it. Tonight they would cosset her, tomorrow too. Colour would come back to her cheeks, the hairdresser would style her hair, the social worker would take her shopping, and in a week she would be a different woman. Then they would send her back to her flat and she would sit watching the four walls, except on the day she came to the Day Centre.

In the end she would resort to a razor blade or cleaning fluid in order to return to the only source of warmth she knew. If he had any real depth of compassion, he would end her pitiless existence. Except that when she smiled he sometimes saw a glimpse of the woman she could be, if he could only get it right.

'You get some rest. We'll talk on Monday.'

He was at the door when she called out, 'Have a nice weekend, doc.'

He turned and smiled at her. 'I'll try, Jenny. I'll try.'

Ellie boarded a bus in Sunderland town centre, clutching her purchases, feeling alternately wicked and exultant. It would be lovely to have the radio, not to be alone in a silent room any more but have the world at a touch of a button. It had only cost £7.99 and would undoubtedly be tinny, but it was a radio. She had also bought a cardigan, a blouse and skirt and a T-shirt, all in the covered market and none of them costing more than £5.99, but the possession of a change of clothing seemed to make a huge difference. If she had stayed in the grey separates much longer Mrs McReady would really have become suspicious. Besides, she had needed something. Something nice. A present for Ellie.

A woman squeezed on to the seat beside her, shopping bag clutched in fat, be-ringed fingers, and they were off, through lighted shops and on to the bridge with its brilliant bulbs.

'Getting ready for Santy?'

Ellie looked up and saw the woman was looking at her. 'Sorry?'

The woman gestured towards Ellie's bags. 'Been Christmas shopping?'

Ellie smiled and nodded. 'Yes, I like to get a bit done before the shops get crowded.'

The other woman was nodding too. 'It'll be a bull-bait before long. I'm glad my big Christmases are over. We go to the daughter's now and I buy for the grandbairns, but only something small. You can't go mad when you've got seven to cater for.'

Ellie smiled agreement.

'What family have you got?' She was looking at the square shape of the radio, believing it to be a toy.

'I have three,' Ellie said, 'two boys and a girl. Well, she's still a baby really. She's not quite two.'

'They're lovely when they're that age,' the woman enthused. 'That's when they're really yours. Once they get to school you lose them, I always say. Does your hubby lend a hand?'

Ellie was giving a put-upon smile. 'When he remembers. You know what they're like . . . taken up with their own affairs. I think he thinks I twiddle my thumbs all day. You should try it, I tell him, but he just laughs. Mind, I can't grumble, he's very good really. Likes his home, all for his family. I'm very lucky.' She went on romancing until they reached St Peter's and it was time for the woman to alight. She could have continued the fairy-tale to her own stop and beyond. Her head was full of tit-bits about her chauvinist husband and impossible though well-loved children.

'I am a liar,' she thought as she put her packages on the vacated seat and looked out on a fairyland of lights. She had always known she was wicked. Even in childhood she had been aware of her own potential for sin. Now it was coming out.

As the conductor came towards her down the aisle she remembered other bus rides with Gran. '*Sit very still, Ellie, I haven't paid for you. Sit very still or the man will come.*' And once, in the cinema, singing and dancing on the screen and terror in her heart: '*I haven't bought you a ticket, Ellie. Sit very still or the man will come.*' The light advancing, flashing along the row, seeking her out. Naughty Ellie, who did not have a ticket, who really had no right to exist at all. *I am nothing*, she thought.

A woman alighted with Ellie at her stop, and gave a frosty smile. 'You're the new tenant, aren't you? I'm Sarah Summers. I have the off-shot.'

They fell into step, side by side. 'I've seen you about. I would have knocked, only I don't really believe in too much fraternization.' It was said so matter-of-factly that it did not sting. 'How are you getting on with the vampire?' She broke into a fair imitation of their landlady: '"I never boast, but I can safely say I put myself out for my guests. Cast your bread, I say. Be a Samaritan." Samaritan? There was more kindness in Belsen. Still, I shan't have to put up with it much longer. Another year and I'm off. It wouldn't pay me to move now, but I'm tempted sometimes. As for that little worm in the big front! He calls himself a military man . . . three months in the DLI and invalided out with athlete's foot. I've got his measure.'

She looked about fifty, smartly dressed for such a big-bosomed woman with an air of command. As if she'd read Ellie's thoughts she continued. 'I'm an HEO . . . Higher Executive Officer, to the uninitiated. I'm with Social Security now but I've moved around a lot. A woman has to if she wants promotion. Boards are so prejudiced if you're not a man with a supportive wife and 2.2 children. But I've got my cottage. In Swaledale, beautiful spot. I've had it for ten years now, get away to it whenever I can. A year to my pension, and then I'm off.'

Ellie tried to display interest. 'Swaledale? That's Yorkshire, isn't it? It's a lovely area.'

They had reached the gate, gleaming in the light of the sodium lamps.

'It's kept me sane, I'll tell you that. I'd never have stuck this place otherwise . . . or some of the others. There's one like her in every town, fleecing the punters and fancying they're doing a public service. I've shopped her to the Revenue. She must be making a fortune here, and I doubt she discloses a penny of it. Check her books, I've told them – but they don't seem interested in default any more.' There was a wistful note in her voice, as though Mrs McReady in Newgate for non-payment of tax was a consummation devoutly to be wished.

As they entered the hall the faint sound of fairground music followed them. 'And then we had those ghastly lights to put up with – what a waste of ratepayers' money. If I didn't deplore civil disobedience I'd support a rates strike.'

Miss Summers went on her way upstairs, Ellie following dutifully in her wake. 'Knock if you need anything,' she said as they parted on the landing. 'And watch your back with our friend downstairs.'

Ellie put away her purchases and brewed tea. Standing to drink it at the uncurtained window she gazed at the triangle of light that marked the sea-front. It was as though she were standing in the wings, in the comfortable darkness off-stage, where prying eyes could not reach.

Behind her the room seemed suddenly familiar and friendly, her place. No one knew she was here and she had become so clever at invention she could maintain that secrecy for ever if she wanted to. She need never go back. 'Back' was pain, fear and rejection; here in this room, in this street, in this northern town, was limbo. Safety.

Inside her head a voice reminded her that night would come and with it all the terrors of darkness, but she would not listen – until a light sprang up in the house opposite and a figure appeared, arms raised to draw curtains, pausing at the sight of her silhouetted across the way. Ellie scuttled back from the window and then returned stealthily to twitch the thin curtains into place.

It was not the same after that. Peace was destroyed and could not be mended. She thought of going out but she craved the safety of her own territory and, besides, it was cold outside. She was about to get out the gin bottle and pour a drink when she saw the clock: six-fifteen. If she started drinking now she would go on till midnight, or until the bottle ran dry. And she must save the pills until they were really needed.

A shiver of self-disgust ran through her, and then came the impulse to do something, anything, as long as it was positive. She picked up her handbag and went on to the landing. Downstairs a sliver of light gleamed from under Mrs McReady's door. She locked her own door behind her and descended the stairs.

'Come in, dear.' Mrs McReady was painted and powdered, and smelled of tea-rose. Black shoes and fine grey stockings, black skirt and white blouse joined by a black patent belt, a cascade of frills snuggling the chin beneath the painted cheeks. Something was up! Sure enough, she drew Ellie through the door and peeped out and upwards. 'It's all right. I'm expecting Mr Corkhill down for a bite of supper. It's only panna-calty but he loves it with black pudding and a nice bit of ham stock.'

Ellie suppressed a smile. So Mr Corkhill had decided to part with his body in exchange for a mess of pottage. 'I won't keep you. I was hoping I could ring my husband, and I wondered if you had any paperbacks I could borrow? I'm not visiting tonight.' She leaned forward. 'I wouldn't be welcome . . . not with the lot that are going in this evening.'

Mrs McReady nodded gravely. 'I know, dear, I know. You don't have to tell me about families. And I've got plenty of novels in the bedroom. I'll look out one or two while you make your call. It's dreadful being bored, and you with no telly. I'd ask you down but . . .' She smiled coyly to indicate that two was company, and Ellie nodded complete understanding.

She was impatient to get to the phone and amazed at her own need to play-act. It was ridiculous but she enjoyed it, like someone throwing up a smokescreen. While the robot voice at the other end droned on she inquired anxiously about children and dogs, gave a hospital bulletin and, sensing ears on the other side of the door, ended with a declaration of undying love. 'And kiss the children for me.'

'*Kiss the children*': she was going upstairs with a borrowed Mills and Boon under her arm when she remembered. '*Are you pregnant?*' Babs had asked, and she had been momentarily shocked, but only momentarily. She had made sure she would not conceive, and now that she was away from Richard she was safe. At the edge of her mind fear flickered. If she ever became pregnant she would die! She had thought carefully about Richard's proposal, for marriage usually meant children; but Richard already had children. If he had not she would have said no.

Mrs McReady's voice came suddenly from behind her. 'You haven't told me which ward Aunty's in, yet, and Edie Bollon's dying to know.'

Ellie knew she would have to leave. The inquisitorial gleam was in the landlady's eye. 'It's 12. Ward 12,' she said despairingly.

When she got to the landing she saw Mr Corkhill's door quiver and then open a crack. 'Is she there?' He mouthed the words rather than uttered them.

Ellie nodded. ''Fraid so.'

His eyes rolled as his door closed silently.

Tomorrow she would have to escape. She could try to tough it out, but she was no match for Mrs McReady and she knew it. Perhaps she could switch cover stories? Mrs McReady might swallow the tale of a runaway wife in hiding from a brutal husband. But Ellie would feel as though she were maligning Richard. She would have to go. In a little while, when she had had a stiff drink, she would count her money and see what escape could be afforded. If only she hadn't spent so much today.

She poured herself a generous measure of gin and added tonic. Worries were nibbling at the edges of her mind and she thought of the pills tucked away in the case inside the wardrobe. One might bring relief, more than one oblivion.

She walked to the window and looked out towards the V of lights that marked the sea-front. She could take the pills and then walk towards the lights and through them to the dark sea. No possibility of fear or struggle with the pills inside her, only the sea, to bear her gently away. Inside her head she could hear it, sucking on shingle, retreating and then advancing inexorably, bearing everything away. The sea would be sure to take her, no possibility of rejection there.

She felt the whimper rise in her, remembering the pain of rejection. Remembering, but not quite bringing it into focus. No one had mishandled her, struck her, deprived her of food or shelter. What *had* they done, then?

Nothing came to mind and instead Ellie refilled her glass. It was only seven and a long night lay ahead. She pulled the curtains to shut out the sea-front and sat down on the edge of the bed to tune the radio. They were playing a medley from *West Side Story* on Radio 2: 'Tonight, tonight . . .'. She couldn't bear to hear love songs but the drink had reached her fingers and she could not find Radio 4. That was always safe, a human voice, droning away, a friend who made no demands. She moved through bands of static and back again before touching the 'Off' button and consigning the soprano to limbo.

In the welcome silence she reached for two sausage rolls she had bought in a baker's shop. They had been warm when she bought them, now they were cold and hard, the flaky pastry solidified and staining the paper bag. She bit down and chewed, and felt the familiar nausea. Perhaps she was pregnant, after all? That would be the final and fitting irony and, in a way, a relief. No doubt then about what to do – she would drag herself like some monstrous turtle towards the sea.

She filled her glass again, feeling her senses reel and welcoming the feeling. Until you knew you had gone too far there was always the possibility of retreat. When you knew you were drunk and there was no going back, you could indulge yourself, accelerate the decline. There was no point then in doing anything else. She threw back her head to drain the glass and reached for the bottle, easing off her shoes by rubbing one foot against the other. The bed creaked amiably at her weight. If Richard had been here they could have made love to the accompaniment of musical springs. It might have spurred him on so that he took her as he had taken Julia.

She thought of Julia, exulting at the onslaught, arching her neck in ecstasy, Richard's hands on her breasts, the fullness of them spilling between his fingers. *'Did you do it like that with her?'* She had wanted to ask him that a thousand times. *'Is it good with me, Richard? Is it better? Am I best? Am I once in my whole life important?'*

She put out a hand for the bedside table and used the other to guide bottle and glass to a resting-place before she began to cry, drawing up her knees and winding arms around them. Dirty thoughts! She was dirty. The ultimate proof of sin. You couldn't be wickeder than that.

Outside the faint sounds of fairground music drowned the rhythm of the incoming sea.

Paul had felt weary during the crossing but once they reached Paris his spirits lifted. The boy was obviously enjoying it and grateful to him for reacting to his plea: 'Let's do something mad, Paul!'

'What did you have in mind?' Paul had asked.

'Oh, I don't know. Take off somewhere. Somewhere nice . . . like Rome or New York.'

Rome and New York had been unavailable at six o'clock on a Friday night but Paris had been possible. They had boarded a train at Victoria and alighted a few hours later in Paris. The hotel Paul used, on the Boulevard de Clichy, had rooms available. Now they were out on the Paris street, walking together through the scents and sounds of that city, no one remarking when they slipped companionable arms around one another. They ate folded crêpes with their free hands, laughed uproariously over everything and nothing, stopped now and then to press their noses against café windows, deciding when and where to have dinner.

'This is great,' Gary said, grinning so that he looked momentarily like a child. They would laugh and talk without tension, go back to the room that looked out on a Utrillo street in the shadow of the *Sacré Cœur*, and talk again, and love, and keep the walls of their happiness around them for two whole days. *I am entitled to this*, Paul thought and sealed his mind against the inevitability of further pain and conflict and fear.

They had made love and it had been nice, in spite of the hard floor and the girls next door. Now they lay close, both tired but unwilling to break away. 'I love you, Terri.'

'How much?'

'A bit.'

'A bit? Scrooge!'

'Well, quite a bit.'

'Why do you beat me, then?'

'Because I'm a brute.'

'You're right there.'

He turned slightly, so that his lips were against her hair. 'Seriously, Terri . . . I wish we could cut out the slanging matches.'

She curled closer. 'So do I. I don't know why I do it.'

'It's not always you. Sometimes I'm so bloody insensitive . . .'

She gripped him. 'You're not. It's me.'

He chuckled. 'Oh God, if we could keep the postcoital agreement going, we'd have the perfect marriage. All the same, it *is* me. It's just that half the time I don't know what to do for the best. I could iron my own shirts, but when I tried it you took the horrors because you said I was making you feel a failure.'

It was true. That was her dilemma, the dilemma of all working women. She wanted to be all things to him, and when that proved impossible she blamed him for it because blaming herself was too much to bear.

'We've had a lot of extra things to put up with lately,' she said. 'And I'm not very good at accepting that you had a life with Diana. I thought I would be, but I'm not. I want . . . if I'm honest . . . I want it to just dissolve and go away. And that's not possible.'

They had relaxed a little, moved away slightly but the bond was still there. Beneath her fingers his chest rose and fell evenly. She had made him happy and now they were talking together: Terri thought she might die of the pleasure of it all.

'I do remember life with Di – the good bits. And when we talk about the kids I still feel we're a partnership. But I don't love her, Terri, I don't hanker after her. I couldn't make love to Diana now if we were alone in the Garden of Eden in an apple glut. If you could just latch on to that, things would be easier.'

But she would never cease to be afraid. Hearing him talk about Diana even now, she felt threatened. She sought a different topic. 'I've been on edge about Ellie this past week.'

It was his turn to hug her now. 'I know. And I'm bloody ashamed of the way I behaved that night. I just didn't take it seriously . . . I mean people don't disappear. Well, not people you know. I thought it was just something you were exaggerating to get at me. Now I believe it. She's gone all right!'

'I was thinking about her today and I realized what was strange about her. It's as though she'd been ironed out. No creases, no bumps, no fissures, nothing to get hold of. I went round the others who were on the paper in Ellie's time. "What was she like?" I said, and they all looked clueless. "Nice". "Easy to get on with". "OK". Nobody came up with one significant fact about Ellie, except that she'd married money and they wished they could follow her example.'

'Money!' Mike groaned. 'Don't let's think about that.' He was withdrawing from her. 'I'm bushed, darling. Got to get some sleep.' They kissed, the sleepy kisses of satisfaction, and she climbed on to the settee. 'Mike?'

'What?'

'If she was your friend, what would *you* do?'

'Not a lot. I mean, it's up to the professionals now.'

'Yes, but . . . I feel so useless. There must be something.'

His voice was slightly testy and she knew it was time to let go. 'If she was my friend I'd feed every tiny detail into the computer and see what came out: that's my tool of the trade. If you want to do something, use the paper.'

[9]

Sitting at the breakfast table with Mike and his daughters, Terri's conscience pricked her. The girls had been angelic, no other word for it. She would never understand how Diana had produced two such thoroughly nice and well-balanced kids, even allowing for Mike's genetic input.

If she had a child it might take after Mike. But a child was not to be contemplated, not with the new house in the offing. They had appointments to view two today and Sam had given the go-ahead: 'You have to live in it. As long as it's sound and resaleable, it'll be OK by me.'

Across the breakfast table Mike was grinning at her. 'Penny for them.' And then, without waiting for an answer, 'You're thinking about 12 Victoria Close and 14 Denbigh Street?'

She saw the girls grin and raised her eyebrows. 'Who? Me? Would I think about houses? Never!'

Gemma wrinkled her nose. 'If you get a house, can we still come?'

Mike's eyes were on Terri.

'Of course you can, darling. Where Dad and I live is

your home too, you know that.' She couldn't meet Mike's eyes, in case the memory of what she had said on Thursday was mirrored in them. *'Your fucking children have ruined my weekend!'* – That's what she had said, or something very like it. In the end, though, it had worked out.

She turned her attention to the girls again. 'When we get the house, before we do anything with it you two can come and pick your rooms. And advise. Dad'll say, "Paint everything brown so it won't show the dirt." I need some feminine support.' They grinned and she sneaked a look at Mike. He was happy now, not wary as he had been yesterday. She must try to make him look like that more often.

The boys were both at the breakfast table when Richard came down, Mrs Withers fussing around them. 'I thought you'd be sleeping in.'

'Waste of time,' Gavin said matter-of-factly. 'Up! Up!' He was dangling bacon rind over a drooling dog.

'Not at the table, Gavin.'

'Just one more bit, Dad. I've got to make them equal. It's natural justice.'

Jeremy groaned. 'Stop talking rot.' His brother's answer was to lob a pellet of bread.

Mrs Withers was smiling indulgently but Richard, after an initial glance, kept his eyes on his plate. Gavin was getting a little above himself. Jeremy was looking at him, expectantly, and Richard knew what he should do but he couldn't face it this morning. For the first time in his life he had no plan of campaign. Even in Julia's illness there had been a clearly defined course to pursue. He had smiled gaily, filled her room with brochures for coming holidays, met her determinedly calm eyes with equal calm, each of them knowing what they had was slipping away; both silently agreed that death's insolence did not deserve acknowledgement.

This was different. He didn't know how to cope with uncertainties unless they were the calculated risks of business, cliff-hanging moments when you held on until the other chap's nerve went. Paul had said, *'We are dealing with imponderables,'* and he was not equipped for such a contest. He folded the *Telegraph* and put it beside his plate, pretending to read as he ate. Ever since he picked up the boys he had been dodging, marking time. And all the while he had been conscious of Jeremy waiting for him to act. He had not realized how deep the bond between the boy and Ellie had been until now, when perhaps it was too late.

'What do you want to do today?' he said at last. 'I thought we might go for a walk this morning.'

Gavin groaned. 'Walking rots your feet.'

Richard made a mock lunge at him. 'You're a lazy young devil. How do you get away with it at school? They used to hound us out on runs in my day.'

Both boys were grinning now. 'Times have changed, Dad,' Jeremy said drily. There was a faint moustache along his upper lip, but it only served to make him look more immature.

I mustn't fail them, Richard thought. *I'm all they've got*. He had felt like that before, after Julia's death, when an almost fanatical desire to care for his motherless children had overwhelmed him. And then Ellie had come along and he had felt a lightening of the load.

Now they were vulnerable again, and he was not sure of his capacity to function alone again. He needed to talk to them, open his own heart and see into theirs. But he did not have the courage to do it.

Ellie was finishing her breakfast tea when the row broke out. She crossed to the door and opened it a crack. Miss Summers was on the landing, resplendent in pink candlewick and sleeping net. 'I know I left it in there. Of course I know I left it. You followed me in. If you didn't take it, who did?' Ellie felt her cheeks flush. Something had gone missing; she was going to get into trouble.

Mr Corkhill came into view, flapping shirt-sleeves and scarlet braces, wispy hair standing on end, a *Daily Mirror* under his arm. 'What d'you think I've done with it, then, silly old faggot? I'd hardly got in the bloody carzy when you banged on the door. Can't even do me bloody ablutions in peace! There was no soap there, I tell you, except my Lifebuoy.'

'I left it on the basin, a full tablet of Pears, hardly touched.' She was holding out an empty soap box. 'See – there it is. Empty. You can't deny that . . .'

It was obvious that long-buried tensions were surfacing; no two people could get so angry over a bar of soap.

'Listen here, you old cow, no one calls me a thief. There's laws about that . . . this is Britain, not Nazi Germany. What've you got under that nightgown – jackboots? If I took that soap, where did I put it? Up me arse?'

Miss Summers was in full flow when Mrs McReady rose like ectoplasm from down below. 'What's going on here? They'll hear you down the sea-front.' Her face was chalk-white except for the pencilled brows, and her curlers had been hastily hidden by a chiffon scarf, but it was the nylon peignoir with its chewed marabou trimming that pushed Ellie's suppressed laughter to hysteria.

She was about to close the door and give vent when Miss Summers uttered the fatal word 'stolen', and Mrs McReady clutched her chest. 'Oh my God, my heart. In my house, my little palace. The place I've slaved for swarming with police. It's too much! I feel faint.'

One eye was fixed vengefully on Miss Summers, the other hopefully on Mr Corkhill. For a moment he wavered and Mrs McReady got ready to swoon into his manly arms, but discretion prevailed. 'Stick your bloody soap,' he said belligerently, and went back into the bathroom with a rattling of bolts.

Mrs McReady straightened up. 'I hope you're satisfied. A gentleman like Mr Corkhill . . . and over a twopenny-ha'penny cake of soap. I wouldn't demean myself to argue over such a trifle. But then some of us have standards.'

Miss Summers stood silent as marabou and nylon were gathered up for a stately descent. Mrs McReady was half-way down when she pulled herself together. 'At least I pay my taxes!' she called down the stairwell.

'Bugger off,' Mrs McReady said serenely, and continued on her way.

'So I got the number of this old lady's ward and went over to the hospital. Your wife'd been there, all right, pumping the old lady for all she was worth. The nurse thought she was still there, in fact, but when I got to the bedside she'd left.'

'Do you think she saw you?' Richard asked. If Ellie knew he was hot on her heels, what would it do to her? His fingers ached from clenching the receiver, and he shifted it to his other hand.

'No, I'm quite sure she didn't see me. I couldn't have missed her in the corridor. She must have left just before I got there. That's three places I've been now that she's also checked up on. I've got another address here . . . a couple who fostered her. This time if she goes there, I'll be waiting.'

'Don't reveal yourself,' Richard said. 'Follow her if she turns up, and then contact me, but don't scare her. The psychiatrist says that would be most unwise, and I must accept his expert opinion.'

'OK, if that's the way you want it.'

There was exasperation in the detective's voice and Richard sympathized. He was getting the man to run a race with his legs tied together. But Paul was very convincing; for the time being, at least, it would have to be his way.

'I know it's frustrating, but that's how it has to be. My sons are with me at the moment but they go back to school tomorrow. After that I'll be free. I'll join you in Durham and we'll work together. In the mean time, do your best.'

Terri loved the house on sight. It was small but light and airy, situated in a tiny close built in the back garden of a huge Victorian terrace in Acton. 'I love it,' she said. 'It's tucked away like a secret garden.'

Mike was less enthusiastic. 'No one will ever be able to find it. They'll be circling around within feet, and never know it's here.'

I wouldn't want them to find it, Terri thought. If she and Mike and a baby were here, in this tiny house with its cypress hedge and shiny door knocker, she would be content never to see another human face.

'It's not much for 90 thou, is it?' he said.

She sensed he was withdrawing and tried desperately to stimulate his interest. 'It's very compact. And it's got decent units in the kitchen, not like the crap we've got at the moment.' This morning, when she had been trying to do her competent stepmum bit, the cutlery drawer had come off its runners and jammed, and she had broken a nail trying to get cereal spoons.

'You don't buy a house for the kitchen, Terri. Anyway, you couldn't swing a cat in there.'

'I wouldn't want to swing a cat.' *Just heat bottles and purée carrots*, she thought, but forbore to say it. She was becoming broodier by the hour, and if Mike got wind of it he would panic and there would be no move at all.

'Well, you know what I mean. We couldn't get in there together, not and move around, so you could kiss me doing the chores goodbye.'

She couldn't resist a derisory hoot. 'What I've never had I'll never miss. You don't do chores, they don't fit your chauvinist image.'

He shook a world-weary head. 'You want to be married to some men. You don't know the meaning of the word chauvinism – I'm a pearl by comparison.

Anyway, we'd better get on if we want to see the other house.'

As they shut the front door Terri looked around. Victoria Close. 12 Victoria Close. Mrs M. Benedict, 12, Victoria Close, Acton. It had a nice ring. 'I like this one, Mike. I like it a lot.'

The other house was in Haringey, an old terraced house that smelled of damp and ancient bricks. 'Nice window,' Mike said of the stained glass on the landing. Terri wanted to say, 'I couldn't live here, Mike,' but discretion kept her silent. She would have to look at every single house they were offered if she was to argue convincingly for Victoria Close. But she had already lost her heart to the house with its through living-room, its tiny third bedroom, and pocket-sized garden just right for a pram.

'Good-sized rooms,' Mike said, crossing the landing. They had T-fall ceilings and made her think of Ingrid Bergman and plopping gas brackets, but she made an enthusiastic sound. God, a wife had to be devious if she wanted to get her own way. Women always saw things with crystal clarity right at the beginning, but they were forced to go through a tortuous charade until men's thought processes caught up.

'What will Sam think?' she said, trying to sound artless. 'The other house is almost new . . . won't that make it a better investment?' But Mike had his head in a built-in cupboard and chose not to reply.

'That's the original dado,' he said as they came down-stairs. He ran his fingers over the raised flowers and leaves. 'Lasts for ever, that stuff. And look at that arch.' A plaster arch at the foot of the stairs was guarded each side by a female head garlanded with leaves. 'God, that's the real "I am",' Mike said, awestruck. 'You usually find they've chipped it off to put in Godawful wall-lights. This is a gem, Terri. It's largely untouched.'

Terri was making rapid calculations about the cost of bringing the house into the twentieth century, and it was mind-boggling. There would be nothing over for a pram, much less a baby.

They closed the front door and tested it to make sure it was locked. 'I'll speak to Sam tonight and arrange another viewing. We don't want to lose out by being too slow.'

Ellie took her case out first and left it at the corner shop. Mrs McReady had four weeks' rent in hand so she was free to say farewell, but she couldn't face an interrogation. She had pondered saying goodbye to her fellow lodgers and decided against it. It was too complicated and, besides, the dust had hardly settled.

Back in her room she gathered the rest of her belongings, left a brief note with her keys on the pillow, and tiptoed down the stairs. She was sure she would be caught in mid-flight but she made the street safely and sped to the shop to collect her case. She had £78 left: if she had to pay four weeks' rent in advance again she would be penniless.

Leaving the shop she looked back at her former lodgings. She had lived there for almost two weeks, but already it seemed remote. She had decided to look for a new room near to the town centre, in the terraced houses beyond the park, where she had seen bed-and-breakfast signs years ago. Perhaps some would remain.

She had noticed another sign, outside a pub in a side street. 'Gold and silver bought,' it had said, 'London prices'. In the early hours she had sorted her jewellery, and those items she was ready to part with were tucked in the back of her purse. She would try to sell first, and would pawn them if that were not possible.

A bus came along the sea-front and she boarded it, clutching bags and holdall and stowing them awkwardly on the rack under the stairs. Above them, as they moved along the road, the remnants of the illuminations swayed in the breeze, bare and tawdry in the light of day. She leaned her head against the window and thought about what lay ahead. Perhaps she should call a halt, use her remaining money to buy a ticket home, and surrender herself to Dr Weidenek. He had begged her to submit to pentothal: 'narco-analysis,' he had called it, but it was still the truth drug. She could not, dared not, give someone else access to her mind.

Richard had told his secretary to call him at home if necessary, but he knew there would be no problems. Short of earthquake or power failure, Marriner's would go on spinning like the well-oiled top it had become. And there was no real need for him to stick grimly to the phone.

As he looked from the window at his sons cavorting with the dogs, relief swept over him. Fatherly pride, at least, was uncomplicated. He leaned over the sill. 'Give me half an hour, and I'll be ready for off.' Jeremy smiled and nodded, and for an instant Richard saw Julia standing there before him in the winter sunlight.

In the bedroom he pulled on a sweater, and rinsed hands and face in the bathroom. He was rubbing his eyes with the towel when he remembered the photographs of Julia that he had put away at the bottom of his wardrobe on the eve of his marriage to Ellie. Only a picture of Julia with the boys in Capri stood on the living-room mantelpiece. He had left that there as a sign to his sons that their mother's place was unaltered. The colour photograph had faded until their features were indistinct, and he wanted to see Julia again, to check Jeremy's resemblance.

As soon as he lifted the lid of the box he knew they had been disturbed. He had never looked at them since he put them away, he had even forgotten their existence, if he were truthful. Mrs Withers would not have pried – it must have been Ellie. He lifted the frames one by one and put them aside. They were all there. Then he turned to his chest of drawers and looked for the special one he had put there. It was missing! Julia on her wedding day, smiling above stephanotis and lilies. Why had Ellie wanted Julia's photograph?

He made a swift search of the room before he accepted that she had taken it with her. In God's name, why? Perhaps he should mention it to Paul: it was part of the jigsaw, after all. He was putting the box back into the wardrobe when he saw the album. It was not his, and a quick glance showed it belonged to Adele. It was full of photographs of Julia – Julia aged seven with pigtails; Julia at eleven with braces on her teeth and an unashamed grin; Julia, solemn for once, in a school photo; self-conscious in her first high heels. Julia

275

and Adele, arms linked on either side of a tennis-net, rackets at jaunty angles.

He felt his heart lurch at the sight. Julia had been lovely even then, and Adele striking. The other night he had looked at her across the dinner-table, thinking she was good to look at but would not be good to hold. Her forearms were muscular and strong and her hands square. Ellie had been like a bird beneath his hands, fragile to the touch. He had mentioned her then, and had seen Adele's neck glow red beneath the pearls until he changed the subject. Now he looked down at the album. She had deluged Ellie with photographs of Julia and probably with reminiscences, too. She hated Ellie. He should have realized that from the beginning.

Five minutes later he was breasting the rise behind the house, boys ahead of him, all of them laughing at the antics of dogs drunk with freedom. 'You'd think they hadn't been out for yonks,' Gavin said. He was wearing a sweater Ellie had knitted him, a brilliant pink that Richard would never have chosen for a boy. But Gavin had pounced on it with glee and worn it almost non-stop since. Ellie had understood them, and yet she had no experience of children.

They paused on the crest of the rise and looked around. 'England,' Richard said with satisfaction.

'Britain,' Jeremy said automatically. 'England,' Richard repeated firmly. 'If it's all right to be Welsh or Scots, I refuse to be defensive about being English.'

They were moving down the other side now, gathering pace as the ground fell away. 'It's still Great Britain,' Gavin said, hoping for controversy. 'It's the best place.

Everyone wants to get in here and no one wants to get out, so it must be.'

The statement produced the desired effect. Jeremy countered with statistics on emigration as opposed to immigration, and Gavin rose serenely above the facts and stuck to his original thesis.

'I love them,' Richard thought. He had never expected to enjoy fatherhood. It was something you did in the fullness of time to please your wife. But without the boys he'd have sunk without trace. Ellie had decreed that there should be no children: '*Not for a while*,' she had said, the only stipulation he had ever known her make. But a child was growing somewhere, his child, boy or girl. His child under threat, even already aborted. Perhaps that was why she had gone? They had never thought of that.

He halted at a stile. 'I think we should go back,' he said.

Adele followed the girls upstairs, all of them weighed down with packages and dress bags. 'You've been an angel, Mummy darling,' Sara said, but she spoke absently. 'Now, if I can have some peace . . .' She gave Emma a warning glare and went into her room, shutting the door behind her.

'She's doing it again,' Emma said aggressively.

'What?' Adele had put her own packages down and was helping her younger daughter to unload.

'Flouncing off,' Emma said. 'She does it all the time now. Flounces off.'

Adele looked at her curiously. 'Where did you get that word from?'

'Gee Gee said it . . . "Don't flounce off, Sara," she said and everyone giggled. Sara was mortified.' This last was said with satisfaction.

'Gee Gee should retire,' Adele said. 'She was past it in my time – Aunt Julia was frightfully good at imitating her. I know Sara can be a pain sometimes but it's best to ignore her. I wish you could've seen Aunt Julia imitating Gee Gee . . . she was so funny.'

But Emma was delving into her parcels and didn't seem to care. 'They've forgotten Julia,' Adele thought and turned away, disconsolate. She could see Emma in the mirror, fair hair tumbling into her eyes, freckles still prominent on her cheeks in spite of winter weather. She was Frank's child. So was Sara, even in the way she laughed. 'You ought to have your hair cut before you go back,' she said, but there was no reply.

'I might as well not exist,' Adele thought, and began to gather up her parcels.

When she had put away her shopping it was time to prepare for Ellie's call. She unplugged her bedroom extension, hid it in the wardrobe, and left the living-room door open so she could monitor the extension in the hall. Ellie had promised to ring at a specified time but it might be a long wait.

Adele had changed into slacks and a silk shirt but she felt chilly. Outside the lights was already fading, and birds, homeward bound, flew purposefully across the sky. She felt a sudden lowering of her spirits, thinking of the girls upstairs, preferring their own company to hers, and Frank, outwardly an attentive husband but less and less in love with her. She had looked forward to the girls coming home but they didn't want her company.

Last night she and Frank had talked of Japan. He had been querying the florist's bill and she had teased him: 'Take me to Japan, and I'll learn the secrets of ikebana so I can do wonderful things with one bloom and a handful of twigs.' His face had remained impassive and she had tried again.

'Oh come on, don't be an old Scrooge; tell me I can come. I won't be a scrap of trouble. Put me out of my misery.'

He had gone on writing cheques as he spoke. 'If you're in misery, my dearest, it's of your own making. I have never even hinted at your coming to Japan, much less promised. We can't leave Richard alone – I would think you could see that for yourself. One of us has to stay. I have to go, *ergo* you remain. And frankly I'm getting tired of the subject.'

She was saved from further soul-searching by the sight of Sara holding her grey Caroline Charles. 'I found this in your wardrobe, Mummy. It's not as bad as some of your gear. Can I take it back with me? It's far too trendy for you.'

Adele moved away from the phone. It wouldn't do for Ellie to ring while Sara was in earshot. 'Take it back upstairs. Now! Shoo.' She followed her daughter up the stairs, all the while on edge in case the phone should ring.

'All right,' she said grudgingly, when they were safe in the bedroom. 'But I want it back – intact!' Her Caroline Charles went into Sara's case along with her silver gate bracelet and the last of her Femme scent.

'Now is that everything? You always seem to forget something vital, and Daddy or I have to race across three counties before nightfall.'

Sara was indignant. 'Once, Mummy, that happened once! You're always throwing it up. It's not fair. Emma is far more disorganized and you never say a word, just because she's the baby.'

From the adjoining room came an indignant shout. 'Pig!'

Sara was unrepentant. 'Well, it's true.'

Adele felt a sense of impending doom. There was going to be an argument, and Sara would go away hating her. 'Come on,' she said, wanting to sound reasonable and instead sounding ingratiating, 'we'll have time for tea before Daddy gets back. I've got choux buns. You can finish your packing tomorrow.'

Sara was mollified. 'Thanks, Ma, but no thanks. I'm not hungry.'

Next door Emma let out a shout. 'She's fasting, that's what she's doing. She won't touch school food and she lives on the scales in the San.'

Visions of anorexia rose in front of Adele, Sara down to four stone, drip-feeding, amenorrhea, and a mental home. 'You're not fat, darling, you're beautiful.'

Emma had come to the doorway. 'She won't listen. She's besotted with Charlie Grant, from UV1 – that's why she starves. Because he thinks she's obese.'

Sara hurled herself across the room. 'Little beast. He does not! God, you're a creep. I hate you.'

Adele stood in the centre of the room. This was all she needed; she had never wanted St Kit's to go co-ed . . . and now this! Emma fled in a rain of shoes, and

280

Sara turned back. She was fourteen years old and had breasts like a woman of twenty.

'You're not doing anything silly, darling? I mean, I like you to see boys at home, you know that. But at school . . . well, you are being sensible?'

Sara sat down on the bed. 'Mummy, you've gone red. You're not on about sex, are you? Trust you to be miles behind the times. It's purity now; didn't you know? Sex is vile.'

'I didn't mean anything like that.' But they both knew she had meant just that. 'I handled it badly,' Adele thought. 'And I always thought that when the time came I would do it rather well.'

Sara's mood had changed. 'Come on, you're all red and crumpled. You've told me the facts of life, haven't you? Well, leave me to get on with it. I'm not a complete idiot.'

Adele felt near to tears, overcome with the temptation to tell someone, anyone, about the phone calls from Ellie. But Sara would despise her. This morning she had expressed sympathy for her missing aunt: 'We could have been nicer to her, couldn't we? When she comes back I think we should make a super effort.' And Emma had shaken her head: 'She may never come back. I think she's got a death wish; I saw it in her face last hols.'

'Don't be silly,' Adele said, trying to keep a smile on her face. Increasingly she felt as though she were play-acting. Coaxing, cajoling, begging people to like her, frightened in case they would not. She was always on the losing side. Even with Ellie, the balance of power was shifting. A week ago she had had the upper hand, but things had somehow gone awry. Soon the phone would ring, and Adele was afraid the call would take her even further out of her depth.

Ellie had walked for half an hour, dragging her bags, before she saw a bed-and-breakfast sign. On her way she passed the corner shop, where she had once lived with the Harpers. It was no longer a shop; its window had been altered to an ordinary sash and the newly inserted bricks showed up like a scar. She wondered briefly if the Harpers still lived there. Tomorrow she would try to find out. They had been kind in their way, but they had not really cared. All the same, they might know something.

At the edges of her mind the music started again. But Ellie had become adept at quelling it now, and it got no further than the first bar. If she found decent lodgings, with a landlady unlike Mrs McReady, she might let it re-emerge, even encourage it, let the tune roll through to its conclusion, and face the terror that lurked where the music stopped. For now, though, she must put a roof over her head. She mounted the steps of the house displaying the sign and lifted the knocker.

The man who answered was unshaven and apologetic. 'Sorry, love, that notice should've come out last week. We're full. Couldn't get you in with a shoe horn.'

Ellie had put down her bags, now she bent to pick them up and resume her search. 'Tell you what, try No. 9, she takes students sometimes. Don't be put off if she's a bit offhand. She's arty-crafty, works at the art school, but the place is clean. Mind, she might be pricey. Still, you can always ask.'

The owner of No. 9 was young and striking. Black hair sprang from a broad forehead and was pulled back to cascade down her left shoulder. A huge enamel ear-ring hung from her right ear, and she wore un-relieved black except for a matching enamel brooch at her neck. She looked at Ellie critically. 'How long would you want a room?'

Ellie tried desperately to figure out what answer would find favour, but the woman's patience ran out before she had reached a conclusion. 'I can't promise anything beyond Christmas. I may be moving on then.'

Ellie had a cover story ready and it fitted. 'Oh, that's perfect. I really only want something for a few weeks. I may be moving up here permanently, and if so, I'll want to buy. In the mean time I still have my place down south. I don't want to sell till I'm sure . . . I've taken this job up here, you see . . .' She was all pre-pared to rattle on but her listener's eyes had glazed and Ellie's own voice died away.

'I keep myself to myself,' the girl said, obviously relieved. 'I expect you like to do that, too?' It was a warning and Ellie nodded. 'It's £20. Everything con-tained except loo and bath. I have a shower downstairs you can use in an emergency. Do you want to see the room?'

It was light and airy even at dusk, with a window that gave on to the park. There were Mucha posters on the walls and a faded but beautiful patchwork quilt on the bed. 'I like it,' Ellie said. 'Would two weeks do as an advance?' The woman had not asked for references and seemed uninterested even in the money.

She must like the look of me, Ellie thought, but when

she gazed in the dressing-table mirror the face that stared back was gaunt, with blue-circled eyes and hair, deprived of professional attention for too long, that hung round her face like string. She looked round the room: it was nice, so why did she feel such despair? Time and money were running out, but it was more than that. She had run away to find herself and in the process had lost what little identity she already had. There had been nothing to run to, that was it. She was a creature of a cover story now, shadowy and insubstantial. Tomorrow she would spin another tale, tell another lie. 'I am nothing,' she said aloud, and there was no one to deny it.

Lights sprang up suddenly outside in the street, and she switched off the room light. There was safety in darkness, in standing there a ghost in a ghostly room, as vague as the unreal women in the posters, all shadow without substance. The tune started up in her head again, but when it came to the vital line the music stopped, clicking, clicking . . . Ellie started to cry and sank slowly to the floor, feeling the cord carpet harsh to her fingers, reaching out and searching for she knew not what.

The novelty of being in an expensive restaurant had worn off and Gavin was beginning to fidget. Jeremy scraped up the last of his pavlova and licked the spoon.

'You could have another,' Richard said.

Both boys cast an eye at the sweet trolley and then shook regretful heads.

'No thanks,' Jeremy said.

Gavin burped slightly. 'I'd like to, because you

choose the best one and then when you get it it isn't.'

Jeremy groaned. 'What are you talking about?'

Gavin shrugged. 'You know what I mean. It's hard to choose, and when you do you wish you hadn't . . . 'cos the other things look creamier, or something.'

Richard smiled. 'We know what you mean. The other man's grass is always greener . . .'

Gavin looked uncomprehending and changed the subject. 'When can we go?'

A waiter bustled up and began to clear. 'Coffee, please,' Richard said and then, looking at the boys, 'Would you prefer something else?'

'Is it little cups?' Jeremy asked.

'I'm afraid so,' Richard said, glancing at the waiter's pained expression. Coffee here was a speciality of the house, black and strong and served in extremely small quantities.

'I'll have Coke then . . . or the nearest they've got.'

'Me too,' Gavin said, and the waiter turned away. 'Everywhere has Coke,' Gavin added. 'They keep it for the tourists.' He looked at his huge and intricate watch. 'Twenty-four hours more and then it's back to jug.' He sounded gloomy but his face gave the lie to his words. Richard had watched him become bored with home in the last two days and begin to long for school and its companionship. When Ellie had been here, she had known how to occupy them.

He tried to make conversation. 'It won't be long to Christmas.'

'What'll happen then?' Jeremy asked. He didn't mention Ellie, but Richard knew what he meant.

'We'll have a good time. I hope Ellie will be back by

then. Last Christmas was good, wasn't it? Hopefully she'll be back and able to organize us as she did last year. But I can't promise that. I simply don't know what will happen about Ellie. What I can promise is that you two will have a good time. Uncle Frank and Aunt Adele and the girls will be there, and Mr and Mrs Withers. We'll have a tree . . .' His voice trailed away. What if they were still looking for Ellie at Christmas . . . or mourning a tragedy?

'Ellie wanted a tree outside,' Jeremy said. 'Not a bought one; a real tree that was growing but all lit up with lights. She asked Mr Withers about it last year but there wasn't time to fix it up. It has to be earthed and all sorts of things.'

'One more thing I never knew,' Richard thought. Aloud he said, 'We could talk to Mr Withers about it tonight. Start the ball rolling. It would be a nice surprise for Ellie, to find we'd fixed it up for her coming home.'

Across the aisle a woman was staring, looking away when he caught her eye. He realized he had met her somewhere before. 'See,' her expression said, as she leaned to whisper to her companion, 'he's putting a good face on it, lunching his sons, and not knowing where his poor wife is.' He had no doubt her curiosity was well meant, but it irked him just the same. He would have liked to get to his feet and bellow his anger, but you couldn't do things like that.

Coffee came, and Coke in glasses misted over with chilling. 'Could we go to Hamleys?' Gavin said between sips.

'It's for kids,' Jeremy said. 'I'd rather go to the British Museum.'

Gavin's eyes rolled heavenwards. 'Bo-ring! Might as well be back at school.'

'There's a good joke shop near there,' Richard said. 'We can do Hamleys, then the Brit, and wind up in the shop to get some tricks and gew-gaws for Christmas.'

'Gew-gaws?' Gavin said. 'Translation please, Dad?'

'I don't know that I can translate it . . . it means bits and pieces, I think. Odds and ends, only rather complicated, amusing odds and ends. It's one of those words I've always known. I think my mother used to use it.'

'I remember Grandma,' Gavin said. He sounded reflective and his face had grown still.

'What do you remember?' Richard asked, suddenly curious.

But Gavin took refuge in a shrug and it was left to Jeremy to speak. 'She was awfully grand. I mean, more than usual. And everyone was a bit scared of her.' He shifted a little uneasily. 'Mummy used to want us to be good when we went there.' He had been five when his mother died, seven when he lost his grandmother.

'How do you remember that?' Richard asked, amazed.

'I don't know. I just do. And she had pincers for sugar.' He made nipping movements with his fingers, which amused Gavin and made them laugh.

While they were drinking their Coke Richard tried to remember his own childhood. His mother had been kind, certainly, and sympathetic to pain or illness, but he had always been conscious of the limits of her affection. *'That's enough, darling!'* – she had had a special

287

voice for those words, a tone that said, 'No more'. He was brought back to earth by a guzzling sound from Gavin's empty straw.

'Honestly, Dad,' Jeremy said, 'isn't he the end!'

They had not really discussed Ellie, yet – it was not natural, and it troubled Richard. Over lunch they had talked about Nigel Mansell's lost chances of the World Championship, the merits and demerits of *Spitting Image*, and the possibility of go-carts for Christmas, when they ought to have been talking about the absence of a family member. It was up to him to broach the subject but he hadn't been able to find words. Perhaps if he had treated it as a board meeting: '*Gentlemen, as you see from the agenda* . . .' But this was more than an item for discussion, it was the very fabric of their lives. What had Paul said about repeated loss? If Ellie never came back it would affect the boys for the rest of their lives. Though it might not show, it would condition them to loss, and that was dangerous.

Again, his anger stirred. How could she have done this to them, she who had always sympathized with their loss? But even as he questioned her behaviour, he knew his own had been questionable. He had married Ellie for love, because he found in her something he had found in no other woman, but instead of treasuring that difference, exploring and understanding it, he had simply expected her to step into the space that had been Julia's.

'I want to talk to you about Ellie,' he said aloud and saw apprehension and relief mingle on the boys' faces.

'I *hope* she comes back for Christmas,' Gavin said, sounding slightly aggrieved. 'I'm making her a spice

288

rack in Hobbies. It'll be a bit of a waste if she doesn't turn up.'

Hysteria rose in Richard's chest and a terrible fear of screaming aloud, until he saw Jeremy's eyes fixed on him, understanding, reassuring, amused at Gavin's outrageousness but not thrown by it. He pulled himself together. 'I want her back before then, old chap. I want her back now, instanter. If anyone has any ideas on how to bring that about, I'm listening.'

'Why doesn't she ring up any more?' Jeremy said. Richard had asked Paul that same question and received an inconclusive answer.

'I don't know. She did once at the beginning. Perhaps she's afraid we might persuade her if she lets us talk. I don't know. There are lots of things about Ellie I don't know.' Their eyes were on him, wary, and he hastened to qualify his remark. 'Not bad things . . . just things that happened to her when she was very young. I should have taken more interest in them. If I had, I'd have some idea of where she is now.'

Gavin was fiddling with the cutlery but Jeremy was intent. 'Why does that matter?'

'Paul Weidenek . . . that's the psychiatrist, you met him, remember? . . . he thinks she's gone back to the place where she grew up. He thinks she was very unhappy when she was a child and that it's making her unhappy now. I know it's hard to believe, but there wasn't any other real reason for her to go so he's probably right.'

Jeremy was nodding. 'I always thought she was sad. That was why she was so good about things. I mean, she understood if you felt a bit iffy. She didn't say things like . . . well, like Aunt Adele does . . . you know, like counting your blessings and pulling your socks up.'

'Platitudes,' Richard said and after an initial hesitation Jeremy nodded.

Gavin was still shuffling spoons but decided to join in anyway. 'She wasn't like a stepmother. She was too young for one thing and she didn't poison apples and shut us in cellars, or anything.' He looked put out at their burst of laughter. 'It's all very well to laugh, but when you say you've got a stepmother everyone goes "Ugh!" I'm only saying what people say. I put her in my family tree in History and everyone said I was mad.'

Poor Ellie, Richard thought, wiping a tear of almost mirth from his eye, unable to find her proper place even in a school exercise book.

'Could we get some Kentucky Fried on the way home?' Gavin asked. 'There's one in every street in London.'

Adele wore her aquamarine shift and her gold snake necklet. 'It will do Richard good to have company,' she said when Frank raised his eyebrows. 'He's bound to feel lonely sometimes. Anyway, this is a special evening for the children.'

As soon as the words were out she regretted them. The girls had already cried off: 'Not a dreary family gathering on our last night, Mum. Not even you could be that mean! We're going over to the Tryons to listen to records.' No doubt Richard's boys were equally unenthusiastic.

But Jeremy and Gavin were there when they arrived,

handing out sherry and dashing backwards and forwards to the kitchen to report Mrs Withers' progress, or lack of it.

Richard took his seat at the head of the table. *He looks ghastly*, Adele thought, but this time it was hard to blame Ellie. She thought of the anguished voice on the phone this afternoon: *'Give them my love, Adele. Tell them I'm sorry. I'm sorry about everything. I may ring you tomorrow . . . it all depends . . .'* Adele had gone on asking questions but it had been pointless. *She doesn't really hear me*, she had thought and had wished once more that she had not begun the deception.

She looked up to find her brother-in-law's eyes on her. They were bleak, but when he spoke his words were kind. 'I've been thinking about Japan, Adele. I think you should go with Frank. You'd enjoy the break, and there's nothing you can do here.'

Adele beamed her thanks, looking at Frank to see how he felt. All he did was raise his glass in a mock salute. 'To Tokyo,' he said. That was all. Not, 'Marvellous, darling. I want you with me.'

She raised her own glass (Waterford crystal – she had always begrudged Ellie the crystal!). *'Sayonara, Marriner-san.'*

By now, excitement should have been filling her chest, a thousand euphoric wing-beats of it, but there was nothing. This was what she had hoped and schemed for, but it didn't feel right somehow. What had Ellie meant by *'it all depends'*?

'Are you sure you don't want me to stay here, Richard? Something is bound to happen soon.' Frank's expression softened slightly, at least Adele thought it did. 'I would like to go to Japan, I'll admit it. But not if it means leaving you in difficulties.'

Richard was adamant that she should go but Adele hardly listened to his arguments. She felt unreal. She had put so much energy into getting her own way, taken terrible risks to bring it about, but she had achieved nothing. She was not going to Japan because she had manoeuvred it, she was going because Richard had decreed it, which somehow rendered it worthless. And Frank didn't want her there; that much was obvious. For a moment she wondered if he had someone else, but in her heart she knew it was not so. She could have coped with that, fought tooth and nail to keep him. Against the wall of his indifference she had no weapon.

She looked down at her plate, afraid her agony would show on her face. 'Courgettes, Aunt Adele?' She smiled and took the tureen Jeremy was proffering.

The food was perfectly cooked but it turned to ashes in her mouth. She chewed bravely, looking around the room as she did so in case she caught anyone's eye. She had done a good job on the house, no one could deny that. If Frank had given her a free hand in her own home, she could have surpassed all this. But he didn't understand the importance of gracious surroundings. He had made no effort when his parents died, so Julia had got everything – or at least everything that mattered. Not that she had begrudged Julia anything, but she had had Anstruther pieces of her own . . . the kind of thing she herself would have brought to Frank if most of Mummy and Daddy's nice things had not had to be sold. Family possessions, passed down the generations, auctioned off for a pittance. What was left would come to her when Mummy died . . . her train of thought shuddered to a halt in a morass of guilt, and when she looked up, Frank's eyes were on her, cool and speculative, as if he knew the full depravity of her thinking.

As they walked home together, Adele wondered if she should tell him about Ellie's phone call. Not about all of them, just today's. 'I forgot,' she could say – except that no one would believe her. But if Ellie rang tomorrow . . . she could tell them then. Own up straight away and make it seem that she was helping. She wanted to help really. Tonight, looking at Richard's drawn face, she had simply wanted peace for them all. '*It all depends*,' Ellie had said. There was something sinister about those words.

'Frank . . .' She was getting ready to confess when he interrupted her.

'I know what you're going to say, Adele. OK, I'm not going to raise any more objections. If it's all right with Richard, who am I to disagree? I only ask one thing. We're going on a business trip. Five short days. For God's sake don't take half your wardrobe. You make us look ridiculous, sometimes.'

Above them the sky was vaulted and mysterious, sprinkled with stars. Adele walked on over the crisping grass, the tears that had welled in her eyes chilling on her cheeks.

[10]

'Ouch!' The heat from the gas tongs had seared Terri's scalp and she turned to disentangle them.

'God, I hate the smell of singeing hair,' Mike said equably, licking in marmalade from the side of his mouth. They had been awake since five, discussing houses, so breakfast was, for once, a leisurely affair.

'It isn't hair you can smell, it's flesh. The things I do to get beautiful for you.'

Mike shook his head emphatically. 'Not for me. It's a fallacy that women dress to please men. If it were true, you'd go around in G-strings, four-inch heels and Chanel No. 5.'

She aimed at him with her slippered foot. 'Sexist pig! Anyway, it's eight o'clock – we have to decide.'

'We could leave it. Look at other houses.' He was teasing and they both knew it.

'No, we couldn't. It has to be now.'

He raised his eyebrows. 'What's the hurry?'

She kicked out again. 'Because if we don't get Victoria Close I'll die – that's the hurry.'

He shook his head as though in doubt. It was a delicious tease and they kept it going.

'What you're saying, Terri . . . now let's get this straight . . . what you're saying is that I have to decide between the two houses, but whatever I decide it'll have to be Victoria Close?'

She wound the final curl and nodded. 'Yes, that's what I'm saying.'

He shrugged. 'It'd better be Victoria Close, then. I know when I'm beaten.'

She was shrieking with glee and tearing the tongs from her hair. 'I love, I love you . . . do you mean it? Oh, I can't believe it.'

He submitted to her onslaught and then reached for his jacket. 'I'll ring Sam today and say we're ready to go ahead. You're sure you've made your mind up? I mean, won't you miss the period elegance of this place?'

She fell on his neck again, nuzzling him with pleasure. 'I've been happy here . . . give or take the odd row . . . but I'd still like to move to Victoria Close, please. Tomorrow!'

When he had gone she combed out her hair. It looked a mess, and the dye-job was becoming a matter of life or death. There would be no cash for hairdressing if they got the house – but she could always go back to mouse. Nothing could depress her today. Nothing! Except perhaps thoughts of Ellie, and she meant to do something about her this very day.

There was nothing in particular on her agenda. The running series on the new morality was taking up a double page each day this week, and today and tomorrow there was a two-parter on rock stars and their money. She would have to go through the motions, but in fact the day would be free, so she could take an extended lunch hour and go to the Central Register in search of Ellie's antecedents.

She looked at the clock: eight-fifteen. Time to do what she had meant to do last night and find a good snap of Ellie. No use looking for a studio portrait, Ellie had never been vain enough to sit for one. A snapshot would have to do; if she took it in today Pictures might play around with it and blow it up into something usable.

She carried the drawerful of photographs over to the bed and sat cross-legged to search. She and Ellie at Brighton; Ellie with next-door's dog when they had lived in Earl's Court; a flashlight shot at an office party, Ellie on the outskirts holding a tray of glasses. Terri flipped through a dozen more, regretting that she herself had almost always been the centre of attraction. Why had she never got hold of Ellie and posed her? Because she had never cared enough, that was why. She went back to the photo of Ellie with the dog, cuddling it to her and smiling into the camera. Perhaps it would do.

She put it on the bed, bundled the rest back, and was putting the drawer into its hole when she saw Mike's wallet on top of the chest. He must have forgotten it when he changed from his suit. She picked it up, considering whether or not he could get through the day without it. She was still considering as she flipped it open.

Notes loose in the centre, credit and cheque cards in little pockets, a dry-cleaning ticket which looked as though it had been in the stamp pocket since the flood, and the bank slip holding his personal number for cash withdrawals. You weren't supposed to keep it with the card – she would have to remind him of that. She was closing the wallet when she saw the tip of the photograph protruding from the inmost pocket. She pulled, and two snapshots emerged. One of Gemma and Alison, ages about six and seven, clutching buckets and spades and squinting into the sun. And another of Diana, lean and brown in a striped bikini, lying on a towel brandishing an admonitory finger at the cameraman.

Inside Terri, a weight descended, a physical presence cutting off breath. She couldn't bear it. She couldn't, couldn't bear it. Slowly she slid the photographs back into place and closed the wallet. A wail was forming in her chest but it was too painful to let it go in tears. Instead she crossed to her dressing-table and began to line up bottles and jars with methodical correctness.

Ellie leaned her head against the window. Somewhere in the house someone was playing an instrument. Not a guitar, perhaps a sitar. She half smiled, picturing a bearded guru plucking at strings. Life was so strange. She had looked from the window earlier and seen sari-clad women hurrying duffle-coated children to school. In a generation, two at the most, duffles would have won and the bright saris be lost from British streets, which would be a pity.

There must be a number of immigrant families here. Dark little faces had peeped from several windows as she walked the streets yesterday, vanishing quickly behind curtains if she met their eyes. It was curious but all children looked alike – Asian, European, African, there was a universality about them, so that you wanted to reach out for them. But in the end it would not do.

Across the landing the strange music twanged out but the familiar music in her head was drowning it. Ellie shut her eyes and clutched her arms around herself, swaying backwards and forwards. It was there, it was almost there . . . the music and the clicking, and then the sugar bursting, spreading out into the road!

She sat down on the Lloyd Loom chair. There had been sugar glistening on the wet road, turning brown at the edges as the damp took it, and she had looked at the black mouth of a drain and wanted to crawl inside. And the man had run towards her and scooped her up in his arms.

Outside in the street a child was crying. That was real. Inside Ellie's head the images retreated, and after a moment she got to her feet and went on with her preparations for the day. She felt better knowing she had something positive to do, an important task: to buy a pregnancy-testing kit. Not for any special reason. Just to be sure. She had tried and tried to remember the date of her period, but it eluded her. And she must be sure.

There were so many things to think about. Raising some cash for one thing, and then looking up the Harpers. It was fifteen years ago but they were not the type to move around much. And after the Harpers, the library.

Adele was clutched by welcoming hands. 'Darling, we wondered if you'd make it. No news, I suppose? No, well . . . try and forget it for this morning at least.'

Sue was drawing her in to the noise and the heady smell of expensive perfume. 'Everyone's here. Flicky's coming on later, she's on the bench this morning. You know Diana Forbes-Carteret? No? I'll introduce you. She was at school with Sarah Ferguson . . . well, actually she was leaving as Fergie arrived, but her sister was in the same year as Jane Makim. Diana, can I introduce Adele Marriner, one of my oldest and dearest friends? She works terribly hard for us. I'll leave you to get to know one another . . . I see Lady Dobson's arrived.'

Diana Forbes-Carteret was handsome rather than beautiful, Adele decided, and she felt a shaft of fellow-feeling. Around them the charity brigade was in full flood. 'Nothing like animals for arousing enthusiasm, is there?' Diana said, and smiled, revealing flawless teeth. She looked like a young Judith Chalmers and the be-ringed hands clutching her bag were brown and strong.

'Do you ride?' Adele said, accepting a cup of coffee.

'Not if I can help it,' Diana said cheerfully. 'As soon as I was old enough to say no, I did. I was a lousy horsewoman.'

Adele felt a small glow of superiority form inside her, and began to relax.

'Ladies, can I have your attention? The tombola is fabulous, Verity and Agnes have simply laboured over it. We're also going to have an auction, so get out your cheque books.' Their hostess had an ambitious gleam in her eye. This coffee morning must raise a record sum; honour demanded it.

'My husband calls us "Pooch-befrienders",' Diana

299

whispered under cover of her coffee cup. 'He thinks we should give everything to the NSPCC, instead. But I love my dogs. Besides, the tax man should look after deprived kids – God knows he takes his cut.'

'Adele, I'm so glad to see you.'

Adele turned. 'Virginia . . . it must be ages. Do you know Diana Forbes-Carteret?'

Virginia was nodding enthusiastically, looking more like Joyce Grenfell than ever. 'Of course. Old friends. Now, tell me, has the wandering sister-in-law returned to the fold? Everyone's dying to know, but Sue said we weren't to ask. Bosh, I said, Adele's not the sensitive type.'

Adele cast a quick look in Diana's direction. She had the fixed smile of someone who doesn't know what's being talked about and is too polite to inquire. 'I'm afraid my sister-in-law has had some sort of mental breakdown. She's gone off, God knows where, and Richard, her husband, is simply frantic.'

Diana tut-tutted politely. 'He's not Richard Marriner, is he . . . of CBI fame?'

Adele tried not to preen. 'Yes . . . I suppose he is. Of course, she was his second wife. It's not the same, is it? You might have known his first wife – Julia Anstruther? She was my greatest friend. I miss her terribly.'

They were looking polite but uninterested. It was a relief when someone came round selling tickets and everyone dived into handbags. Afterwards there was a quite deliberate shift in the conversation, as though missing relatives were not quite nice. Virginia admired Diana's tan, suggesting it had been acquired elsewhere.

'Hawaii – we got back last week. It's a fantastic place, lush greenery one minute, the next the landscape of the moon. We went on impulse. Robert said, "Where to?" and I just said, "Hawaii", I don't know why, but it was an inspired choice.'

Virginia was countering with Sardinia, where they had a holiday home, and Adele sipped cold coffee and waited her opportunity. 'I'm going to Japan next week. Frank thinks I need a break. It's business initially and then we'll relax. I said, "You don't want me along", but he insisted.'

'Japan?'

They were looking suitably impressed and Adele warmed to her theme. 'What does one take for Japan in November?' It was all shushi and sumo wrestling after that.

'It's never been off television lately . . . Japanese this, Japanese that. Oh, you are lucky! And who's their designer, Kenyo? Kendo? No, that's a martial art . . .'

Inside Adele a small knot of worry had replaced the glow. If things went wrong and she didn't get to Japan, everyone would know Frank preferred to go without her. If they learned of Ellie's phone calls, she would not only lose Japan, she would be cast into outer darkness.

It was noon and Terri was about to go to lunch when panic erupted. 'I don't believe it!' Stephen was tearing his thinning hair.

'Believe what?' Even without knowing, her own voice was panic-stricken.

'We've got to pull the pop-money piece! The ex-manager of Bogus 4 got an injunction this morning.'

Panic subsided in Terri's breast. 'Can't we just lift out the Bogus 4 section and pad the rest?'

Stephen's face contorted. 'Are you mad? That's the guts of the piece, the only juicy bit. Pull that, and there's nothing. Nothing! What've you got . . .' He looked around the Features section. 'Anyone, everyone . . . I need 1,500 words *now*. It's for page sixteen, 1,500 Grade A words. God, I'll kill myself before I'll tell him we've got nothing. He's always on about forward planning. Jesus Christ, tell me there's *something* we can use?'

Heads were shaking all round, and one or two consulted watches.

'If I had time,' Greta said vaguely.

'I've got something,' Terri said. It was fate. The piece on Ellie was on her desk, the blow-ups from Pictures attached. 'It's my piece on the industrialist's wife who went missing.' Stephen's face had fallen, but she went on. 'I think it's strong enough, and I've got a picture.'

She picked it up and handed it to him, crossing her fingers behind her back that he would use it, hoping in her heart that he would not and would thus save her from the possible consequences of publication.

Stephen was reading it quickly, eyes flicking along the lines. 'Well . . . it might do.' Around her there was an audible exhalation of breath. Panic over! 'We'll put it in, and if the Editor throws it out that's his fault. Give it to Subs, Terri . . .' He looked around. 'And for God's sake, get to work, all of you. We should be prepared for this kind of eventuality and we never sodding are.'

Terri sat down at her desk when she got back and

reached for the phone. 'Well done, Terri,' Andy said from the opposite position.

'And thanks,' Greta added. 'I was having visions of Herr Flick walking up and down, flaying us all for dereliction of duty. You know what he's like about us being lazy sods. We can't all be workaholics like him – he's got no private life; we have!'

Andy nodded a gloomy head. 'Trust us to get an asexual editor. Other papers have lechers or queers, but we get one who only talks about it. That's why he's such a bloody sadist.'

Terri grinned and then waited for the ringing tone to end. 'Richard Marriner, please.' A moment later she was through to Richard and telling him what had happened.

'Yes, Terri, please go ahead. Whatever the consequences, get it in.'

Terri shuddered slightly, thinking of how impossible it would be to stop it now, even if Richard had wanted her to. 'Time is running out, Terri, and I welcome anything . . .' There it was again, that suggestion of a time limit.

'Richard, what do you mean by time running out? Ellie's not ill, is she?' There was a long pause and Terri wondered if she had offended him by being too inquisitive.

'Ellie is pregnant, Terri. She doesn't know, and Paul Weidenek is anxious we keep it an absolute secret. It would be disastrous if she got in touch with someone and they blurted it out. But I think you need to know, and I trust you.'

'I'm going out,' Terri told Greta as she put the phone

down. 'If there's going to be flak about my piece, I don't want to know. Anyway there's something I've got to check on. I'll be back after lunch.'

A cab was disgorging at the door, and she stepped inside it. 'St Catherines House,' she said, and sat back as the cabbie weaved into the traffic. She tried to read the adverts on the undersides of the tip-up seats, but tears were blurring her vision. It wasn't fair; life wasn't fair. Everyone had a right to a baby, everyone. The photograph of Diana came into her mind – lithe, beautiful Diana who had twice sat proud in the bed while Mike thanked her for the gift of life. Flushed with childbirth, smelling of milk . . . and getting back her fucking figure into the bargain.

She sniffed and wiped her nose with the back of her hand. At least she could help with Ellie's baby. Sort things out and keep Ellie safe. Perhaps they would ask her to be a godmother. She would have to watch her language if they did, Mike was quite right about that. It was just so effing difficult. If they got the house, that would help. The dear little house with the shiny front door and pocket-hanky lawn that simply cried out for a swing. And she did have a share in Mike's daughters, a tiny, tenuous hold on their lives. It was better than nothing.

Half an hour later Terri was looking down at Ellie's birth certificate. Ellie had been born on 8 June, 1959 at 19, Park Street, Toxteth, Liverpool, and named simply Elldis. The father's name was given as William George Rowe and the mother as Dorothy Mary Rowe, formerly Baxter. Her father had been a foreman joiner, and Ellie's birth had been registered on 13 June, Registrar

David W. Pollock. It was all as Richard had said, but seeing it in black and white helped.

She sat and looked at the information, trying to link it with her friend. Liverpool had never been mentioned, not once. 'I'm a northerner,' Ellie had always said, a trifle apologetically as northerners were apt to do – unless they were militant and rammed it down your throat. Liverpool was 'north', but that was not what Ellie had meant. They had all assumed she would go north, to Durham or Northumberland. What if she had gone west, to Liverpool? Was even now walking the streets of Toxteth? But Liverpool was a huge throbbing city; it would be like trying to find a needle in a haystack. All the same, it was worth a try.

Terri copied all the details into her notebook and made her thank-you speech to the clerk. Outside it had started to drizzle and she searched her bag in vain for a headscarf. If she didn't find the money for a perm soon she would begin to look like Medusa. As usual when it rained in London, the cabs had disappeared or drove past with their flags down. She turned up her collar and made for the nearest tube. She was nearly there when an idea struck her, and she turned to retrace her steps.

Ellie had decided to sell the huge gold ear-rings she had worn on the day of her departure. The board was still there: 'Gold and silver bought. London prices.' She needed the money and the ear-rings were no use to her. She went inside.

Three others were waiting on seats ranged against the wall, a nervous young mother with children at her knee, a middle-aged man with a stick, and an elderly woman clutching a shabby plastic handbag in gnarled fingers. Ellie felt a wave of compassion. To be old and forced to sell your treasures to a man in a pub, his tools spread out before him, a watchglass screwed in his eye like Cyclops!

The vendor at the table got up and left the room, and the young mother broke free of her brood and moved forward. She produced a broad gold wedding ring and proffered it. 'It got too tight,' she said and Ellie saw that a cheap eternity ring occupied her wedding finger.

The man examined it with the glass, then put it on the tiny scales. 'Fifteen,' he said.

The woman's face had fallen. 'It cost three times that.'

He shrugged in a take-it-or-leave-it way, and she bit her lips and nodded. As she shepherded the children out Ellie saw there were tears in her eyes.

The next customer limped to the table and produced several flat boxes from his inside pockets. The gold and silver man was already shaking his head. 'Commemorative coins . . . not worth what you paid for them. Keep them for your grandchildren, that's my advice.'

The would-be seller was disposed to argue. 'That's a 1953 Coronation five-shilling piece. There won't be many of them around.'

'I know what it is, sir. It's still not of great intrinsic worth. You could try a specialist coin shop, but they'll tell you much the same.' His tone was weary, and he had obviously been through all this a thousand times before. The other man was closing his boxes, all fingers and thumbs now in his embarrassment. 'Sorry,' the silver man said.

'Thank you very much,' the limping man said in far from grateful tones. As he made for the door the elderly woman slipped into his seat and opened her bag, but it was not some gimcrack trinket she produced: it was Aladdin's treasure. Gold chains, identity bracelets, rings, brooches, a gold lighter . . . the man examined each one solemnly and named a price. She nodded agreement and wrote the sum down on a list. 'Sixty.' 'Forty-five.' 'Only twenty there, Mary, I'm afraid. It's only nine.'

So she was known to him, and this was a regular occurrence. Ellie felt the hair at the nape of her neck prickle. There was more going on here than ordinary buying and selling. Instinctively she got to her feet and made for the door.

'I won't be long, madam,' the man called out, unwilling to lose a client, but by then Ellie was in sight of the door and did not stop until she had gained the street. She window-shopped until she had recovered her composure, and then caught a bus across the bridge. She still needed to raise some money and she had seen a pawnbroker's sign there on a previous bus ride.

The shop was dark and surprisingly cluttered, but the woman behind the counter was bright-eyed and shrewd. 'We don't go for costume stuff,' she said, when Ellie produced the ear-rings.

'They're gold,' Ellie said, and received a disbelieving stare.

The woman took one and turned it round in her

hand. She picked up a magnifying glass and examined it closely, then unscrewed a tiny bottle and dabbed with an applicator at the back of the ear-ring. The result apparently surprised her and she looked at Ellie closely. 'Have you got a receipt?'

Ellie shook her head. 'No, but they're mine. They were a gift.'

The woman pondered. 'Just hang on a minute.'

She vanished into the recesses of the shop and Ellie looked around. There was clothing on a rack, a leather briefcase, a trumpet, numerous boxes and paper bags all tagged and labelled.

The woman came back, a man in tow. He looked hard at Ellie and then at the ear-rings, put them on a small scale and looked at Ellie again. She realized they were worried about stolen goods, and grew reckless.

'They're mine, if that's what you're worried about. My sister came over from America, she's married to a GI. Money's no object, you know Yanks. She gave me these as a thank-you gift, but the fact is I'm cleaned out with the expense. Americans have to live like lords.'

She was into her stride now, face beaming with remembered pleasure of the visit, brow furrowed at the punishing cost of it all. 'I wouldn't dream of parting with them . . . well, she'll expect to see them when she comes over next time . . . I just need something to tide me over. I'll redeem them next week when my husband's salary cheque comes through.'

'Salary cheque' had a good ring and produced the desired effect. Ellie gave a false name and address, and left the shop with £45 in her bag.

*

Terri had been looking at it for five minutes and still she couldn't believe it. 'Marriage solemnized at St John's Church, Toxteth, in the City of Liverpool on 16 June, 1985 between Gordon Churchill, aged 27, Bachelor and Engineer and Elldis Rowe, age 26, Spinster and Clerk.' For the tenth time she checked the details. Same name, same age, same father's name. There was no real doubt: eighteen months before she married Richard, Ellie had married someone else!

It didn't make sense. Terri had decided to check the certificate of Ellie's marriage to Richard, just in case there was some significant detail. Instead she had turned up this.

She scrabbled in her memory. Where had Ellie been the summer before last? June: she herself had been in Brussels for the Euro-parliament piece then, so Ellie could have been in Liverpool. But why? Why keep it quiet? Why take up with Richard? Why, in God's name, commit bigamy? There hadn't been time for a divorce.

Unless . . . unless there was some terrible, valid reason why this first marriage had not worked out. They set you free at once if the reason was good enough. Terri copied the details into her notebook and shrugged into her coat. She must not say a word to anyone. Not until she had found Ellie and given her a chance to explain.

Paul looked down at his papers to avoid the social worker's hostile gaze. 'Do you realize the danger this child is in?' she said. Her mouth was a tight line and he would bet her knees were pressed together under the table.

'*Could* be in, Mrs Jackson. *Could* be in; let's not pre-empt our inquiries.' He seemed to spend half his life now holding back rampant social workers. Jargon had taken over discussions; case conferences were in danger of becoming sessions for rubber stamping. It sometimes seemed that hysteria was the norm.

'Chair, I'd like my anxiety recorded, please,' Mrs Jackson said. The chairwoman cast an admonitory glance at Paul and directed that the objection be recorded. Paul could never understand why someone who refused to be called a 'man', preferred to be called an inanimate object, but he had learned the importance of terminology.

'Madam Chair, all I am asking is a little time. Whisking this child out of its home environment could be a recipe for disaster. I think we are too quick nowadays. The child has not claimed it is being abused, there is no medical evidence of abuse. It is failing to thrive, certainly, and I am as anxious as anyone else about that, but I want to find out the real reason before I prescribe treatment. Mrs Jackson is accusing this father of sexual deviancy on non-existent evidence.'

According to Mrs Jackson all men were sexual marauders. God help Mr Jackson, if he still existed. Paul looked around the table, hoping to find one mind at least half open. The Health Visitor met his eye and shuffled in her chair.

'I think Dr Weidenek has a point, Chair. I've had the Coxons on my books for nine years, since the first child, and I've never had the least reason to doubt either parent. They're feckless, certainly, but that's all . . .'

Paul relaxed. He had been prepared to hold the bridge alone, but it was nice to have help.

Five minutes later the Coxons had a respite and he was gathering his papers. 'If that's all, Madam Chair . . .'

Outside the sky was darkening and as he unlocked the car the street lamps came on, shining weakly in the half light of afternoon. Gary had promised to be home tonight and he must make sure they had time together. He couldn't face another scene. He had two weeks' leave coming up: if peace could be maintained until then they could get right away from everything. Then they could talk, work out a better *modus vivendi*.

He nosed out of the hospital car-park and into the traffic, wondering what he was going to do about Ellie Marriner. He couldn't go on holiday unless she had been located and he had had a chance to sort out the pregnancy; that much was certain. First he must decide whether or not to involve the police officially. Then when Ellie was found, it would be up to him whether or not termination was offered. Would she wish to escape this baby, or cling to it like a drowning man to a straw? He had seen that happen in similar cases, usually with disastrous results.

There was something else he must do before he could escape to the sun: visit his parents. Paul sighed, thinking of their pride in him and the burden it placed upon him. 'We've never had a professional man in the family,' his mother had confided once in her soft Welsh voice. 'Proud they'd all be if they knew.' There was satisfaction in her voice, the satisfaction of one who has married an alien against advice, and seen it turn out for the best.

He smiled, remembering their faces at his degree ceremony, twin beacons in a sea of beaming parents. But there was no possibility of their understanding about Gary, about any of it. And there was a limit to how long he could continue to lie.

Seated in the reference library, Ellie had worked her way through April and May 1961, and had found nothing. She had no idea what she was looking for, so every column inch had to be scrutinized which made for agonizing slowness. A picture of a child abandoned in an apartment store caught her eye: 'Does anyone know this girl? She says her name is Louise,' ran the headline, but the child was at least four. She herself would have been two in 1961. A few pages later she came upon a follow-up story, showing the child had been reclaimed by her teenage mother.

The idea of a nineteen-year-old having a four-year-old daughter intrigued Ellie. How old had her own mother been? She had never thought about that before; mothers did not have a particular age in the imagination. Grandma had seemed old, but that too might be a figment of her imagination and no true indication, anyway, of her mother's age. What if she had been a teenager who had simply tired of an infant encumbrance? But in her heart Ellie knew it would not be that simple.

In the early hours the idea had come to her from nowhere, to look up the local paper for the years 1961 and '62. In the cold light of morning it had not seemed quite such a good idea. Still, here she was, bound copies of the *Echo* for April to June 1961 in front of her.

She looked around the reference library. The other browsers were mostly students completing assignments or old-age pensioners come in for a warm. A man in a shabby raincoat was perusing *The Financial Times* with the eye of the *cognoscente*, and an orthodox Jew in the corner, his serene face framed in long ringlets, had a heavy leather-bound reference book open in front of him.

There was a clatter as someone dropped a book and all eyes swivelled. Only the Jew read on, undisturbed, and Ellie felt a twinge of envy. Perhaps if she believed in God she might find peace. But it hadn't saved the Jews in Belsen, or the Catholic martyrs in Elizabeth's England. The librarian had been gone for five minutes, fetching July to September, labouring away for the second time in some subterranean dungeon, unearthing papers that had not been disturbed for a quarter of a century and might disintegrate at the touch of a fingertip.

Perhaps Ellie should get to her feet and tiptoe away before they came? It was a wild-goose chase, after all. She didn't know what she was looking for, and there might not be anything to find. She wasn't even sure if 1961 was the operative year. She had appeared in Belgate in 1962, but the events that brought her there might have happened long before that. She was giving a margin of a year and beginning in 1961, but ten to one the year she wanted was 1960 or even '59, the year of her birth.

At the other end of the room the doors swung open

313

and the librarian appeared, a huge leather-bound volume in her arms. She looked around for Ellie and then bore down on her. 'There you are, 1961, July to September. Let me know when you're ready for more.'

It was strange to be leafing through events she could not remember. John Kennedy featured prominently but the local news looked surprisingly familiar – crime and punishment, flower festivals and school events. Ellie turned page after page, scanning headlines, looking for something, anything that might be of interest.

A few editions on she came across a report of a house fire. Four children had been left alone while their parents went drinking, only one had survived. She closed her eyes trying to summon up the memory of fire. Once her mother had hung her vest on the fireguard to air; it had been forgotten until it smouldered and filled the room with the smell of charred wool. And her mother had stood in the middle of the room and cried, holding the scorched garment to her mouth. But that was all she could remember.

The following day the paper gave more detail. The survivor had been a boy, Michael, aged three.

When she came to the classified sections she went carefully down the columns looking for Rowe or Baxter, her grandmother's name. There was nothing. An hour passed and she was still in August. It was eleven o'clock and her mouth was dry. 'I'm just popping out for a coffee,' she told the assistant at the counter. 'I'll be back to start again in twenty minutes.'

Outside the sky had darkened and wind was blowing leaves from the park along the pavements. There were antique-style lamps along the pavement edge and neat chains hung between posts as a railing. Crossing the road to a department store, Ellie made her way through tiered rows of richly decorated china to the lift. She had coffee and a scone with jam, her first food of the day, but it lay uneasily on her stomach again and she regretted her extravagance. As soon as she was finished she got to her feet and went to the cloakroom. A young woman was sitting on a chair in the corner, nursing a baby. She smiled apologetically at Ellie and then looked down at her child. Ellie's eyes followed the down-bent head and saw, half hidden by the woman's coat, that the baby's mouth was clamped voraciously to its mother's nipple. The sight shocked her and she turned to an open cubicle, not drawing breath until she was safe inside and the bolt shot home.

Wickedness! She felt tears begin and put a hand to her mouth. Mustn't make a scene. Babies were sin, and ultimate sin must be paid for. She put out a hand to the cistern and pulled the handle. Water gushed, making noise enough to let her cry.

Back on the library steps, she paused. Why go inside again when there were more important things to be done? There was a chemist in the market place, but she wanted somewhere more private.

She made her way towards the outskirts and found a shop in a side street. There were two girls behind the counter and a mother and child buying cough medicine. Ellie pretended to study the cosmetics until they were served and then she moved to the counter.

'I'd like a pregnancy-testing kit.' She tried to look pleased and anticipatory, and the assistant smiled as she rattled off the brand names.

'Which is the simplest?' Ellie countered. 'I've got my hopes up so much I'm all fingers and thumbs.' She was slipping into her role and the assistant responded.

'Is it your first?'

Ellie nodded. 'Yes. And I don't want to tell my husband if it's a false alarm . . . so I thought I'd check.'

The assistant ranged the boxes on the counter. 'They're all pretty easy to use . . .'

To add authenticity to her performance, Ellie browsed along the baby shelves before she left the shop, clutching her purchase. 'Let me know the good news,' the girl called, and Ellie nodded.

'Keep your fingers crossed it's positive.'

It was dark outside and drizzling now, and the streets gleamed. Ellie hurried towards her lodgings, looking for a phone box, clinging to the fiction of the young mother because the truth did not bear thinking about.

Richard had made his mind up to call on Paul on the way home. He needed to talk to him before going north, and besides, he wanted to warn him about Terri's piece appearing in the newspaper. Perhaps he should have checked with Paul before giving it his blessing, but it was too late to worry about that now.

He parked opposite the terraced house. Lights were on in the hall and on the first floor, so someone was home. Weidenek was a bachelor but that did not mean he lived alone, not nowadays.

Richard's hand was over the bell when he heard Paul behind him on the steps. 'Richard! What's happened?' He looked taken aback and Richard hastened to reassure.

316

'Nothing. No new developments. But I've made a decision, and I'd like to know how you feel about it.'

Paul was fumbling with his keys. 'Come in and we'll talk.'

Richard followed him into the hall. 'I mustn't be long, I've left the boys in the car.'

They were moving along the hall when there was the crash of feet above them on the stairs.

'Paul? Sorry, old love, but I'm in a tizz. We've got a booking tonight . . . out of the blue.' The boy saw Richard and stopped midway down the flight. He was young and blond, tight jeans, a shirt open to reveal a hairless chest, cuffs flapping to show a gold bracelet that matched the chain around his neck. 'Oh! Didn't know you had company.' His tone was surprisingly hostile, and Richard saw Paul tense.

'Richard Marriner . . . Gary Redmond. You've got a gig, Gary? Good! I won't be long, then you can tell me all about it.'

He wants to get rid of him, Richard thought, but the boy was in no mood to be disposed of.

'Don't hurry for me. You never do and I don't want to die of shock tonight. Not till I've done the gig.' He looked at Richard. 'Have you come to see his etchings? All the dear little bunny rabbits and furry friends? Or perhaps it's the tapes – that's his real passion. He doesn't let me hear them, I'm too young.'

Comprehension was flooding Richard and with understanding came pity, not only for the situation but for the sight of a man he respected so obviously at a loss. He looked Gary in the eye.

'I haven't time to see anything tonight, I'm afraid.

Or hear anything. My wife is Dr Weidenek's patient. I've come to check something out, and then I'm off. Nice to meet you.' It was a dismissal and it worked.

'Come into the study,' Paul said, and switched on the light. They were there, the wildlife miniatures Richard had noticed last time. As Paul moved about, depositing files, switching on lamps, Richard picked one up. 'They're most attractive.'

For the first time the other man's face lightened. 'That's a Kathleen Nelson . . . I like her work. Now, what momentous decision has brought you here?'

'I'm going north, Paul, as soon as I can clear my desk.'

The psychiatrist frowned. 'I thought your brother was going off to Japan?'

Richard put the miniature back in place. 'He is, and I've suggested he takes Adele. I'd rather leave Mrs Withers in charge while I'm gone. The detective in Durham thinks he's on to something with the foster-parents, and I want to be there. And there's something else – Terri Benedict has written something about Ellie for her paper. It appears tomorrow. I gave the go-ahead . . . I thought it could do no harm. Was I right?'

'I'd have said no, but it's done now. We don't want her hounded, Richard. And I still worry about that detective. If I thought he'd just locate her and report back to us, I'd be in favour. But if Ellie is "apprehended" it could be disastrous. If you find her, leave her alone; let me know, and I'll join you.'

Richard felt his throat constrict. 'Thanks,' he said.

Paul shrugged. 'Wait until you have cause for gratitude before you thank me. I mean to make things right for you if I can.'

'God help him,' Richard thought as he came down the steps. There had been an almost tangible tension in the house, and it was a relief to get back into the car.

Terri and Mike arrived home simultaneously. 'Good day?' he said, relieving her of her shopping bag and fumbling for his key. He was still in the buoyant mood of the morning and Terri did her best to respond. She had thought about the photographs in his wallet all day, and decided she could not mention them. She should not have looked through his wallet, and he would have every right to be furious if he found out that she had.

There was another reason for maintaining silence: the photograph was the genie in the bottle – unstopper it, and there was no knowing what damage might be done. However much it might hurt, she must simply tough it out. She was not going to tell him about Ellie's marriage certificate, either. Not until she had checked.

'Come on then,' she said. 'What did Sam say?' Mike was setting the table while she put lamb biriani in the microwave.

'I saw him at lunchtime,' he said, continuing to place mats and cutlery with methodical exactitude.

'*And?*' she said, setting the timer.

'And?' he said, unable to conceal his grin.

'And what?' she shrieked. 'What did he say? Is it OK?'

Mike put down the last fork. 'Of course.'

Her squeal of delight ricocheted round the kitchen. 'Oh God, Mike! I can't believe it. I love it, I love it, I love it. And we'll make the girls a super room. Oh, I love you, I love you.' She was beating him round the head with the wrapper from the biriani.

'Don't go over the top,' he said mildly. 'It's only a house. And by the way, I promised the girls we'd take them to see that *La Bamba* film next week.'

The microwave pinged and they sat down to eat.

'You know that piece I did about Ellie? Yes, you do . . . I told you about it. Anyway, it's out tomorrow. Stephen's plans fell through, and it was the only thing handy, so it's gone in. I checked with Richard, and he was keen. And he told me something. It's a dead secret so don't tell anyone.'

Mike emptied his mouth. 'Who would I be likely to tell?'

'Well, you never know. Anyway, Ellie's pregnant.'

Mike gave a soundless whistle. 'So . . . what does that mean, then?' He filled his own glass and held out the bottle. 'More plonk?'

She pushed forward her glass. 'Yes please. Well, in a way it doesn't make much difference. But on the other hand, it makes it more important to get her back quickly. He says . . . Richard says . . . she doesn't know. And mustn't know! He says the doctor . . . the shrink . . . thinks it could be disastrous if she finds out before he's there to help her.'

Mike shook his head. 'They get some daft ideas, doctors. Of course she must know already. That's probably why she went. Is it his?'

Terri was affronted. 'Of course it is. Don't judge

everyone by your own standards, chum. And don't be so sure she knows. People can block things out.'

She got up to get the tutti-frutti from the freezer, thinking as she did so that she was doing quite a good job of blocking out her own feelings. A baby, a tiny, loose-limbed, red-faced creature with fingernails the size of sequins and blue, unfocused eyes. She wanted one, but she must block out that yearning. The cookie had crumbled and ruled out motherhood, and that was the way it had to be.

'I went to the Central Register Office today,' she told him when she sat down, choosing her words carefully. 'St Catherines House. Richard had sent me a copy of Ellie's birth certificate, the shortened version, and I looked up the original entry. She was born in Liverpool. Liverpool! And she never mentioned it. I was thinking I might dodge up there if I get the chance.'

'What for? I'm all for lending a hand and that sort of thing, but Liverpool . . . God, you'll need danger money if you go over there. It's a cesspool.'

'Sometimes, Mike, you are so ill-informed! If you weren't taking me to Victoria Close I'd leave you. Liverpool is an up-and-coming city, packed with talent, dripping with culture . . .'

He finished for her '. . . and just bustling with warm-hearted Liverpudlians. Bring on the violins.'

'Well, anyway, I'm going. It's a slim chance but you never know. It's all very complicated, but someone there may remember something. I mean, Ellie could be up there now, looking herself. She might be wandering the streets, for all I know. I've got to try at least. And I'm not being altruistic – I want Ellie back home and out of my hair so I can wallow in the delights of house-owning. And decorating. And carpeting. And buying expensive furniture.'

He was nodding and joining in. 'And being evicted for non-payment of mortgage. And going to jail for debt. And driving your husband up the proverbial wall. What a good idea! Come here and givvus a kiss and stop your blather. And if you have to go to Liverpool, make it a day trip. I can't stand a night without you.'

She could have been utterly, blissfully happy if it had not been for her worries about Ellie. And the thought of the wallet, nestling against his heart, and the photograph which had pride of place there and which was not a photograph of his second wife.

Frank had been decidedly tetchy at breakfast, Adele thought, so she must get him in a good mood tonight. She went through to the kitchen and put the lamb to spit-roast. Solange had prepared the vegetables, so there was time to give a face-lift to the flowers and uncork the wine. If only Ellie would ring. She looked down at her hands, flexing and unflexing fingers to ease her tension. She was living on tenterhooks now. It wasn't fair!

She couldn't communicate with Frank, that was the trouble. In her whole life the one person she had felt close to, been truly happy with, was Julia, and between them there had never been a need for words. They had been friends, best friends, growing closer all the time. And it would have gone on like that.

She was pushing back the cuticles on her large, oval unpolished nails, when the phone rang.

'Adele?' Ellie's voice was soft and breathless with apprehension. Who else did she think would be hanging on the other end of the line? Silly bitch! It was time to dispense with kid gloves.

'Ellie, where exactly *are* you?'

It didn't work. Adele changed her tactics, playing Ellie like a trout, allowing her line, then reeling in, letting her go again, waiting for the moment to swing and land her catch. But the moment never came, and Adele felt her anger rise. Frank would be home soon. 'Ellie, pay attention . . . you sound half-asleep. Look, we can't go on like this, it's affecting everyone. Now, pull yourself together and tell me where you are. I'll drive up in the morning . . .' But even as she spoke she could sense Ellie withdrawing.

'Give Richard my love, Adele. The boys too. I can't face ringing them, but I want them to know I loved them.' And then the line was dead.

'*I loved them*': past tense. What did that mean? Had Ellie uncovered something grisly? Or discovered she was pregnant? A woman knew; she always knew. It did not take missed periods or discoloration of the nipples; you knew, in your mind and heart, that you had conceived. If only she had had the nerve to come out with it: '*You know you're pregnant, Ellie. We all know, so you might as well come home and get on with it.*'

But if something nasty happened . . . If Frank had walked in on that phone call . . . For a terrible moment Adele considered the possibility of crossed lines giving her away, and had to laugh aloud at her own stupidity. All the same, she was playing a dangerous game.

She looked at the receiver. She could pick it up now and tell Richard about the call, say it was the first she had received. She would be in the clear then. If Ellie turned up after all and said anything about having made previous calls, would they put it down to her state of mind? Adele bit her lip as she calculated the possible effects of revealing that Ellie was in touch with her. If she relayed Ellie's message to Richard, would the whole thing be reactivated? Would they all leap around like bloodhounds, tongues lolling at the prospect of the prodigal's return, and tell her to stay home instead of going to Japan, and prepare the fatted calf? What if she stayed silent, and something terrible happened? No one would ever know she had played any part in it. All the same . . .

She went through to check on the lamb. She put a light under the potatoes and added seasoning to the savoury cabbage. A knob of butter on the top, and the lid back on. Not quite time yet to start it off. She laid the table, nudging silver and crystal into place as she heard Frank's car grinding to a halt on the gravel.

'Darling . . .' His cheek was cold and male and she kissed it again.

'Let me get in, then. It's more like December out there.' He was shrugging out of his jacket as though she didn't exist. Adele turned away, remembering Julia, confident on the eve of her wedding: *'We'll be happy for ever and ever, Del. Both of us, you'll see. I don't believe in bad luck.'* Even when Julia was dying she had gone on making plans, but it hadn't saved her. And her prediction for Adele had been equally awry.

She poured gin and French into two glasses, and sat

opposite Frank as he reached cold hands to the fire. 'Good day?'

He was chewing on his moustached upper lip and she could tell he had things on his mind. 'Average. How was yours?'

At seven-forty-five Gary stormed through the hall, throwing obscenities over his shoulder and taking the stairs two at a time to bang the bedroom door. The promised gig had been cancelled. Paul pondered the advisability of switching off the tape-recorder, but it couldn't always be peace at any price. Besides, he must come to a conclusion about Ellie. It could now be only a matter of hours before the fact of her pregnancy forced itself upon her. Before then he must decide whether or not she was a danger to herself and should be hunted down. The police were waiting for him to give a lead, and the detective was blundering around up there, muddying the water and encouraging Richard to join in the chase.

Paul had wanted Ellie to be free, prayed for her search to reach fruition, but he had always known there might come a time when he had to act for her protection. God help him if he got his timing wrong.

A few moments ago the final tape had ended. Paul looked down at the pad in his hand. The conclusions were pitifully few:

(1) There was some area of her infancy secret even from her conscious mind.

(2) That secret was bound up with her parents, whom Ellie feared had been criminal or insane or both.

(3) In some way her predecessor, Richard's first wife, Julia, had reactivated Ellie's fear of the past. When she had talked about Julia it was as though she had known her all her life and feared her for the same length of time.

(4) She had a distaste for child-bearing, a distaste that amounted to a revulsion. Twice she had called it 'the ultimate sin'. They were not her own words, obviously, but derived from whom?

(5) She was motivated by a desire for paternal affection. She did not see men as sexual beings: Paul had sensed that from the beginning. There had been no trace of flirtation in her manner, something he was used to in women patients. She seemed to fear men, and had no faith in her ability to please them, but still she yearned for a father figure. This was how she had seen Richard in the beginning. It was the change in her feelings for him that had acted as a trigger and sent her running for cover.

(6) She was not keeping in touch any more, which was both significant and frightening.

Above, on the landing, a door opened and slammed. Feet pounded on the stairs, Paul put down his pad with a sigh, ready to face the storm.

'That's it, that's fucking it. I'm tired but I can't go to sleep because if I do you'll wake me when you come up and I'll be awake the rest of the night. You're selfish, selfish through and through. And you're old. You've forgotten what it's like to live . . . fucking tapes, that's life for you. Vi-bloody-carious pleasure! You're a voyeur and a sham, and I hate you!'

Gary balled a fist to strike the door and when pain whitened his face he did it again and again anyway. Paul moved towards him, holding out placatory hands. There was sweat on the boy's brow and a spot erupting on his cheekbone. 'I've finished now, Gary. Calm down . . .' In spite of himself, he felt stirred by the fury. He wanted the boy. Wanted him now.

But Gary had turned and was mounting the stairs. Today he had been disappointed and Paul had been less than sensitive. Tonight had not been the night to put Ellie first. Except that for Ellie there might not be time to spare.

As Paul stood in the hall, wondering whether to follow Gary or allow a cooling-off, he wondered why Ellie and Richard and their happiness were so important to him. Perhaps he wanted for them what he would never obtain for himself, a loving and stable relationship.

The phone rang and he heard Gary lift the bedroom extension. The next moment he was careering down the stairs again, gibbering with delight. 'We've got another gig, a club gig. Oh God, I've prayed for this. The guys'll be here in ten minutes. You'll have to help.'

'Shall I come?' He wanted so much to enter the boy's world.

Gary paused on the stairs, considering. 'OK. But I've got to dash.'

Paul went into the study and began to clear his papers. Five minutes later Gary was back. He paused in front of Paul and struck a pose. 'How do I look?'

The vest top looked grimy but Paul knew that was

intentional. 'Good. Great! A bit swashbuckling . . . but that's what you're after, isn't it?'

Gary ran curved fingers through his hair to make it spikier. 'It isn't dry yet. God, I've got cheap hair. Cheap bloody skin. Do I look all right?'

Once again Paul reassured him. 'Now, where is this place? I don't want to get lost.' He was regretting suggesting to go, if the truth were told, but there was no way of extricating himself now.

'Follow the van. I'd say come with us, but there isn't room. You will change, won't you?' Gary was eyeing Paul's suit anxiously.

'Jeans and sweater do?'

The boy was already half out of the door, like a cat on a hot tin roof at the prospect of a gig. 'Yeah. Anything. Just don't look like Old Father Time.'

'Why not?' Paul thought as he changed. He felt like Father Time. Older if anything. He had looked forward to some peace tonight; now he was in for three hours of unmitigated torture. He had been to a club gig before, so he knew what to expect. Gary's group was filling in for another, more established, band so they would need all the support they could get. And if it went well there would be rapport between him and Gary, for a while at least, so it was worth making the effort.

A roadie was in the hall as Paul came downstairs. There was something about a rock group and their attendants – they moved with the rapt expressions of acolytes at a shrine, all knowing what they must do and doing it precisely. Paul climbed into his car and let the engine idle while the last drum was packed into the van and the roadie ran round to the driving seat.

Gary shut the front door and took the steps two at a time in his haste to join his friends. It would have made sense for him to ride with Paul, but Paul had known better than to suggest it. He let out the clutch as the van moved away and fell into place behind it.

The club was dark and empty. Paul took a seat at one side, feeling awkward and anxious not to embarrass Gary. They were setting up their equipment, moving like well-tuned machines, helping one another where necessary, the roadie at everyone's beck and call. Behind Paul the shutters of the bar rolled up. 'Want a beer?' He bought himself an exorbitantly priced half of lager and resumed his seat.

It took another twenty minutes to finish setting up, then it was time for the sound check. They played a few bars, playing badly, so that he winced. Then they tuned and retuned, and tried again. Gary was moving microphones among his kit, floor tom-tom, bass, snare, tom-toms and high hats. 'I know them all now,' Paul thought, and smiled in the darkness.

A row had broken out on stage, something about acoustics and the mixing desk. The lead singer was waving his arms, and Gary was nodding agreement. When it was settled the singer leaned over to pat Gary's shoulder and Paul's teeth chinked on the rim of his glass.

A few moments later the first customers arrived: jeans and Wrangler jackets for both sexes, spiked hair in all the colours of the rainbow – and ruby red, here and there cycle leathers. And all of them young, drinking beer, laughing uproariously and sometimes casting a curious eye at the old square in the corner.

Gary came to speak to him and he saw the boy was embarrassed. 'There are two sets, about forty-five minutes each. The interval's half an hour. We can't drink here, it spoils the image, so I won't see you till the end. Sorry about that.'

'Where are you drinking?'

The boy was evasive. 'I don't know yet. Somewhere out the back, I'm not exactly sure. You'll be OK here.' He was grinning. 'Brought your ear plugs?'

Paul smiled back. 'I should have. Good luck. Play them up a storm.'

He watched the boy's thin figure make its way back to the stage, swaggering a little and tossing his head in the manner of a Rolling Stone. Where would it all end? Tonight he had met Richard's eyes and seen pity in them. The PA system crackled and the house lights dimmed. He settled down in his seat and gave himself up to the beat.

[11]

Ellie sat by the window all night, sometimes dozing, more often looking out on the silent street. Behind her on the dressing-table stood the glass she had used for the pregnancy test. She had watched in disbelief as the stick turned pink. It was unmistakable. She had looked away and then back, sure she would find the colour unchanged, the test negative. But there was no mistake.

In the end she had wrapped herself in the quilt and curled up by the window, afraid to lie down in the bed lest terror overtake her. Instead she had laid her forehead on the cold windowpane and watched the street, silver in the moonlight, then grey and ghostly in the half light of dawn.

The milkman had rattled along, stacking his crates just below her; twice policemen had gone by, patrolling in pairs, and once in a cruising panda car. Ellie had dozed and woken to see a perky dog sniffing from gate to gate, finding a discarded package of fish and chips and wolfing them with gusto. And still she had come to no decision.

It was wrong for some people to perpetuate

themselves in children, wicked even. She had always known she had bad genes. She should never have married Richard, never allowed herself to love him. Now this conception had come upon her by stealth.

As the sun came up at last she roused herself to reach for her bag. Inside, in a velvet-lined box, was the ring Richard had bought her on their engagement – a huge diamond, picking up light even in the darkened room. Sold, it would bring money enough for an abortion. She had seen advertisements in the paper, so she knew where to go. But was that what she wanted? Was there not a better and more comprehensive solution. She opened her bag and fingered her pills, running them through her fingers. The right mix would mean an end to all of it – a clean sheet for Richard and the boys, oblivion for her.

She was still pondering when the street door opened below her and a man came out, wincing at the sudden onslaught of cold air so that he turned up his collar and thrust his hands deep into the pockets of his donkey-jacket. He turned back to the door, smiling the foolish and indulgent smile of a lover, and Ellie felt her own lips curl in sympathy. She could not see the object of his affections but she saw his lips form 'I love you' before he set off down the street. No one had ever said that to her. Not once in her whole life. She had waited for Richard to say it, but words had never come.

'I love you.' She was crying as she uttered the words, not knowing for whom she intended them. 'I love you,' she said again, hearing the front door close and the stairs creak as the one who was loved crept back to bed.

*

Paul was drinking coffee and listening to the morning news on the radio when he heard the front door open.

'Get it over, then!' Gary said, flopping into the chair at the kitchen table and slumping until his head touched the back rail.

Paul stood up and reached for another cup. 'Coffee?'

Last night, when the gig had ended, Paul had waited in his car while Gary helped to dismantle the equipment and bundle it back into the van. He had waited until one o'clock and then had driven round to the rear, knowing the van would not be there but praying he would be proved wrong. The back street had been empty, the doors of the club bolted and barred. He had driven home, resignation gradually replacing hurt. It was not until he saw the boy's discarded clothing scattered around the bedroom that pain and humiliation had threatened to overwhelm him.

Now, though, he was calm and not disposed to respond to provocation. There could be no backing down, whatever the consequences.

Opposite him, Gary's lip curled. 'I know you're dying to tell me what a shit I am. Go ahead. You're right, I'm crap – I know that. But I've got to be free, Paul. I've never pretended anything else.' He waited, hoping for some response, but Paul went on drinking coffee not out of a desire to snub him, simply because he had no counter-argument.

'We went for a jar last night, someone's pad. One jar, then I was coming home.'

It was too much. Paul felt his fingernails crucifying his palms until he raised his fist and brought it down on the table with such force that the cups rattled in the saucers. 'You left me sitting there . . . Dumbo, your unwanted hanger-on. You left me there. You didn't say you were going on somewhere – you went off. Did you laugh in the van? "See the poor old sod sitting there under the street lamp. Silly old bugger, serve him right!"?'

This was not the way, but he couldn't help it. What the hell, he was going to lose out anyway. Might as well make it quick.

'You dumped me, Gary, like a worn-out shoe. In a way, though, you did me a favour. It doesn't work, you and me. You've given me a lot, I'm grateful. But I can't go on like this, never knowing whether you'll blow hot or cold, turn up or vanish. I want you to go. Please. Take as much time as you need – pads are hard to come by, I know. I'll help with money. But I want you out. I think you owe me that much.'

The boy looked at him viciously for a moment and Paul felt fear rise in his throat. And then Gary was standing up. 'You bloody worn-out old poof,' he said and turned on his heel.

When he was alone in the kitchen Paul got to his feet and opened the fridge to take out the cheese box. He cut the square of cheddar into minute pieces and mixed it with chopped peanuts from a carton. The birds were waiting on gutters and ledges, the starlings bolder than the rest. In the beginning he had tried to arrange it so that sparrows and tits got preference. But he had learned that there was nothing you could do. Nature would dictate the terms, the birds accepted that.

He rinsed knife and chopping board and put them to drain, washed his hands and dried them, spreading the hand-towel over the back of a chair to dry, then he went to his study to collect Ellie Marriner's file. From the cabinet the miniatures beckoned. Tonight, when he came back to the silent house, they would console him. He found himself standing in the centre of the room, clutching the folder to his chest, fighting the impulse to run upstairs and beg forgiveness.

In the end he went out to his car. He was supposed to understand the human mind, but his skills were useless when it came to his own affairs. There he was no better equipped to communicate than any other man.

Terri got a seat in the tube and subsided into it gratefully. They had kissed goodbye when Mike left, checking his wallet was in his pocket. 'Mustn't forget it again,' he had grinned, and the impulse to confront him had almost overwhelmed her.

The train rattled to a halt and a woman got on, clutching a child in her arms. No one moved, and she tried to hold the rail with one hand and the child with the other as the doors closed and the train lurched forward.

'Sit here,' Terri said. 'No, come on. I get off soon anyway.'

A boy was sitting opposite looking at her. '*Sucker*,' his expression said, and she turned away.

Last night they had made love. Good love, even a little frenzied. But as she responded, incited, shouted her gratitude at his ministrations, she had thought of

Diana – the first and foremost wife. Was that what had driven Ellie away, the inevitability of second place?

'God, you're a demanding woman,' Mike had said when they lay, breathing quickly, heads still swimming.

She had made one final demand. 'Was it like this with her, Mike? As good as it is with me?' In the darkness her lips had formed a silent plea: *'Lie. Please, please lie! I can bear the truth if only you will lie about it for my sake.'*

But he had groaned and turned away. 'Don't start all that again, Terri, for God's sake! Let's get some sleep.'

When she arrived at the office she picked up a copy of the paper from the pile by the newsroom door and turned to page sixteen. It was there, Ellie's face, six inches by four, young and vulnerable, the dog removed so that she seemed to be appealing from the printed page. 'Have you seen Ellie Marriner?' the headline said, and the piece had been printed uncut, as far as Terri could see.

'He likes it,' Stephen said when she reached her desk. Relief made him look like a boy. 'He wants you to do a follow-up. People are already ringing in. I've put Pam on to note the calls and liaise with you. It's come at just the right time, Terri. News are pushing for our pages, so we've got to keep on the ball.'

'I'm glad you feel like that, Stephen.' Terri put her bag down on the desk and reached for her railway timetable. 'I want to go to Liverpool, I might have a lead. I'll ring in every chance I get. If it comes good, I'll phone Copy. I'll be able to use whatever I find anyway because it's background, but with a bit of luck I might get a breakthrough.'

'I don't know, Terri, Liverpool?'

She sighed. '*Liverpool*, Stephen. *Not* Ecuador. I can be there by lunchtime and back for tea. And you never know what I might turn up.' But whatever she turned up, she would give it to Richard first and the paper second, and to hell with the consequences.

'What about the calls? Who's going to deal with them?'

'Put anything hopeful on to Richard Marriner's office,' she said and buried her face in the timetable.

Richard had spent the previous evening packing and collecting pictures of Ellie, even searching her drawers for childhood snapshots. If Terri's article had the desired effect, all the papers would be clamouring for photographs. Scenting disaster, probably. Preparing double-page spreads on a dead woman before death was confirmed. Now he switched off his razor, shook the shavings into the sink and swilled them away. The water eddied and swirled, catching the fine grey dust into the vortex at the plughole.

He realized he was frozen there, unwilling to move away. He had longed for morning, but now it was as though inertia had settled on him like some terrible wasting disease. He wanted to do nothing, think nothing, simply lie down in a green meadow or a white bed and close his eyes until it was over. He switched off the mirror-light and went back into the bedroom to get dressed.

Driving towards Slough with the paper open on the

passenger seat beside him, he glanced from time to time at Ellie's picture. He had almost forgotten how she looked. And in the last few weeks, before she left, she had looked different somehow, unless that had been in his mind's eye. Perhaps he too had been different, withdrawing from a situation he could not comprehend. If only he had said, 'I love you, Ellie.' Just that. But he had never uttered that phrase in his life. 'I love you,' he said experimentally, and then looked guiltily at a passing car as though he could be overheard.

A picture of Paul came unbidden into his mind, as he had seen him last night, bemused, unsure of himself, humbled by a boy hanging over a banister and making remarks that had an undertone of viciousness. So Paul was homosexual, and he had never realized it. How little the reality resembled the myth perpetuated by the media. His own reaction had surprised him: he had not felt disapproval, much less revulsion. If anything he had experienced a fellow-feeling for a man in torment like himself, locked in a relationship that might bring disaster, and probably would. As they had said good-night afterwards, the psychiatrist's eyes had been wary. *He must wonder how I'll take it,* Richard thought. Impossible to tackle it head on. If he tried he would wind up being appallingly insensitive. When Paul came north he would let him see how grateful he felt towards him, how unchanged his feelings were by the revelation.

Ellie had roused herself to leave the house but once outside there was nowhere to go. No point in going to

338

the library – the situation had changed, and it was the future she feared now, rather than the past. She had thought the past might engulf her, but what was growing inside her was far more dangerous. Perhaps she should go to the Harpers? Someone might have told them something all those years ago, something that would help. She needed help. Time was running out. Sooner or later Richard would track her down to take her back, and she couldn't let that happen.

Ellie walked towards the park. It was cold now, the heel of the year. Grass was losing colour and dead leaves were curling to dust instead of scurrying before the wind like living things. Men were emptying a flowerbed, pulling up annuals that clung to life, throwing them into a barrow, their red and yellow heads protruding. She had a sudden impulse to rescue them and cram them back into the wounded earth, but when she halted beside the barrow the man straightened up and looked at her strangely, so that she was forced to move on.

She passed the bowling-green and the lake and came to a shelter. Inside, the cream-washed walls were scattered with names, lovers' names. She could take out her lipstick and write 'Ellie loves Richard' on the wall. Her fingers touched the wooden seat, scarred by knives. 'Ellie loves Richard but Richard loves Julia'. She had lipstick enough for that but she couldn't remember the spelling. She had taken another pill before she left the house, which had dulled the ache in her heart, but her mind was now blurred at the edges. Not so blurred, though, that she could not remember the photograph. She had held it in her hands and gazed on Julia. Julia in white. Julia on her wedding-day. A perfect bride. A proper wife. A once and only wife.

She sat down in the shelter and folded her hands in front of her. A yard away a man was reading a newspaper. As if it mattered. She felt a profound disinterest towards newspapers now. The rumblings of the stock exchange fall, Prince Charles in hunting gear, Russian soldiers watching British war games, the usual trivia about the rich and would-be famous. Always the same mix. He was folding the paper when she saw her own face staring back at her. Instinctively she turned away, feeling her cheeks flush and her heart race. She put up a hand to make sure her spectacles were there and fingered her hair, lank and greasy and in need of a trim. It was all right. The park was almost empty and no one cared. She might as well be invisible.

A bird hopped on to the seat beside her, cocking its head on one side in appeal. If she had had bread she would have broken it into crumbs, but she had nothing. For some reason she found this sad, overwhelmingly, unbearably sad. She was too tired to cry but her eyes ached. Perhaps the pill was not going to work after all. She was opening her bag to take another when she realized that without water she would never swallow it. The bird took flight at the movement, flying off with a scurry of wings, and the man went too, leaving his paper behind him.

After a few moments Ellie reached out and turned the pages until her own face, huge and grinning, stared up at her. 'Have you seen Ellie Marriner? I want to know because she is my friend . . .' She did not need

340

to seek out the by-line. Terri, oh Terri! If she could speak to Terri, perhaps it would be all right.

She got to her feet, leaving the paper on the seat, and stumbled towards the park gates. There were two telephone boxes there. She would ring the paper and hear Terri's voice. They had been happy together . . . she shook her purse out on to the ledge and sorted silver, stabbing out the paper's number without the 01 prefix so that she got a continuous high-pitched tone and had to re-dial.

'Terri Benedict please.'

A ringing tone, and then a strange voice: 'Features, Miranda Frazer.'

'I'd like to speak to Terri Benedict.'

'I'm sorry, Terri is away on an assignment. Can I help?'

Ellie put down the phone and turned back towards the park. Silly to think there was anyone who could help. There was no one. No one in the whole wide world.

Terri gave the cab driver the address of the house where Ellie had been born, and sat back in her seat. She had been to Liverpool before so she was not surprised at its pleasant streets, the cheerful faces on the sidewalks, the signs of affluence. The media depicted it as a dump; the reality was different. It had unemployment problems, but it was a city with pzazz and it knew it.

She had wondered if Park Street would still be standing, but the cab driver seemed to recognize the name. As the cab threaded the streets she watched for her friend, hoping she too had come to Liverpool – but that was crazy, really. If she had stayed in London she might have done more good. Still, it was too late now. She must see what, if anything, was to be found here and get back double-quick. Mike had been more understanding about Ellie lately, but there were limits.

The cab drew up at a neat terraced house, differing from the others in the street only in the colour of its paintwork, which was black and white and looked as though it had just been washed down. It looked, in fact, like the home of newly-weds. God, it was twenty-eight years since Ellie's birth – there might have been ten different occupants since then.

Terri climbed from the cab and turned to the driver's window. 'Could you hang on? I don't expect to be long. In fact, I don't know what I'm doing here.'

He was looking dubious and she fumbled in her bag. The meter said £3.20 and she handed him a five-pound note. 'Take this and wait for me. Please. I won't scarper, I promise you. And I want to go back to the station eventually.'

He shrugged. 'OK, it's your money.' He picked up a newspaper from the front seat and shook it open. If he was going to wait, he was going to relax.

Terri turned back to No. 19 and walked up the short path. The bell was an 'Avon-calling' chime, and the girl who opened the door was nineteen or twenty, a pretty girl in a mohair jumper and tight jeans.

'I wonder if you can help me?' Terri said, searching for the right approach. They would think her crazy!

'I'll try,' the girl said, grinning at Terri's obvious discomfort.

'I'm trying to trace someone who was born here about twenty-eight years ago.'

The girl frowned. 'Here, in this house?'

Terri nodded. 'Yes. Her name was Rowe – I don't suppose you've heard of the family?'

'Sorry. We've been here for eleven years, but before that it was the Halroyds.' The girl shook her head. 'There's no one you could ask, either . . . they're all newcomers around here. I suppose we've been here the longest.'

Terri thanked her and climbed back into the cab. 'Offerton Street,' she told the cabbie. That had been Ellie's address on the marriage certificate. It was worth a try.

In Offerton Street she rang the bell of No. 4 and stood back, telling herself to keep calm. Ten to one it would be a dead end. The door opened and she felt a sense of anticlimax – she had been expecting Ellie to open the door, which was crazy.

'I'm sorry to bother you, but I'm trying to locate a friend of mine. Her name is Elldis Rowe.'

The girl's face creased into a grin, and she ushered Terri over the step. 'Well, look no further. She doesn't live here any more but you'd think she did 'cos she's never away.' She raised her voice. 'Ellie! You're wanted.'

The door at the end of the hall was opening and Terri felt her breath catch in her throat. Ellie *was* here.

The woman in the doorway was holding a child in her arms, its curly hair half-obscuring her face. She shifted it to her other arm.

'But I've never seen you in my life before,' Terri said, and lowered her bag to the ground.

*

'It's good of you to come, Paul,' Richard said. 'The paper is getting calls, most of them crank calls, but one or two will probably bear checking.'

The intercom buzzed and he flipped a key. 'I've got an MP on the line, Mr Marriner. He says he met your wife in Durham.'

A moment later Richard was listening to Dave Smith. 'She was calling herself Caroline Shaw, said she was a novelist. I didn't pay much attention . . . ships that pass in the night, you know the sort of thing. Anyway, something made me check at the desk, and the name she'd given there was different. I didn't think much of it at the time . . . *nom de plume*, that sort of thing, but it stuck in my mind. Odd sort of woman . . . well, that's how it seemed . . . I thought she was a bit barmy, if you must know. And then I saw this paper today. That's her, I said; take away the spectacles and that's her.'

Richard picked up a pen. 'It's good of you to get in touch. Can you give me the name of the hotel? The Dunelm Arms. And that was the night of Monday 20th? What name had she given the receptionist? *Julia?* It was definitely Julia?' Richard knew then that there could be no mistake, but he still had to ask: 'You're quite sure it was her, I suppose? You'll appreciate that time lost on a false lead . . .'

At the other end of the line there was a bark. 'I'm not in the habit of sending people off on wild-goose chases . . . I've told you I sat at a table with your wife, and that's a fact. Make what you like of it.'

'What do you think?' Richard asked when he had given his thanks and put down the phone. Paul was nodding. 'It fits. And her using the name "Julia" puts it beyond doubt. I thought she'd go north, and Durham was the logical place for her to go. On the spot, but just big enough to hide in.'

'He said she checked out the following morning,' Richard said, 'so I suppose this information is already out of date. Still, the detective has the foster-home staked out. I've told him not to move until I'm there, so you don't need to worry.'

He picked up the internal phone. 'Frank? Things are moving quite fast now . . . yes, Terri Benedict's article. Yes, more hopeful . . . I've had an MP on the line who says she stayed in the same Durham hotel as he did last week. Not one of nature's charmers, but he seemed sure of his facts. So I'm going up there. No, I'll be all right. I've got Paul with me at the moment . . . he'll come north if I need him. Leave the Japan arrangements as they are – if this firm can't function without us for a few days, the sooner we find out the better. And for once, Frank, I wouldn't care if we went to the wall.'

He put down the phone. 'Now,' he said, 'I'll ring the boys and I'm off.'

The intercom buzzed again and Richard pressed down the switch.

'It's the *Record* . . . they've got notes of a sheaf of calls. What do you want me to do?'

Paul waved a hand to attract Richard's eye. 'Leave them to me. I'll go over there on my way to the hospital, and see what they've got. You get up to Durham, and ring me as soon as you arrive. And take it easy . . . I think we're almost there.'

When Paul had gone Richard walked to the window, looking out but seeing nothing. There were a dozen things he should be doing but he felt a sudden and terrible fear. If he went to Durham and found her, what then? And why had she used Julia's name? Had he failed Ellie, made her feel so insecure that she had felt the need to step inside another woman's identity? It must be that, there was no other logical explanation.

He turned at Frank's signal and opened the door.

'You're alone?' Frank moved inside the room. 'Good. Now, I prescribe two stiff drinks and a pow-wow. Tell me what I can do to help.'

It took only a few minutes to thrash out the practical details, but they were loath to part. 'I wish I could come with you,' Frank said. 'In a way it's more my thing than yours. I was always the doer, you were the thinker. I used to envy you, you know . . . the way Dad depended on you. He was proud of me, the games bit, that sort of thing. But he respected you.'

'I've failed, Frank.' It was a relief to say it aloud. 'I've done well by Marriner's, and I'm proud of that, but I've failed Ellie, and lately I've wondered whether I failed Julia too. I didn't talk to them, you see. I felt it all, but I couldn't communicate it. And now there's this mess.'

It was Frank's turn to walk to the window, putting hands into pockets, speaking with his back to his brother as though it were easier that way. 'First of all, you didn't fail Julia – I never saw a woman more content with her life. And at the end you did what she wanted. She never liked to chew over and analyse things, that wasn't her way. "Be happy, take and enjoy": that was

Julia's code, and it was a good one. And you were brave through it all, Rich. Don't ever underestimate your courage.

'The situation with Ellie is different. It's outside your control, in a way. She has her own hang-ups, you didn't create them. So you could have been a better communicator? I suppose so. But we were never encouraged to communicate, were we? "Stiff upper lip, no fuss". "Enthusiasm is not done." I rebelled a bit; perhaps not enough. You conformed.'

At the desk, Richard stirred – this was coming too close to home. But before he could speak Frank turned. 'It was mother. It irked her that our money came from trade, so we had to behave like aristocrats! It's all so unimportant, so bloodily inconsequential! And I see it all happening again, in my own marriage.'

Frank stopped then, as though he was straying from the point, and came back to the desk. 'Anyway, what I'm trying to say is, don't blame yourself. Go and find Ellie, and don't agonize too much. You've done your best, and that's all any of us can do.'

It had come at last, and the reality was worse than her fears. Adele had picked up the phone, knowing it would be Ellie and hoping it was not, knowing at once that something was desperately wrong. 'Ellie, please. I can't hear what you're saying. Slow down, Ellie. Please . . . I can't help you if I can't hear.'

Ellie was either drunk or deranged. 'I can't let it happen, Adele. Try to understand. It's unforgivable. And it doesn't matter. If you have none to make you laugh, you'll have none to make you cry – that's what

Grandma used to say. So you see I can't let it happen I'm just not sure how . . .'

She knew about the baby! 'Ellie, listen to me . . . I want to come and get you, Ellie. Where *are* you? Are you in an hotel?' No, there had been STD pips at the beginning. 'Ellie, are you staying with someone?'

There was a long silence, and then her voice, calmer . . . 'I have a room. I used to play in the park, beside the lake. Now I can see the trees from my window.'

'Are you still in Sunderland? Give me your number, in case we're cut off. Please, Ellie . . . give me your address. I won't tell, I'll come myself. No one will know. I'll help you. Just give me the address, Ellie.'

'I had to get out, Adele. I couldn't bear the music.'

Oh God, she really was raving. 'Ellie, do you know what's wrong with you, why you must come home?' She wanted to say 'pregnant' out loud but she couldn't take the risk.

'Oh yes, I'm pregnant, Adele. It's so sad, isn't it? Take care of the boys.'

'Ellie . . . Ellie . . .'

But the line had gone dead. Adele could hear the au pair in the kitchen clattering pans, but there was no help there. She must talk to someone. She pressed the receiver rest and dialled.

'Frank . . . I've just had Ellie on the phone!' The relief of telling was exquisite, but she had to be careful to cover her tracks. 'No, she sounded very upset but it was just the usual . . . "give my love to Richard, take care of the boys". No, she didn't say where she was, just that she was all right. But she sounded awful, absolutely awful.'

The news that Richard had already gone north was a relief. He would find Ellie, and then it would be all right. And no one could blame her – not now that she had told the truth.

But it was not the whole truth! Long after Adele had collected coat and scarf and was walking towards the quarry, she was still guilt-ridden. Why had she got into this desperate situation? If they found Ellie, they would discover she had lied over a period of days. And if they did not find Ellie, if they came too late, she would never be able to live with what she had done.

It was getting dark and the dusk seemed like a judgement on her. Puddles along the pitted lane reflected the leaves of the hedgerow trees. Adele started to whimper. Perhaps if she went to her mother . . . but even as she considered it she knew how useless it would be. *'It's no use coming to me, Adele. If you will get yourself into these situations you must get yourself out of them.'* Around her the banks were shrivelled and lifeless, here and there a plant turning red, in one last, defiant affirmation of living. Adele thought of her father. At his funeral they had sung, 'O love that will not let me go'. But he had gone. He had gone and left her. She looked at the landscape, eyes misted with tears. Her father had loved her and he had been brave, trying to keep up a front while everything slipped away. He had been an awful old fraud, really, always pretending, just like her. But he had loved her. The only person who ever had.

Terri sent away the taxi and together they checked the details on the birth certificate to see if there were two

Ellie Rowes. But the certificates tallied absolutely. 'So she had your birth certificate,' Terri said at last.

The real Elldis Rowe, now Churchill, bounced her baby on her knee for a moment, then came to a decision. 'Pat, take the car keys off the hall table and fetch mam.'

She looked at the baby and then at Terri. 'You take this one, and I'll put the kettle on. We need to sort this lot out – it's worse than *Brookside*. My mam's at a church coffee morning. She'll know what's what when she gets back.'

The baby was warm and damp and quite enchanting, fingering Terri's scarlet fingernails with hands like tiny starfish. On impulse, she caught one of its hands and carried it to her mouth. It laughed aloud at the planted kiss, and she did it again and again, until she was almost savage in her fervour. Oh God, she wanted a baby so much. But instead she would have a house: 12, Victoria Close. The Benedict residence. And she must think of Ellie not babies, and try to sort out this muddle.

'She's taken to you, all right.' Ellie Churchill was back with a tray. 'Have you got a family?'

Terri shook her head. 'Not yet.' The front door saved her from further discussion.

'Now then, our Ellie, what's all this?' Mrs Rowe was eyeing Terri with suspicion. 'I've got no sense out of our Pat, no sense at all. Will someone tell me what's going on?'

Terri tried to marshal her thoughts. 'I have a friend called Elldis Rowe. She's married now, her name is Elldis Marriner. She went missing ten days ago but she left behind a birth certificate, which we thought was hers. Now it seems it belongs to your daughter.' The woman was bridling. 'No, please . . . I'm sure it *is* your daughter's . . .'

'Well, I should hope it is. Elldis was my maiden name. We called the first girl for my family, and the second after his mother.'

Terri smiled. 'It's an unusual name.'

Mrs Rowe nodded. 'It is, and why anyone should want to pretend it was their name . . . well, it beats me. You say she's a northerner? I came down from Durham when I wed . . .'

There it was, the link! 'You came from Durham, like Ellie . . . well, the person I thought was Ellie. Could she be a cousin, a niece?'

Mrs Rowe was thoughtful now. 'How old is she, this friend of yours?'

Terri shrugged. 'I thought she was twenty-eight. She's about that age. Does that suggest someone?'

Mrs Rowe began to unbutton her coat. 'Is that tea, our Ellie? Pour it out while I collect meself. This is a nice carry on, and no mistake.'

Ellie had meant to go to the Harpers. Instead she found herself in the market square, sitting on a honeycomb-shaped seat beneath trees heavy with red berries. She looked up at them, enjoying them until she heard a titter: two girls were passing by, laughing at the sight of a foolish woman craning her neck to watch winter trees. She looked down at the ground, watching the scurrying feet of shoppers. The windows of the stores were already decked for Christmas and she leaned her head on her hands, unwilling to acknowledge the glitter.

'Are you all right, love?' The woman's eyes were kind but bright with curiosity.

'Yes, thank you. Just a little dizzy.' Ellie swayed as she got to her feet, and the woman put out her hand. 'I'm all right, I assure you.' She heard the slur on 'assure' as she saw the woman's face stiffen. 'I can't be drunk,' she said, 'I haven't had anything to drink.' But the woman was already hurrying away.

It must be the pills. She had taken two – or perhaps three. And it was a long time since she had eaten. Perhaps she should sit down again and wait for another Good Samaritan. 'Who am I?' she could say and feign amnesia. Then they would take her to a white bed in a white ward and be kind to her.

But they would not stop the cancer growing within her. *'Babies are sin, Ellie. A living, breathing proof of sin.'* She heard the music start in her head, and tried to stem it, but it was breaking through. Ahead of her, Ellie saw a shop doorway and then a pub. Stained glass and darkness. She stumbled over the step. If she could get a drink she might stop the music before it got to the part where it clicked . . .

Faces were looming over her. 'It's all right, love. You fainted. Just lie still while they fetch you a drop brandy.' It was making her splutter and someone was taking it away. 'Who are you, love? What's your name and address?'

Ellie tried not to smile, but it couldn't be helped. *Who am I? Now, that's the sixty-four-thousand-dollar question.*

They were looking in her bag but they would find

no help there. There was no help anywhere – but at least they had stopped the music. Ellie closed her eyes and pretended to sleep.

Paul's clinic had been due to finish at four but he had spent an hour at the newspaper and started late. The last patient left at five-fifteen and he said goodbye to the charge nurse, carried the folders back to Medical Records, and made for the main door. Richard would be arriving in Durham soon and would ring when he was settled, so the sooner he was home to take the call, the better. He had a list of sightings of Ellie in his pocket. Tonight he would work out which to follow up, and tomorrow Richard could make a start.

Paul walked towards his parking spot, a consultant's perk, but it was empty. Had he left the car somewhere else without thinking? He turned slowly, surveying the ranks of cars, seeking his own. He had turned full circle for the second time when he realized the car was gone, and knew who had taken it. At first he felt a terrible anger and then a weary resignation. 'You owe me,' Gary would say if challenged. 'You owe me.'

It took twenty minutes to find an empty cab, twenty stomach-churning minutes while he worried about Richard's call, about his car with an angry boy at the wheel, worried most about how to handle the inevitable confrontation. The car didn't matter, nor the inconvenience – in an hour it wouldn't really matter that he had had to come home by cab. But the gesture mattered. The boy was uttering a challenge, and how he formulated his reply would be crucial.

Paul was fitting his key into the lock when the phone

began to ring, and he went through a terrible fingers-and-thumb struggle, finally leaving his key in the lock of the open door to sprint to the phone. 'Yes, Richard. I've just got back.'

At the other end of the line he could hear Richard's anxious voice, but the words made no impression on him. His eyes were fixed on the doorway to his study, on the tangled mess of tapes, the splintered glass and twisted frames of his wildlife miniatures, scattered on a floor that had the appearance of a battlefield.

Terri got back to Lime Street with twenty minutes to spare. Buying a paper and some peppermints took care of the change problem, and she made for the telephones. Mike first – but there was no answer at his office, and no one at home when she rang there. He must be in between.

Marriner Engineering was still working, but it was Frank who took her call. 'Richard's gone north, Terri. He's going to the Dunelm Arms at Durham. I've got the number – you can get him there tonight.'

He whistled when she gave him a brief outline of her discovery, and promised to keep in touch.

Terri rang the paper next, and promised a future piece. 'I'll ring in again tomorrow and we'll talk. Yes, we'll definitely get something out of it, Stephen, but it's too good to hurry. No, I can't give you anything now. I've got to think it through.'

She tried her home number again, getting out her address book while it rang and checking for the Northumberland number. When she gave up, she re-dialled and heard the old stringer's voice on the other end.

354

'It's Terri Benedict here . . . you remember? . . . yes. Look, sorry about the noise but I'm ringing from a railway station. I'm sorry to bother you again but I've got a name that might mean something to you. Mariella Richardson?' She held her breath in the silence and then, as he began to speak, her face cleared.

'Yes. Yes, that's what they told me. Yes, I'm coming up in the morning. Can I? Oh, thanks! Yes. About eleven . . .'

She wanted to finish the conversation and try Mike again, but she couldn't afford to offend Charlie. When at last he hung up, she had one minute left to get to her platform. She gave the phone a last regretful glance and started to run.

The Dunelm Arms was old and beautiful, but Richard could not imagine Ellie in these ornate surroundings. A message from Jackson, the detective, was waiting for him when he checked in, and he decided to go straight out again. The journey to Sunderland took twenty minutes but he fretted all the way, imagining Ellie at the Harpers' door, the detective laying hands on her, and disaster ensuing.

Jackson was waiting in a dark-blue Cortina. Richard paid off his cab and slipped into the passenger seat. 'I had to hire this,' the detective said. 'I needed a lookout post.'

Richard shook his head irritably. 'I told you not to worry about expense.'

The Harpers' house was in a cul-de-sac at the foot of a hill. The houses were modern with neat gardens and tidy windows. 'They had a general dealer's shop,'

Jackson said. 'Did quite well out of it, by all accounts. Retired three years ago and bought this place. She's the driving force – younger than him. They fostered three children in all, and your wife was the first. There was some talk of adoption, but it never came to anything. Now, your wife has been moving from one old haunt to another, so she's bound to wind up here.'

'Have you seen anything while you've been waiting?'

The man shrugged. 'Usual comings and goings. No sign of Mrs Marriner.'

'She could be inside,' Richard said suddenly.

Jackson nodded. 'Possible, but unlikely. I checked them out, and they don't strike me as the hospitable type. Well, *she* doesn't. Want me to knock and suss things out? You said not to move, before.'

Richard was reaching for the door handle. 'I'll go myself.' No use in agonizing over it. If he didn't do something soon, he'd go mad. He closed the wrought-iron gate behind him and walked between neatly pruned roses to the front door.

'Mrs Harper?' Her beige sweater matched her beige and white checked skirt. Her hair was lacquered into a neat cloche and there was a lacy handkerchief tucked into the fancy strap of her gold watch. Richard didn't like her. 'Forgive me for disturbing you. My name is Richard Marriner.'

She was looking him up and down and apparently approved of what she saw. 'Well, whatever it is you'd better come inside. No sense in letting the heat out.'

There was a plate rack round the tiny hall, filled with colourful plates, all modern, all matching. Everything matched. When she showed him into the sitting-room it could have been the window of any High Street furniture store, down to the Turner print on one wall and the wall-lights on another.

Mr Harper put aside his evening paper and rose to greet the incomer.

'Richard Marriner. It's good of you to see me. Perhaps I should explain – I'm trying to find my wife, whose name was Elldis Rowe. I believe you fostered her some time in the 1960s?'

'1968,' Mrs Harper said. She had seated herself on a Dralon-covered chair, bony knees together, neat brown feet side by side. There were faint scorch marks under the beige nylons, and a blue vein just below her knee-cap. No comfortable lap there for Ellie to snuggle down on. Poor Ellie, she hadn't been lucky with her life's companions.

The man had reached for the morning paper and was turning to Ellie's photograph. 'Did you say Marriner? I thought she looked familiar. Little Ellie – well, I never.'

'She wouldn't come here,' Mrs Harper said suddenly. 'Well, we hardly knew her. It was a mistake taking her in the first place. We were too tied. I couldn't give the supervision, and in the end she was a handful. I told them, and they took her away. So she wouldn't come back again.' Her tone was flat but her eyes were agitated.

'She was with you for two years,' Richard persisted, turning to Mr Harper. 'Is there anything you can tell me?'

The man cast a furtive glance at his wife. 'Well, not really, not to add to what my wife has said. She was quite a nice little girl, but as Esme says, we were tied.

The shop . . . and I had a wholesale then. She used to like to come in the van, make herself useful . . .'

He might have said more but his wife had risen to her feet. 'We haven't seen her for fifteen years or more. We read about your wife in the papers, but of course we didn't connect it. I'm sorry we couldn't help.'

She had put a hand on her husband's shoulder and Richard saw her knuckles whiten as she pressed. Whatever the Harpers knew, they were not going to tell.

'If she should show up or contact you in any way, would you ring me?' Richard scribbled down the number of the Durham hotel. 'I may move through here tomorrow or the next day. It depends how we go.'

Mrs Harper took the card and put it on the tiled mantelpiece beside another china plate on a wooden stand. Richard couldn't help feeling that when he was gone she would throw it into the fire.

Adele had taken extra care over dinner, hounding Solange and putting the finishing touches to it herself. She dressed and made up carefully, but to her own eye the face in the mirror looked furtive and unhappy. Frank would question her about the phone call, and when he did what would she say? As he came through the door, she noticed the gazetteer she had used to check on Sunderland lying on the sofa table, and put it hastily behind a cushion.

'Gin and It, darling? I've made moussaka – I thought we'd just have something simple.'

Frank took the drink and grunted a thank-you.

'You look tired,' Adele said, but he didn't reply. He

put his head against the back of the sofa, closing his eyes and stretching his legs. She wanted him to mention the phone call so that she could demonstrate innocence. Instead she looked at her perfect oval nails, touching thumb to middle finger, seeking words, safe words. 'Did Richard ring the boys?'

His eyes opened. 'Yes.'

'How did they take it?'

'They were jumpy, so Richard said. Poor little beggars, they've had no security since Julia died.'

He seldom talked about Julia, and Adele felt her eyes fill with tears. Now was the time to tell him the truth. But he was speaking again. 'We haven't done all that we might have done, Adele: Terri Benedict has been more use. Driving back I thought about it, about death. About me with the girls if it had been you instead of Julia.' He looked serious, severe even, but he did not look stricken, talking about losing her. Adele's impulse to confess shrivelled.

'We did all the conventional things when Julia died: "We're standing by you, old chap, you only have to ask!" – all that sort of thing. But we never really tried to see inside Richard's head. And then Ellie came along and, if I'm honest, I thought, "Oh good! Old Rich won't have to go without . . . or get it from dubious sources." And Ellie was a nice little thing. I know you resented her, but that was par for the course. And then she went, and we all carried on as though nothing had happened.

'Christ, if we'd been civilized we'd have held a wake – but no, we went on doing utterly mundane things, making utterly pointless conversation. You went on

359

and on about Japan! Japan, Japan . . . you'll be pleased to know that's still on, by the way – unless Ellie turns up dead. And after what Terri's discovered she well may. Still, as long as we send a suitably sized wreath . . .'

'*I know where Ellie is, Frank. At least, I think I do. And I think she's in trouble . . .*' Adele could hear the words in her head, and they were quite simple, but she couldn't say them aloud. She was too afraid.

'And there's something else, Del. God, it's all coming out now. Richard told me today that Ellie is pregnant. She doesn't know, apparently – at least, they think she doesn't know.'

She must register amazement. He must never, never know the truth.

Mike was furious, just as Terri had known he would be.

'I tried to ring you, I tried and tried. But it was leave it or miss my train.' The sink was full of pots and pans, a half-eaten omelette was on the draining board, a crust of wholemeal bread on the rim of the plate.

He gestured around him. 'This isn't marriage, Terri. This is not what I call loyalty. I knew you had a career; I admired you for that . . . for not being like Diana, expecting to be kept. But at least she made the occasional meal, and I saw her from time to time.'

If only he had let her explain about Ellie . . . but it was too late now. She would never forgive him for that crack. The fatigue she had felt in the cab fell away and energy suffused her. 'So you miss Diana? Well, you don't surprise me, I knew you missed her. I've seen

360

the little shrine in your wallet. Your precious little home-maker in her best . . . no second-best . . . bikini.'

Mike should have looked guilty, but instead he looked faintly surprised.

'*I'm* your wife, in case it's escaped your notice. I am your fucking better half, but *I'm* not there, tucked away so you can have a sneaky look now and then. You utter bloody crud, speaking to me of loyalty and carrying that bitch's photograph around. Ever since I met you you've been telling me what a ten-dollar whore she was . . . yes, you have, don't deny it . . . even with your best friend. She took you for everything you had, but she's there in your wallet, your beautiful first wife who I wish with all my heart was your only bloody wife!'

She was weeping now, tears of fury, as he took the wallet from his jacket on the back of the chair and searched through it for the photograph. 'This . . . this . . . is *this* what you're on about? I didn't even know it was there, that's how important it is!'

He was tearing it into pieces, but that was not what she wanted. 'Oh God,' she said aloud, 'I wish I had never laid eyes on you.'

They had gone outside the curtains to discuss her but Ellie could hear enough to know they were puzzled. The nurses had gone through her bag and pockets, solemnly recording every item, trying to get her to speak, gasping when the ring had emerged from its box, looking at one another and then at the cheap clothes on the bedside chair.

They had held up the pills: 'Have you taken any of

these, pet? Doctor needs to know. Come on, you can tell us. Tell us your name, chuck.'

But she had pretended not to hear. She was enjoying this total inactivity, not even lifting an arm, sagging when they lifted her from trolley to bed, letting them roll her like a log from side to side.

If she stayed like this, totally immobile, she would die eventually. And she was not really pretending – she did not know who she was, had never known. She had felt more comfortable as Mrs McReady's lodger or the sister of a GI bride than she had ever felt as Elldis Rowe. Perhaps it had all been a dream, all of it, the park in childhood, Gatcombe Street, London, marriage to Richard . . . all of it had had a dream-like quality. Perhaps she had never lain in Richard's arms and felt him enter her and cry 'Julia' at the final thrust. But one thing was certain: whatever happened, Julia would survive. She always won in the end.

[12]

Adele managed to hold on until the first bird cheeped in the darkness, rehearsing how she would tell him, changing and rechanging words to find an acceptable formula. But new and uncomfortable thoughts kept intruding and eventually, alone in the darkness, she acknowledged the truth.

She had not only loved and revered Julia. She had also feared, and sometimes resented, her for being an adored daughter, a favoured pupil, a happy and secure wife . . . simply for being there, because while Julia was there she, Adele, would always be second fiddle. And then Julia had died, and that had given her the chance to come into her own – until Ellie had come along and threatened her position once more. But Ellie had never in fact been a threat. *She is more alone than I*, Adele thought, remembering the story Frank had recounted last night.

She shifted on the window-seat as cramp took her legs. The garden was dark and mysterious below except for the lawn, which was silvered with frost, a white arena. And the fox, picking its dainty way around the outskirts again, paused to sniff the air, shaking a front paw as though in dismissal. Adele felt a sudden fierce affinity for the lone beast. Perhaps it was a vixen, a mother like her, making mistakes in an effort to protect what it valued most?

Adele pictured herself telling Frank the truth a thousand times. In the end, as the dawn chorus started, she woke him by switching on his bedside lamp. 'Frank, I think I know where you can find Ellie.'

He raised himself on to one elbow and smoothed back his hair with the other hand. 'What are you talking about, Adele?'

She sat down on the edge of the bed. 'Ellie has been ringing me for days, Frank. I don't know why I kept it quiet, but that doesn't matter now. The important thing is that I think she's in real trouble, and we ought to get to her quickly.'

Frank stared at her but didn't speak, and that was more frightening than a torrent of abuse. Instead, he pushed her aside and got out of bed. He walked to the Teasmaid and altered the clock, and as he went into the bathroom she heard the kettle start to hum. She had wondered if she would regret telling him, wish in the first moment that she could snatch back the words. But she felt nothing, no regret, no remorse. Nothing.

He came back as the water boiled and began to fill the teapot. He stood with his back to her and the familiar body was suddenly that of a stranger. At last he turned and handed her a cup. 'I want everything, Adele, every minute detail. Now!'

Paul had cleared up the night before, sweeping up the tapes and broken glass, putting the ruined miniatures on one side. Now he carried his coffee into the study and sat down to assess the damage.

The snow goose was gone, irreparably scarred by broken glass, but the winter hare had survived, and the harvest mouse too, apart from the imprint of a heel on one corner. He pictured the fury that had gone into that orgy of destruction and felt his own fear rise up in his throat.

At seven-thirty he put what might be reclaimed into a drawer and went upstairs to get ready. It was going to be a heavy day, and he had not had much sleep. He soaked in a warm bath for a while, closing tired eyes, then he turned on the cold tap and lay until the drop in temperature forced him to leap from the bath and towel himself dry.

While he shaved he thought of the calls that had been made to the newspaper. Seventeen people claimed to have seen Ellie Marriner in places as far apart as Broadstairs and Maryport. If Richard was to chase them all up, it would take a month. So he would have to make a selection of some sort. When he had made more coffee he sat down with the list and studied the entries one by one.

A vicar in Bridlington thought he had seen Ellie sitting at the back of his church the day before yesterday: possible. A Mrs Raeburn from Birmingham had given tea and biscuits to a gypsy who had very white skin and spoke with a broken accent: probably not. A landlady in Sunderland had had a mystery woman staying while receiving hospital treatment. Not Ellie, she wouldn't have gone within miles of a hospital. Two teenagers from Twickenham had sat behind Ellie on a London bus: wrong area.

When Paul had finished he had four possible leads, none of them in the north-east of England. It was seven-forty-five: Richard would ring any time now.

As if on cue the phone trilled. 'Richard?' He listened as Richard told him of Terri Benedict's Liverpool journey, pursing his lips in silent amazement as pieces clicked into place.

'All this happened in Sunderland, Paul. The detective is watching the foster-parents' place, and I was going there again this morning, and then Frank rang ten minutes ago. Apparently Adele has been in contact with Ellie for days. Don't ask me to explain her behaviour, it's inexplicable. Watching us all worry and suffer, and all the time in contact secretly! I feel sorry for Frank . . . however, he's wrung everything out of her now. Adele says Ellie sounds in a bad way. She's supposed to be in Sunderland, in a room near a park with a lake, and put with the other story that makes sense. Adele says she hasn't got a precise address, but that may be another untruth. I'm going there now. Could you come? God knows where I'll start.'

'I'll have to tie things up here, Richard. Give me a few hours. I'll travel down tonight at the latest. In the mean time, I think I may have something. The paper had a call from a Sunderland landlady which I discounted, but now I think you should check it out. It's a Mrs McReady.'

There was a pause as Richard wrote down the details. 'OK, I've got that. At least it's a place to start. There's one other thing, Paul: according to Frank, Adele thinks Ellie was either drunk or drugged most of the time. What does that mean?' There was anxiety in his voice.

'I don't think we should place too much credence on anything Adele says. We'll talk about it when I see you. Can you check back with me in a couple of hours? I'll know by then – say ten-thirty. You'll find me at St Chad's.'

When Paul had put down the phone he reached for a medical directory and then re-dialled. 'Hallo, this is Dr Paul Weidenek of St Chad's Psychiatric Hospital, Brent. I'd like to speak to your senior psychiatric consultant. I think that's Dr Max Schofield? Oh, well, put me through to him. Just one thing . . . do you cover the whole Sunderland area? You do? Good.'

Terri and Mike had not spoken a word to one another until she was ready to leave. He was still in bed, back turned to her, as she put a cup of tea on his bedside table. 'I'm off now. I'm going north, I don't know when I'll be back. Ellie is up there and Stephen wants me on the spot. I'll ring when I know what's happening.'

Mike didn't move or speak as Terri left the room, and she didn't care enough for it to upset her.

Now she sat looking from the train window as London fell away. They passed a golf course and she saw three women in animated conversation as they walked to the next green. What would it be like to have leisure, time to gossip and play golf, and have a rich stockbroker husband to pay for it? She was never likely to know. Ellie must have looked from a train window and seen all this. Except that they didn't know if she had travelled by train. They didn't know anything. She had uncovered an extraordinary story in Liverpool, but trying to match it to Ellie, quiet, gentle Ellie whose voice hardly rose above a whisper, seemed impossible. Perhaps they had never really known Ellie. Perhaps she was like a Russian doll, round and imperturbable on the outside, opening to reveal a dozen different selves inside? And when the last self was revealed, what would it be like? Someone to love as they had loved Ellie? Or a stranger?

Terri put the imponderable on one side and thought about a more immediate problem – the promised outing to the cinema with Gemma and Alison was tomorrow afternoon, and the girls were taking a day off school specially. She couldn't spoil their treat by taking part with Mike in a hostile silence, much less a war of words, but how was either of them going to pretend that nothing was wrong?

The train rattled into Peterborough and she waited until passengers had mounted and dismounted before she went to the buffet for coffee and a cheese salad sandwich to ease the pangs of indigestion that had troubled her since yesterday.

Back in her seat, she thought about Mike's daughters. Could she ever see them as hers? When they were there, in front of her, she liked them, even loved them a little. Gemma's face was changing as she moved into adolescence, and it had touched a chord in Terri, recalling her own teenage vulnerability. Alison was still a little girl with wispy pony-tail and a gap-toothed grin. Yes, in the flesh they were eminently lovable; it was when they were out of sight that they became a threat, weapons by which Diana could maintain and strengthen her hold on Mike. Terri closed her eyes on a picture of him, tousled and vulnerable, raising himself on one elbow in the early morning to tell her he loved her.

But as the train sped on the picture changed into the disapproving Mike of a dozen rows: *'You have a vicious streak, Terri. I've always suspected it. Now I know.'* Her coffee had grown cold and the cheese sandwich mushy. She pushed them away and turned her face to the window.

It was a long time since Ellie had felt so content. Why hadn't she done this before, closed lips and tongue and refused response? It was absolute power. Their eyes watched you, begging for answers, turning to bafflement, then irritation, then hostility, and finally to resignation. At breakfast time they had tried to tempt her to eat: 'Just a little. For me. Come on, it'll do you good. Please. I'll get wrong off sister if you don't eat anything. Come on, just a spoonful. Look, everyone else is eating. Elsie can't wash up till you finish. I'll have to take it away, mind. Oh, well, it's no good saying you're hungry later on.'

She felt quite happy lying there once they left her alone. She could hear a constant hum of conversation and laughter, but she was not part of it so it called for no effort. She still felt cold and nauseous but that was small price to pay for the high bed with its crisp sheet tucked in so firmly that it held her in a comfortable vice. She watched patterns of light on the glossy ceiling as clouds came and went outside the window. Eventually she discovered faces in the pattern of the curtains around her bed, faces that could be made to vanish and reappear at will simply by narrowing her eyes.

At some time in the morning a doctor came, young and earnest in a too-big white coat. He carried out an examination, apologizing all the while that the nurses had to pull her about to make it possible. 'If you would only tell us your name,' he said tentatively, and for the first time she was tempted. He was just a boy, Jeremy seven or eight years on. But he would only tell someone else, and besides, if she gave them anything . . . anything at all . . . they would never let it rest. So she held her tongue.

The nurse who put her back to bed when the doctor had gone was in her thirties, stocky and determined. 'You're making things very difficult, you know, and all for nothing. They'll find out in the end, they always do. I've got better things to do with my time than look after someone who's pretending to be a dummy. And don't tell me it's anything but an act, because I'm not as green as I'm cabbage-looking. We'd all like to get into bed and have a bit of rest. I've got three bairns at home when I come off duty. What'd happen if we all decided to pack in and lie down; you tell me that?'

Getting no response, she gave Ellie's pillows a final thump and exited, swishing the curtains behind her. What would happen in the end, Ellie wondered, a tiny sliver of fear stabbing her brain? They wouldn't let her refuse food for ever. They might put a funnel in her mouth and pour disgusting pap down her throat. She had seen that happen on television.

She was still worrying when the curtains opened and a woman doctor came in. She had a turquoise silk shirt under her white coat and smelled delicious. 'Hallo,' she said, drawing up a chair. Her hand on Ellie's was warm and soft. *This one is the dangerous one*, Ellie thought and geared herself to resist.

'Your hands are cold.' The doctor was chafing them between her own, taking them one at a time. 'I wish I knew your name. It's difficult to talk to someone when you don't know their name, but I do want to talk to you. I think you probably feel awful and you'd like me to go away? No? Look, my darling, I have to talk to you today because you're having a baby. You know that, don't you? Babies are my business, you see. And besides, I quite like them. I'm a wee bit worried about this baby of yours. Nothing specific, but you haven't been taking care of yourself, have you? And that's not good for your baby.'

Poor baby, Ellie thought dispassionately, condemned to be living proof of sin. *'You're the proof of sin, Ellie, no getting away from that. It's not your blame, poor bairn, but if it hadn't been for you . . .'* If it hadn't been for her the world would have gone on spinning on its axis, the sky would not have fallen. Now it was time for punishment.

Above her the doctor's face was anxious. 'I want to help you. You and the baby. Won't you give me the chance?'

Ellie closed her eyes but left her hand inside the two warm ones. 'All right, then,' the doctor said and went on stroking.

Terri loosened the neck of her coat.

'Sit yourself down.' Charlie, the old reporter, pushed

the cup towards her and then unscrewed the cap of a bottle of Bell's whisky. 'Yes – no?' He held the bottle above her cup and she nodded.

'Yes please.'

The coffee and whisky was wonderful and she settled back in her seat as he began.

'It was 1958, the beginning of it. I was on the *Journal* news desk then. A fire started in a house in Sunderland, and there was a kid there alone. A little girl. They could see her at the window, screaming, but by the time they got her out she was dead.'

'And her name was Julia?' Terri was still unable to accept the coincidence of names.

The old stringer shrugged. 'It might have been, I don't remember. Anyway there was an inquest. The child's father was a long-distance lorry driver, away in Scotland. The mother was a colliery lass gone wrong. Not wicked, not by today's standards, but a bit loose. They were often like that, too much chapel in their upbringing, so they went a bit mad when they got the chance.

'Anyway, she'd taken up with a Yank, a GI. He was sightseeing in Durham on Gala Day, and he and the child's mother struck up a friendship. The night of the fire he'd come north again – he was being posted back to the States, so this was goodbye. She tucked the kiddy up, and went out. When she came back the bairn was dead and the house gone.

'I remember her at the inquest, she was in a terrible way. As for the father, he looked as though he'd been pole-axed. Just sat there, never saying a word. I don't think he'd known a thing about it, he thought she was at home like a good little wife and mother while he was out winning the bread . . . and then this! Anyway, that was that – accidental death. The coroner let her off lightly and warned of the dangers . . . you know the drill.'

Terri put down her cup. 'What happened next?'

Charlie was filling his pipe, tamping in the tobacco. 'As far as I was concerned, nothing. They weren't news any more after the inquest. But, unbeknownst to everyone, the mother was pregnant. Another girl. Her husband stood by her, but I don't think he ever believed it was his kid. They went on living in Sunderland, in a terraced house near the sea-front, a nice, ordinary area. But according to witnesses she'd changed, couldn't forgive herself for what had happened to the first child. He could never trust her again . . . and he didn't like the kid.'

Terri stirred. 'That was Ellie?'

He nodded. 'Mariella Richardson, that was the kid's name. Daft, if you ask me, but I've heard worse by far. To get back to the story, the husband kept on accusing his wife, up-casting things. No one knows exactly what happened, but one day the kid was found in the street, crying her eyes out. The mother was in the living-room – strangled. He got life.'

'And what happened to Ellie . . . Mariella?'

He shrugged. 'I don't know. The mother's family took her, I suppose. I remember her grandmother in the court, like a graven image.' He drew on his pipe. 'There is someone who might be able to help you further . . .'

*

The front door was opened before Richard had a chance to knock.

'Do come in.' She was a tiny woman, balanced on enormous heels, dressed in a girl's outfit that sat oddly on an elderly woman. 'I'm Irene McReady. And you're Richard Marriner. I've read all about you, and I do want to help. You could've knocked me down with a feather when she went, Mr Marriner. I never boast, but I will say I keep my tenants. It's not the money I mind, though it'll be weeks before I can re-let, what with cleaning and what have you. No, I don't care two pins about the rent, it's the way she went without a word.'

Richard was taking out his cheque book but she ignored it. 'I was relieved when I read the paper. "That explains it," I said. "Poor thing, she's not responsible."'

He was writing a cheque. 'That should cover it, I think.'

'Oh, I couldn't,' she said. 'I shouldn't have told you,' but she took it just the same. Richard doubted that Ellie had left owing a penny, but if he judged Mrs McReady correctly he would get nothing out of her until money was out of the way.

She blinked at the sum. 'It's not this much,' she said.

He waved his hand. 'Please. For your trouble.'

She got to her feet. 'Well, you must have a sherry.'

The sherry was nauseatingly sweet, the gold-encrusted glass mercifully small. While Mrs McReady filled her own glass and resumed her seat, he looked around. Was this where Ellie had sought refuge, this over-decorated doll's house with a wrinkled vulture for

374

a janitor? 'I'd be grateful for anything you can tell me, Mrs McReady. My wife has not been well for some time and we're anxious to find her as soon as possible.'

She drew in her breath, causing the cascade of ruffles at her neck to quiver. 'Well, where to begin . . . I'm a widow, Mr Marriner. There'll never be another man for me, but that's by-the-by. I have one or two paying guests . . . very genteel people. We're just like a happy family, although I say it myself. Never a cross word.

'Well, your wife turned up on my doorstep. My name's a byword round here for keeping a nice home. "Do take me, Mrs McReady," she said. "I've got an old aunt in hospital and I need to be on the spot." I really didn't have room, but she begged and pleaded. I'm not given to boasting, Mr Marriner, but I do know my Christian duty. "Come in, my dear," I said. "Don't worry about rent at this juncture. We'll manage somehow."'

Profound distaste was growing in Richard. 'Did she go to a hospital?'

Mrs McReady pursed her lips. 'Well, that's the problem. Went out regular as clockwork, morning, noon and night. I sent a beautiful plant for her aunt, I'm very green-fingered. "Give Irene a toothpick, she'd get a tree from it," that's what my Fred used to say.

'But my friend, Edie Bollon, her daughter's the matron at the hospital and she couldn't trace an aunt. Of course you can't be sure, there's more than one hospital. Which brings me to another point. You'll be staying in Sunderland till you find her? Well, I want you to

consider my home your own. There's room upstairs
. . . we could come to some arrangement. I'm not
interested in money.'

There was a china figure on a side-table, an old
cobbler mending shoes. Richard fixed his eyes on the
figure and tried to stem an irrational desire to roar with
laughter. He looked at his watch: ten-thirty. 'I wonder
if I could use your phone?' There must be a phone
although he couldn't see one.

A crinoline lady lifted her skirts to reveal a bright red
handset, and he dialled Paul's number, to hear the
psychiatrist's excited voice.

'Richard? Good. I've got news for you. Don't worry,
it's not life and death, but Ellie's in hospital – the
District General. Well, I'm almost 100 per cent sure she
is. I rang the Psychiatric Consultant in Sunderland,
just on the off-chance, and he knew of an apparent
amnesiac admitted yesterday. Right age, colouring, et
cetera, shabbily dressed but carrying a diamond soli-
taire ring which they estimate at two or three thousand
pounds. Ring them now, Ward 25.'

When Richard put down the phone, he turned.
'Thank you for your offer, Mrs McReady, but my wife
has been located.' He should be feeling something –
relief, satisfaction, any emotion would do. Perhaps
when he got outside, feeling would come.

Terri paid off the cab and looked around her. The pub
was newly painted with a beautiful sign, the Lamb
and Flag. She walked into the saloon bar and up to the
counter. 'I'd like to speak to Mrs Dinsmore, please.'

The barmaid looked Terri up and down for a moment. 'I'll see if she's in.' She put down the glass she'd been polishing and vanished behind the fixture. There was the pounding of feet on stairs and a muttered conversation.

For a town-centre pub it was remarkably spruce but comparatively empty. One or two men in business suits were sinking a mid-morning pint, and an old man in a raincoat sat at the end of the bar.

'She says to go up.' The barmaid lifted the flap and Terri passed through, skirting wooden crates and bins to pass through the door to the stairs. A woman was leaning over the banister. At first glance she looked like a girl, but as Terri mounted towards her she saw that the golden hair was candy floss, the face raddled. But the mouth was wide and generous, and the eyes twinkled.

'Now dear?' she said, in a voice that had been mellowed by years of booze and cigarettes.

'It's good of you to see me, Mrs Dinsmore. I'm Terri Benedict. Charlie Pringle gave me your name. I'm hoping to pick your brains.'

The woman gave a bellow. 'You'll have to find them first, pet. Haway in off the landing and I'll see what I can do. How is the old bugger? I've known Charlie for thirty years. Tell him I miss him coming in to cadge a pint.'

The sitting-room was surprisingly pleasant, apricot walls and a chintz three-piece with matching curtains. A white poodle rose to greet them, and Terri let herself be sniffed and approved.

'All right, Pepsi, you can go back to sleep,' the woman said. 'Now, what can I get you, love? I've got

377

most things up here, and there's a well-stocked bar down there if you want something exotic.'

Terri settled for a Drambuie on the rocks, and loosened her coat. 'I'm trying to help a friend of mine, who's gone missing. Charlie says you knew her years ago, that her mother was your friend.'

The woman's eyes were wary. 'What's your friend's name?'

Terri put down her glass. 'Mariella Richardson.'

The woman seemed to slump in her chair. 'My God,' she said, 'little Ellie.' She drained her glass and went for a refill, proffering the bottle to Terri. 'No thanks,' Terri said, 'not just yet.'

'What do you want to know? I haven't seen that bairn for years. Not since . . . well, Charlie'll've told you.'

Terri nodded. 'I need to know as much as I can about Ellie, about her mother and her grandmother.'

Mrs Dinsmore's eyes hardened. 'What for? You're not from one of those muck-rakers, are you? Because if you are I've got nothing to say but *out*!'

Terri shook her head. 'No. I am a journalist but Ellie Marriner . . . that's her married name . . . is my friend. I'm helping her husband to find her, and we're running out of time. She's come up here to trace her childhood. She has lots of pills with her – well, we think she has – she's pregnant, and if we don't find her soon it could all go wrong. I need to piece together her background so that I can get some idea of where she might be. I will write it up for my newspaper, but that will be after she's safe and well . . . and with her permission.'

The woman looked at her shrewdly for a moment

and then her face softened. 'OK, I'll tell you what I can.'

She settled herself on her cushions. 'We were girls together, Marjorie and me – that was Ellie's mother. No harm in us, just daft and neither of us much for schooling. Girls weren't in those days. Her family were strict . . . well, her mam was. Religious maniac, my mam used to say.' She laughed. 'Not like my mam. "Do what you like, Molly, but keep your hand on your halfpenny." And I did!

'We went down south together to work in an hotel, 1949 it was. We were there a year and a half, and then we came back north. I got a job in a pub and wound up marrying the landlord; that's how I got into this trade. He was twice my age, but he treated me all right. Margie married Joe eventually, 1952 or 3. He was on the buses then, but later he went long-distance for the cash. She fell for a bairn straight away.

'Well, you know what happened: she did wrong with that American, and her kid died in the fire. It preyed on her mind. I never had kids – man proposes and God disposes, doesn't he?' For a moment her face fell.

'Anyroad, when Margie found she had another on the way it didn't seem to register. All she thought about was the dead bairn, Julia. Fancy name, but Marjorie was like that – very fanciful. I went round there one day and the table was all set for a party. "What's this, then?" I said, and she said, "It's Julia's birthday." Just like that. For a dead bairn! My flesh crept, I can tell you.'

'What happened when the new baby came along?' Terri asked.

Molly Dinsmore shrugged. 'No difference. She looked after it, had it christened . . . Mariella, what a name! I mind on at the christening her mam said, "Another of your daft ideas, our Marjorie." Hard as the hobs of hell her mother was, and no mistake.'

'Was she still obsessed with the first child?'

The woman was refilling her own glass, and Terri accepted another for herself. 'Absolutely. Bill was alive then, my Bill . . . he said there'd be trouble and there was. Every time you went round she'd be playing the gramophone: "Julia loves to hear the records," she'd say. There was a power cut once, and she filled the place with candles: "Julia can't stand the dark ," that's what she said.'

Terri closed her eyes for a second. Poor Ellie, playing second fiddle to a dead child. 'What about the father?'

Molly Dinsmore's snort was graphic. 'Him! If he'd been any other man he'd've buggered off and left her. She might've pulled herself together, then. Made a new life. But he had to stay to rub salt in the wound.'

'What was his attitude to Ellie?'

'He behaved as though she didn't exist. She'd come to his knee . . .' the woman's eyes had filled, '. . . she'd come to his knee and look up, and he'd just ignore her. Not put her away or smack her, or anything – just stare right through her. I wouldn't have treated a dog like that.' The poodle cocked one bright eye at her and then snuggled down again.

'What brought it all to a head in the end?'

'I don't know. It was bound to end in misery, a situation like that. But I never thought it'd end in murder. It just happened: he came home and accused her of seeing another man. She never went across the doors after that fire, so he was wrong there. But one thing led to another . . . I'm guessing here, because there were no witnesses. Only the bairn.'

'You mean Ellie saw what happened?'

'I don't even know that. But she came out into the street crying. Someone went in and found Marjorie dead, blue in the face and her tongue sticking out, and him just sitting there. "I did it," he said, and that was that. The police took him, Marjorie's mother took the bairn. He got life, and Marjorie was cremated. That's the last time I saw Ellie, at the crematorium. I went round her grandmother's the next week but they'd both gone. Vanished.'

'What happened to Ellie's father?'

'He got life. Didn't even ask for the circumstances to be taken into account. He wanted to go to jail, if you ask me.'

They sat on in the chintzy room, drinking and talking. 'My God, you've opened me up today,' Molly Dinsmore said as Terri got up to go. 'I haven't thought about all this for years. But I've never forgotten them. I hope you find her.'

Terri was half-way down the stairs when Molly spoke from the landing. 'There's one more thing.'

Paul had found someone to take his clinics and dictated all essential letters. Now he was trying to pack a case for his journey north, but everywhere he looked there were traces of Gary and it did not make for concentration. It couldn't have gone on much longer, he had always known that. Now it was a question of accepting.

And there were compensations. He could follow his own pursuits without guilt. He could travel, get in a car and go, without frantic phone calls home in case the elusive gig had turned up. He could get on with his paper on Mauser's Syndrome, which had fallen by the wayside and could now be revived. And he need not be afraid any more. It had teased and tantalized, that hint of menace: there had been a certain thrill in abasement, but he had had enough of it.

Downstairs he emptied the fridge, turned it to 'defrost', and rang for a taxi. While he waited he telephoned Richard. 'I'm on my way. You've seen her? Good. I'll be with you tonight. Yes, please, that would be helpful. No, I've arranged to stay as long as necessary. However, I've spoken to Ellie's doctors, and there's no medical reason why she shouldn't be moved back here . . . I suggest we postpone decision until we have all the facts. There may be things to do up there, I simply don't know at this stage . . . She is? Good! I think Terri has a rapport with Ellie, and she may prove useful. Now, I must go or I'll miss my train. I'll see you later.'

A Wrangler jacket was on the hallstand. When he came back he would pack everything of Gary's and leave it at the band's rehearsal rooms. He opened the drawer of his desk and looked at the remains of the miniatures. This afternoon they did not look so pathetic. It was as though they were beginning to revive in the darkness, as they would have done in nature.

Outside in the street a horn blared. Paul shut the drawer, took a last look around and picked up his bag.

*

Richard had managed to get a suite with a view of the park. The hospital had moved Ellie to a private room and he could see her at six o'clock, by which time she might be awake. Last time she had been asleep, like a figure carved in alabaster.

'We've had to give her medication to counteract certain deficiencies and she's sleeping now,' the doctor had said. 'As far as we can make out she hasn't eaten properly for some considerable time. She's dehydrated and she had taken some tablets, not enough to do any harm but enough to slow her down. Now that you've confirmed her identity, we can make progress.'

At five o'clock Frank rang. 'Are you sure you still want me to go to Japan, Richard? I'm not happy about leaving.' No mention of taking Adele. Richard would have to let Frank know that it did not matter now, that there had already been enough misery, but he had an uneasy feeling that nothing he could say would stem his brother's fury. And probably no point now in Adele's going on the trip – they needed time apart.

'Yes, Frank, I think you should go. I want you to go. There's nothing you can do if you stay. I mean to bring Ellie back as soon as Paul gives the go-ahead – he may want to admit her to his own wards, I don't know. But the best thing you can do is get to Japan, nail the deal and get back. And Frank . . . take it easy on Adele.'

There was no direct answer and Richard had not expected one. 'OK Rich, I'll go then. Give Ellie my love, and take care of her. I know you will.'

Richard ordered afternoon tea and was tipping the room-service waiter as Terri arrived. 'Sit down,' he said, 'you look exhausted. Have some of this tea.'

There was a small frown on her face that betrayed her weariness, and he felt a shaft of fellow-feeling. 'I'm glad you're here,' he said, and handed her a cup.

Terri sipped for a moment and then she began her tale, starting with her discoveries in Liverpool and ending with the Lamb and Flag. 'My God,' he said when she'd finished. 'My God! No wonder Ellie broke under the weight of that burden. To play second fiddle to a dead child, with parents who begrudged your existence! Paul will be here tonight and he wants to see you. You can stay over, can't you? I've booked you the next-door room, and you can use this sitting-room.'

Conflict showed on Terri's face, and Richard knew he was asking a lot.

'OK,' she said at last. 'I'll need to make some calls, but I'll stay. Now, tell me, when can I see Ellie?' And then, remembering, she pulled a face. 'I forgot one thing when I was telling you Ellie's story. It's something I think you should know.'

Adele was unable to meet Frank's eye when he came home. She had expected a tirade but he was icy and silent. She sat opposite him at the dinner-table, moving her own food around while he picked at his, conversation confined to 'More beef?'

'No, thank you.'

'Pudding?'

'I've had enough.'

At the end of the mock meal he got to his feet, still wiping his mouth, threw down his napkin and left the room. Adele sat on while Solange cleared, and then followed him upstairs. 'Frank? Please let me explain.'

'I don't want to talk about it, Adele. And I forbid you to petition Richard while I'm away. It won't do any good. He may forgive you, but I'm afraid I can't.'

He was moving around the bedroom, throwing things into airflight bags open on the bed. She followed him at first, until he turned on her.

'I'm tired of you, Adele, tired of your airs and graces, your eternal chip on the shoulder. Your father made money and lost it like any other trader, but you've always behaved as though your family was blood royal robbed of a crown. You're not upper crust, Adele – if you were you'd think a lot less about what you are. It's the middle class who are obsessed with their origins; above and below, it doesn't matter a damn. Julia had more blue blood than the rest of us put together, and she never gave it a thought.'

Julia, Julia, always Julia. Adele put her hands together to hide their trembling.

'My grandfather was a mechanic. Dirty, oily hands, Adele. And I'm really rather proud of him. I loved you once because you were a bright, witty girl who was always pleased about something. But you've become a bore, Adele. And now I find you're spiteful into the bargain.' She couldn't bear any more but there was no escape. 'No, I think "spiteful" is probably an understatement. The time you've wasted could have been dangerous to Ellie, even lethal.'

She made the mistake of trying to excuse herself. 'But I didn't know *where* she was, Frank, I was trying to find out. I wanted to be able to give you and Richard something concrete.'

He straightened up from his case and stared at her.

'Don't perjure yourself, Adele. It really won't make any difference. When I come back from Japan we'll decide what's best to be done. There are the girls to be considered, they're the only thing that matters now.'

He carried his bags to the door and turned. 'I'm using Sara's room tonight. I won't disturb you in the morning.'

No use running to him to plead or beg forgiveness. He already despised her; she could see it in his eyes. 'Will you ring me when you get to Japan? So I know you've arrived safely?'

He did not turn round as he spoke. 'I'll see. It will depend on the time difference. No point in ringing in the middle of the night.'

Adele walked to the window when he had gone and looked down at the garden, grey and shadowy in the half light. Tonight, if the fox came to share her vigil, she would howl her misery and watch its ears prick at the sound.

Her breath had frosted the pane. She put up a hand to wipe it clear but instead wrote J-U-L-I-A, watching the letters until they disappeared, one by one.

There were lights in the strange room when Ellie woke, and the curtains were drawn so it must be night. They had moved her while she was sleeping. How long had she slept? How many days or weeks? Perhaps, like Rip Van Winkle, she had dozed for a hundred years. She would have liked to ease herself upon the pillows, but there might be hidden eyes in the room. Perhaps that was why they had moved her here.

A nurse came in, smiling. 'You're awake then. That's

nice. How about some ice-cream? Or a cup of tea?' A tube in Ellie's arm was attached to a bag of colourless fluid. 'It's only a drip,' the nurse said, seeing her eyes flicker. 'Can't have you dehydrated – not when you've got visitors.'

Ellie kept her face still but inside her there was turmoil. Not Richard. Not the boys. Not Terri. Above all, not Dr Weidenek who knew her inside out. But it was only the nice doctor, in a pink shirt this time with a cameo brooch at the neck. 'Hallo, Ellie.'

Alarm bells! They knew her name.

The doctor was taking her pulse and it was racing enough to give the game away. *'Watch the light. Ellie. Concentrate on the light and ask God to forgive you.'* *'You are the wages of sin, Ellie, and that's the sad fact.'* The light was bright so that the doctor's head became a blur. And then it was slipping away to be replaced by another head.

'Ellie? Ellie, it's me, Richard.'

She could feel his hand on hers, willing her to respond but she would not. 'Oh Ellie, I thought I'd never find you.'

The light was shimmering and tears, traitorous tears, were threatening to betray her.

'Don't, Ellie. Please don't cry.'

And the second head, swimming back on the other side now. 'Let her cry, Mr Marriner. It's the best thing that could happen.'

[13]

In the early darkness, Adele heard the car draw up at the front door, and then Frank's step on the landing and stairs – but she did not leave her room. Some instinct told her it would be counter-productive, and in the long watches of the night she had done a lot of thinking. She had thrown away her marriage for a whim, for five days in Japan, most of which time she would have been jet-lagged anyway.

The bond between her and Frank had been fragile for a long time, but it was her obsession with the Japanese trip and her willingness to lie to obtain it which had been the final straw. If she were to save her marriage it would mean hard work and long-term planning. She would have to earn her place again. It was a sobering thought and it kept her immobile in the window-seat as the front door opened and closed, and the car started up in the drive.

She got up then and went into the bathroom, filling the tub and pinning up her hair before she discarded nightdress and dressing-gown and walked to the full-length mirror. Her own reflection stared back at her, body slim and still firm, neck crêpe-ing slightly, face . . . she moved nearer and stared. Face anxious, that was it! She had been running after the bus for all her adult life, never quite catching it. The gaunt woman in the mirror defied her to contradict that, as steam dimmed the glass and then obliterated her reflection.

After a moment Adele put out a hand and rubbed, revealing her face again, staring herself in the eye. She had wanted power all her life and had never, ever possessed it, except in those first heady moments when she had introduced Frank to sex. She had been a novice too, but instinctively she had known what to do. It was she who had guided his fumbling hands, drawn him into her, not caring about the pain because she could sense his gratitude and his dependency which had made her feel all-conquering.

Her face was disappearing once more, and she turned away. She must get him back. It was all she was good at, being a wife. But for now, she needed comfort. She bathed quickly, pulled a robe over her still-damp body and went in search of her jewel-box.

Terri woke to a feeling of satisfaction. It was more than finding a lost friend, it was the feeling of a job well done. At seven o'clock she made tea and carried it back to bed to watch breakfast television. Frank Bough was still in command, making her feel safe in spite of the various headlines of mayhem and disaster. She snuggled down to enjoy. Breakfast would not be delivered until eight-fifteen: last night she and Richard had agreed that a late start would be highly desirable.

Paul Weidenek had looked pale, she had declared herself bushed, and Richard's cheekbones were standing out like prows in a face grey with fatigue.

This morning she felt better, eager to see Ellie and play her part in breaking the news. Would Ellie find it a relief to know it all at last? Or would there simply be too much to take in? Terri had wondered whether they should tell her only part of the tale, and Richard had looked to Paul for decision. The psychiatrist had been firm.

'We tell her everything. She has lived with uncertainty for too long. She has to start trusting us, and if she senses we are being less than truthful . . . besides, how much would we withhold? Which segment? No, I've weighed it up. She's physically weak and ideally I'd like her to have two weeks of rest, good food and a thorough cleansing of drugs and alcohol. But two weeks more in limbo would be immeasurably damaging to her already fragile grip on reality. So I want her told now, and I think Terri is the one to tell her. I am an inquisitor in Ellie's eyes. She is in love with you, Richard, so there are inevitably emotional overtones. Terri is simply her friend: it should be Terri who guides her through that unpleasant labyrinth which is her past.'

It was a fearsome responsibility, but outside the sun was shining. Terri decided to take a walk in the park after breakfast. It was ages since she had walked in a park, she and Ellie together, bare armed and legged in summer, kicking at leaves in autumn, mincing gingerly over ice in high-heeled boots in winter and watching for the breaking of hard earth that presaged bulbs in spring. The years passed too quickly, and a year when you did not walk in the park was a wasted year.

She showered and dressed, and then downed orange juice, muesli, croissants with jam and butter, and one slice of toast, purely for greed. It was lovely to have breakfast served up on a tray. Still munching, she looked at the clock: eight-twenty-five. Mike would be in the kitchen now. She picked up the phone, dialled 9 and then her home number.

'Mike? It's me, Terri.'

He did not sound welcoming. All the anger of the day before yesterday was there in his voice. 'You haven't forgotten about taking the girls to the movies this afternoon, have you?'

She tried to sound placatory. 'No, I haven't forgotten, Mike, but I'm afraid I won't be back in time. Ellie has been found, but I'm still needed here.'

'You're needed here, too, Terri. Here, with me. A united front, remember? "I'm your wife now, Mike," remember? "No one else but me, Mike." You can't have your cake and eat it, Terri. Either you're my wife and you put that first, or you're not. The girls are expecting you; you can't let them down.' He didn't say 'or else', but it was there in his tone.

'Mike, please be reasonable. Ellie is my best friend, and I'm the only one who can help her . . . well, the best one to help her. Try to understand. I'll have time to make it up to the girls, and I will. But this day is vital to Ellie, this one day. You can't expect me to walk out on her now. And besides, there's the newspaper to consider.'

The moment she said that she knew it was a mistake.

His voice, which had been rough with anger, turned suddenly silken. 'I see. What you're saying . . . correct me if I'm wrong . . . is that I must put you first, above the girls, above Diana, above everything. You, on the other hand, will slot me in wherever and whenever it's convenient.'

'It's not like that, Mike, and you know it. But I can't be bothered to argue. I'll be home as soon as I can . . .'

She had intended to say 'I love you,' but he had rung off so there was no point. And she didn't feel loving any more, even if he had still been there.

Paul walked in the park before breakfast, smiling at pigeons milling around for morning crumbs, gazing into the green depths of the lake for signs of life. There were islands in the middle and a cobblestoned shore. A balustrade ran along its northern edge with stone lions couchant at intervals. Paul leaned his arms on a leonine back and let the sun warm his cold cheeks. Sunderland seemed a nice town, its people friendly. Perhaps now that he had some freedom he could explore the country of his birth.

'I'm forty-seven,' he thought as he walked along the lake's edge. 'Forty-seven years old.' There were compensations to growing old, a dampening down of fires, a greater appreciation of the rare . . . but he was not old enough for that yet, and not sure he wanted to be. He turned towards the park gates and lengthened his stride.

In the main street shops were opening for custom, but he could hear sea-birds and see them sometimes, wheeling above. Coming to a bridge, he saw that the river mouth must be near. There was a crest on the bridge and a motto: *'Nil Desperandum. Auspice Deo'*. If his rusty Latin was right it meant 'Never despair. Trust in God', as good a motto as any.

He took a roundabout way, keeping an eye on his watch, passing through a market square with red-berried trees and a clock on a pole beside the railway station. Now that he was alone he could leap on and off trains at will, visit towns and cities, learn and explore. A fine rain was descending and he turned up his collar. Any minute now he must turn back.

The antique shop was in a side street, selling second-hand jewellery, some of it beautiful and priced accordingly. A porcelain bowl, a beaded evening bag, a vase that might be Clarice Cliff – and there, in a silver frame, the badger. Old Brock, black and white amid brambles. He went inside, heart racing, drawing his cheque book as he approached the counter. He must have it, whatever the cost.

'It's a Nelson, isn't it?'

The assistant looked bemused but checked the signature. *'K. Nelson, 1981.* Yes, that's right.'

Paul wrote out the cheque for £95 and watched as she wrapped it in tissue. It was a beginning, a replacement for what had been lost.

When he came out the rain had ceased and there was blue sky to the west. His father had always pointed out blue sky, spinning one of the Polish folk-tales handed down from his mother and his mother's mother before her. The Polish nation was rich in folklore and that tradition persisted, whatever the regime. He knew all the tales by heart, but there would be no child of his to tell them to. Inside his pocket his fingers closed around the miniature.

Gold-ornamented lampstands stood outside the imposing library. Paul had seen them lit last night and had wondered if they were original. Now, in daylight, they looked what they were – good reproductions. But they were beautiful in their way, and someone had cared enough to put them there. He smiled at a little boy in a bobble hat pulling his harassed mother along by the hand, and then he broke into a lope. Mustn't keep Ellie waiting.

Richard could not believe the time when he awoke, picking up his watch from the bedside table to check that the clock did not lie. Nine o'clock! It was the first time in an age that he had slept through till morning.

He lay for a moment, reliving the events of the previous day, planning ahead. Today they would talk. Tomorrow a light aircraft would be ready at Newcastle airport at two o'clock. By four they would be in London, where Ellie would probably be admitted to a private room at St Chad's. 'I think it's best,' Paul had said when they arranged it. Richard had been unable to hide his disappointment, and Paul's brow had clouded. 'She has an enormous hurdle to take today, Richard. For a little while I'd like her to be under supervision. Besides, if she agrees, I want to try narco-analysis with sodium pentothal. Terri has the bones of the story, but only Ellie can put flesh on them.'

Richard had felt relieved that the burden of telling Ellie would be Terri's, and guilty at the same time. If he had cared enough to ask, to explore gently . . . if he had talked to Ellie of his own past, both before and with Julia, they might have made her voyage of discovery together.

He swung his legs out of bed at that point. Lying there castigating himself for his shortcomings would benefit no one. He passed a hand over his chin and felt stubble. Janet had warned him last night that the papers were up and running. It was dangerous to meet the press, even industrial correspondents, when you were less than par – he knew that of old. He went into the marbled bathroom and drew back the shower curtain.

When he had showered and shaved he caught himself whistling and was amazed by it. They were not out of the wood yet, not by a long chalk. He had packed without interest so it was a struggle to find a matching shirt and tie, but he dressed as carefully as he could, wondering if he should take Ellie flowers and deciding against it. He couldn't afford to look like a lovesick boy. When she came home, though, he would fill the house with flowers, piling them on every surface. *If* she came home. What had Paul said, a week or a month ago? *'I don't know what the new Ellie will be like. I'll tell you one thing, though, she will no longer want you as a father figure.'*

He pushed unpleasant thoughts aside and rang Avebury School. The Head was relieved to hear the news of Ellie's safe return.

'Tell the boys she's fine and will be home in a few days. I'll collect them then, if you agree, so that they can see her for themselves.' When he had put down the phone Richard buzzed the hall porter and ordered a dozen red roses.

*

The baby doctor had sat by Ellie's bed for half an hour. 'You're not my patient, not officially, but I've taken a fancy to you so they're humouring me.' She was older than Ellie, thirty-five perhaps, and her hands were bare of rings. 'Does she have a lover?' Ellie wondered. It would be nice if she had but it didn't really matter. Very little mattered.

The doctor talked of everyday nothings, skirting the real issue until Ellie was forced to speak out. 'I want to have this pregnancy terminated.'

She expected shock and horror, but the doctor simply nodded. 'I thought you might.'

'I have reasons.'

Again the doctor was nodding. 'Most women who have their pregnancies terminated have reasons.'

Ellie was silent for a moment, weighing possibilities. 'Would you terminate it for me? Is it legal?'

'If there is reason to believe the baby poses a threat to a mother's physical or mental well-being, then it's legal. I think we could make out a case, if it's what you really want.'

Ellie wanted to nod vehemently but somehow she couldn't. 'I don't know what I want.'

The doctor smiled. 'That figures. That's why I hope you'll wait, just for a little while. We estimate you're eight weeks pregnant, so you can take a week or so to sort out your feelings. I promise you it will be your way in the end.'

'Is it all right – the baby, I mean?'

The doctor raised her eyebrows. 'I think so. As far as I can tell. We'll know better when you've had a scan . . . if you decide to go ahead, that is. But I think you should talk to your husband. It . . .' She hesitated, suddenly less assured.

'It's his baby,' Ellie said. 'That's the one thing I'm sure of.' It was Richard's baby – somehow she had not thought of that. She had felt it as an extension of herself, growing from within her almost of its own volition. But it was Richard's baby too.

'They want to take you south tomorrow,' the doctor said. 'Dr Weidenek can't be away from his other patients for too long and he's anxious to keep you under his wing. Is that what you want?'

If I want to stay she won't let them take me, Ellie thought. *I am important to her.* Or was it the baby that had aroused the doctor's interest? *'The wages of sin.'*

'What's amusing you?' the doctor asked, intrigued; and then, seeing the tears, 'It's all right to cry, Ellie. We all need to cry sometimes.'

Richard handed Ellie the roses awkwardly and then, seeing her indifference, he lifted them and put them on the locker.

The nurse who had shown him in swooped. 'Roses! Lovely! I'll find a vase.'

They were alone now, and he sat down by the bed, seeking the right words. Paul had warned him against emotion but that warning was unnecessary. He never could voice his feelings.

'Terri is here, Ellie. And Paul Weidenek. Don't bother to talk, I know you're exhausted. They're coming over later, hoping you'll want to see them. Especially Terri. She's worked very hard to find you.'

Ellie showed no reaction, and he hurried on. 'She's

managed to find out quite a lot about the past – before the time you remember, before you were born in some cases. She's willing to tell you about it . . . if you want to know.'

He was about to despair when she spoke. 'Are the boys all right?'

He nodded. 'They're fine. Longing to see you.' If she refused to come home there was nothing they could do, Paul had told him that.

She looked white and tired but that was to be expected. Her arms were lying on the folded coverlet. He put out a finger and touched her wristbone. It was small and insignificant beneath his finger. 'You need building up.' It was a silly thing to say, but for the first time there seemed to be a slight reaction. 'It's cold outside.' That was a bloody silly thing to say. What else was there? 'Trumper misses you. Dasher too, but especially Trumper. Paul and I walked them the other night, miles and miles. I think they were glad to turn for home in the end. The fox has been round again. Remember the fox?'

She was nodding, but without real interest. *She's going through the motions*, he thought. *Still the old Ellie, not wanting to give trouble, to make waves.* He looked at his watch. The others were not due for half an hour: how would he fill the time?

'The boys were home for the weekend. We did the usual things. I took them to the British Museum. We ate out quite a lot, got takeaways . . . you know what they're like. We went for a walk up by the quarry one day. The weather's been quite good. They miss you, Ellie.' A note of anguish was creeping into his voice. He mustn't let it.

Her lips were moving and then she spoke. 'Did you do their tuck?'

He nodded. 'Mrs Withers did it for them. Enough for the whole school.'

He was silent then, until the nurse reappeared with the roses. 'There now, aren't they lovely? No one ever sends me flowers like that.' She put them on the locker and rearranged a stray bloom. 'It's time to get up, Mrs Marriner. I'll get your clothes.'

Ellie sat up and Richard decided that was a good sign.

'Perhaps you'd wait outside, sir? We won't be long.'

But as he left the room he noticed that Ellie did not look at him. It was as though he had never been there.

'I thought you'd be in Japan by now, Adele.' Her mother's voice was only mildly surprised. 'Well, you'd better come in, but I'm afraid you can't stay long. It's my bridge afternoon and we're going out to lunch first. On Eleanor . . . it's her birthday. Do you want coffee?'

They went through to the morning-room, her mother carrying the tray. 'Sit down, dear. I can't bear it when you follow me round. This is such a tiny house.'

It was not a tiny house, Adele thought suddenly, it was a very nice house by most standards. They had made up their minds to hate whatever replaced the old home, and so the house had been condemned. But it had its points.

'It's only instant, I'm afraid, as we're in a hurry,' her mother said, 'but I've given you the last of my florentines.'

'I don't want sweets,' Adele thought, 'they don't

399

make up,' but she took the biscuit just the same and bit into it.

'You'd better tell me what's happened,' her mother said, hitching up her wool skirt to reveal still-elegant legs. 'I gather this is not a social call.'

It had been a mistake to come here. Adele tried to think of a get-out, a cast-iron excuse for Frank's leaving her behind. She could say Ellie's reappearance had necessitated one of them staying, but it would be a lie. It was cold in the room but she knew better than to ask for a fire.

'Frank didn't want me to go with him to Japan. That's about it. We're not getting on.'

Her mother drank carefully, then set her cup down.

'Is it bad?' She might have been asking about a fault in double glazing.

'Pretty bad.'

'I hope you won't do anything foolish, Adele. These things happen in every marriage. Is there someone else?'

Adele shook her head. 'No, we managed to foul up entirely on our own. Wasn't that clever of us?'

'There's no need to be flippant, Adele. I'm sure I don't understand you. Any other girl would give her eye teeth for what you've got . . . and you mustn't contemplate divorce, not with the girls coming up to marriage. Modern weddings are so complicated, with no one knowing who's supposed to sit next to whom. You've got to ride it out, that's all, and be clever about it. Cook for him whatever he likes, and do watch personal hygiene. It's easy to get slack, and these things are crucial.'

Adele let out her laughter, letting it roll on and on, revelling in it until her mother's voice cut through it like a whip. 'Stop that at once! At once, do you hear!' She had risen to her feet and was moving to the fireplace, standing there like a prosecutor. 'Do you think I'm going to let you throw it all away? You little fool, I might have known you'd make a mess of it.' She turned her back on her daughter, placing both hands on the mantelshelf.

'I've never talked to you about the past, Adele, but perhaps I should've done. I wanted you to feel secure, so I kept quiet. And I wasn't proud of my background. You never knew your grandparents. Your father's parents were dead when we married – they were decent enough, but they're not important. I never knew my father. My mother swore she did, but I doubt it. I was a bastard, a by-product of one of her many affairs.'

The florentine had congealed in Adele's mouth, nuts and cherries locked in a gluey paste as her mother continued.

'I was little Cicely Edwards whose mother kept a beauty-parlour above a bicycle shop. By day she anointed the ladies of the district, by night she bedded their husbands. I was conceived by accident and born in spite of everything she could do to prevent it. She was a gin-soaked hag when I finally got away from her. Maudie Edwards, the neighbourhood joke. And I swore, I swore to myself, that I deserved better and I'd get it.

'I worked in a hat shop. I was pretty, I watched what people did, the right people, and when I moved on I changed my class. I became upper-crust come down in the world. There was no shame in being poor in wartime. I went into the WRNS. The other girls thought I was something special, and I played on that for all I was worth.

'Your father was a naval rating, but he had charm and he looked the part. Above all, he was someone I could push. I knew I would have to do it myself, for I'd never have married into a good family once they looked into my background. So I took your father and I made him. *I* was the business. *I* worked. *I* acquired. *I* bought the gracious house and restored it, furnished it piece by painstaking piece. I made money hand over fist, but I had to be discreet. Women of my chosen class weren't supposed to *do*, just to *be*. My God, I fretted sometimes, itching to do things myself because I'd have done them better.

'Your father went along with me, and in the end he came to believe it all. It went to his head. That's why I wanted Frank for you, because he was strong. Your father was weak. He let everything I achieved slip through his fingers.' She looked around the room. 'So I've come to this.'

Adele's hand had strayed to her mouth. Now she took it away. 'Did you ever love Daddy?'

Her mother's hands fell to her sides as she turned. 'Love him? My dear girl, haven't you realized . . . there is no such thing as love.'

In the car Adele felt the need to cry, but tears would not come. She was passing St Andrew's church and on impulse she turned in at the gates. Ten to one it would be locked . . . but the door gave at a touch and she was inside before she saw the stooping figure by the altar. The vicar's ghastly wife!

'Mrs Marriner, what a nice surprise. Were you looking for the vicar? He's not here, I'm afraid.'

The face, with its incipient moustache and weather-beaten cheeks, was suddenly kind. 'I expect you'd like to sit down. I feel like that myself, sometimes.' She looked more dishevelled than ever, but her eyes were kind. 'Sit yourself down and draw breath – yours is such a busy life. I must see to my jobs. I'll be in the vestry if you need me, but if you want to slip out before I come back . . . well, I shall hope to see you again.'

The church was shadowy and cold, and Adele fixed her eyes on the altar. She was alone now, alone with God, if such a being existed. She wanted to pray but the only words she could think of were, *'Yours is such a busy life.'* But *I don't do anything*, she thought, *nothing at all*. And probably she never would. That was reason enough to cry, but she could find others if she tried. Perhaps she should pray for a new deodorant – according to her mother, that was all you needed to repair a broken marriage.

The church windows were red and blue and gold, conventional stained glass, but they were of poor quality. Perhaps she could endow a window, a glorious blaze of colour sacred to the memory of the first Mrs Frank Marriner? Frank would marry again, no doubt about that. She would be quietly pensioned off and he would begin again. She would never see him, except when the girls married and they put on a charade – everyone did that now, even the Royals. And Snow would go: Frank would not be mean, but there would not be enough for stabling. She would have a neat suburban semi like her mother, nothing more.

She looked around. It was a poor little church, really. Threadbare kneelers, plastic runners in the aisle, the altar almost bare now that it was not buried under flowers. Perhaps she could find religion and, through it, consolation? But she knew enough about it to know you couldn't find it; it had to find you.

Her mother's face appeared when she shut her eyes, and she opened them again. She couldn't think about that now. Not yet. *Please help me, God.* No, that was wrong. *Please help Ellie. Don't let me have harmed her. Let things work out. Give me a quiet mind. For once in my life, give me peace.*

There was no divine light, no clash of chords, just a gentle clatter of vases from the vestry as the vicar's wife fumbled her way through the week's flowers.

Well, that's something I can *do,* Adele thought, and got to her feet.

'Hallo, Ellie.' Richard had warned Terri to expect little response, but Ellie gave a half smile, so that was something. 'I brought you some soap and talc. You like Rive Gauche, don't you? Anyway, that's what you've got, so make the best of it.'

A definite smile now but no attempt to touch the package.

'Paul is outside, with Richard. He's very dishy, isn't he? Paul, I mean. And Richard too. Oh God, I'm blathering!' She knew what she wanted to say . . . it was beginning that was difficult. *This is the most important assignment I've ever had*, she thought and was suddenly afraid.

Ellie laid her head back against the chair and closed her eyes before she spoke. 'Richard says you've been checking things out.'

Terri felt a flood of relief. It was out in the open! 'Yes, Ellie. Do you want me to dive straight in?'

She licked her lips as Ellie nodded, seeking an embarkation point.

'Well, first of all, your name is not Elldis Rowe.' Her friend's eyes widened at that. 'It's true, Ellie. You are not Elldis Rowe, you never were.'

Wheels were screeching on rubber in the corridor outside but Ellie seemed not to hear. 'Who am I?'

It took half an hour to tell the tale, Ellie interrupting the flow now and again to question Terri until at last the nub of the story was out. 'And so you went to your grandmother. It was the logical solution just at first, it suited everyone. When someone decided to put the thing on a proper footing, they found your grandmother had left Sunderland. She'd vanished, lock, stock and barrel, taking you with her.

'I don't think she meant to evade the authorities, she just wanted to protect you from publicity, from the stigma of what had happened. But to do that she had to give you a new identity. You were three years old; she'd need a birth certificate when you started school, and for other things. She had a niece who'd left the north-east and married a Liverpool man. Their daughter had been born the week after you and christened Elldis Rowe. Your grandmother applied for a copy of that child's birth certificate, and used it for you. She didn't register for child benefit, I expect she was afraid to do that. There must have been times when she was short of money . . . but it was worth it to protect you. I've talked to people who knew her, Ellie. They say she was a hard woman, but she loved you.'

Tears were coursing down Ellie's cheeks. 'She said I was the wages of sin.'

Terri shook her head. 'That was wrong of her, but she probably thought it would go over your head. It would have done with most kids, but I think you were different. You had to grow up the hard way. Living with your mother's obsession with your dead sister, Julia, and then . . . what finally happened. I think you blocked it all out, but it left its mark. That's Paul's province and I don't pretend to understand it all, but I've got a vague idea of how it must have been.'

Ellie had started to shiver, and Terri picked up a white honeycomb blanket from the bed to cover her. 'That's about all. You were taken to a village a long way from your grandmother's own, and away from Sunderland too, where your parents had lived, so when your grandmother died you were taken into care. No one questioned the birth certificate and you became, to all intents and purposes, Elldis Rowe. I think she probably chose that name deliberately because she could go on calling you Ellie. If you'd been suddenly called something else you might have queried the name-change, and someone would have twigged. But you remained Ellie, and at three years old you accepted what you were told – that you were born on 8 June in Liverpool, that your father deserted you and your

406

mother died. But the truth was there, in your head, like a time bomb.

'And then, once more, Julia came into your life – another Julia, but enough to trigger your unhappy memories of a dead and perfect predecessor. It was coincidence, but it must have been awful for you.'

'She seemed to be everywhere.' Ellie closed her eyes briefly. 'If I opened a book, she was there on the flyleaf. There were photographs, too, hundreds of them, or so it seemed. And her initial on towels and table-linen. J for Julia. I couldn't understand why it upset me so.'

'Let's face it, Ellie . . .' Terri said, '. . . God, I'm glad you're Ellie: I couldn't have called you Samantha or Jean or something . . . let's be honest, being a second wife in any circumstances can be traumatic. It's fine if you're sure of yourself, but if you have an Achilles heel you suffer.' She was quiet then, thinking of Diana.

'There's one more thing,' Ellie said suddenly.

Terri sighed. 'I was afraid you were going to ask me that.'

Paul sat with Richard and Terri in a corner of the dining-room. No need to lower their voices – most of the other tables were empty, and piped music provided cover.

'This is gorgeous,' Terri said, cutting into thick slices of lamb. 'I didn't realize how hungry I was.' They were all eating, drinking. Paul even felt a little hungry himself. He looked up to find Richard's eye on him.

'What do you think?'

Paul took his glass and sipped, to buy time. This was always the doctor's dilemma, steering between the fostering of despair and the encouragement of false hope. 'I'm cautiously optimistic, Richard. We've inched forward today, but there's still a long way to go.'

Terri laid down her knife and fork. 'Inched? I think we've galloped. This morning Ellie believed she was Elldis Rowe. Now she knows . . . *knows* . . . she is Mariella Richardson, and it hasn't thrown her. I was expecting hysterics or total disbelief . . . I know how I'd have reacted. But she accepted it. That seems like a giant stride to me.'

'Of course we've made progress, Terri,' Paul said. 'And neither Richard nor I underestimate the part you've played. But what has happened is that we have given Ellie a set of facts. She accepts them, but does she relate to them? When we get back to London I want to use pentothal to let her remember for herself. I suggested it long ago, and she said no. I brought it up again tonight and she said nothing. Now, that *is* a step forward!

'I need to . . . I think you'd call it getting inside her head. However much we lay out the facts, if she retains in her subconscious any misinformation, we'll have trouble. The worst thing that could happen now is that Ellie should greet us tomorrow, apparently together and anxious to get home. That would be papering over the cracks, and it would be fatal. I don't think that's what will happen, so you needn't look so worried, Richard. Terri, you look suddenly like a little girl who's just been robbed of her favourite toy. Let me fill your glass.'

They talked of practical things then. 'We should be through by noon, shouldn't we?' Richard asked. 'I've got a plane laid on at two. We'll be back in London by four.'

Terri was taking a meringue glacé from the sweet trolley. 'I'm indulging myself tonight,' she said cheerfully. 'It's back to Marks and Sparks and the microwave tomorrow. All the same, it'll be nice to be home.'

Paul smiled at her enthusiasm, but shook his head to the trolley. There would be no welcome home for him. A silent house, an empty fridge. For a moment he allowed himself to think of former reconciliations, of blazing rows and walkouts which he had believed to be the end, only to hear the radio in the kitchen when he got back the next day. But this time was different. It was not that he could not forgive the destruction of things that had been important to him, it was that he couldn't face the inevitability of further conflict. He had made up his mind. 'Tell me about your house, Terri,' he said, and relaxed a little as she prattled cheerfully about her hopes of a house with a garden.

The men carried their coffee into the lounge, but Terri excused herself: 'I want to wash my hair, and I must ring Mike.'

Paul could see more questions trembling on Richard's lips, and it depressed him. He didn't have answers yet. All the same, the questions would come and he would have to field them as best he could.

'I've been thinking about this baby,' Richard began. 'After all that's gone on in the last few weeks, what are its chances? You talked to that obstetrician, Dr Hethcote. I wondered what she had to say?'

'She thinks, as far as anyone can tell, that the foetus is unharmed. The human embryo is tough, you know.

But it's early days, Richard. Ellie has asked about termination, saying that's what she wants. Dr Hethcote is a typical baby-doctor, she'd rather save than abort. But she believes Ellie's wishes . . . once we know what those wishes *really* are . . . should be respected. Ellie's been through a lot, and I don't think we're entitled to impose childbirth upon her against her will. On the other hand, there are also consequences of abortion, which is a traumatic business . . . we must weigh up the possibility of her future regret. All I ask of you . . .'

He never finished his sentence. 'Dr Weidenek?' The receptionist had left her counter and was moving towards him. 'I have a Dr Hethcote on the line.'

Paul would have preferred to take the call alone but he knew when he was beaten. He talked to the obstetrician with Richard standing a foot away from him, not trying to conceal his anxiety.

'I see . . . that's good.' He tried to signal that all was well but Richard's eyes were agonized. 'Yes . . . Nine o'clock . . . Thank you so much.'

He put down the phone and turned to face him. 'Dr Hethcote called in to say good-night to Ellie, and Ellie told her she wants the narco-analysis now, before she leaves the north. It's arranged for nine tomorrow morning. I'd've had to do it in hospital, anyway, for fear of an adverse reaction.'

When Terri heard Mike's voice she knew straight away that something was wrong.

'I read your piece about Ellie, Terri. Someone at the office shoved it under my nose. I've been a sod; worse than that I've been a stupid sod. I'm sorry.'

She was taken aback by an apology when she had been expecting further aggro. 'It's OK. It's as much my fault as yours. I should've explained properly.'

'Is Ellie all right?'

He sounded so penitent and down that Terri's throat constricted in sympathy. 'She's fine. Well, considering all the circs. I'll tell you all about it when I get back, and you won't believe half of it . . . but she's alive and well, and we're hoping to get her straightened out. Richard's here and Ellie's psychiatrist. You'd like him.'

'Good,' Mike said. 'Well, don't overdo it. I want you back in one piece.' He sounded so *down*. What on earth was wrong?

'I'm OK,' she said. 'Marvellous food, plush accommodation, limousine travel . . . I'm living it up, here, brother. You should be so lucky.' She was dying to ask him what was wrong, but she daren't.

'That's about it, then,' Mike said slowly. 'As long as Ellie's OK . . .'

But that was *not* all, she could sense there was something else. 'Are you all right? And the girls? How did the outing go?'

The outing had been postponed. 'Diana wouldn't let them take a day off school . . . and I wanted to wait till you were there, anyway. We all did.'

There was a pause and then . . . 'Terri?' This was it, the crunch! 'Sam rang tonight. He's pulling out of the deal.'

So that was it: goodbye, Victoria Close. Dear little house. Poor Mike, how he must hate telling her.

'It doesn't matter, darling. I never really believed it, so I'm not going to die of disappointment. I've been

411

thinking . . . the flat is fine really. When would I find time to clean a house? And we could buy a convertible sofa for the girls, a really good "put-u-up". You'll see, it'll all work out.'

If this had been telly or a Meryl Streep movie she'd have had eyes glazed with tears while she spoke these brave words, but this was real life and in real life big girls didn't cry. Well, not about houses, anyway.

[14]

Adele would have liked to go for a walk when the sun came up; better still, to saddle up Snow and ride for miles. But once again she couldn't leave the telephone. She had spent hours trying to work out time-changes and had ended up totally confused. Frank was in Japan by now; he had said it would take fifteen hours door to door, so he must have got there at eight o'clock last night. If he had been going to ring, he'd have done it then. All the same, she couldn't take the risk. She seemed to have spent half her lifetime waiting for the phone to ring.

She carried coffee through to the living-room and opened the French window on to a bare and frosted garden. *'We'll have French windows in every room so we can give marvellous parties. Everyone will want to come and when the room gets crowded they can just spill out on to the terrace.'* Julia had always had such good ideas. But life had taken care of the parties. After the first few years they had only gathered for Christmas and funerals. Julia had died at Easter, and the sprouting of the garden had somehow seemed obscene in the face of her death.

Above Adele a plane was passing on its way to Heathrow, soundless, miles up in the sky. Later today Richard would bring Ellie back. If she came straight back to the house, what would they say to one another? Would Ellie, too, have turned against her?

The phone rang and her cup clattered in its saucer as she raced back into the room.

'Hallo, Adele.' It was her mother. 'I'm ringing to ask if you've heard from Frank.'

Adele forced herself to be civil. 'No, Mother, and I must ring off. He could ring at any moment.'

She had almost given up when the call finally came.

'Adele?' He sounded as though he was in the next room.

Her head was moving from side to side for some ungodly reason, but she managed to keep her voice steady. 'Frank! You're there. How was the flight?'

'Tedious. I was shattered when I got here. What's the news of Ellie?'

'She's coming home, well, coming south . . . I don't know yet whether she'll come back to the Garth or go into Dr Weidenek's hospital.'

'Good. I was wondering. Well, mustn't linger. What time is it there?'

'Eleven . . . eleven in the morning. What time is it with you?'

'Eight o'clock in the evening. I'm going to turn in now. Give my love to the girls.' And then, when she had almost given up hope . . . 'I'll ring again. Cheerio.'

She would get him back. They'd had something once, he'd said so himself. She would work and strive and win him back. She started to laugh suddenly, and then to cry, and then a combination of the two. It was crazy, but all she could think of was Scarlett O'Hara vowing to regain Rhett Butler's love – even if he didn't give a damn!

She poured herself a brandy, the decanter chinking the glass as her hand shook. There was a *Movies Themes* LP somewhere, with 'Gone With the Wind' as one of the tracks. In a moment she would play it, and pull herself together.

Ellie had relaxed now, and Paul tucked her arm inside the blanket and put the syringe back into the kidney dish.

'Ellie, can you tell me what year it is?'

'1987.'

'And the month?'

'December.'

'Are you married, Ellie?'

A second's hesitation. 'Yes.'

'What is your husband's name?'

'Richard. Richard Marriner.'

'Do you love him, Ellie?'

The eyes were drooping, the voice becoming monotone. 'Yes, I love him.'

'Do you love his children?'

An almost imperceptible movement of the head there, as though she did not want to answer. 'I love them, but they don't belong to me.'

Too soon to mention the baby growing inside her. Paul stayed in safe waters until she was deep under the influence of the drug and he could steer her back to childhood.

'How do you feel about Julia?'

Hesitation and then, 'She designed the house, it's her house really. Richard has photographs of her. She's so beautiful it makes me want to cry.'

'Are you beautiful, Ellie?'

A small frown as though she thought the question irrelevant. 'I'm not beautiful like Julia. Her name was in the flyleaf of the books: "Julia Margaret Anstruther."'' There was still reverence in her voice, but no anguish. He could safely take her back.

'What happened on your birthdays, Ellie, when you were a very little girl?'

'I didn't have a party. I might have one some time, Mammy said. But it had to be for Julia this time.'

'Why, Ellie?'

A pause and then the voice, childish and resentful. 'Because Mammy said so.'

Julia, Julia, the name cropped up again and again.

'Do you love Julia?'

The answer was unfettered by any inhibitions. 'I hate her. If Julia wasn't here I could get on Mammy's knee.'

'Would you like to do that, Ellie?'

'Yes.' Quite matter of fact. No pain, no regret. When Ellie woke she would not remember questions or answers, but he would have cut free the debris so that it could float to the surface and be dealt with.

'Tell me about your name, your proper name.'

'I'm called Mariella.'

'What does your grandmother say about your name?'

'It's another of Mammy's daft ideas.'

He half smiled as he made a note: her grandmother must have been a redoubtable woman.

'What happened on the day your mammy died, Ellie?'

If there had been normal emotion in her voice, listening would have been almost unbearable. 'Mammy said, "Go out and play." But I was frightened because Daddy was angry. Mammy wouldn't listen to him when he shouted. She put the record on, the one I liked. He got very angry and she made the music louder. I was in the kitchen and I could hear Daddy shouting and I could hear the music until it started to click. I waited for Mammy to put it right like she always did, but it went on clicking.'

There was a long pause. 'I looked through the crack in the door . . .'

Paul closed his eyes, thinking of the child alone in the silent kitchen, the record stuck in a groove, repeating and repeating. 'What happened then, Ellie?'

'I went into the room. I wanted to get on someone's knee. Mammy was in the chair but she wouldn't wake up, not even when I tried to make her. Her face was all funny and she wouldn't listen to me. I didn't like it.'

'Where was your father, Ellie.'

'He was sitting in the chair.'

'Did he say anything?'

'No.' She fell silent now.

'Go on, Ellie.'

'I was crying.' She was suddenly reluctant and the words came slowly. 'I couldn't get the front door open. I tried and tried but it was too high.'

'Why didn't you go out of the back door.'

'I couldn't go past Mammy again. She looked funny.

I didn't like it. I got a chair and climbed up. It took a long time to get the catch off. It made me cry and it hurt my fingers. There was a man in the street, the man from the corner shop. He was putting the orders in his van and he dropped the sugar. It went all over the street, and the rain made it turn brown, but I didn't get wrong.'

It was warm in the waiting-room, isolated from the morning bustle in the ward. Several times Richard walked to the door and looked across to Ellie's room but there was no sign of activity and a passing nurse gave him a warning look. 'It will be quite a while, I'm afraid. They mustn't be disturbed.' Twice she offered him tea or coffee, and the second time he said yes, sipping the lukewarm yellow tea gratefully.

'Mumbo-jumbo' – that's what his father would have called narco-analysis. And to him Paul would have been a 'witch doctor'. One of his aunts had grown strange during the menopause and his father had simply advised her to 'pull her socks up', even on his visits to the private room he had paid for in an exclusive nursing home that specialized in the eccentricities of the rich. His mother had gone to extremes to keep his aunt's illness a secret, and the whole subject had been taboo.

What Frank had said was true. Richard fought against feeling disloyal as he reviewed his upbringing. He had been taught so many things but not how to live, not how to communicate, to comfort his wife or tell his children they were loved. As for this . . . he looked around the hospital room. No one had taught him how to stand by one wife on a journey into death or another on a sortie into nightmare. Ellie was not mad. The human mind was an organ, like kidney, liver or lungs. It must be as capable of going wrong under stress and equally deserving of treatment.

He tried to analyse his feelings about Ellie's coming home. Paul had refused to make a decision: 'I want to see what happens this morning. And I want to know what Ellie wants. I'll take her into St Chad's if that seems best; if not, you can take her home and let your Mrs Withers give her some TLC.'

Richard had looked blank and Paul had explained: 'Tender loving care, Richard. Best medicine in the world.'

If Ellie came home, *when* she came home, he would care for her himself. All the doubts of the last few weeks had been swept away when he looked at her in the hospital bed, plain and white-faced, hair scraped back, skin sallow above the unflattering hospital night-gown. He had never loved her more.

'I wonder how we'll see this in ten years' time?' he had asked Paul. 'There have been times when I've wondered if I'd survive it, and other times when I've felt quite detached from it, as though it were happening to someone else. All the while I've gone through the motions for other people, giving orders, making polite conversation, putting a good face on things, doing whatever I thought people would expect of me. But I was just acting a part.'

Their eyes had met. 'We're all acting,' Paul had said, 'all of the time.'

*

419

Terri was firm when she rang in to the paper. 'Yes, I'll be in in the morning, Stephen. I know you're under pressure, but this hasn't exactly been a picnic . . . I can't help that, Stephen. They *may* all be front-paging it, but they won't have the whole story. Richard has promised us an exclusive . . . I'm flying home this afternoon and I'm going to bed . . . Yes, I thought you'd sneak sex in somewhere! I'm going to bed to *sleep*. I'll set the alarm for six in the morning and by the time we go to press you'll have a masterpiece . . . Yes, Stephen . . . Yes. If you don't let me go I'll miss the plane! . . . God, if I told you I'd broken both legs and my spleen had ruptured, you'd still say you needed the copy.'

Already the words were swimming around in her brain, her hand itching to put pen to paper, and it made her feel ashamed. Ellie was on the floor above going through some kind of mental excoriation, and she was down here planning a scoop. And getting a buzz from it, if she was honest. *You're in a dirty trade, my girl*, she thought and swung her bag on to her shoulder.

Ellie was coming out of the drug now. In a moment she would become aware of what she was saying, but still she would be powerless to hold it back. The 'truth' drug did not make you tell the truth, it robbed you of the ability to formulate a lie. 'Do you want your baby, Ellie?'

'I don't know.' There was more, and Paul waited. 'I think I do . . .'

Paul took hold of her hand as he saw her eyes open

and move to meet his. 'That wasn't so bad, was it?'

Ellie smiled, but it was an uncertain smile. 'It didn't take long.'

He nodded. It was two hours since they had begun, but no need to tell her that now. 'I want you to lie there for a while. Sleep if you like. Later on I want you to have some soup or scrambled egg, something light. I'm going to take Richard and Terri to the hospital canteen. Afterwards we'll go on your visit, and then we'll all go to the airport. Is that what you want to do?'

'I think so. Am I going home?'

'It's up to you. For the next few days things will occur to you, facts you never knew you possessed. Bit by bit you'll build up the true picture . . . and I'll be there whenever you want to confer. You can come into St Chad's, or you can go home with Richard. I know Mrs Withers is waiting there like a mother hen.'

There was a real smile now, even if it was a small one. 'And the dogs? I'm longing to see the dogs.'

'Home it is, then. And I'm sure the dogs are there and waiting. But you can change your mind at any time, remember that. Richard understands, so don't be afraid to say what you want. He's waiting outside. Do you want to see him?'

Ellie thought for a moment. 'Not yet. I think I'll close my eyes for a while, and then I'll see him.'

The old Ellie would have said yes for fear of giving offence, Paul thought. Perhaps he was witnessing a sea-change.

The hired Bentley with Richard at the wheel turned in at the cemetery gates. They had managed to elude the press, and the road behind them was empty. 'It's first left, and left again,' Terri said, and Richard turned obediently.

They got out and walked between the stones. There it was, the small white headstone! 'Julia Marjorie Richardson, aged five years. Dearly beloved daughter of Marjorie and Joseph Richardson.' And then, at the bottom, 'Until the morning breaks and the shadows flee away.'

'It's very tidy,' Ellie said, looking at the newly turned earth.

'I think that's the policy here,' Terri murmured, fingers crossed at the thought of Richard's tenners handed over yesterday for an instant face-lift. She looked at her watch. 'I don't want to hurry you, but we don't have much time.'

Ellie looked pathetic, still in a cheap camel coat, her head and shoulders covered by the warm wool shawl Richard had picked out this morning from the hotel gift shop. 'Just a few more minutes.' There was finality in her voice, and no one argued.

She turned away at last and they made their way back to the car. 'Turn right at the gates, Richard, and carry on to the roundabout,' Terri said. 'I'll tell you when we get there.' It was one-fifteen: if they weren't careful, they'd be too late.

'Shall I stay in the car?' Richard said when they drew up at the school.

'I think so,' Terri said. She climbed out and took Ellie's arm. 'You're sure you want to do this?'

Ellie nodded. 'Yes, please.'

'OK, then. Let's walk along here. There's a seat.'

Terri waited until they were seated on the wooden bench. 'If he does the same as usual, he'll come round the corner any minute now. He brings his grandchild . . . well, step-grandchild, in its pushchair to wave to the other child in the playground. He does it every day.' She had done her homework carefully, but it could still all go wrong.

'Is that him?' Ellie's voice was filled with disbelief. 'He's old.'

The man was stooped, and white hair showed beneath the checked cap. 'He's in his late fifties,' Terri said. 'But he hasn't had an easy life. He was in prison for fourteen years: you have to take that into account.'

The man was talking to the baby in the pushchair, bending to unbuckle it and lift it up to the bars where another child, tiny and duffle-coated, was climbing to say hallo.

'He never spoke to me,' Ellie said flatly. 'If that's him, he never spoke to me. It's strange, but I can remember that now. I'd go to him, and he would turn me away.'

Terri tried to think of something to say that would not be crass. 'Perhaps he's trying to make amends?'

They had agreed that neither of them would speak to him. 'You can always contact him later,' Terri had said.

'Do you think he really was my father?' Ellie asked now, the past tense sounding quite deliberate.

'I don't know, Ellie, and I don't think there's any way of finding out. Does it matter?'

Ellie shook her head. 'I'm not sure. It probably

doesn't, but I'll tell you better when I've had time to think.' They got to their feet and walked, arm in arm, back to the car.

'All right?' Richard asked anxiously, following Ellie's eyes to the scene at the railings. The children had vanished from the playground and the man was strapping the baby back, kissing its forehead as he did so.

'Yes,' Ellie said, and climbed into the car.

Paul and Terri followed Ellie and Richard out on to the tarmac, the plane looking small and somehow flimsy at close quarters. Inside it was surprisingly roomy and there was a stewardess to settle them in. *Marvellous what money could do,* Paul thought. A moment later they were airborne.

'Can we come back?' Ellie said suddenly. 'Not now, but some time?'

Richard was looking ridiculously pleased. 'Of course we can. We will,' he said and then looked to Paul, who nodded slightly to show he too had noticed the 'we' and thought it significant.

They were fairly silent on the flight, each with their own thoughts. They had coffee and tiny sandwiches of smoked salmon and egg mayonnaise, and then it was time to disembark.

'OK?' Paul asked, and Ellie nodded. He noticed a little colour had come back to her cheeks. 'We begin tomorrow,' he said, leaning to kiss her brow. It was unprofessional but this was not an ordinary case. 'Remember what I said about things floating up in your mind.' She was nodding so the process had already begun. 'This morning we opened the door, Ellie. It'll all be a bit jumbled at first, but gradually it will fall into place. Some of it may hurt but you can cope with it and I'll be there to help. When you know it all, you'll begin to understand your own motivations. That's when you should make decisions, not now.'

'I can't thank you enough,' Richard said, when Ellie was safe in the first car and Terri had sped off in the second. He took Paul's hand and then gripped his arm. 'I'll expect a large bill and I'll pay it gladly but . . . well, we're friends, I hope. Something more.'

'Yes, something more,' Paul said and climbed into the waiting limousine. As they left the tarmac he wondered what he would find when he got home. More carnage, perhaps – Gary still had a key. Or a penitent, begging forgiveness and another hand-out. Perhaps the house would be quiet, empty except for the woodland creatures, licking their wounds in his desk drawer.

He unzipped the pocket of his bag and checked that the badger was still there, then he settled back to enjoy the journey. However things turned out, it was good to be going home.

The Witherses were on the steps, trying to subdue dogs who were wild at the sight of their owners. Dasher was not sure whom he had missed most, but for Trumper there was only one mistress. Ellie put her face against the massive head, trying to keep her mouth from the loving tongue.

'Steady,' Richard said, 'you'll have her over in a moment.' And then, to no one in particular, 'I think he's glad to see her back.'

Ellie looked up at Mrs Withers. 'Has everything been all right?'

'Oh yes, Mrs Marriner, now that we've got you home everything's fine.' She was turning to Richard. 'Mrs Frank asked me to ring her when you got back, sir.' Adele, Ellie thought, of course. Adele should be here. But Richard was shaking his head.

'I'll deal with it, Mrs Withers. I don't think we want a houseful tonight. Is my brother OK?'

Mrs Withers nodded. 'Apparently, sir. He's arrived in Japan and he's been in touch.'

Glances were flashing between them but Ellie was too tired to care. 'I'm going to ring the boys, Richard. Will I catch them between tea and prep?'

She had been curled on a chair by the fire for a while, sipping tea and refusing a dozen varieties of cake, when she realized what had been strange about her homecoming. She had not felt safe nor happy – there was too much still to be resolved for that. But she had felt certain of her right to do things if she chose. When she had said she was going to ring the boys it had never occurred to her that anyone would argue. And that was strange.

On the other side of the fire Richard appeared to be relaxed in his chair, but his hand on the arm was tense and each time he spoke his head came up slightly as though he needed to jerk into action. Poor Richard. It would be nice to offer him reassurance, but for the moment she had none to spare.

They ate at seven-thirty, from trays, and then Richard followed Mrs Withers to the kitchen and told her to go home. 'You've been wonderful, but we don't want to make her feel like an invalid. I can manage now, and I can always ring you if something crops up.'

'Well, as long as you will, sir. I'm that pleased to see her back, but it'll be a long haul. She looks drained.'

Ellie was still sitting by the fire when he came back and he wanted to go to her and take her in his arms. Instead he said, 'Were the boys pleased to hear from you?'

She nodded. 'Yes. Full of tales of their exploits and looking forward to Christmas. Jeremy says we're having a lighted tree in the garden?' So she meant to be here at Christmas: 'We're having a tree,' that was what she had said.

She had changed into a white jellaba and it made her look almost ethereal. Richard was debating whether he could cross to her chair and kneel at her side when she stood up. 'I think I'll go to bed now.'

He followed her out to the hall. 'Shall I come up with you?'

Ellie was using the banister to haul herself up. 'No, thank you. I'll take my time.'

He watched her for a moment. 'Would you like me to use the guestroom? It's no trouble.'

She kept on mounting. 'Thank you, Richard, but there's no need. I may be asleep when you come up. I expect you're taking the dogs out as usual, so I'll see you in the morning.'

It was now or never. If he didn't find the words now he never would and it would all go wrong again. '*I love you, Ellie*' – that was all it needed. If he didn't hurry she would have reached the landing and he would have to shout. Jesus Christ, what was wrong with him?

He opened his mouth. 'OK, if you're sure you'll be all right, I'll just take them around the garden.'

It was useless. He would never be able to tell her now.

Terri and Mike had climbed into bed, equally tired; but lying there in the dark, tiredness seemed to have left them.

'Are you disappointed about the house?'

'I'll survive.'

'About the photo . . .'

'It doesn't matter, Mike. I was wrong . . . it's just that I get scared, sometimes.'

He slid his arm under her shoulders and drew her close. 'Idiot! I'd forgotten it was there. Admittedly I should have got rid of it in the beginning, but somehow it seemed, well, disloyal. Is that crazy?'

'No. It had every right to be there, and I was wrong to make such a fuss. Diana was part of your life, an important part. I've got to accept that. I'm your future, she's your past – so I'm the lucky one.'

She would always be afraid but she would have to learn to be brave. 'At the moment he dies,' she thought 'Diana will flash through his mind. But I'll be the one by his bed, holding his hand.'

'What are you laughing at?' he said and she chuckled.

'I wouldn't dare tell you.'

He was kissing her now, his free hand moving to cup her breast. 'I love you, Terri. The last two nights without you nearly drove me mad.'

She put up a hand to his, moving it to the relative

safety of her waist. 'Mike, I hate to tell you this, but I forgot to pack my pills. I haven't taken them for three days.'

His face was against her neck. 'I know. I saw them on the bedside table yesterday.'

She lay for a moment, unable to believe her ears.

'You know what that means?'

His hand was moving up again. 'I think so.'

'But how would we manage?'

'If we wait till we can manage, Terri, I'll be too old to bring it off. You want a baby, don't you? When you told me Ellie was pregnant, you looked like a Victorian waif with your face pressed up against the sweetshop window.'

'Was that when you decided?'

'No, I decided last night. Now can we get on with it.'

'It might not work.'

'Then we'll just have to persevere, Terri. It'll be an ordeal, but I'll grit my teeth.'

Ellie had bathed and changed and was ready for bed, but she couldn't settle. She sat at the dressing-table and regarded herself. 'Mariella Marriner': it was a mouthful, but she liked it. She sat on for a moment and then crossed to the window. Across the darkness a light glowed in an upstairs window. Poor Adele, obviously she and Richard were at loggerheads. She would have to smooth things over.

Suddenly she realized her hand had dropped to her belly, curving itself in the protective gesture of woman with child. Had Julia done that, here in this same window, looking forward to the birth of a son? How proud she would be of the boys now that they were growing into men, each of them splendid in his own, very different way.

Impulse carried her across the landing to look at their neatly made-up beds, their books and posters. She must remember to replace Jeremy's penholder. At Christmas she would fill their stockings, hear them suspend breathing for fear of spoiling the fun, see their exultant faces in the morning if she had chosen well. Poor Julia, to be deprived of so much. But she lived on in her children, in Richard's memory, and in the house she had created out of love.

Ellie moved on to the landing, thinking of Richard's wife, young and in love, running up and down the stairs of her new house, her face alight with laughter. Somehow she had become more substantial than that other, infant Julia. And less to be feared.

She was feeling a little giddy as Richard appeared below.

'Ellie!' He was standing on the bottom step, his face determined. 'I love you, Ellie,' he said.

And then, relief making him bold, 'We'll leave this house, if that makes you happy.'

She held out her hand to encourage him to mount the stairs. 'Come to bed, Richard. We'll talk about it tomorrow.'